Praise for

THE ELEGANT GATHERING OF WHITE SNOWS

"A rallying cry for the empowerment of women, Radish's novel is also a celebration of the strong bond that exists between female friends." —*Booklist*

"[Kris Radish's] characters help readers realize they are not alone in the world and their struggles have been or will be experienced by other women." —*Albuquerque Journal*

"A message of hope, renewal, and the importance of female friendships." —*Duluth News-Tribune*

"Kris Radish's idealism shines through in this tender and often funny story about eight Wisconsin women who, without provisions or a destination or any kind of plan, decide one day to leave their homes and walk, embarking on a journey that transforms them, their lives, their families, their communities and their country." —Mako Yoshikawa, bestselling author of *One Hundred and One Ways* and *Once Removed*

"I wish I could buy a copy for every woman I've ever met. I am so in love with this book, the women's stories, and their relationships with each other."
—Susan Wasson, Bookworks, Albuquerque, NM

"A group of women, meeting informally for years, have shared secrets, joys, heartaches, losses, and pain. When one confesses she is pregnant and that the baby is not her husband's, the confession draws the women into a life-altering step that affirms the bonds of female friendship."
—*Booknews* from the Poisoned Pen

"A story of friendship and empowerment." —*Library Journal*

Also by Kris Radish

THE ELEGANT GATHERING

OF WHITE SNOWS

Dancing Naked

AT THE EDGE

OF DAWN

Kris Radish

BANTAM BOOKS

DANCING NAKED AT THE EDGE OF DAWN
A Bantam Book / January 2005

Published by Bantam Dell
A Division of Random House, Inc.
New York, New York

Book design by Virginia Norey

Bantam Books is a registered trademark of Random House, Inc., and the colophon is a trademark of Random House, Inc.

LIBRARY OF CONGRESS CATALOGING-IN-PUBLICATION DATA
Radish, Kris.
Dancing naked at the edge of dawn / Kris Radish.
p. cm.
ISBN: 0-553-38263-2
1. Self-actualization (Psychology)—Fiction. 2. Separation (Psychology)—Fiction. 3. Married women—Fiction.
4. Adultery—Fiction.
PS3618.A35 D36 2005
813'.6—dc22   2004055060

Printed in the United States of America
Published simultaneously in Canada

www.bantamdell.com

BVG   10 9 8 7 6 5 4 3 2 1

Occasionally, like a fine breeze, there are women—Amelia Earharts, Eleanor Roosevelts, Gloria Steinems, Mother Teresas, Audre Lordes, Margaret Sangers, Susan B. Anthonys, Wilma Rudolphs, Sojourner Truths, Emma Goldmans—hundreds of wonderfully brave, fine, glorious women who followed their hearts on a journey of great courage.

This book is for every woman who dared—even if the daring was something as seemingly simple as starting over.

They would tell us all to do it.

Dance naked—go ahead.

Acknowledgments

Every book project is a journey that includes cargo as precious as the fingers that helped me write this story.

On this journey my editor, Kate Miciak, gave me tickets to everywhere. She saw where I needed to go and set me free. Kate, you are a fabulous co-pilot.

Susan Wasson delivered the maps, felt my spirit, breathed in my words—you are a gift from every goddess, Susan, and I will always be grateful.

Sally Miller Gearhart and Jane Gurko stood out in the pouring rain, in the dead of winter and when it was a hundred degrees in the shade, to give me comfort, shelter and a kiss on the face. You are as important to me as the fuel that keeps me in the air.

Linda Fausel listened as I recited the route. Never told me to turn back. Believed. Your name I whisper as true friend.

Mary Catanese documented every turn and was always there, sometimes with little warning, when I needed her help. Mary, I worship you.

Susan Corcoran and the Bantam Dell wizards put all their magic into one bag and continue to create miracles that would astound even the most road-savvy women warriors. I appreciate every single step.

My sister, Maureen Zindars, always listened, never judged and keeps the door unlocked. If I loved you any more, Pooter, you would not be able to breathe.

Lynn Vannucci took a parallel route, met me in midair and the wind from her lovely laugh and beautiful heart kept me going when I wanted to tumble to earth.

Andrew and Rachel, son and daughter to the gypsy, handed me off to the elements, waited patiently for my return, sent me gifts wrapped in their very souls and when we hit tremendous turbulence—held on. Your flying lessons are almost finished and you know I would crash-land in a heartbeat to save your lives. You are both everything.

And at the very end of the journey Madonna Metcalf appeared riding high on the horizon and waved me into the terminal so I could refuel for the next journey. How lucky am I.

Lastly, there is only one man I would ever invite to a Reverse Bridal Shower—my father, Richard Radish. He always told me I could do and be whatever I wanted. I chose "writer," and for him, and that gift, my heart will always be dancing. I love you, Dad.

And for every woman who has yet to dance naked—throw yourself a Reverse Bridal Shower and race for the edge of dawn.

1

I wanted to watch.

This was by far the most bizarre feeling that I have ever experienced in my entire life—all forty-eight years of it. I wanted to watch. What I should have wanted was to kill, to mutilate, to hack with a sharp butcher knife, to maim and claw and slice over and over again until I saw blood and the screaming ended and there were sirens outside the bedroom window. I should have wanted to pull a hidden revolver, one of those slick babies that fits into the palm of your hand and startles unsuspecting victims, from inside of my white Bali bra. I should have wanted to move quietly around the room with a powerful look of raw hatred flashing from my gray eyes and with a multitude of weapons spilling out onto the floor. But no. There would be no flashy pistols or loud cries. This would not be a simple scenario that involved a sad moment of passion-induced violence, because what I wanted was . . . to watch.

My heart was pounding so rapidly, I could see my blue shirt jumping up and down. Jesus. I could feel it in my throat. It touched the edges of my skin and moved like a snake into my veins until it was in charge of everything I did, who I was, where I was going. It was a red mass of vessels and tissue as soft as a baby's arm, it was a tiger prowling just under the edge of my skin everywhere, creating music—a beating drum, rising smoke, naked dancing women, sweat at midnight, and I wondered for a moment as brief as a winter sunset if they could hear it. It didn't matter if they heard it or if the entire population of the free world heard it, because I could not stop. I edged closer to the door until I could see—them. Them. I know it was a them and not simply a he. It was a couple. A them. A her and a him.

It was the sound that had propelled me up from the basement, where I had been struggling to understand why in God's name or the Goddess's name, or whomever it was controlling my divine destiny, I had never thrown away all those yellowed papers that stuck out in the lines of boxes that had been propped against the side of the wall for the past twelve years. The sound was a kind of tapping, a foreign echo that seduced me like a brilliant lover. It was not loose change dropping onto the bathroom floor or books falling off a shelf or an alarm clock being pushed off the edge of the dresser on purpose. It was a thump against the wall. Constant. Regular. What the hell? I put down the papers and quietly moved up the basement stairs and stopped just before I could see the edge of the kitchen counter.

I was not supposed to be home. This is why I stood frozen with one hand on the basement wall and the other hanging at my side. Someone was probably trying to break into the house. Why not? Suburban neighborhood. Everyone working. Regular patterns of coming and going. There had to be some good stuff sitting on top of dressers, that's what a savvy intruder might think about this lovely neighborhood where some rich slobs drove Saabs and there were hot tubs in many backyards and the kids did not ride a bus to school. If it were a robber he would be sorely disappointed when he found sweat socks, two jogging bras and a wad of Kleenex on top of my dresser. No diamonds or gold bands. No tennis bracelets. One antique chest that came from my great-grandmother and represented my entire inherited fortune, a fortune they would never be able to lift without the help of a small crane. Pretty much what he would find would be twenty-three years of accumulated junk, one new car with a bumper sticker that said *Thelma & Louise Live,* some silver spoons under the sink that I would never finish cleaning, a row of tattered books probably worth thousands of dollars, but it's been my experience that most robbers are not that literate, my daughter's Barbie Doll collection stuck away in plastic boxes from the local drugstore, a pitiful selection of moderately prized booze and a doorknob from my old college that I considered one of the finest objects that I owned. "Shit," I told myself as I took a step into the kitchen, "it can't be a robber. They'd have better luck stealing from the Goodwill store."

In the kitchen, I could tell the noise was coming from upstairs. This is the moment when I also remembered that my car was parked one block from my house because I had been working with a co-worker on a special project and that because I almost never work on special projects out of the office, no one in the entire world would expect me to be at home on a Thursday morning in June at 10:38 A.M. rummaging through boxes in the basement and listening at the edge of the steps for the sounds of ax murderers sharpening their blades.

When I got to the top part of the house, I expected one of the alarm clocks to be going off or a television set to be turned on or a leaky faucet dripping stones the size of golf balls instead of water onto the tiled bathroom floor. Maybe the flag had fallen off the roof or a hunk of siding was banging against the side of the house, begging to be released. I certainly did not expect to see a woman's naked foot moving up and down on top of my bed.

It was a slender, beautiful foot. I imagined it was as soft as my own and warm and that the man—undoubtedly my husband—whose fingers I had seen slide down to touch the top of the toes, was thinking how sexy the foot was and how he wanted to inhale it and place her beautiful feet against the sides of his thighs.

This is when my heart stopped thumping explosively and I knew that I wanted to watch. Whatever was happening, whatever they were doing, whatever they had on or didn't have on or were holding or touching or eating—it didn't matter because I wanted to watch. I had to watch. Sex. Someone was having sex in my bedroom and it sure as hell wasn't me and I had to watch it.

A kind of calm settled over me. Perhaps there was a name for this pre-I-Gotta-Watch version of sexual voyeurism that had captured my very being. Maybe I was treading some new water that I could share with my colleagues at the University. My mind raced as wildly now as my heart had just a breath ago. I wanted to watch and I was going to watch. This yearning propelled me forward with a rush of power and sureness unlike anything I had ever known in my life. I was brave and strong and I was going to watch no matter what happened. Nothing could stop me. Nothing.

Her foot was more than lovely. I noticed this again as I slithered to the edge of the shelf, where I had a terrific view directly into the mirror above the dresser on the far wall that I had once begged Bob to move. Hello, lovers. There was a view of the bed where I had slept not more than four hours before. They were not on my side of the bed. "How nice," I wanted to mutter out loud. "Maybe I should go get a cold drink and an energy bar," I thought to myself like someone who is about to go into a movie and does not want to be disturbed during the best scenes. This is where my body began separating itself from my mind. This might be what the Green Berets and Navy SEALs do. Snap of the

fingers. I am invisible. My feet are a cat's paws. Swift and sure.
They will never see me if I can maintain this level of high mental
control. That's what I thought. Suddenly, I was invincible.

My husband was on the bottom. This was also a startling fact.
The last time we had sex—could I remember when?—I am certain he was on the top and I am also certain that the sex lasted a
good three minutes before he fell off, rolled over, patted my ass
and fell asleep. Enough of him: back to that delicious foot.

Nails painted the color of a frosty pink geranium; a slender
ankle that looked as if it could give way to a calf that had been
shaped by years of exercise. I had to see this. I had to see the rest
of her leg and I edged myself flat, belly to the carpet, slithering
like a snake across floor covering that had seen trails of baby
poop and vomit from the high school dances and the last half-
decent lovemaking session that I ever expect to have in my life. I
must have looked like a fool and I couldn't have cared less.

The damn mirror was not low enough. I would have to slink
around to the other side of the door, where I could get a full-on
view of my husband making love to the geranium woman.
Should I risk it? I had to think about this, which, I was about to
discover, was the reason for every screwed-up mess that touched
the edges of my life. I had to stop and think if I wanted to risk
getting caught so I could watch my husband making love at
ten-something in the morning to a woman who was definitely
not me.

The fact that I decided to go for it should count for something. Really. It was a ballsy move so unlike me that it came fast
once I talked myself into it. I simply walked past the door. One
huge step and there I was. I could stand at the far side of the door
just at the end of the hall where the wall turned a corner before
Katie's room and watch. I could watch. Of course, they might

see me. But I wanted to watch so damn bad, it didn't matter. Breathing, work, my kids, food, wine, my latest research project, world peace—nothing mattered but watching.

My need to watch was an ache that moved across the small of my back and down into the tops of my legs. Sweat was running down the insides of my arms and my stomach was on fire with such a desire that a brigade of hungry near-death wild dogs could not have pulled me away.

So I started to watch. Jesus. Just Jesus. I would wonder later why the hell they didn't get a hotel room or if they had planned it and how long I had been so goddamned stupid or why he picked someone who looked so much like me or how many others there had been or when the moments of my life and marriage and world had started fraying at the edges until they met in the middle in a tangled mess of nothing, but for those moments, one and then two and then ten or fifteen, I simply stood there with my hands hanging against the seams of the denim skirt I had worn every Thursday for ten years and I watched.

The geranium woman was naked except for her blouse. It was red and looked like it was made of expensive silk. Unbuttoned, it hung against the sides of my husband like a bright tent protecting him from sun and wind and the sand I would one day want to grind into his eyeballs. Her hair was long and dark blond, kind of what mine might look like at that length. I did not have the pleasure of seeing her eyes but I imagined they were also dark and that she had high cheekbones and flawless skin. I did not hate her. I would never hate her. I would hate him for a very long time but never her, although I might never understand some things about her and what she did and how she did them. I might. I could. I would try.

She had a perfect ass. It was the ass of someone who has not had babies and who works out five days a week and could go to the spa without having to worry about picking someone up from play practice or sorting through the damn dry cleaning on the way to the grocery store for the third time in one day. She was not very tall and once when she rose up off of my husband I could see that her breasts were simply average—small rounded mounds of flesh—and not like mine. My rather glorious forty-something breasts are large and firm even though I have nursed two babies and did not wear a bra for eleven years during a very crucial period of breast growth. The geranium was riding my husband like a seasoned jockey and he was wild with sexual happiness, bucking against the red tent, with his hands pulling at the brown, terribly frayed bedspread that I had been meaning to replace for the past five years.

My friends think Bob is handsome. Some of them have warned me for years that he is ripe for an affair. Some of them have told me that they have seen him having lunch with beautiful women and getting into cars that appear to be going nowhere and that he often seemed way too happy for a man pushing fifty who has a so-so job in a community where hope of advancement means moving to a real city in a real state where there are real jobs and buildings taller than the four-story giant in our downtown. Bob was just ordinary Bob to me, which is part of the problem I realize now, but then, that day, he was the pumping machine and I was the woman in the hall who wanted to watch.

"Oh," they both took turns moaning, and I suddenly wanted to moan with them. It would hit me later when I was woozy with vodka how absolutely insane and risky and not-like-me wanting to watch had been but I do have to admit that I was a little turned on. What a delightful feeling that was after all those months of celibacy when sex was something I might have seen after eleven P.M. on the old television or a vague memory from the past or a flicker of heat that passed quickly from my mind to my hips and then was gone just as fast. Sex? Making love? The mere thought, the simple word and now this real live sex act was throwing me into near ecstasy and there I stood watching this glorious woman rock the socks off of the man I had been married to for twenty-seven years.

The geranium rose up occasionally. She moved fast, like a machine that had just gotten back from a terribly expensive overhaul, and I wondered how long she could go on like this before Bob called 911. Once Bobby's little penis came out and they were frantic to get it back in there. I had all I could do but to rush in and help them. "There," I would say. "Now, you kids behave, and you, Ms. Geranium, you stop being so damn wild. Bob has high blood pressure."

I didn't talk or move or think of anything but what I was seeing from my perch in the hall. I stood there watching for what must have been about fifteen minutes, because Bob came fast, and then I realized they would be flopping over onto their backs and then they would have a perfect view of the bedroom door, where I stood watching them making love or having sex or just fucking around. Take your pick.

Of course, I knew when Bob would come and what he would sound like, and when he started that low groan I knew it was just about over, but I wanted to see what the geranium would do because it was hard for me to imagine that she was going to come like this too. I was certain this was a woman who needed focus and attention and direct work in just the right location. I was correct. Well, maybe I was right, but if she did come she was sure thinking, "Is that it?" because in about three seconds flat she pushed off of him and I leapt across the entrance to the doorway, a deer dancing in the headlights, and I was gone and almost certain they had not seen me.

Gone. Now what? Would they rumble in the sheets for a bit? Would they hurry up and get the hell out of there? And me? Would I race to the basement? Would I hurry up and get the hell out of there?

I have always hated the word *fuck*. Saying it was one of the few things that would make me punish my children. But now I could think of nothing else to say. I had just watched some fucking. I was certain that within a short period of time I might go fucking nuts and I had no idea what in the fuck to do or where in the fuck to go but I wisely decided that I should get the fuck out of the house and fucking vanish. And that I also needed to do this fucking fast.

When I closed the side door and bolted through backyards toward my parked car, like I used to in high school after I toilet-papered a lawn or threw eggs onto some car windows, it hit me. It hit me hard and brought me to my knees in Gloria Sorensen's yard just under the oak trees and I wanted so desperately to lie down there and roll into the garden and past all the houses on my street and into someplace where no one would ask me why I was rolling. I wanted to roll to Egypt or Cuba and out past an endless blue ocean and I wanted to grab both my children and take them with me and maybe throw the old books and the doorknob into the mix and then just roll away.

Instead, I slowed my running to a fast walk and calmly sauntered into the office at Anna Jorglinson's house and said, "I couldn't find the files and my daughter just called and needs me to pick her up from school," and then I got into the car, put the key into the ignition, turned it on and drove fourteen blocks to the Kmart parking lot, where I pulled in between a Subaru with a canoe rack on top of it and an old black Buick that looked as if it had rusted into the space next to the light pole. I didn't cry or move or even think. I sat there looking into the backside of the

Big K and counted sixteen men and women and one goofy-looking family, who had on clothes for winter and not for summer, walking into the health food store next to Kmart, which was bound to go out of business any second. I sat there for forty-eight minutes and then I reached into my black bag and pulled out my cell phone.

I held my tiny black-and-silver phone against my chest for another thirteen minutes before I could remember how to dial it. I pushed the numbers that would connect me to Elizabeth's phone and then I left her this exact message: "It's me. I just watched my husband making love to a woman who looks like a geranium on our bed. I cannot remember how to drive the car. I cannot remember who I am. When you get this message, please call me."

Then I waited. Three planes flew past and a swarm of confused geese, who were so messed up by the ever-growing ozone layer and backwards tides and El Niño's sister-in-law that they never bothered to fly south or north anymore. I think I rolled down the window once and tried to talk to them. I sat there for a long time and then the phone rang. It was Elizabeth.

"Where in the hell are you?"

"Let me think."

"What? You don't know where you are?"

"A parking lot."

"Jesus, Meg, look for a sign. Look around."

"Oh, Kmart. I'm at Kmart."

"Can you drive?"

"I have to pee."

"Don't leave. I will be there in five minutes."

I forgot to hang up the phone and a soft buzz drifted through the air and then the phone went dead and I started laughing then and could not stop. When Elizabeth pulled up I was still laughing and the windows had magically rolled themselves down and she touched me on the side of my face and I looked into her eyes and I saw an ocean of light, beams of salvation from beyond the last cloud, the whisper of a sky the color of blue that I saw once off an island near Maui. Elizabeth has the most beautiful blue eyes I have ever seen and I adore every single thing about her and there she was saving me.

"Come on," she said gently, opening the car door and walking me toward her little red Honda. We pushed aside books and clothes and a pile of hangers and then I sat down. She locked my door and took my phone and found the keys on the floor, and then she drove off and turned to me once with the biggest smile on her face and said, "So you watched, huh?"

And then I told her the truth, the whole truth and nothing but the truth.

"I wanted to watch."

2

Elizabeth's house is an oasis of complete chaos. Nothing works or fits or matches. When you open the door to her life, her world, her kingdom—it looks at first glance as if someone ripped off the front window and took a handful of everything, threw it in the air and then turned and ran as fast as possible before it all hit the ground and splattered.

Even Elizabeth looks as if she has been thrown together in a hurry by a group of crazed orphans. Her reddish, blackish, brownish hair is streaked with somewhat awkward strands of gray the color of the sky following a tornado and it always lies in a tangled mass on top of her head. In the sixteen years I have known her I have never seen her unpin it but I have imagined what it must look like. Birds unnested. Swallows rising from the crown of her hair in astonishment for the first time since their birth. Airplanes having to find a new landing strip. Lost explorers surfacing for the first time in decades. Amelia Earhart pushing her own unkempt trusses from her head and announcing, "I told that drunk to make sure we had enough gas."

This beautiful woman named Elizabeth has a wild kindness about her that attracts every woman in town and every man for a ten-thousand-mile radius. Women who get off of buses downtown with nothing but hope in their eyes have found their way to her doorstep. Once a car full of gypsies broke down in front of her house and before dinner they had a tent set up in her backyard and a hundred people stopped by for a juggling show. Last year I met a perfectly normal-looking man who was asking every person he met on the street, "Could you please tell me if Elizabeth Rapalla lives near here?" Her three sons, who never knew their three separate fathers, are allowed to dream and dance and live as if there are no rules. These boy-men never speed, are unfailingly polite, always seem to make the perfect choice and they treat their mother like the Queen that she is. They are scholars, athletes, gentle souls of the universe—and some of the finest young men I think I could ever know.

There are men in Bosnia and Cincinnati, and three that I know of in New York, who would kill and rob and steal just to be able to sit and look into Elizabeth's eyes for five minutes. She has not lived with a man or a woman since I have known her but there is no way to keep track of her lovers, the people who love her, the people who want to love her. She has a degree in economics and works as an administrator for a huge national nonprofit organization that gives money to quiet geniuses, poets who live in trailers, women who are researching a cure for breast cancer on a shoestring and at least one group of doctors who performs abortions for young girls and women who have been raped.

She also tells fortunes. Elizabeth can simply touch your hand, look into your eyes, place her fingers against the side of your pulsing temples and tell you why you turned left instead of right and to give that guy on the fourth floor a second chance. I have driven by her house at midnight, only to see her sitting right in the center of her front window holding the hand of the local bank president. A week later there was a priest sitting there and then a woman who was at least eighty years old was in the same spot just a day later. Men, women, teenagers—everyone, it seems, ends up sitting in Elizabeth's kitchen or pushing close to her around the old wooden table by her front window. She has a gift for reading the lines in our faces and hands that we refuse to see. It is a gift, and a gift that makes her so much extra money that she supports at least three unwed mothers I know of and countless other causes and people and places that think of her as the goddess that she is and will always be.

Today, she is my goddess. We have pushed aside plates and what looks like a dish of dog food, three cigars and some bright pink socks so we can sit at her kitchen table. I am helpless. A widow. A woman who is about to face a future that is almost as uncertain as the past she has just witnessed throbbing on her own sweat-saturated bedspread.

"Sweetheart," Elizabeth says, pushing back strands of my tangled hair and lightly running her fingers across my cheek. "This is quite a day for you."

"I just went home to find the files from the Brimley case and I heard this noise..."

Elizabeth listens intently. Her gorgeous eyes are focused on my own eyes, and she does not let go of them. I keep talking but a part of me holds her and our eyes are locked and there is no one else in the world but us and I cannot stop talking. Falling. I am falling and I think that if I talk, Elizabeth will hold me up and I will be just fine.

Finally, she stops me when I begin telling her about the lovely ankles of the woman who was on top of my husband. She finds the details unnecessary, and perhaps she is right, but I want to keep talking because if I stop talking I will fall off of the chair and hit my head on the edge of the table and I will be in a coma for the rest of my life and who will finish raising my beautiful, almost-grown, sometimes smart-ass teenage daughter? Who will tend to the flighty and occasional needs of my son, who is cruising through life fairly estranged from his family?

"You look like shit. Should I slap you?"

This is what Elizabeth does. She says something that on a regular day would make most people say, "What the hell? Are you nuts, lady?" But on the day she chooses to say it, anything and everything she says sounds perfect. "Can I stick pins in your eyes?" "Certainly." "If I get up and leave the room and come back with a whip, would it be okay if you let me flog you fifty-six times?" "Oh, sure." "When I count to ten I want you to disrobe and to tell me sixteen good things about the way your body looks, as we are sitting in full view of ten thousand members of the United States Air Force." "Sounds good to me."

"Sure."

That is what I say because a small, very small—about the size of a baby's booger small—part of my mind knows that she knows this is exactly what I need.

Elizabeth slaps me. Hard. The sting of her hand against my face and the feel of her fingers, six rings and knuckles the size of marbles hitting the bone underneath make me cry. My tears start slowly and then build to a crescendo and all the time Elizabeth is simply sitting there as if she is waiting for a train to stop so she can get on. The very hand she has used to bring me back from my wanting-to-watch moments is now wrapped around my wrist. It is my anchor. I need an anchor. Any moment now I am about to become undone and float out to sea, where I will surely die while a gaggle of seagulls peck out my eyes. My body is at the table and I am standing against the refrigerator with my arms crossed against my breasts and I am going to watch myself fall into pieces and descend into a cavern of seemingly hopeless resignation.

Elizabeth wills me to fall with those huge eyes of hers. Her eyes are swimming in a sea of champagne, a liquid so golden that it defies description. Her head, wrapped in a frayed red bandanna, looks as if it is on fire, and I fall into her, hoping that both of us will sink together to the bottom of this cold, dark place where we can breathe water and kick against sand that has never seen human flesh. I cannot bear to be alone, and in the morning when I see the marks my fingers have left on her arm I will realize how desperate I have become in such a short period of time.

She does catch me, whispering in sonnets that come from a poetess I will soon come to love:

> *"my heart*
> *on pause*
> *the electrifying truth*
> *the reality*
> *of my spare breath*
> *beating its wings*
> *against*
> *my stilled soul . . .*
> *waking slowly now*
> *i can learn*
> *to dance*
> *naked*
> *and swift*
> *music*
> *moving*
> *like*
> *the wild song of summer . . .*

i will
dance naked
when i first
learn
to walk…"

Her own breath is a warm shower against my face and we have fallen to the floor and Elizabeth is finishing the poem, but I can no longer hear the words. We are swimming on the bottom of that sea and I have something bottled up so deep inside of me that I am terrified to let it go. The world would flood and thousands of people would die and there would be no space for walking and sitting and only water. This something bottled up in me is a solid block that is unmovable. It is lodged halfway between my chest and my throat and I know that it will take major surgery and thousands of plunges into the depths of this ocean to dislodge it from a place that has wrapped its hands and feet and mouth around the core of who I am and what this thing has made me.

We rock on the floor until my sobs surrender. The well is not dry but it is tired, and Elizabeth begins whispering into the side of my face. Her words travel like tiny spiders into the web of my hair and then to my ears.

"Oh, sweetie, you have so many places to go, so much to learn, so many people to cradle in your own arms."

She stops in between each proclamation, and I cannot move. It is only possible to listen and nothing else. Listen. I am not really alive. My flesh is warm and soft but my spirit, the heart of who I am and may someday become, is a frozen block of ice the size of Alabama. If I move my hand to the center of my chest, I feel the frozen walls of caverns as deep as forever. I am freezing.

Cold as hell. Elizabeth goes on and I listen because I am searching for a warm spot, just a whiff of her breath on my face.

"This day is a gift," Elizabeth tells me in that husky prophetess
voice of hers. "You cannot see it that way now, Meg. It will take
you a while—but not as long as it took you to get to this place.
You will see mountains explode and birds fly without wings. In
weeks you will see colors you never knew existed and the sides of
buildings will call your name."

Once, she shifts her hip against my back and I remember, with
a touch of reality, that she once fell and broke her leg while she
was parasailing in the Caribbean. She spoke of it only once.
Never limps. Ignores the occasional pain that I imagine remains
as sharp as a knife rubbing up against the inside of her bony
spine. The hard floor does not stop her and I move as close
against her as I can get and I never want her to stop talking. Her
voice is a cradle and I want to be held and rocked and tucked
into bed on the back of a soft white summer swan.

"Meggie, we don't have to talk of everything now, but I have
to ask you one question. Just one more question."

"Just one?"

"It's a big one."

"I'm ready."

"Why are you crying?"

Tucked away behind years of life that have stacked up and
blocked out the sun and my old list of dreams and the way I used
to take my checkered purple bedspread and fall asleep in the tall
grass behind my grandma's old house in the country is a memory of what I really wanted. This memory flashes to the front of
my mind and for a second it seems as fresh and young as it did
when I was sixteen and the world stretched in front of me—endless and possible, wild, free and so forever. I want to tell Elizabeth
this but I am afraid. I have been afraid for so long that I cannot

utter a word. So afraid that years of my life have been frozen in a parade of sameness and routine.

She strokes the side of my face and pushes my hair behind my ears and she asks me again and then again, "Why are you crying? Why are you crying?"

"It's not because of Bob," I say.

I move up onto my side so that we are facing each other and lying in parallel lines on a floor that has seen some of the most interesting feet ever created. Elizabeth is so wise that I imagine she knows what I need to say and do and feel, but she remains silent, and then I tell her what she already knows.

"It isn't about the watching or Bob or infidelity or marriage or any goddamn thing."

Elizabeth smiles and touches my hair again. I am frightened, scared, terrified and exhausted at the mere thought of what lies ahead, and I want to crawl under the kitchen table and stay there for ten years. Elizabeth's visitors could drop me food and gently place glasses of milk and water at the edges of their chairs. Life would be simple—hard, but simple.

"More?" she asks, stretching her legs. "Tell me more and then we will move to a comfortable spot and you can talk or cry or yell or do anything you want all night long."

"It's me," I say slowly, holding each word in my mouth and then tossing them around with my tongue and lips before I let them go into Elizabeth's ears. "The crying is just for me and there are miles of rivers and lakes and oceans dammed up behind this pseudo-life that has claimed me. Miles and miles."

"Ahh...," Elizabeth says, smiling as wide as a river herself. "And so it begins."

"It begins, Elizabeth, and I have never been so terrified in my entire life. I am frightened and scared and I don't know how to begin. I don't know which foot to put forward or how to turn on the car or move my arm. How did I regress like this, Lizzie? How in the hell did this happen?"

She closes her eyes and pulls some Magic from her mind. I want to crawl inside that space behind her eyes and see how this works, but I am too scared for even that, too scared for anything.

"Everything is so simple. Now, from this moment on you will do what you have to do, what you must do, by remembering that we have just the present. Just now. You must settle into the idea of change and you can only do that one moment at a time. There is no grand plan except the one you create, and you have lost your sense of creation, oh beautiful Meggie. It is not that far of a reach to touch what you need, what you might remember, because here you are and there are hundreds and thousands of women who will never slide to the floor like this and surrender. Those women will cascade through one day after another with a simple wish of happiness that they will never be bold enough to find."

"Elizabeth, I am so damn tired. I am so tired."

"I know, sweetie, I know."

Somehow we manage to get off the floor and she drags me into the living room that is such a delightful garden of books and flowers and rocks and sticks and stones that I feel a lightness soar through my weary bones. My tiredness is a weight that I have dragged with me for so long, it is hard to move. Elizabeth has a futon that flips out into a bed in three seconds and she tells me to stretch out, which I do without hesitation. I quickly sink into another world. A world where there are thick blankets colored in purple and red. A world that smells of patchouli and has glasses on every table and towels lying in plush piles near the bathtub. A world where the door is not locked and where people come and go and leave notes of love and passion on the kitchen table. A world where anyone who enters can say and feel and be and do whatever they want and where you can sit on the roof and read a book at midnight, wear shorts when it snows or plan your outdoor exercise routines for only the days when the weather is bad, because you like it that way.

A world of passion and light. That is what I crave. No schedules or routines that mix politely with the plans of the people in your life who have no consideration for what you need and want. A world where someone, just once, says, "What can I do for you?"

Elizabeth comes back with two martini glasses that are about the size of a Miami cruise ship. She orders me to drink and sets down a pitcher of liquid that I know will ignite the lining of my stomach and send me into a place of total confession and exotic boldness. Then she lies next to me and asks me what I thought about while she was gone.

"Someone saying just once, 'What can I do for you?' "

"Oh, no, this is where you missed the boat and plane and the whole damn train. It's not them. It has nothing to do with them and everything to do with you."

"What?"

Elizabeth sets down her glass and molds her hands around mine, which are glued to the stem of my own martini glass. She squeezes me so hard that I am terrified I will drop some of this liquid gold—some of my salvation, the ribbons of diamonds that I will use to ignite me so I can take some kind of step forward.

"We make our own choices every single moment. Happy or sad. Married or single. Alive or dead. Miserable or content. Successful or not successful. Your life choices have nothing, absolutely nothing to do with anyone else. How dare you or anyone give away the power to be. Bob and Katie and Shaun don't make you happy. The frigging new car doesn't make you happy, or the house or the job or flying to Paris."

I am listening but I need another sip. A large sip. She releases me and goes on.

"Bob was pretty happy today. Bravo for Bob. He did something that made him happy, something that he wanted to do. He took care of himself."

"It sure looked that way."

"When was the last time you did something that made you happy? When?"

How could I answer this? Women aren't supposed to be happy. We are supposed to save the world and then do the wash, fill out college applications for the kids, order grass seed and walk to the store in a snowstorm for more milk. We burned our frigging bras, saved a few whales and a fraction of the environment and then we did the damn ironing while the guys barbecued. Nothing seems to have changed in a hundred years. I can't even remember the last time I thought about the mere possibility of being happy.

"Jesus, Elizabeth . . ."

"Women have blown it big-time," she answers for me. "You know now that you have to start over, don't you? You have to learn how to crawl and then walk and then run and then fly. What the hell were you thinking giving yourself away like that?"

She is angry, just a little angry, because Elizabeth never gets angry like most people get angry. Her skin flushes just a bit. She is an amazement, and I drink my martini, which tastes like Christmas—a touch of evergreen and mint, one snowflake and an olive laced with gold, incense and Santa's garter belt—and pour another one, and I suddenly feel more exhausted than I ever have in my entire life. I need to make sure my daughter, Katie, is safe and I have to call in to work and there is Bob, wildass Bob, and then the next fifty years of my life. Half of my life. I have half of my life to live. Oh my God.

"Half of my life," I say out loud.

"What?"

"I have half of my life floating around out there waiting for me."

Elizabeth doesn't say a word but I notice her eyes light up a notch and a breath of something wild leaves her chest. She listens and I ramble and ramble and sip and sip again and I see something, not very clearly, something like a ship so far away you wonder if it isn't the wine or the bend of the horizon or the past meeting the future right there where your eyes happen to be resting for that one second. I see a glimpse of something moving so slowly, I imagine I could catch it if I barely crawled, but I cannot bear yet to reach out and touch it or see it or understand what it is. Please pass a baby blanket.

"You are starting," she says, like a professor nodding to a class of freshmen. "Crashes, wrong turns, be prepared. But also be ready for dancing."

"What?"

"Naked dancing."

"What are you talking about?"

"The shit is about to hit the fan, Meg darling. Lives are changing as we speak. When you leave this house, as you must eventually, everything you know will have changed. Bob. The kids. Your job. Your role in life. All of this because of your watching. It can be a glorious relief. Wonderment. Naked dancing at midnight with flames of fire or at the break of dawn when the air is fresh and hard."

I am feeling woozy with the vodka but I almost get it. I put one hand on Elizabeth's thigh so that I can steady myself, and then I imagine me dancing naked—C-section scars, fifteen extra pounds around my middle, veins popping out like adolescent acne, dips and curves replaced by a melting pot of middle age, hair gray at the roots, scars from elbow to chin—and I am not quite sure if I should laugh or cry.

Elizabeth looks over at me and sees my eyes crinkle with deep thought, notices the questions lying right there, and she tells me to imagine it anyway. "Just imagine it."

I do.

The light is perfect and there are miles of red desert cliffs. All of my nails are painted to match the ribbons of a summer sunset and are perfectly filed. My hair has been bleached by the sun and hangs in perfect curls down the center of my back. My skin is the color of whole wheat bread. It is the glorious moment before day surrenders—hands in the air, clouds drifting fast—into the dark eyes of night. I take off my shorts, shirt and sandals. This act does not bother me. It does not matter if anyone sees me. I do not care. The music drifts in on the edges of the night air, musty, wild, scented with the smell of sage from the desert. It is never loud, and surely I am the only woman in the world who hears it. I hear it and I begin to dance. I dance for five, ten, fifteen then twenty minutes. I dance until it is as dark as it will ever be and the sky is littered with stars, and when I finally stop and look up, a crowd of ten thousand men and women begin clapping and the sound rumbles in my ears like an explosion in my own head.

"Dancing naked at the edge of dawn, Elizabeth. I can imagine it, but can I do it? Can I?"

My hands are in hers. She has moved to face me. I may never sleep or eat or walk again.

"Drink up, sweetie. Drink up. You are going dancing."

3

1963

The noise is a raging wave of mingled voices that wakes Margaret from a dream where ponies are dancing and she is talking to the sky. Her father's voice is the loudest. It is a deep siren that is laced with the words *No* and *Never*. She has heard the voices like this since the day she turned seven just three months ago. The house had been filled with her aunts and uncles, cousins running from room to room, a tub of beer on the back porch and her brothers swinging from the trees and stealing the birthday balloons so they could fill them with water and drop them onto the front sidewalk.

Her Auntie Marcia was the last to leave and was also Margaret's favorite person in the entire world. Her present that year from Aunt Marcia was a pocketknife, because "Girls need them too," and Margaret slipped it from the small white box and held it to her chest as if it were a piece of gold. She never put it down and when her auntie asked if she would walk her to the car she kept the knife in her right hand and noticed her auntie smile when they held hands and touched the knife together.

"The world is yours, honeybunch," Auntie Marcia told her

before she jumped—Auntie Marcia always jumped, never simply sat—into her small red car. "You are seven now and next year I want you to tell me all the places you will travel to when you are a grown woman. Start a list tonight and then next year we will go for a ride in my red car together and you will tell me."

That night Margaret decided she would have everyone start calling her "Meg," because she now had a pocketknife and because she was seven years old, and then she started her list. Her parents were woozy with the beer and the shots of whiskey Grandpa Frank had poured, and as she was writing down the word *Africa* the noise started.

Meg put down her number 2 pencil and she listened. Her parents were in the kitchen and it was hard to hear and it was an unusual sound. No one yelled much, except the boys, around her house and she had never, ever heard her mother raise her voice like she did that night. She stopped writing after the letter *i* because the sound scared her. Her fingers found the cool edge of the red Swiss Army knife that was under her pillow and she touched it like she used to touch her blankie and the doll her mother threw away two years ago.

"No," her father yelled. "Goddamn it. No!"

Her mother cried then and Meg wanted so very much to pull open the longest blade of her knife and walk down the steps and into the kitchen and tell her father to stop yelling, but she was scared. Really scared. She pulled open the blade in the dark, memorizing how she had to touch the long blades first and then the tiny scissors, and she sat there wishing the yelling would stop and that she could finish writing the word *Africa* and that her auntie would pull up in her cool car and jump onto the porch and run up the steps and save her.

She heard her brothers get out of bed and open their bedroom door. They tapped on her wall and she moved just an inch to tap back. It was their signal, their secret code. She tapped two times which was the signal for A-OK and then she waited.

Two doors slammed and then everything was quiet, but Meg did not put the knife away. She waited again, heard Grant shift in the top bunk, and she desperately wanted to finish writing. She was thinking of Africa more than the loud voices and she was imagining a line of tents and hats shaped like domes. It was hot and men with skin the color of her brown shoes walked with rifles and there was the scent of smoke everywhere. Night was falling and from the flap of her safari tent she could see a round sun, huge, huge in the sky like the one she saw in *National Geographic* the last time she went to the dentist. Meg imagined herself riding elephants and resting behind a bush as a lion raced to feed off a dead zebra.

Her mother moved like a lion in that African jungle. She quietly opened the door and looked startled to see her birthday girl in bed, a knife in one hand and a pencil in the other.

"Honey . . . ?" her mother asked in one word that was at once a question and a way to find out if she had heard.

Meg did not speak. She closed her knife, put down the pencil and opened the covers so her mother could climb in beside her. They never spoke but her mother pushed Meggie into a ball and curled around her and within minutes was asleep. Meg could feel her breath against the back of her neck and in the morning she would smell like the beer that seemed to pour from her mother's lungs and tangle in her hair. She would also wake with the knife in her hand, her fingers stiff from holding on, and the faint notion that she had been someplace far away and could never, ever get back home.

The yelling never seemed to stop after that. Two nights would go by and then it would happen again. Her parents did not say anything about what happened after ten P.M. and her brothers, except for that first night of wall tapping, acted as if they had been struck deaf.

Three months after her birthday the mingled noises are especially loud, and in the middle of the pony dream Meggie's mother comes into the room but Meggie does not pull back the covers.

"Margaret, can I sleep with you?"

"My name is Meg."

"Okay. Are you mad?"

"You have to tell me now."

"Tell you what?"

"Why is he so angry, Mommie? You have to tell me."

Meggie's mother wears tiny, black plastic glasses that always slide down onto the top of her nose. She is a wisp of a woman who barely weighs one hundred pounds and when she stands near Meggie's bed with her hands on her hips she could pass for her own child. Her hair is short, so short that when Meg reaches up to touch her and pull her onto the bed, there is nothing to hang on to and Meg ends up grabbing her mother's ears.

First her mother sits. She winds her fingers inside of Meg's, closes her eyes and tells Meg the truth.

"I want to go to college and your father wants me to stay home."

Meg, who constantly dreams of Africa now and Cuba, where there are dancers who throw flames, and of travel with nothing but her pocketknife and a road map from her auntie, does not understand what her mother is saying.

"Just go. Is there something wrong with college?"

Meg does not see the tears right away but then she notices a wet line that runs down her mother's face, crosses at her chin and moves like a quiet river onto the top of her chest. Meg instinctively brings up the yellow sheet from the place where her worlds of beating drums and wild sunsets live, so she can wipe off her mother's face.

"Your father thinks that women, especially mothers, should stay home like his mother did."

"Do other moms go to school?"

"Yes."

"Mommie, can I go to college?"

When her mother turns to look at her, Meggie sees something that she has never seen before. Her mother is not soft and kind but suddenly hard and mean, she looks fierce and powerful. Meg holds her breath waiting for something terrible to happen.

"You *will* go to college. You will do and be whatever you want to be, if I have to sell everything we own. You will go to college, Margaret. This is about me and what your father thinks. It has nothing to do with you."

Meg, who has a pocketknife, two brothers who have made her rough and wild and a spinster auntie who has shown her a tiny glimpse of the world, does not understand.

"Can't we both go, Mommie?"

"I can't. I give up. I can't. I can't choose. I just can't anymore."

In the morning Meg wakes before her mother. Each morning now, she pushes her hand under the pillow to see if the knife is there. She just wants to feel it. When she turns she sees that her mother has the knife. She is turned away from Meggie and her feet have tangled in the sheets so they are halfway down the bed. The knife is lying at the edge of her open hand, just out of reach, and Meg cannot bring herself to lean over and grab it.

So she waits for a very long time until her mother wakes up and then Meg reaches for the knife quickly, as if it is a baby lying helpless in a burning building and she must save it. She is so anxious just to touch it again, to feel the weight of it against her fingers, to know that it is there, and for a moment nothing else exists. When her mother sees this she looks away quickly as if she has never seen or touched the knife herself. She looks past Meg and she focuses on the horizon, which isn't really there because there is a line of trees blocking the view just at the edge of the long sidewalk.

4

My daughter tells me she cannot choose and I have a memory so sudden and real that I place my hand against the side of my neck because I can feel my mother's breath there whispering, "I can't choose, baby, I can't." Katie comes to me at Elizabeth's house a bundle of nerves and confusion and the moment I see my daughter march up to the front door my heart drops into the pit of my stomach and begins swimming for light, for shore, for a place to land and then hide quickly. I drop my hand and begin to head for the closest landing.

Katie is seventeen and even though I burned incense to the Eye Goddess while she was in my womb so that she would have her father's deep blue eyes, the goddesses laughed and gave her my gray eyes and a mass of blond curly hair to prove that I had absolutely no idea what I was asking for. She is beautiful, smart, independent and very pissed off at her mother. Her father has chosen not to tell her that he has been screwing around, and I am sitting on a fence that will impale me no matter which direction I fall. If I tell her the truth, she will at first not believe me and then hate both her father and me. If I lie, I will hate myself. Which way shall I fall?

I have been living at Elizabeth's for almost three weeks, sleeping on the futon, having Katie drop off clothes, trying to negotiate an emotional and physical path toward a place of peace that I cannot see or describe or even desire. I am depressed, confused and simply want to be—just be. Elizabeth has moved around me, touching me lightly, engaging me in conversations that try very hard to open doors that I want to lean against with the edge of a two-ton cement mixer. If I open the door—then what? I cannot bear to put my fingers on the handle and pull it open. I cannot.

She has been gracious and patient and has allowed me to limp in place, lick my wounds and to settle into a routine that has become disgustingly ordinary. Sleep, drink, barely eat, go to work, talk a little bit, cry and then start all over again. I have lost ten pounds very quickly and the bags under my eyes are in serious danger of taking over my entire face.

"Come on, baby," Elizabeth whispers. "When was the last time you made a decision that was just for you? Think before you answer this one. Think."

I cannot answer, because there is no answer, and I hate her for asking and love her for asking and all I can seem to do is cry and respond with a vague form of grunting that has replaced all my spoken words. I am so depressed, I have started wearing the same outfits to work two and then three days in a row, and now there is Katie launching herself at me from Elizabeth's front porch.

She wants me to come home. This is an option I never considered until she forms the words and then spits them, really spits them, into my face.

"How can you do this to *me*?" my daughter says.

Before I can respond, she explodes in a chorus of rage that

would give the Mormon Tabernacle Choir an excuse to embrace Catholicism.

"One day my whole world changed. You run away from home—and isn't that supposed to be what I do?—and then I end up running back and forth, and all you can do is fucking *cry*. Get over it, Mom. What about my life? You are the mother—not me. What is wrong with you? Mom, stop it. Just fucking stop it."

Her words fly into the surface of my skin like blades of hot steel. She needs me at home. Who will do this and who will do that, and while she crucifies me in Elizabeth's hall I remember how her brother once emotionally disappeared just as she now sees me disappearing. One day he was kissing me in the kitchen and the next he was spending the night at Andy's and then Josh's and then back at Andy's, leaving me cryptic messages on the answering machine, plotting a future that selfishly did not include me or anyone else who might have the same last name and then eagerly brushing off any criticism of his behavior with a sweep of his hand and the words, "Mom, get over it. I'm growing up."

I want to grow up too. I want to grab my daughter by the arms and then slap her face like Elizabeth slapped me.

"You selfish hussy," I would tell her. "Don't you see what I gave up for you? Don't you know your father screws around and that I am unhappy and am trying hard to figure out what to do to get happy? Don't you think it's a little selfish to want me there so you have warm muffins in the morning and someone to iron your dress before the prom?"

I don't tell her this, because Katie is breaking my heart with a series of sobs that could drown an entire army and I am consumed with an ocean of guilt the size of the *Titanic*. I cannot bear to see what I have done to her.

"What do you want, sweetie?"

"Come home, Mommie. Please come home."

When Katie was a little girl and I was working at the University, she would call me the second she got home from school every day. Her voice was sweet and cool and so tiny I could feel it resting in the palm of my hand when she spoke. She called me "Mommie" then. For years and years she called me "Mommie," and it always made my heart twist into the shape of wedding ribbons, pearls, cascading fireworks.

"Mommie, I'm home. When are you coming home, Mommie? I miss you, Mommie. Sometimes it's scary here alone."

Katie is still sobbing when I pull her into my arms and whisper, "Oh, baby," into her ear.

As I hold her I want to slice open my chest with something sharp and long and show her the dark shadows that have all but strangled me into an eternal coma. I want to tell her that I am so unhappy I want to lie down and never get up. I want to tell her that I am going to slip and fall and tremble and then fall down again before I learn how to walk but I cannot tell my baby those things. There is a huge part of her that is just that—still a baby, and she needs me and I am a mother. *I am a mother.*

"Okay" is what I say instead. "I'll come home."

These three words will prove to be terribly expensive and those words and what happens next will end up eating out all but the last inch of my heart, but I do it—so I think—for my baby.

Elizabeth is not home when I leave. I could not begin to tell her what I am doing, because I am obviously out of my mind and I would not be able to look her in the eye. Both her eyes. Her wise, beautiful eyes. She is out raising money to prevent George W. Bush from decapitating a woman's right to have an abortion while I gather up my clothes, the few books Katie brought me and no self-esteem because what little I have left is tucked in between my legs like the tail of a frightened dog. There will be hell to pay later and I will go into debt paying it. I will nearly end up in the poorhouse paying for it. I will sell pieces of my heart and the wind on my face and my left ovary and a night of the best sex I could ever have to pay for that hell.

When I turn quickly to leave Elizabeth's house, what I see is a rainbow. Colors from the edge of the hall through the kitchen and onto the ceiling that blend together in a wave of singular fineness. I know it is a mistake to leave before I close the door but there is this limitless battery in my head that tells me over and over, "This is what women do—they sacrifice." And I back out of the door slowly because I don't really want to leave. I want to stay and bring Katie into a house that feels just like this, but instead I back out and Katie leads me to the car like a little puppy who will go anywhere with strangers who have cookies, and within six minutes I am right back where I started.

It is a foreign land, this house I have lived in for all these years. I know my way home blind but when we walk into the kitchen through the back door by the garage I feel my skin crawl with uneasiness and I see the basement door and remember the boxes and the climb up the steps to watch the sex in the bedroom and I fight an urge to run as if I am a recovering addict who has just spotted a large bottle of free gin. Katie knows none of this, and I step back into my old life. I am slipping on an old shoe, but there is something lodged in the tip of the toe.

I walk slowly past the stacks of magazines on the chair by the front door, my fingers trail across Katie's old jacket, my blue wool sweater, a photo of my son that tips to the left a good inch every time someone opens the front door, the worn edges on the corner by the stairs leading up—*there*—every inch of this house, my life, memorized.

"You okay?" Katie asks me as we shuttle my clothes upstairs and I pause at the entrance to the bedroom. My feet have decided to stop. There is no moving forward.

Katie has her father's height but everything else belongs to me. The color of her hair, the slant of her chin, the way she grabs her forearms when she is nervous, her weight and how her mind wraps around issues of complexity and then rips them apart with fangs as long as the drill bits on an oil rig. She is right down the middle on the right brain–left brain scale and when she pauses like this I know it is because she cannot decide if she should follow her heart or go work up a pie chart to see what to do next.

"I'm fine," I lie. "But..."

I am stumbling big-time. What the hell is wrong with me? Katie is old enough. I am old enough. What is wrong? What is with this huge pause in everything I do and say and feel? Have I been doing this forever? Have I ever stopped to look?

"Mom...?"

All the windows in my life are shut. I feel a wave of combustion that is building like small tsunamis. Air, light, air. The essentials have disappeared. Katie is not yet wise enough to see that something gigantic is amiss. That is the reason I cling to for returning to this hall, this life, to these unanswered questions.

"I'm going to crash in your brother's room."

"Oh."

She thinks she gets it. She must think there was some huge fight that was patterned after the last Gulf War that rose up fast and then collapsed when someone ran to hide. That would be me.

"Katie," I boldly say. "There are things you need to know. I'm a mess."

"I got that part."

"Katie..."

"Mom...?"

"I'm sorry."

"For what? Leaving?"

"No. Not for leaving but for what might happen next."

Could I have suffered short-term memory loss in such a brief period of time? Everything is suddenly unfamiliar. It is as if I cannot remember simple things like how to walk to the phone or make a decision or express my inner feelings. Once, just after an old college friend had finished his PhD and was working as a clinical psychologist, one of his old classmates called him, stoned out of her mind. She was at a local gas station and could not remember how to get out of the car. My psychologist friend tried talking her out of the car.

"Roll down the window first, sweetie. Get some air. Can you do that?"

"Maybe. I'm not sure."

"Now gently pull up on that little button you see. Can you see it?"

She couldn't remember how to pull or push or move. Dialing the phone had been a miracle. My friend got into his car, drove to the gas station and literally picked her up, put her in his car and took her home.

That is me. I am stoned on myself. How in the hell am I going to get up off Shaun's bed, initiate a conversation with Bob, remember how to urinate?

I am an assistant professor of social work at the University. I write grants and talk to famous people all over the world. I research legal cases for people who pay the University a great deal of money for my services. Once I testified in front of Congress and winked at Hillary Clinton. I can stand up in front of three hundred graduate students and tell them they are full of shit and that they will never get jobs because they don't know how to spell and cannot do basic research. I can make babies and direct political campaigns and run three miles without skipping a beat. I held my grandmother's hand to my own healthy breasts when she was dying of breast cancer and I have been to the funerals of friends, my favorite aunt and a neighbor man who blew me a kiss five minutes before he was hit by a car. I was once nearly raped in a parking garage and have a scar that runs down the inside of my left thigh from where I fell on the glass from my car window when I hurled a rock through it to get the attention of a cop who was breezing past drinking a can of Pepsi—I will never forget that can of Pepsi. All of this and more, so much more, and I cannot get off the goddamn bed.

I think I need help. Elizabeth will be pissed even though she would also forgive me forever, so I lurch for the phone in Shaun's bedroom and I call Bianna. She is a funky spirit-guide woman who worked with me at the University for just a few weeks, felt the "repressed" energy of our academic world and took off so fast you'd have thought there was anthrax on every desk. Bianna now connects the living to the dead. Really. This woman has a master's degree in marketing and has worked for everyone from the Girl Scouts to the Harley-Davidson Company and she now runs a business aptly named "Rising from the Dead," where she swears she can help people by reconnecting them to loved ones who have died.

Bianna does have a gift. She's definitely intuitive. She hears the phone ring before someone dials her number. She can predict illness and weather and events like major traffic accidents, political disasters and a marriage and life that has fallen apart at the seams, the collar, the hem and the buttonholes.

"I will come to you," she announces as if she has been waiting for my call.

"I think that would be a good idea, because I cannot get off the bed in my son's bedroom."

"Is this the son who no longer lives there?"

"Yes?"

"Then it is not his bedroom. This is a no-fault state, darling, half the bedroom is yours and half now belongs to your husband."

"Husband."

"You are still married, and very confused. Did you not see this coming?"

"Apparently not."

"Meg, you are a bit of an ass."

"An ass?"

"Yes, and you have forgotten how to form your own sentences. Do you want me to bring Elizabeth?"

"Elizabeth? No. Don't call Elizabeth. I was at her house for three weeks and I came back here ten minutes ago. She'll kill me."

"Well, this explains everything. Don't you get how messed up I am either?"

"I cannot even drive a car. Are you kidding me?"

Bianna, believe it or not, is more—what? More normal than Elizabeth. She is married to a man, childless, accepted by everyone from the local garden club to the sports boosters at the high school, who have her speak once a year at their breakfast meeting. She makes house calls. She has a small office downtown with a little hand-painted sign and people think of her the same way they think of the local dentist, the guys at the bakery and everyone in town who belongs to the PTA.

Bianna drops the bomb just when I am thinking how she will save me.

"You did not let me finish," she says loudly.

"What?"

"I will come to you when you are ready to listen. You are not ready to listen."

"What?"

"See."

"This is not the time for humor," I say, raising my voice just a bit. "I will pay you. I need a house call."

"You need to think. You need to sit in that bedroom or go for a walk and think."

"Think? What the hell should I think about?"

"What you want and how you ended up on a bed in your son's room, which is really not his bedroom, calling a psychic to make a house call when you are one of the most intelligent women I have ever met."

"Bianna . . . something, give me something."

The pause is terrifying. I am underwater and waiting for someone to pass me a thin line of air. Just a simple breath. That's all. Then I will be able to get out of the car by myself.

"Meggie." My name is a sentence. I hear it and my eyes cloud.

"I never say this," Bianna continues when I don't speak. "It goes against everything I believe in and know to be true. But you have to do this—and this is all you get from me until you are ready, and you will know when you are ready. You have to take a giant step backward."

"What?"

"That's it. Backward. It's a terrible word. I never use it, but your case is extreme."

"I've gone backward instead of forward."

"You are too analytical. You have to go back before you can go forward. So get off the bed. Go look around. It will be raining in days."

She hangs up. That's it. I would say "Jesus Fucking Christ" but I hate those words, especially all in a row like that, and I am pretty sure Jesus is a woman who is too busy for this shit. Raining in days? Backward?

"Get up," I tell myself. "How hard can that be?"

I have to trust someone and it may as well be Bianna and it's pretty obvious that I have no clue.

My legs miraculously move and I shuffle around the bedroom that I should have made into an office three years ago. Should have? Shaun has left everything in his bedroom except his clothes, a radio and the book of poetry he read like a Bible. He spent the entire last year of high school in this room, at the houses of his friends Andy and Josh, and at school. Then he left. Angry, a loner, closing in on a life path that will fuel his need to understand how everything works and is connected. Where did I fail him? How did I fail him? Did he see me moving toward this terrible place of uncertainty? What secret did he never share?

Katie interrupts me. Her presence awakens something mildly psychotic in me. If she weren't in my life, I would not be back in this bedroom. Would I have ever come back here? Damn it. Damn her.

"What do you want?" I snarl.

"Geez, Mom, I was just checking to see if you are okay."

I snap. Just like that. She freezes in place.

"No, I am not fucking okay. Are you kidding me? Okay? How the hell can I be okay? Your father screws around with other women. I hate this house and my life and what I do every god-damn day. I'm a robot. I have no idea who I am. Not one little clue. I'm lost and confused as hell. Look at me, for crissakes, Katie. I'm standing in my son's old bedroom looking at pieces of a life that no longer exists. I am not fucking okay, do you get that? I AM NOT OKAY."

By the time I am finished I am screaming. Katie has been struck dumb. She is standing in front of me with her arms hanging at her sides as if they have been severed and any movement will make them fall off and drop to the floor. Her beautiful mouth is wedged open just an inch. Her eyes are as big as bike wheels. I can see her heart trying desperately to get outside of her body. It is thumping against her chest and her shirt is rising and falling, rising and falling each time her heart pounds to be released. Has she ever heard me scream like this? I think not, and I feel water spilling over the dam, but this is nothing. Nothing at all. The dam will break eventually, but I cannot go on. Katie has not moved and there are tears running down her face. I do what I always do, what every mother does, what I cannot stop myself from doing.

"Baby, sweet baby. Come here."

Katie is in my arms and sobbing into my shoulder. Her weight against my chest is solid and warm. I say nothing. We cry together for a good five minutes and I let her go first. She pulls back just slightly and I wipe the tears from beneath her eyes with my fingers. Everything about her is familiar and soft. I know how her tears fall toward her chin and where they will land. I know she wants everything to be perfect and that she is desperate to get good grades so she can get into a college that I will never be able to afford. I know how she sleeps with her left leg pulled up as high as it will go and an old pink stuffed kitten wrapped in her hand. I know she loves storms and hates the dark and that she's never had sex but is on the pill anyway because, well, just because. I know her. She is my baby, and what in the hell am I doing? What am I doing?

She talks and the sound of her voice is a tranquilizer. Something to grab on to, something to swallow, a tonic to keep me on some kind of small but equal plateau.

"Mom, do you remember the day I called you from school because I got my period for the first time and I was nuts and thought I would die or something?"

"Of course I remember."

"What I remember is running from English class to the health room and thinking that if I could not get you on the phone that I might die. Really. I was terrified and sick and there was no one else in the world that I thought could help me."

"Sweetie..."

"When I heard your voice it felt as if your hand was moving inside of me, Mommie. Do you remember how I cried when we talked?"

"Yes." I close my eyes and I can see the red skirt I was wearing that day, the way my hand trembled as I was rising from my chair to reach for the car keys so I could go get her.

"I cried because it was the first time I realized how much I loved you and how much you meant to me and I'm so sorry that I never told you."

My heart stops. I can feel it grind to a halt, and then brace for that second when you can choose to keep breathing or simply remain at ease forever.

"It wasn't your period?"

"Maybe just a little, but I'll never forget you being there when I called and coming for me and putting me on the couch and how we went to dinner and celebrated because I was a woman. Do you remember what you said that night?"

"I don't remember anything today."

My heart is barely cranking. I am mesmerized.

"We were clinking our water glasses and you looked me in the eye and you said, 'Katie, there hasn't been one single day my entire life that I have not rejoiced because I am a woman.'"

"What was I thinking?"

"Mom, you said it and you meant it and now it's time for you to act like a woman."

My heart lurches forward as if it has been struck by a cargo ship. Who turned my baby into a guru?

"Katie, I don't want to hurt you, and I am afraid. I'm afraid I might hurt you and I might make the wrong decisions and that you will never forgive me."

"What do you want, Mom?"

"I have no idea, baby, no idea at all."

Bob comes at me walking on objects so light and thin I cannot see them. Cotton, water, the breath of a baby—those are all heavy. He floats around me asking what I want and need and saying once very quickly that he is sorry, and I realize on the third day that I could use this entire situation to my advantage if I only cared, if I could only remember why I married him and what I am doing in this house and how to turn off the light switch. I have floated myself to a place that is one level above la-la land. I work and eat and sleep, and sometimes if I remember I do something terribly remarkable like answer the phone or buy groceries. I can't know if anything is changed because I can't re-member how anything was before . . . before I wanted to watch.

"Do you want to see a therapist?"

This from a man who still asks me to go bowling and who has missed birthdays and anniversaries and who would most likely be hard-pressed to remember the color of my eyes if I turned around and he was not looking directly into them. But do I see him? Did I ever see him? Do I want to see him? There are hun-dreds and thousands of miles between us and I am so exhausted, I cannot—do not want to—go more than one inch. One single inch, and what will that do? Nothing. Not a damn thing.

"A therapist?" I respond without moving.

He looks at me and I see a blank television screen. Maybe the tail end of a cartoon with dogs and cats dressed up like people.

"Why?" I ask.

He is thinking. I imagine him scrambling around inside of his head, lifting up curtains, peeking under the couch, searching desperately for a pile of sentences that he can put together in an answer.

"I thought we could try and work this out."

"Work this out," I repeat back to him. "Work this out."

"Yes," he says forcefully. "People go to therapy, talk about things, see where they are headed. It happens all over the place. In fact, it's happening right now in dozens of places right in this city."

A spark of anger rises inside of me. I think I could hit him. Really hard with the back of my hand on the edge of his chin so his head pops up. I actually have to hold my hand so I don't do it. I could actually hit him.

"Is that what you want, Bob?"

He doesn't hesitate, which is a bigger part of the answer than the answer itself.

"I'm not sure."

My response comes as quickly.

"I will go to a therapist, but I will not go with you. I have to go. But, Bob, this has nothing to do with you. Nothing at all."

There is a look of tight confusion galloping across his face. I can hear thundering horse hooves and the room is suddenly filled with dust from dozens of legs pounding in the stampede.

"I'm sorry, Meg," he fairly whimpers. "Jesus God, I'm sorry."

Once I loved this man. I could not wait to see him on Friday nights and the simple thought of him made me weak in the knees. We made babies together and I cried in his arms. One night, so long ago I could not begin to reach back and pull out an exact time, we stayed up for two entire days reading poetry to each other, making love and then reading more. Was I twenty? Who was I? What was I doing? Did I really love him?

Questions are piling so high around me, I have to stop myself, otherwise I will not be able to get out of the room. The door will be blocked shut, the windows sealed; any form of escape will be obliterated.

"Bob," I finally whisper, but I do not go to him.

He looks up and what I see is him in that bed, our bed, and the woman under the red tent and his knees bucking and his head pushed back against the headboard and the bed moving and I slowly begin to back away from him.

"I can't help you now."

He says nothing.

"I can't help you, Bob."

"I'm not sure I understand, but I do understand that I deserve nothing from you right now, Meg. Nothing at all."

"You will have to leave me alone," I demand. "I don't know what will happen. I don't know anything right now. Do you understand that, Bob?"

"Yes."

"Fine" is the last thing I say or will say to him for a very long time.

Katie calls late Friday and says she wants to stay overnight again at her best friend's house. I say yes and at the same moment am choked by a wad of panic that begins boiling in my stomach and rolls to the top of my throat. I am going to be home alone. Again. The quiet of my nights in the house, his house, someone's house, has risen up to haunt me, and in every room there are laughing echoes taunting me with voices I can barely hear.

"What?" I ask the walls through the beating drum of my own heart. "What do I do, where do I go?"

My feet listen. They know what to do. I push some money into my pocket, dislodge the house key from my ring set, lace on my tennis shoes and I start walking.

In three blocks with the summer air blowing in across Lake Michigan, sounds of neighbors putting away their grills and the rumbling conversations from open car windows, I realize with a great deal of glee that I am lonely. Maybe I have been lonely for a very long time. The house walls. My schedule, the absence of a husband, my daughter's exploding life—I am alone more than I realized.

"Not tonight," I say out loud. "People. Just some people."

I diagnose my malaise as loneliness just as the RadCalf Wine Bar and Café appears at the end of the block. Before I can talk myself out of going into the bar alone, before I remember how many years it has been since I went into a bar alone, before I realize the last time I was in the café was a year ago with Bob, who looked mysteriously happy when I had just gotten back from a conference, I pull open the door and walk inside.

The ambience always makes me smile. Scattered tables, old wooden floors worn thin from years of all the neighbors' footfalls, soft lighting and, most important, many open seats at the bar. I order a glass of Merlot and snuggle in to listen to conversations other than the ones I have been having inside of my head—alone.

Before I finish my second glass, another one arrives, and the bartender tells me the woman around the corner bought it for me.

"What?"

"Over there." The bartender points and the woman—vaguely familiar, short brown hair, T-shirt, no makeup—smiles and salutes me. Without thinking, I wave her over, realizing as I do so that wine is a wonderful narcotic that can make the timid very, very bold.

It is a stretch to remember who she is, and as she wobbles from her seat, I smile, because she is just one drink beyond tipsy. "A friend," I think. "Someone to flush away another hour with, someone who might listen, a kindred spirit, who hopefully will forget everything we say in the morning."

I am quickly embarrassed because the woman tells me her name is Jane Souley and she has lived at the end of my block for at least a year and we have spoken maybe twice without even exchanging names.

"I think I'm drunk," she says, beginning the conversation, and I laugh and tell her that's what I am apparently trying to do.

We quickly stretch, as women do, into that paradise of female familiarity—kids, jobs, periods, and touch fast, very fast, on that gliding force that bonds women everywhere. We are similar and yet totally different. Jane touches my arm. We are women, sharing hearts, time and everything—we are women sharing everything. We laugh, and then just like that, she begins to cry.

"What is it, Jane?"

"I'm so fucking unhappy...and..."

"Jesus," I think to myself. "She's worse off than I am. Who is she? What is she trying to tell me?"

"And...what? Jane, what is it?"

"I know you."

She tells me this and she looks away and now she is crying harder. I lift my cocktail napkin to her eyes and have this sudden urge to wrap her in my arms and let her cry until she is finished. This woman *needs* to cry. She needs me, and in a strange, awesome way, I need her, especially tonight.

"What is it?" I repeat.

"You might hate me when I tell you."

"I doubt that."

"But I like you, Meg. I have, like, no friends. My husband left ten months ago. I . . . I have to tell you."

I'm ready. I think I am ready, but when she says it slowly, I am not really that ready.

"I know you from your picture."

"My picture?"

She nods. Her speech has slowed to that place where drunks lie low and their words gather in rows at the back of their throats. A place I want to be.

"The one in your bedroom, on the dresser." She looks away and cries harder.

"You were in my bedroom?"

She nods again.

"When?"

"Ten months ago. Just after my husband left."

Oh my God. She slept with Bob.

Jane tells the story in halting sentences and I still do not take my hand off her arm. She was walking. He picked her up. They talked. I was at the damn conference and when I got back he took me here, here to this very café. She never did it again. She's been crazy ever since. What are the chances? What in the hell are the chances?

When she turns to look at me after the story, I wonder what other pains are lined up in her heart. She looks pathetic and I cannot hate her or let go of her arm even though I can barely sit myself, even though I am also lost, even though I have no idea what will happen tomorrow or how I will make it to the end of the week. I think only that she needs me and that I have already let Bob slip from my hands and that we most definitely need another glass of wine.

"I had to tell you, Meg. I almost died when you walked in. I am not like that, you know, sleeping with neighbor men, but I just got so messed up. I'm still so messed up. Why are you here? Why aren't you trying to murder me?"

I tell her, leaning in so we can support each other. We share our stories in sentences that dip and sway just like we do when we straddle the sidewalk down the block and to my house. We laugh thinking what it would be like to have Bob come in and find us talking in the kitchen, and then I put Jane to bed in Katie's room because she has left her key locked in her car, and when I turn to leave she takes my arm and she asks me if I will be her friend, because she will be mine.

"Yes," I say, "I need you too, I do."

My dreams that night are laced with shadows and questions and in the morning when I remember the night before I race to the bedroom and there is Jane, arms wrapped around Katie's pink kitten, her head tilted toward the door, pillow on the floor, and I tell myself she is real, that I did something, one good thing, and that whatever happens next will be okay. I tell myself this over and over, and then I do what I have done maybe thirty thousand times.

I make the coffee and I wait.

5

Dr. Cassie Breckwith has six stuffed dogs, a drum, a lava lamp, a pile of broken pencils, stacks and stacks of files, and an ashtray full of marbles sitting on top of her desk. Off to one side I swear to God there is a slab of concrete with a nail through its center, two Folgers coffee cans filled with dirt as black as midnight and an empty beer bottle. It's all lovely stuff and my mind is whirling. There are no cutesy-wootsy posters on the walls advocating the benefits of peace or love or anything in between. The couch is a sagging lump of green corduroy. There are no psychiatric magazines or pill bottles anywhere. The window has a full view of the asphalt parking lot, and when I walk into her office the first thing I see is her bending over a stuffed chair and whacking at a fly with her shoe. I like her instantly.

"Damn vents let in everything from mice to these flies," she tells me, slapping like a wild woman at a fly that is admittedly the size of something that should not be able to fly at all.

"Need some help?"

She laughs loudly. It is a machine gun. This woman has one of those infectious laughs that makes you want to start cackling, which is exactly what I do after she says, "That's what I'm supposed to say."

I have never been to a therapist and from the get-go with this woman I am immediately sorry that I have not discovered how screwed up I am much sooner. Dr. C has a kind intensity that overshadows everything and I watch her walk around her office and immediately know what her entire life must be like. She never makes her bed and there are always dishes on the counter. She was married, may still be, and has grandchildren who love to come over because she doesn't give a damn if the house gets messy. She drinks something with whiskey in it, loves to watch old movies and she has a beautiful singing voice. I have no idea if any of this information is correct, but I decide to latch on to it and make it real. She's what all our grandmas would call "a real peach."

The preliminaries are already down on paper. Husband. Affair. Unhappy. Married young. Unhappy. Two kids. Works at the University. Unhappy. Fairly decent support system. Confused and unhappy.

She begins by leaning forward in her big chair, touching one set of fingers to the other and telling me how remarkable it is that this is my first trip to a therapist. "That's something," she exclaims as if she has just found a missing hundred-dollar bill.

She makes me laugh again. Her polyester pants and long cotton blouse, her pinned-up hair that dangles out in strands from behind her ears and her row of gold rings, one on every single finger and thumb, are a miracle of comfortableness for me. "Talk," she commands me. We are just going to talk and everything stays in this room and there isn't one damn thing she hasn't heard, and I am free to say, do or be anything I want.

"If only I knew" is what I say first.

"You look like hell. Have you been sleeping?"

Without even realizing it I start crying. "I look like hell because I feel like hell," I weep. There is Kleenex and water and her hand reaching out to hold my arm—a steady beat against what I perceive as me swaying and about to go under.

I cannot answer even one of her questions, so we begin even more slowly than I imagine she imagined, what with me being supposedly intelligent and all.

I tell her where I was born and how my mother made such a huge deal out of me going to college that I could not stop going to college and that's why I have two master's degrees and three-fourths of a PhD and never really left the university. I even tell her about Jane and the bar and how I think I may be losing my mind. We waltz on and on like this for almost forty-five minutes, when I suddenly blurt out a fact that is apparently astonishing only to me.

"I never did what I wanted to do."

What I expect is the good doctor to clap her hands together, prepare a bill and send me on my way, but she does not. Instead, she tells me a secret. She leans forward so that her face is two feet from mine and I can look right inside of her.

"Twenty-three years ago, I got up one morning and knew I had to change my life. I had become an old woman at the age of thirty-seven. I was fat, drank vodka for breakfast, and I was working as a waitress at a restaurant."

I am just a bit astounded.

Dr. Cassie tells me in rapid succession that she left her husband, went back to college, almost starved to death, had to ask for help from her parents, raised her daughter pretty much alone and spent eleven years—eleven years—getting her PhD in clinical psychology.

I can only think to ask this: "Why that morning? Why not the week before or the following year?"

Dr. C has probably told this story a hundred times. It apparently does not get easier to tell it, because I see a wave of sorrow move across her face as deep as her own soul as she does so.

"That morning I hit my daughter," she tells me, looking away, remembering the slap again, the soft skin of her baby against her hand, the look on the little girl's face, the instant realization of a horrific mistake. "I had never hit her before—never—and that morning I hit her so hard, I knocked a tooth loose."

I want to touch her and tell her that I know how she feels but I already get the point of the story and I have sensed her humanness from the moment I walked in the door. I know that her daughter was not harmed and that she never struck her again and that the slap propelled her to move away from who she had become to who she wanted to be. All those college years are finally coming in handy.

It's my turn.

"When you watched your husband making love to another woman, what was going on inside of you, Meggie?"

"I think I left my body and was just, well, watching. I remember thinking that the woman was too beautiful to be with Bob and that she would probably not have an orgasm and I was worried that the bedspread looked tacky."

The doctor laughs and leans forward again, and I can feel her breath on my face.

"What else?"

"After that, I fell apart. After I left the room and was running through the yards."

"Why? What were you thinking then?"

"When I started to run, everything changed. I felt something smash against my chest and I realized, well, you know."

"I don't know, Meggie—you have to say it. Can you say it?"

It is a confession. I see that. The uttering of something so deep and dark that once it surfaces, you and the people around you may suffocate. To me it is horrible. Horrible to think that years of my life may have been a lie. To think that I may have missed the boat, the plane, the bus and anything else that moves. My stomach lurches and I have to force it to stop six inches from the edge of my throat.

"I didn't care that he was fucking someone else."

"What else?"

"I got excited."

"Sexually excited?"

"A little bit, which in my case is really something."

"What else?"

"You are relentless," I tell her, looking to that same spot on the window where Dr. C focused when she told me about her daughter.

"Once you say these things, a long white sheet falls over them and they slowly disappear," she tells me, so softly I can barely hear her speaking. "It doesn't mean it will get easier right away, but it's a start. You know it's the beginning."

I want to begin something, but there is this strange sensation that if I begin something then something ends, and I am hanging on to everything so tightly that I can feel my fingers swelling. There are rope burns on the palms of my hands and there is a pool of blood right where I am sitting.

"Can you say it?"

"It's a couple of things and it's everything. I am running through the yard and it wasn't the sex thing, it was that I didn't care and that I had no idea where I was running to."

"You were lost?"

"I've been lost for a very long time, and I just don't want to be lost anymore. I need to figure out how to be happy. I cannot remember the last time I was happy."

The good doctor is smiling. When I finish talking, she moves back into her chair and begins tapping her fingers together again.

"There," she says loudly. "You have had your slap and now you begin again."

There is a wave as high as forever about to crash on top of me. Begin again. How in the hell do I begin again?

"How?" I whimper. "How do I do that?"

"Well, we just started. Now we get to work. There will be no more passiveness and waiting and there will be wondering, but you have to agree, right now, here, Meg, in the next second, to work with me and to remember what it felt like when you were floating around in that bedroom of yours. Can you do that?"

"It's not my bedroom anymore," I remind her.

"I take it that is a yes?"

"Yes."

There. That's it, then. We are out of time, which is mildly irritating but also a relief. During the next five minutes she asks me to make what she calls a "Life List." "Write out your whole life, all the people in it, places, everything you can think of, put it all down on paper. Then you must look at each item, and this may take a while, and decide what goes and what stays."

It's just on paper, she adds, so I can change my mind when I get to the real part. "The real part?" I ask.

"Yes, that's when you actually begin discarding things."

All righty, then.

"Can I sit in the lobby until next week?" I ask her as we both rise to leave.

"There are already fifty-six people living in the lobby. All clients of mine. There's no room left, but if someone jumps out the window I will be sure to give you a call. You just never know when there might be an opening."

I laugh but I also want to cry. Now I actually have to leave the building and get into the car again, and when I manage to do that, I steer myself over to Elizabeth's house, which is the only place I can think of where I might find safety, shelter and a glass of wine before noon. I am worried about the list, not to mention the next fifty or so years of my life. Worried as hell. And now, on top of everything else, I also worry about Jane.

Jane has entered my life like an out-of-control band saw. She needs constant attention, and oil in all the right places. I cannot wait to give her Dr. C's card. I cannot abandon her either. Suddenly, we are both swimming toward an unseen shore and I'm the one pulling the raft. Sweet Jesus. Poor me. Poor Jane.

Halfway to Elizabeth's, I realize that I have left my purse on the floor in Dr. C's office. Now what? This kind of thing has been happening to me since the day I watched Bob and the geranium woman. Maybe some kind of secret powder was released and I'm doomed to spend the rest of my life looking for things that I have lost. How ironic. Yesterday I forgot to turn off the iron, lost my car keys and could not remember if I parked in front of the building or behind the building. I am so distracted, I suddenly think, I should not even be driving a car.

My purse is sitting on a chair in the waiting room when I get there. It looks just a bit lonely, and when I go to pick it up I decide to sit in the chair for a while. Just sit. I could be in a dentist's office. Magazines are on the table. A photograph of geese flying over a long cornfield is tipped to one side above a long table by the door. I move my hand to the wall behind me, where I know there are several offices where psychologists listen and then listen some more, with their fingers tapping against the sides of their chairs, legs crossed, words rationed out like pieces of old bread to starving birds. I think of the piles of secrets and the damaged souls and hearts and minds that must have reached some interesting conclusions just beyond my fingertips.

"Touch the wall," I wonder to myself, "and will I feel a beating heart, the swell of a heartache, the devastation of a lost love?" No one is in the office, so I get out of the chair and stand with my back against the wall. It does not matter to me that I am in this suite of offices and that someone could come in at any moment or that my own doctor could walk back and see me caressing the wall and have me committed. People do worse things than fondle a portion of a room.

I close my eyes and place my palms against the wall, fingers spread, and I listen through my skin for those beating secrets. I sense the rumbling announcement of an avalanche of emotion, but is it theirs or my own? The wall is moving into my hands, a slow cascade that seems to be pushing me out into the room. There is so much hidden in the fabric of walls. So much. Heartaches and healing hands. A secret sorrow released from its cage and into the arms of a kind and smart woman who will throw it out the door so it lands in the lobby, where it will be swept away after hours. But in the corners, some of the secrets linger and there are piles of transparent tears that cling to each other longer and harder than their former owners kept them melded to their souls.

I know also that the swirling mess of my life must be nothing compared to some of the tragic complications that have walked past my chair. Death. The loss of a child. Suicide. Incest. Rape. Lost love. Mental illness. My pain is a simple scratch compared to what I see when my hands are pressed to the wall.

"How easy to feel guilty," I say out loud.

A woman comes into the waiting room. There are dark circles under her eyes and she cannot bring herself to say hi to me. She looks at the door that leads down to the offices and I think she must be deciding if she is going to stay or run back out the door she just came into.

"Hello," I say. "How are you?"

She catches my eye for a second and I see the breath go out of her. Is she on medication? On the verge? Accustomed to coming into an empty room? Or maybe she can see through my skin and into my dungeon of terror. Maybe.

"Fine," she responds, and I see that she decides to sit and stay. I think she will stay. This makes a sigh, wide and long, leave my own chest, and that mother spot in me, the spot that brought me back home, that keeps me weighted to a place that can no longer be ignored for the deep pit of its uncomfortableness, makes me want to reach out and take her hand. I am a toucher; there is no doubt about that. It has gotten me in trouble plenty of times with babies at the mall, young boys on the verge of adulthood— why is it no one wants to touch adolescent boys when that is the one thing, simple and true, that they so much desire?

Shaun was fourteen when I discovered this. My son was in one of his constant angry and selfish stages where speaking to someone who had the same last name took way too much energy. One day he kept bumping into me. We'd be in the kitchen and he'd brush against my arm. We passed in the hall and he reached out to grab my hand. After about fifteen encounters like this, I lunged at him as he ran to catch a ride downtown with his father. I pulled him into my chest and he fell against me in a movement that can only be called surrender. My fingers waltzed through his hair and I felt his sweet breath against my neck. He let his arms glide across my back and for ten seconds he was my boy again. Then the car horn beeped and he was gone.

We never talked about that, but it happened again and I

started going into his room at night and he let me massage his hand, and once I dared to sing him a song from the days when he was a boy.

This did not last long. Shaun bounced into a darker phase after this and pulled so far away from me and everyone else he knew that I have not seen him come back since. I know he will. He will drift and move closer and pull away again, and then one day he will show up and find me and maybe he will tell me what it is that he has buried so far away from his own heart. It is something I count on, otherwise I may go blind with worry. I want my son back. Someday.

My waiting room companion shifts abruptly to the left and makes me realize I am still in my psychologist's office. It takes me a second to remember why, and pulling that thought into focus exhausts me. It simply exhausts me. I cannot remember ever being this tired. When I think about it, my feet and hands and face and bones and blood and skin—every piece of me that I can touch and feel and visualize—aches. Wouldn't it be funny to be lying on the floor when Dr. C comes into the waiting room for this woman?

Which she does, of course, the second I have this thought. The doctor looks startled to see me there.

"My, you moved in fairly quickly."

"I came back for my purse and then I sat down and now I realize that I am almost too tired to drive."

The good doctor looks away and addresses the other woman. She puts me on hold by raising her hand as if she is trying to direct traffic.

"Sydney, can you go wait in my office and get your usual beverage and I will be right with you?"

The woman rises, looks at me as if to say, "You thought I was the crazy one," and disappears down the hall.

Dr. C stands in front of me, hands on hips, that hair hanging wildly behind her ears, and waits for me to say something. I have no clue.

"Doctor?" I ask.

"Meg, are you okay?"

"Maybe not."

"Is there someone you can call?"

"I already called her once. Do you think she will come get me again?"

"Who is it?"

I tell her. Everyone knows Elizabeth. Maybe she has been lovers with Dr. C. Maybe she has been a patient. Maybe it's her wild and wide reputation.

"She will come."

Dr. C moves forward. She touches me on the shoulder and tells me she is a bit worried.

"I just came back for the purse and then I sat down and then I started thinking and that woman walked in and I realized that people don't touch anymore, not enough. People don't touch just to say something like, 'Hi, how are you,' because we are all worried about lawsuits, and then my mind realized that my body was exhausted and then—"

"Meggie, can you stop?"

"I have no idea, Doctor. I think I may be exhausted or having some kind of breakdown. What is wrong with me?"

"Nothing is wrong with you, sweetheart, but you are suffering, right now, right this instant, from something known as depression."

"Wow."

She laughs when I say "Wow," and her laugh is so damn infectious, I begin laughing too.

"Meg, I think you need a break, but I need to go help my other patient now. Call Elizabeth. If she cannot come, then you must promise me that you will wait for fifty minutes until I am finished. Can you do that?"

"Yes. I think I can dial the phone, just don't ask me to do something like get up and drive a car."

"Meggie, I have Elizabeth's number and your cell phone number. I will call you tonight and give you some instructions, and I want you to think about whether or not you would take some medication."

"Really?"

"Maybe, not necessarily, but maybe."

"Can I just drink a little bit?"

"Sometimes that makes it worse. Are you a good drunk or a bad drunk?"

"Life of the party, baby."

"Maybe you shouldn't drink, unless you want to jump off Elizabeth's back porch, naked."

Ha! I knew it. She's been to Elizabeth's house. I am already thinking that I will just sip some wine to keep me calm while I wait for her to call me. She pushes her hand into my shoulder, not hard, but very firmly.

"I know who you are and that you will do what you say you will. Call Elizabeth now. Drink if you must. Wait for my call."

"What?"

I say this like a drunk would, slurring my words, and she pushes off from me and swims to her next patient. "Bye-bye, Doctor," I think to myself, and then I sit for a few minutes.

I never just *sit*. It is something so rare that I must actually focus on sitting. I have no idea what will happen next. The patterns of my life are dissolving one by one and I am not certain what to hang on to. The thought of being alone has never occurred to me. Not once in all of the years I have been married. I am never alone. A-L-O-N-E. I silently roll the letters around inside of my mouth and wonder what it would feel like to say them out loud.

"I am alone in this office," I say like the most quiet whisper in the world, so softly that tiny birds and small people and clouds with ears cannot even hear it. Someone could be sitting on my lap and they would not hear it.

I cannot say it again. The word has been lost. I do not even know what it looks like or remember what it felt like to say it two seconds ago. What is that all about? What is anything all about?

Minutes pass and I do not move. When I hear a voice rise in anger and then extinguish itself, I know I must get out of the room before the good doctor and Sydney tiptoe back into the waiting room and discover my secret.

Elizabeth is home. She says, "Of course I will come. Do not move. DO NOT MOVE."

I do not tell her where this office is, but she gets here in twenty minutes. My goal now, besides not getting drunk and taking any antidepressants, is to find out how these two babes know each other. How hard could that be?

Elizabeth has on black tights, a denim shirt that is apparently posing as a dress, cowboy boots and a baseball hat. She is also smoking a cigar in a building that is, like every building in America, smoke free.

"Hey."

"Hey."

"We sound like a bunch of guys," I tell her.

"That's a stretch," she tells me as she lifts her shirt to expose her breasts.

"Jesus!" I scream.

"That perked you up."

"You look pretty perky yourself."

"Wanna roll?"

"Elizabeth?"

"Yeah, baby?"

"Please tell me it's all going to be okay."

She comes over to touch me. Her hands on my face are a soft kiss at midnight, three bottles of French wine, a morning when I do not have to get out of bed, cardinals singing on my windowsill in spring, warm sheets in winter, clean sheets anytime, someone else cleaning the bathrooms, and everything grand and glorious that will definitely not be crossed off of my Life List once I actually make one.

"You have no idea who you are, how beautiful you are, where you are going—do you?"

"No."

"Listen, sweetie, listen to this."

"I'm listening. Really, I might be an inch away from nuts right now, but I am listening."

"You couldn't be nuts if you tried. Still listening?"

"Yes, Elizabeth."

"Everything is going to be okay."

6

1967

Sister Aloysius has a fabulous trick that has worked so well on the bad boys that third- and fourth-graders line up in anticipation at recess to see who will be next. Her voice sounds like the voice of God, not that anyone at St. Monica's Grade School has ever heard the voice of God, but they know because Father Geparski told them it would be deep and strong and full of power, and if Father says it, then that's it—it's true. That's Sister Aloysius for sure, because her voice is deep and strong and full of power and she is always ready to whack someone upside the head.

Here is what she does. Every day it's almost always someone different, except you can pretty much count on the fact that John Blakeman, Stevie Black and Martin DeBuris will get whacked several times a day because they are such terrible sinners. Sister likes to back them into a corner or against a wall. A wall close to a good corner is like the best place of all. Everyone knows what she is going to do, but there is something about this nun that scares the living hell out of the entire world. She has a river of meanness that is so deep, there is no bottom. Her bottom does, however, edge out on the cliffs of Hell. That is one thing everyone at St. Monica's knows for sure—the cliffs of Hell.

Sister likes to sneak up. Everyone knows that too, but no one is ready. How can you be ready? Jesus was not even ready. He knew, but was He ready? Well, maybe He was ready, but we won't know for sure until we ask Him. So she sneaks up and grabs her daily pick by the collar. Everyone had a collar back then, and this was in the days when you could get whacked or punched or, as we know now, sexually abused, and it was okay because they were teaching us the Fear of God, so violence, well, that was okay. It was okay to be violent.

Sister grabbed them and then she always had a book in her right hand, a very hard and solid book, and she would smack them in the head. Right in the head. Honest. She would smack them in the head, and when they had their eyes closed and would place their hands on top of that now painful place, she would step on their feet. She wouldn't just step on their feet, she would STEP on their feet until an explosion of pain made these boys, and an occasional girl, forget about the awful ache in their heads and wonder if they would ever be able to walk again.

Meggie Callie knew about this and she walked on a tightrope every single day she attended St. Monica's. One false move at St. Monica's and you could be a dead duck or possibly crippled for the rest of your natural born life. Meggie had straight A's and her best friend's mother was the volunteer English writing coach, which usually meant the boys got help to prepare them for the rigors of high school and the girls wrote poems, but sometimes the girls did boy things, but not often enough. Hardly ever.

Meggie had no idea that Sister A had been listening to her talk on the playground, in the bathroom and everywhere else there was a place to hide and listen. What Sister heard Meggie Callie say was that she was going to college and she was not going to be a teacher or a nun or work at a grocery store. She heard Meggie Callie say that she was going to be a doctor or maybe an astronaut or someone who traveled, like an anthropologist, who could look at how people lived and study their habits and determine things that no one else knew.

Once Margaret Joan Callie even had the nerve to say that maybe she would run for some kind of government office so that she could change the world. She didn't want to be President, Meggie said one day behind the old bleachers, but she did want to be a politician who listened to people and who was there one day when someone decided to call, and the Senator would be right on the phone, saying, "Hey, how are ya?" Meggie also had the audacity to mention the fact that she wondered sometimes if there really was a God.

This was a horrible sin. It was the worst sin. Meggie was talking to Cynthia Ann Hanlon and she had questions about everything.

"Would God want us to be scared like this all the time?" Meggie asked her quiet friend.

"I don't know," said Cynthia, who would later get pregnant in tenth grade and eventually end up married three times.

"Think about it," urged Meggie. "We are afraid in church—I mean, what if the chapel veil slips off—we are afraid to not go to church, because we could be struck dead; we have a book of rules as long as this sidewalk, and if we don't memorize them then we are also going to rot in Hell."

"I never thought about it. . . ."

"Well, does this sound like the kind of thing a kind and loving God wants us to do?"

Meggie didn't wait for an answer now because she was on one

of her "things" and there was no stopping her, or the big ears of Sister A, who was trying hard not to reach out and slap this hussy of a girl upside the head.

"Sometimes when I am going to the bathroom I wonder if I am even doing that the right way, because it's rule this and rule that. No wonder people just sit in the pews and shut up, because there are new rules every week."

Cynthia looked at her friend in amazement. She was more worried about Robert Fleischman's new pants than she was about this stuff. Who cared?

"We're just supposed to do it, you know?" Cynthia pointed out flatly. "Maybe they don't even know if we screw up. I mean, it's not like someone is watching."

"That's what they want us to think. Remember when we studied about mind control and stuff like that in science?"

Cynthia looked around just to see if anyone really might be watching. She didn't want to listen anymore. She wanted to go find Bobby. He had on the greatest pants.

"Are you leaving?" Meggie asked.

"Yes," Cynthia said, and she was gone.

This is when Sister A sprang into action. She was so furious that the hair under her veil was soaked and sweat dripped down the back of her neck. If there wasn't a commandment that said, Do Not Kill, she would have her hands around Margaret's meaty and evil little throat in a second.

She came around the corner so fast that Meggie had no idea what hit her, and she was definitely hit. Sister A backhanded her across the face, and there was an instant welt on her right cheek the exact size of Sister's knuckles. The slap took the wind out of her and for a moment she thought she would faint.

No words were spoken. Sister A grabbed Meggie by the arm

and dragged her across the gym, down the brown-tiled hallway, and threw her, actually threw her, into the teachers' lounge. No one Meggie knew had ever been into the teachers' lounge, and this is where Meggie discovered that nuns go to the bathroom. This is where she also discovered the potential cruelty of the human heart.

The room was empty. Sister Aloysius backed Meggie against the concrete wall and pushed her face against Meggie's. Meggie could see down her throat and she sensed something so horrible that she had a hard time breathing. Evil. She sensed something evil.

"Who do you think you are?" the nun hissed. "Do you really think you can be who you want to be? Do you?"

Meggie could not speak. She was afraid she was going to wet her pants. She prayed, because prayers were supposed to save you, but there was no saving her from Sister Aloysius.

"Girls are nothing, absolutely nothing. We are here to serve the men, the priests, the men who will be lawyers and politicians and who will always rule the world. We clean the bathrooms and take what is left. What makes *you* think you can have the kind of life you talk about?"

There was no answer from Meggie, who was crying like she had never cried before. What if Sister was right? What if she couldn't be who she wanted to be?

"Your A's mean nothing and your talk means nothing. Until you humble your spirit, you will have and be nothing. Girls? You are crazy. We are dust on men's feet, and it's time you realize your sinful ways and *beg* God for forgiveness."

Begging was something Meggie thought she could do just then. She did not want to be hit again, and she wasn't. What happened next was worse than hitting.

Sister A opened up the supply closet, the closet with no lights in it, no place to sit, no bathroom, and she pushed Meggie inside of it. Without a word, she locked the door and left.

Meggie stayed in the room for five hours. She heard people moving outside the door and heard the bus leave, but Sister Aloysius knew that Meggie walked home. Meggie cried and she prayed and she begged God to forgive her and she promised that she would do whatever it was He wanted her to do. She didn't have to go to college and save the world. She didn't have to go to law school. She would cook and clean and do whatever she had to, if only she could get out of the dark and scary room. She promised over and over again, for what seemed the longest moments of her life.

When she heard the door unlock, she waited before she pushed it open, and then she ran all the way home.

Margaret Joan Callie never told anyone about what happened that day. She never spoke to Cynthia behind the bleachers or anyone else ever again about what she believed or didn't believe. She sat perfectly still during Mass and she slowly carved away the edges of her dreams until they fit into a box that was designed by someone else.

7

My Aunt Marcia drove to Mexico with a car full of friends in 1959. She told me they packed the trunk with blankets, canned food, spare car parts and the dying echoes of their parents, who all but tried to tie the bumper of my aunt's used Buick to the side of my grandma's house. Women just didn't do something like that.

"Jesus, honey, they thought we'd get fried into some beans and rice, and they'd never see us again." My aunt laughed as she told me the story when I was a teenager. "When Gretchen, Joannie, Barbara and I turned the corner to leave, hours before dawn, we saw your grandma, Barbara's mom and three neighbors standing in the middle of the street holding their bathrobes closed and weeping into each other's arms."

"What was it like?" I asked her, wishing with all my heart that I'd been the last thing they had put on top of the spare tire.

"Oh, Meggie, it was a miracle of colors and tastes and scents and sounds. We slept on beaches at the edge of communities where people had never seen a white woman before. We roasted chilies on open fires and bought matching silver rings and bracelets from a man who kissed each one of us as he put the rings on our fingers."

Aunt Marcia said they danced in the streets with other women and children during a birthday fiesta while wild doggies nipped at their heels, and when their radiator exploded, they spent two weeks camping behind a village store that gave them a breathtaking view of mountains that turned purple every evening.

Twenty years following that three-month trip, she still wore her silver ring and the thick silver bracelet, which she touched constantly, slipping it up and down her wrist from the tip of her knuckle to the middle part of her arm. I believed there were secrets in the bracelet, memories from the trip that she could remember and bring to life whenever she touched it.

"Tell me again about the dancing dogs," I would ask her every single time I saw her, and then, because I knew she would never say no, I would watch her caress the grooves in the bracelet with the tips of her fingers as if she were rubbing specks of silver into her own flesh.

I remember listening to her stories about this particular trip to Mexico with my eyes closed. I had seen the faded photos from old *National Geographic* magazines and I could see in my mind the dogs jumping and my aunt and her friends moving in a circle and then the dust would fly and the dogs would go wild when the men in the streets pounded harder and harder on the backs of their guitars until no one, even the doggies, could stand another second.

Something really wondrous happened on that trip and every single thing that happened was remarkable. I know it like I am beginning to know all my missed chances. My Auntie Marcia had pushed through some kind of invisible barrier that kept most other women home and tied into place so that if they tried to run they would dig a hole that got larger and larger until they disappeared and suffocated on the dirt they'd kicked up with their own heels. Auntie Marcia never suffocated. She was wild and free and there was not one thing about my aunt that did not seem dangerous and extravagant.

My mother looked at her the same way I did—with eyes of wonder and envy. My mother who had stapled herself to a lifestyle that I thought eventually might kill her. My mother who could never quite seem to let go of the rope holding her boat to the safe dock and who then passed the rope on to me. Rope burns be damned, because neither of us could ever figure out how to let go.

When my auntie died, I asked for the bracelet and the ring. My mother brought them to me weeks after the funeral. She told me that she had found the ring and bracelet wrapped inside of a Mexican silk scarf and sitting right on top of my aunt's dresser.

"She must have taken it off right before she left for the hospital," my mother said, sobbing with such grief that she fell into my arms. "She left a note for you sweetie. She wanted you to have the bracelet and the ring. How did you know?"

How could I not know? My aunt tried so hard to show me her spirit so that I might catch on fire as she did. She all but took me by the hand and into all the corners of her world so that I could see what I was missing. I held that ring and bracelet a hundred times growing up and rubbed the softness of the metal into my skin, memorizing what each curve of them felt like, their weight, how my aunt never let them tarnish. They became everything that she was and had experienced and everything that I had once longed to be.

I sat down to open the cloth package because my own well of sorrow at the loss of my glorious auntie made me weak and lost, and when I peeled back the layers of red and blue and green tissue paper, I saw that she had polished the jewelry and there was another note. My heart exploded and I could feel an ache for her and what we had rise inside of me so fast and furious, I thought that I might be sick.

My mother's hand moved to my arm, but she turned away when I opened the note.

"My sweet, beautiful Meggie, how wonderful we have been and what a gift you were to me all the years I lived after you were born. You were the daughter I never had, the challenge of my wild soul and the light in my eyes. Your sweet laugh and your stacks of books and your questions and all those ideas kept me alive months and months when I wanted to go away. Do you know that, sweetheart? Remember the stories from Mexico? You loved the damn story about the dancing dogs and I loved to tell it to you. I want you to have this magic bracelet, for it really is magic, and this beautiful ring too, and I want you to go see the dancing dogs. Your mother will have some money for this trip. I left it in my account for you, and you are a young woman now and it is time for you to go. Inside of the money packet there are vague instructions to the village where the girls and I stayed. It will be an adventure for you to find it. When you do, someone there will remember the dogs, and their grandchildren may still be dancing. Ask, please if Pancho Gonzales Quintana is still alive, and go see him. He will show you something that will help you, because you have always needed just a bit of help, Meggie, and you are too damn stubborn or afraid to see where you really need to go. Do this for me. You must take someone with you, but it cannot be a man. You must invite a close girlfriend or two and you must remember the stories I told you and watch for the orange sky and the twinkle in the eyes of all the beautiful men who will look at you as you walk through town in your purple skirt. Meggie, never be afraid. Fear can wash away

your dreams and fill up all the corners of your heart. You can
drown in your fear. Do you hear this? Someday you will have
to begin living, and how you do that will be a huge surprise to
you because it will be like nothing you ever imagined.
Nothing at all.

I want you to dance, my little darling, and always carry
my love for you, which you know is endless. Even after this
sad body of mine moves away, my love for you is endless.

Love,
The Mexican Queen

Today I am on a plane with the wildest woman I know and my
new sidekick, Jane. Elizabeth has her hair tied up in a rainbow of
ribbons and she is wearing shorts, really short black denim
shorts, with those damned cowboy boots, and we are going to
find the dancing dogs. Dr. C ordered me to leave my life. "Take a
break or I'll make you take medication," she threatened the night
she called me after I could not leave her office. "Do not go alone,
but go. You must go."

Jane has latched on to me and to Dr. C and even though I feel
as if it is the blind leading the blind and the deaf and the dumb
and the terribly foolish, she—by luck of the draw and distance
from relatives and because her husband really was a royal asshole—truly has no one but me. Well, now she also has Elizabeth
and parts of Aunt Marcia and anything else she can squeeze out
of us. Right after Jane moved to our neighborhood from Boston,
her husband took off. He left her a note on the table, half the
cash, a car and signed divorce papers that had been in the works
for months. After Elizabeth and I settle her soul, we will begin a
nationwide manhunt for this man and drag him naked behind
our car through the next women's festival. In the meantime, I am
supposed to be Jane's guiding light, and I take great comfort in

being around her, because she is much worse off than I am—or so I think. She has a kind of innocence that Elizabeth and I cannot ignore. We have looped her into our circle and we have promised to stand with her until she can fly on her own. Today Mexico—tomorrow maybe, just maybe, Chicago.

Dr. C ordered me into some kind of forced retreat, and only then did I remember the trip money. I never went to Mexico like I was supposed to. There was school and my father blocking the door and then I got married so damn fast, but I'd kept the money. I could not bear to spend a penny of it, and when I showed my aunt's note to Elizabeth, she said, "If you don't take me I will never speak to you again" and within thirty minutes we had tickets to Mexico and neither of us could bear not to invite Jane, who sobbed for twenty-six minutes when I called to invite her.

It was much easier to rearrange my life for fourteen days than I could have imagined. I had plenty of vacation time coming from my job, my daughter only needs me occasionally now that I am back near her nest, and I am so estranged from my husband, I cannot imagine he would miss me if I never bothered to tell him I was leaving. When I did tell him, I am certain a huge sigh of relief passed from his stomach into his throat and he nearly wept for joy. Getting ready for Mexico took my mind off the fact that I am an inch away from going nuts and have totally lost my personal identity—not that I had one to begin with.

Preparing for an all but abandoned adventure was not easy, but I could not have picked two more wonderful traveling companions. Jane was so glad to be doing anything, to get a break from her job search, from trying to sell her house and from the dungeon of her marriage, she obeyed us like a trained bird. Elizabeth set the rules from the moment I asked her to go on the trip, and the more I thought about it the more I liked the rules.

"Sweetheart," she said, leaning into me and pulling my face next to hers, "there are no rules."

"Okay," I stammered, because the idea of no rules had never entered even the outer edges of my mind. Not in the past twenty years anyway.

"And, this is very important."

"What?"

"What happens to us, where we go, who we meet, anything at all—it stays with us."

"We can't even tell the doctor?"

"We cannot even tell the doctor, unless you desperately need to say something that might save you from madness, and then it has to be in vague terms, like 'I felt free,' or 'I had the greatest orgasm of my life.'"

"Are we going to have orgasms?"

"God, I hope so," Elizabeth said, laughing as if her throat were on fire.

Jane turned white during this part of the discussion, and I simply reached over to touch her hand. What happened to Jane? Did she miss the '70s? My. My. My.

"Do you have any idea how long it's been since I even said the word *orgasm*?" I asked Elizabeth.

"You are a disgrace to womanhood, darling," Elizabeth said, more than half seriously. "Do you have an idea how important it is to talk about sex, have sex, and to simply say anything sexy as often as possible so the world will realize that it's women and not men who need sex?"

"This conversation could be endless," I said, shuddering. "And we have to catch a plane."

Which is what we did, and when I felt the rise of the wings and the grinding of the airplane tires being sucked into the bowels of the airplane as we started our journey, I asked Elizabeth to hold my hand and I felt, through her fingers, the long dark veins of my Auntie Marcia and the whisper of her promises and a long sigh sliding from inside of me that came from a place so deep and old and tired that I imagined it was a fairly large pit that was close to the very bottom of my heart.

Blue is a color, I realize the moment I wake up for the first time in my life in Mexico, that pulls at the inner circle of my soul, and the color of the water that I see from my bed is like no blue I have ever seen. It is aqua and navy and turquoise and it nails me to the center of my soft cotton sheets as if I am lying on a crucifix.

"Jesus," I whisper to myself in a half-prayer, half-astonished kind of way. I do not want to wake Elizabeth and Jane, who I imagine are sleeping off the six shots of tequila we had at two A.M. when our bus finally found this isolated resort.

But Elizabeth is already gone and there is a note on her pillow. Jane does not look as if she has moved in thirty-four years.

Pee and then walk naked down the beach until you find me.

It has been so long since I have been naked or thought of taking my clothes off other than to change them. I am trying to remember if I even bother to strip when I shower.

"Surely she's joking," I tell myself as I follow the instructions to pee, slip on my stretched-out bathing suit and pray to God Elizabeth has coffee, wherever in the hell she is sitting—hopefully not naked. One step at a time, please. Mexico today, naked in maybe—what?—three years or so.

I am so drunk with the blue and the morning light and from the sound of the waves and from the feel of the already warm sand against my pale skin that I am not at all startled to see Elizabeth sprawled in the sand with her breasts pointed toward the sky, and what looks like a piña colada in her right hand.

"You could get arrested for that," I say.

"You are the one who is indecent," she says without moving.

This is when I look around and realize that I am the only woman on the beach that has on a bathing suit.

"Where are we, sweetie, the Isle of Lesbos?"

"No. Look again."

I see men, who are unfortunately wearing bathing suits, but they are very tiny and revealing bathing suits and on second glance I see that the women, nine out of ten of them anyway, have on bottoms.

"Oops."

"You are overdressed—again."

"Goddamn it, I so much wanted this to go smoothly and I want to be popular like all the other girls."

Elizabeth laughs. It's that big-geese-flying-south laugh that makes me lunge for her glass so I can feel the same way, but instead I end up with a breast in my left hand.

"That makes up for the overdressing," she says, sitting up on both elbows. "You *are* overdressed, you know."

"Oh no." My voice is a pitiful mix of sadness and terror.

"Not yet, but within a few days you just may want to take off your bathing suit. Americans are such assholes about their bodies. There isn't anything sexual about what is happening on this beach. Besides, it's about time you looked at yourself from the outside as well."

"Will you be embarrassed if I just sit here with my suit on for a while?"

Elizabeth knows my self-esteem is in the crapper and that I half believe that she really might be embarrassed if I don't strip.

In reality, she wouldn't care if I wore a frog to the beach or came down here and organized a Tupperware party. But I need so much reassurance that I cannot even joke about being naked on a beach in Mexico where the likelihood of me meeting someone that I know has about the same odds as me knowing in the next five minutes what and who I want to be when I grow up.

"Sit," she commands, and I sink into the arms of the warm sand with extreme gratitude.

By noon I am already getting the hang of this cosmopolitan, non-American life. There are no other Americans at our small resort and there is a stated nonchalance to eating, walking, moving, whipping off tops and smoking and drinking that has me feeling a bit boozy before I even bother to sip the South of the Border booze. Elizabeth made all the plans for this trip and I suspect she has a hidden agenda that has me eventually sleeping with a man from France, his sister-in-law and two long-lost uncles. I very quickly fall into a rhythm of total and complete relaxation unlike anything I can ever remember. I become a virtual physical and emotional captive to my surroundings—the constant and glorious sun, the stunning blue, the way everything seems slower and gentler, that warmish, scented breeze that drifts across the beach from some island miles and miles offshore, the way the men run their eyes up and down my body and then boldly lock into my own eyes, the way I have already forgotten what brought me to this paradise in the first place. How quickly I have been seduced.

Jane finally sees the light of day just after one P.M. and wanders onto the beach like she is looking for something she lost. We say hello to her and she turns slowly to look at us, and she says, "Who the hell are you two?" We laugh and let her sink into the sand. She is hours behind us—hours and days and maybe years.

Elizabeth tells me I must go to a place where I can examine my Life List. "It's right there," she says as we sit on the edge of the wharf, imagining what secrets lie buried out there in the miles of open sea, and then she pushes on the insides of my wrists with her warm fingers. "It's close to the skin now. I have already seen it travel down from your heart and past that tough bend in your elbow. It's very close to your fingertips."

"Most people would think we are crazy if they heard this conversation," I tell her. "But I think I know what you mean. Maybe we should just stay here for the rest of our lives, eating fruit and having your men bring us rum-laced drinks."

"Don't get too comfortable. We're leaving in the morning."

"What?" both Jane and I shout.

"We are off to find the dancing dogs in the morning, and that's why it's so important to work on that List today, and one other thing."

My heart pounds just a little and for a second or two I put myself back in my real life and the sky goes dark and I have a very clear vision of the level of my unhappiness. There is Bob standing behind me with his arms crossed, a counter filled with dirty dishes, my daughter talking on the phone, a pile of terribly boring reports stacked to eye level on my desk and something so odd that I close my eyes to focus on it—a calendar that extends on forever, and every single day has something written on it. My life planned out by everyone but me.

Elizabeth holds my hand when I begin crying. She tells me that the color of my tears has changed and that she can tell these are now new tears.

"This is new anguish," she says, tasting one of the tears. "Fresh salt. Now you tell me."

It is perhaps remarkable to remember the moment when you wake up. It is perhaps remarkable to be able to step outside of your mind and body and see your flaws and missteps and yearnings. It is remarkable to be able to put your finger on your own pulse and to say that you suddenly understand that unhappiness is a choice and that everyone, even you, can change direction, or better yet, find direction at any moment in your life.

"I have to remember the color of everything, Elizabeth, don't I?"

"You can, but what is important, I think, is to remember that something remarkable happened and that something remarkable can happen at any moment for the rest of your life."

Jane is taking silent notes. She has not moved but she is listening.

She is good, this Elizabeth, who wears a brightly patterned piece of Mexican cloth draped around her and tucked into the narrow of her breasts to keep it from slipping off. She is already stunningly beautiful because of the power over her own life that she has always seemed to possess. For the first time in weeks I want to hold her in my arms instead of having her hold me, but I am certain I am not ready to hold the weight of anyone by myself—not yet. I can hold a small part of Jane, but I cannot hold all of her either.

Jane has turned to watch me and her hand, slow at first, has moved to touch my leg. She has not seen me cry. I have been the weight to tie her down, and this is my moment. If she can learn from it and lean into me even more, that is fine, and the strength I get from simply knowing that I need this moment this time washes over both of us.

"Everything has to change, doesn't it, Elizabeth?" I say.

She is smiling, and I can see her eyes crinkle up when her sunglasses slip down just a bit.

"What do you think, sweetheart? Does everything have to change?"

"Here is that moment," I say to myself, "that moment I will always remember not for what I see with my eyes but for what I know is the necessary ingredient for my survival." I take the moment and I hold it cupped in my hands not so gently. My grip is firm and smooth and kind, but it is also solid—because I know. I think I really know.

"Everything has to change."

When I say it, I see a brigade of dancing Mexican women twirling past me with their skirts flying. Dolphins leap from the sea. Little brown-skinned boys and girls laugh in unison. The sand sifts itself into dozens of castles. The sky twirls itself into the shape of clapping hands, and Elizabeth sails from the wharf and slides across the gentle waves of the ocean, totally naked while she jumps rope with the cloth that was once her dress.

8

Linda is driving a Jeep that is so old, portions of the back floor are missing, there is no tailgate, and if there ever was a top it was destroyed long before the Second World War. Elizabeth is in the back end, wearing a jogging bra—thank God—with one leg on one side of the largest hole and the other leg on the other side of the hole. Jane sits next to her, holding on to the roll bar with both hands, and her eyes are open so wide, I am certain they'll pop out. I am in the front seat with a bandanna wrapped around my head in do-rag style, hanging on to what there is of the dashboard while we fly down what appears to be the only main highway between here and Houston, Texas. We are in the heart of the Yucatan Peninsula, in search of the wild dancing dogs, men and women who will yip and holler like the doggies without giving such action a second thought and any kind of memory scent my Auntie Marcia may have left in this hot, dusty and terribly exotic country.

The woman driving the Jeep is so stunningly beautiful and sure of herself, I can barely focus. When she showed up with her long legs and tanned skin and perfectly bent baseball hat in front of the resort at six A.M. just as the clouds on the ocean lifted and the sun began to filter through the trees by the swimming pool, I wanted to slap myself because I felt as if I were in a movie.

She is our guide-friend, local jungle expert and woman of the world. She has come to take us on an adventure to see the doggies and God knows what else. She is a friend of a friend of a friend of Elizabeth's, and the fact that she has beautiful blond hair, legs that are longer than the entire length of my body and this aura of confidence has me spinning. I want to be just like this woman when I grow up. I will have to take up weight lifting, grow out my hair, move to a foreign land—anything seems possible when I watch her move, anything.

"Welcome to my world," she said as her way of introduction, and then she grabbed half of our bags in one arm and we were flying before I could close my mouth.

Linda, Elizabeth tells me as we walk toward the Jeep, is an archaeologist who came to Mexico to help unearth the unbelievably important ruins at Coba, an area of shallow lakes covered by decades of jungle growth that includes an amazing twenty thousand acres of an ancient civilization that we are about to enter as part of the doggie search. When the Mexican government cut off funding for major archaeological projects in sites such as Coba, Linda was unable to leave because she had fallen in love with the land, the lakes, the sky—apparently every ounce of the peninsula. Now she hires herself out as a guide, sometime digger, a friend to searching women as she waits for the skies to open so she can find more hidden treasures.

Call us "the Barking Females"—women in search of dogs. There are sleeping bags, a tent, bundles of water and food wrapped in tarps in the Jeep. I am certain that we will run into Thelma and Louise around the next hairpin turn and I pray to any living thing who will listen that I might not just be ready, but worthy as hell.

Miles and miles from the resort, where there were wonderful things like flush toilets and ice cubes and food prepared for you while you sat on the beach, we turn right and are instantly enveloped inside trees unlike any that I have ever seen. They are a tangled mass of green leaves and roots so thick that it becomes darker with each mile. Occasionally there is a break in the darkness and a slice of light pushes out in the dirt road where someone tried to claim a patch of ground. Because my Life List has been put on hold most of my dull life—okay, all of my life—I have never been to a place where people have to scratch the ground to clear a space to live. I have thought about those people from time to time, but to see a small hole in the horizon and scattered pieces of lumber, piles of garbage and a trail leading off to the next village—it changes everything.

I am an educated woman. I have studied and planned and read more books than the average person, but now I realize quickly that I have missed more than a world of experiences. Something harsh and angry rises up in me when I realize this true fact. It is one thing to live, but it is another thing to *really* live. Why have I been so afraid? Where did my wires get crossed?

We bounce along and I glance back to see Elizabeth lost in her own thoughts, and I suddenly remember the days in high school when I had such brilliant but silent dreams. I kept pages and pages of notes, most of which I wrote down during classes that I considered way too boring for my attention, and my notes were filled with a passion that seems to have gotten lost in all the days and nights of my life that have piled so high I have not been able to breathe.

Once, Mark Cotrel read my pages of notes. Mark was a pompous jackass of a boy who was blessed with a body and face that made girls do things that were terribly embarrassing. I adored

Mark, loved him, wanted him and would wet myself if he so much as said "Hi" when he sat next to me in American history class. He often asked me what I was writing and I never would tell him. It was just "stuff." Poems about climbing mountains and counting the seconds until graduation so I could leave and how I wanted to someday be driving down a jungle road in a Jeep with two women who could kick ass without even blinking.

Mark took my binder one day when I got up to go to the bathroom, and I was frantic after class because it was missing. When I stepped outside the room he was waiting for me.

"Here," he said, eyes down, pushing the book into my hands.

"How the hell did you get this?" I seethed through my teeth, forgetting about his hair and teeth and beautiful shoulders.

"I took it. I'm sorry."

I wanted to kill him. My rage was such a strong emotion that I was struck dumb. I was on the edge of a huge and dangerous tide that could have washed me into a place that I might still regret today. I felt violated, raped, exposed. I may as well have been standing in the hallway of my pathetic high school totally naked.

"I'm so sorry."

"What?"

"It was wrong. I am so sorry."

"That is my life in there," I said. "*My* life, and it's private."

"It's beautiful."

He stunned me. It was a second slap in the face and again I could not speak.

"I write poetry too," Mark said, "but I've never told anyone. People would laugh. What you write is beautiful."

I could not take my eyes off of his face. I saw his lips moving but my mind was floating somewhere up there on the green ceiling in the hallway outside of the history room. He went on and on for a very long time. The last thing I remember him saying was that he would especially remember the poem about walking away from one place to another, unless I wanted him to forget it and then he would never even look at me again.

"Remember it," I said when my voice came back, "and do something remarkable with your life, Mark."

I never saw Mark after we graduated, but friends told me that he went to nursing school and now lives and works in San Francisco at a hospice for men and women dying of AIDS.

And me? I give lectures, watch my husband make love to other women, and it has taken me half my life to remember the verses from my own poem. But I remembered. I finally remembered.

Elizabeth must have been watching me think. Damn it. I can't get away with anything.

"What?" she shouts into my left ear.

"What would we do without the word *what?*" I think, because it seems as if I am always surrounded by that word.

"Thinking and remembering," I throw back to her.

She nods and then shouts to Linda: "I need to pee."

Linda whips her right index finger into the air and stops the Jeep right there in the middle of the highway.

"There you go," she says. "We might as well all pee, because we have one hell of a ride in front of us."

Okay, then.

I try and act like I know what I am doing. Linda jumps out, goes to the front of the Jeep and drops her drawers. Elizabeth takes the left side. Jane just sits in the Jeep. I went to college. I figure I can handle the right side just perfectly. This is why I never went on the camping trips with Katie's Girl Scout troop. What was I thinking? You can apparently go to the bathroom anywhere, at any time, with anyone you want to. If only I would have known this sooner I would have saved myself countless hours of time. Time that I spent needlessly looking for an indoor toilet facility. I cannot believe how my life is changing.

We are all back in the Jeep quicker than it would take three men to pull up their zippers. Jane decides to hold it—which has pretty much been the main theme in her life.

"Before we go, I want to know where we are going," I say rather boldly.

"To see the doggies," Elizabeth answers. "But that's going to take a few days."

"We are driving right through the heart of the peninsula," Linda tells us. "If you tried to walk left or right—well, it would take you pretty close to forever to get anywhere, but you'd die from thirst and there's a very good chance something might bite you that has a poisonous mouth."

"You can't scare me," I say. "I know where we are going, but *where are we going?*"

Linda looks at me very closely. I'm not sure if she believes I have lost my mind, if I'm looking for a mall or want a chilled margarita.

"You have beautiful eyes," she says.

"What?" There's that damn word again.

"There are specks of brown in there. I've never seen that with eyes so gray."

"No one has noticed that in years," I say. "Years."

"No one has looked. Or you wouldn't let them."

That's enough. I feel like I might blow apart. A woman like me can only take so much honesty in one day.

"Look, I'm having a nervous breakdown. Where are we staying tonight?"

"You are not having a nervous breakdown," Elizabeth pipes in. "You just got jammed up, about—what?—twenty-six years ago, and it took something to pop you loose."

Linda is looking at me like I'm supposed to say something, and I have a sudden urge to just laugh. So I do.

"Look," I say, barely able to speak, I'm laughing so hard. "I'm in the jungle with a couple of goofballs looking for wild dogs while I caress my dead aunt's bracelet, because I flipped out and realized my life was a mess when I saw my husband making love to another woman, so is it too much to ask where we are going to stay—tonight?"

"Just down this road another forty-eight miles," Linda says, through her own laugh. "It's a village where some Mayan friends of mine live and where someone might remember your aunt."

"Really?"

"Your aunt was here more than once and she stayed for long stretches of time."

"Are you kidding?"

"I think I know the main village where she lived and worked, and my friends in Tiapiacantio will help us."

Elizabeth has her hand on my shoulder and I realize in that instant that the entire world must be filled with unsaid secrets that lie under trees and inside pockets and behind hidden doors. This is how men get away with having three wives and why bodies disappear and why there is a show on television called *Unsolved Mysteries*. My aunt is an unsolved mystery that is a double mystery because I did not know she was a mystery.

Auntie Marcia, oh, Auntie Marcia.

Linda cranks up the Jeep and we bounce down a road that has never seen the hard edge of a road grader or felt the backside of a bucket filled with hot tar. When I turn my head, I see that Jane and Elizabeth are holding hands. Jane always needs to hold on to someone. It is impossible to go more than 20 mph, but that is okay because my mind races with the possibilities my aunt and her mysterious life have given me. Was she part of some Mexican underground? Maybe she married someone down here and had a baby who is now a blond woman about five years younger than me.

"Imagine," I want to shout to Elizabeth, "while I was charting numbers in the back room of a building that was painted beige from top to bottom and doing mundane things like folding towels and sweeping out the laundry room, my aunt may have been knitting together the fabric of a life that I cannot comprehend. Who was she? Who am I? Where in the hell are we going?"

I have been to California and to New York City and I have taken the train to Denver through the plains and into what seemed like the very sides of mountains that were at first small specks and then suddenly touched the edges of clouds. When the kids were in junior high school, Bob and I took them in the old Dodge van to Arizona, where we peered over the edge of the Grand Canyon—not too close, of course—and saw into the dark belly of an earth that seemed so deep and large that I was stunned down to the center of everything that I was. I wanted to walk down there really, really bad, and I let Bob talk me out of it.

"You could just spend a night at the hotel without me and I'll hike down and take the mules back up," I'd pleaded with him like a little girl asking for another candy bar.

"You can't do that."

"I have to do it," I told him. "There's something down there that I have to see."

Bob got scared when I said this. Come to think of it, he got scared when I said lots of things, and so he took what I said and made it seem like something else until I could not recognize it and I completely lost track of what I was saying or what I wanted or needed.

I have a memory of the moment when I caved in that defined everything about me for years and years after that. We had rented a room at a hotel on the edge of the park that had a small swimming pool and looked out across a field covered in sagebrush and spring flowers that were so beautiful, I wanted to eat them so that they would always be a part of me.

The kids were playing in the pool and Bob was standing in front of me with his arms crossed in a defiant male sort of way that reeked of the word *power,* and he was blocking my view of the desert. I wanted to tell him that the center of the earth was just a few miles away at the very bottom of the Grand Canyon and that I had to, simply had to, rush down there and put my ear to the ground—next to the raging waters of the Colorado River. I wanted for him to look into my eyes and to see that I knew something, like where the gold was buried or the cure for cancer or who really killed John Fitzgerald Kennedy. I wanted for him to see *me*—see me and then reach his arms around behind me and pull me into his chest so that I could bury my face against him and hear his beating heart, which would contain the last clue to what I was supposed to find at the bottom of the Grand Canyon.

But Bob did not move. In the last corner of my mind, that turn before everything clouds over, I heard the kids screaming and splashing and playing Marco Polo for the fifteenth time in a row and I knew they were safe, and then I moved around the backside of Bob, grabbed the open bottle of wine that we had been drinking, said simply, "Okay, Bob, I won't go," and I hiked out into that field.

I did not go far, just over the rise, which stretched out for a very long time and which I made believe came to rest at the edge of the Canyon, which led to a huge drop-off. Then I began to cry.

Something broke loose for just a while as I sat there—I felt as if I had lost something, that someone I had loved for a very long time had died and that I would never ever get over my loss. My tears moved into my stomach and through my chest, and when they emerged out of my eyes, it was a flood that tasted, I imagined, like the water that might have splashed up from the Colorado River—cold and harsh and free, so goddamned free.

I never did drink the wine that day because I cried so long and so hard that it was impossible for me to pick up the bottle and move it to my lips. My grieving for that lost moment, for the chance to smell the inside of the world, never seemed to leave me. One hour passed and then another. My hands fumbled through the earth where I was sitting and I found small rocks that I put into the pockets of my shorts, rocks that I convinced myself had magically lifted themselves up from that place by the river that was roped off from my life. Rocks that had been where I wanted, desired, needed to go. I piled ten, twenty and then thirty of them into my pockets without thinking. Little Grand Canyons filled my shorts pockets until there was not another rock within reach, and then when I had cleared away all the space within arms' reach, I could no longer cry.

The desert at dusk is a place that claimed a part of my heart. My wedge of sorrow must have taken several hours to put itself back in the place where it had been resting for so damned many years and I must have gone to that time-warp place where everything but your immediate emotions disappear. There were no kids and no canyon and no Bob and no loss of dreams. It was just those rocks and me and the desert air that filtered into my lungs with the ancient whispers of a people and a place and time that would never have said no to a walk to touch the heart of all that is.

In the Midwest, where I live, the horizon is an unobtainable screen filtered by trees and low hills and cornfields and factories that were built before the inception of zoning regulations. On the Grand Canyon desert rim, there is no horizon. The world seems like the endless circle that it is, and when the stark colors of sand and darkening sky collide, I can imagine that people might drop dead with the pains of visual ecstasy. I had never seen anything like it and I accepted that sunset, that piece of the world where I could stand without anything blocking my horizon and see one side of the world touch the other, as my consolation prize for not being able to walk to the bottom of the Grand Canyon.

Bob never said a word that evening as I walked into the hotel room, kissed the kids and then emptied all of my rocks into one of those paper hotel glasses. I touched each rock, twirled it around in my fingers and then rolled each one of them up inside of one of Shaun's dirty T-shirts.

My world and life have been filled with so many unspoken words that I think I should have choked to death on the high level of constipation. I can feel the tense moments that moved between Bob and myself as I passed behind him and into the bathroom. I can remember how I moved to the edge of the bed when he tried to wrap his arms around me that night on the saggy hotel bed and how I could not bear to sleep with the window closed. Instead, I slept with one rock in my hand that night and listened for rushing water and the cries of the voyagers and Anasazi women who were looking for the remains of their drowned men along the shores of the raging river. I thought about the choice I had made—and it had been my choice not to go in spite of the crushing forces of the world and all of the Bobs in it and I had no pity for myself. I was ashamed that I was lying in bed instead of climbing up the steep canyon path with a flashlight in my hand, exhausted but filled with the rush of what it must be like to touch the center of the world.

Some part of myself that had risen up to see if it was safe to escape, to chase after a dream, to live how it wanted to live had crawled back down right inside of me, but only to a deeper place. I closed my eyes in that bed and saw myself as a real woman, a defined woman, as a woman of the world might see me, and I pulled the covers around my head in an embarrassed, hurried movement that I hoped would make me invisible.

My own babies were burned to a crisp from the desert sun and sleeping with wide smiles on their faces, resting like angels with visions of their own wild desert dreams, which made my tears begin again. All those unspoken words and Bob rolling over toward the closet door and me sailing through the night sky to peer over the edge of the cliff that kept me from being in a place I needed to be so badly that my entire body—my entire life—ached.

9

1970

There are six boys dribbling balls on the basketball court in
the gymnasium at Park Ridge Grade School, where everyone
gathers on Saturday afternoons to hang out, flirt and see what
free food the school recreation director will bring that day. Even
the kids from the Catholic school and the Lutheran school
come, because they don't have a gym to hang out in, and if they
didn't come, there would only be about six teenagers hanging
out at Park Ridge.

It is the year before high school and on a Saturday in this
town if you are thirteen or fourteen there is nothing to do but
hang out, wish for the acne to recede as quickly as possible,
babysit, cut the grass and talk about what life will be like tomorrow and the next day and the week everyone gets their driver's li-
censes. There is also endless talk about high school and all the
frightening possibilities life holds once everyone walks out the
door of this particularly horrendous grade school where boys
and girls who look like grown men and women still eat lunch in
the same cafeteria with first-graders who cannot tie their shoes,
because there is no junior high in this small town.

At least there is Saturday, when anyone can come hang out at the gym and where parents, for some insane reason, think that their adolescent children are safe. Thank heavens they do not know what Maura Bridget O'Hara (whose parents are about as Irish as the King and Queen of Spain) does behind the bleachers to any boy who is willing to drop his pants, and there is usually quite a waiting list. Maura is the only girl at this gym allowed to participate in any kind of sport, and what she does is not listed in the score box of any local newspaper.

And really, it is only the boys who play ball.

The girls, even in gym class, are still playing dodgeball and doing archery—"Cock your arrows, stand . . . stand . . . point, let fly"—because Title IX has not been written into law yet and the home economics classes are filled with girls whose mothers insist they learn to cook and sew and bake, because there are no other choices. The girls do not have many choices at all.

Some of the girls, like Pam Wochinski, have tried to get the rules changed. Last November Pam walked right into the principal's office with her plans for girls' basketball and volleyball and track all written down, along with the names of parents who had volunteered to coach, and she got the same answer everyone else had ever gotten when they tried to include girls in sports. Mrs. Samuelson, who rode horses all over the world and competed with men, tried to get the rules changed, and they said, "No. That's just the way it is."

This answer did not satisfy Pam or Kaye Marie Smith or Meggie Callie. Meggie was not so much attracted to the athletic side of the aisle as Pam and Kaye, but she could not say no—a problem that would haunt her most of her life—when they asked her to help them.

These two girls were born to do something with a ball besides draw it or kick it over to one of the guys. Pam and Kaye were strong and tall and they did not walk—they glided. Zena would have had her hands full with these two girl-women. Pam and Kaye could beat any boy at any playground game and they followed football and baseball and basketball teams from California to New York as if those duties were part of a religious commandment. Meggie had absolutely no idea what they were talking about.

"Did you see Johnson last Friday night after he got pulled down near the forty yard line?" Pam would ask Kaye during the two-hundredth-plus sleepover at Meggie's house.

"It was his," Kaye moaned with pure anguish. "It was his, and what did he do?"

"He's an ass," Pam shouted. "They need a woman in there to call the plays, run the plays, take the ball over the line. Do you hear me, Johnson—OVER THE DAMN LINE."

Meggie liked these two girls even if she had no idea what they were talking about. They were spunky and did things that she wanted desperately to try but something was just not there—like coordination, self-determination and willpower. Why these two little Amazons even liked Meggie was beyond her, but then, she usually ended up being the brains of their Let's Play Ball group of athletic wannabes. She wrote down their plans and their pleadings and their proposals and then started all over again each time they got rejected.

"Those idiots," she spewed along with her two jock-like friends. "They had a chance to make history, and look what they did."

"No shit," Pam said the last time their proposal for girls' sports got rejected. "I can't take much more of this."

These three girls and thousands of girls like them—girls like Patty Winset in Wisconsin, who could throw the football faster and harder and straighter than any boy in the entire state; and girls like Rebecca Johnson in Kansas, who had such a natural talent for soccer that one brave coach actually let her fill in when one of the boys was sick; and girls like Ann Pagonis in California, who could take a basketball and put it in a hoop that was so far away that grown men, former professional players and every boy who had seen Ann at neighborhood pickup games sighed with envy—these girls were in the trenches with Pam and Kaye and with nonathletic Meggie, the all-season team manager wannabe.

For all the hundreds and thousands of girls who wanted to play and then walked away in defeat when someone said, "You can't," there were just enough Kayes and Pams who could not walk away from the glorious feel of a ball rolling over their fingers in a perfect arc or the way the club or bat felt when they found its sweet spot and moved it like a song against another ball or the way they felt after a three-miler when their hamstrings wanted to roll over into their heel cups and their sweat-drenched shirts stung when they came back into the hall.

All the girls who cried themselves to sleep because they could not play would have loved to watch Kaye and Pam and almost-Meggie that afternoon in the gym in that small town-city where the smell of testosterone often made grown women sick to their stomachs and girls who had the gift for the sporting life angry as hell.

Meggie was a follower, she could admit that and she would have admitted it even back in 1970 when she stood at the edge of her grade school gym with Pam and Kaye—well, not so much with them as just a little behind them, when Pam told John Stevenson that the girls were going to play ball.

Stevenson was the geography teacher who made a measly five bucks an hour to handle the gym on Saturdays, and that was just enough to help him with his car payment, and that's all he really cared about. John Stevenson also had a few gambling debts he didn't want his wife to know about, but how in the hell he was going to take care of that with the five bucks an hour remained a mystery to him even the day the guys from the inner city slit his car tires and pounded the living hell out of his trunk because he owed them $750. But back on October 1, 1970, his real problem was those three girls standing at the edge of the gym who looked as if they wanted to eat him for lunch.

"Mr. Stevenson," the tallest one said. "We want in on this game."

Mr. Stevenson laughed. The three girls took a step forward.

"We said, Mr. Stevenson, we want in the game. We play. We know the game and it isn't fair that we have to just stand here while the boys play."

The other girl, the one in front, not Meggie, moved her foot back and forth as if she were drawing a line with her toe. She had eyes that were as black as coal, and Mr. Stevenson had always admired the way she could take a ball into her hands and turn it, spin it, place it anywhere she wanted to—even though he had never allowed her on the court. Sideline play. Strictly sideline play.

"Girls, now, I think you can play, but the boys get the gym and you can—"

The first girl cut him off.

"What? We can stand here and serve drinks and clean the bathrooms and wipe up their sweat? It isn't fair. We want to *play.*"

Mr. Stevenson was not ready for what happened next. That Meggie girl stepped back and every girl who had ever come to the gym all the months he had been recreation supervisor stepped in a line next to those two girls. They all had balls and they all began bouncing them. Someone remembered years later that there were twelve girls—almost every teenage girl in town under the age of sixteen.

The boys took a step back. Some of them whistled, and Kaye, who was clearly the leader, looked at Jake Gilbert, the star of the eighth-grade team, in the eye until she bore a hole in his face and he looked away. Jake stopped whistling and the gym grew silent.

"Girls, it's not in the rules."

"Write new rules!" one of the girls yelled.

"Yeah," another girl shouted. "Write new rules."

The boys and Mr. Stevenson took another step backward and the girls did not move. But they did begin to chant, "New rules, new rules, new rules, " very softly and politely while they dribbled those damn balls.

Mr. Stevenson felt a long bead of sweat begin to roll down his rather large back, past his shoulders and into the smooth crack of his ass, which showed every time he got up from the gym floor. He wasn't scared, but he was something close to it.

"Girls ... ," he tried to say.

The girls did not want to listen. They bounced their balls and they chanted "New rules" over and over again, and then something remarkable happened for just one moment. One small, beautiful moment that changed so many lives. No one will ever really know how many lives were changed by the sound and sight of that ball moving off that one girl's fingers in the grade school gym, where there were rules—so many rules.

Kaye suddenly moved forward and the floor cleared. She moved across the gym floor like a dancer. She moved the ball between her legs and behind her back and over her head without missing one single step. She went from one side of the gym to the other without ever stepping out of bounds, and the music she moved to was the bounce, bounce, bounce of the balls of all her girlfriends.

No one moved. The boys stood frozen in place and Mr. Stevenson continued to sweat at such a profound rate that his wife would end up throwing out his clothes—and eventually him when she found out about his gambling habit.

No boy had ever moved the ball like this. No one had ever seen anything like this magic moment, and for one minute and then another not a single breath of air was sucked into any set of lungs in that gym. No one breathed. No one could breathe.

Meggie watched too. She wanted to be Kaye, strong and sure and true, but she was too terrified. She wanted to hold something in her hand that was magic and toss it into the air and then catch it again. She wanted everyone in the gym to see her as she really was and not as the girl who always took notes and stood to the side. She wanted to be . . . something . . . but she just could not do it.

Kaye was a dancer and a poetess and the greatest female athlete who ever existed. She played ball that day for the girls who were never allowed to run and who watched with a hunger in their hearts that made them physically sick. She was beautiful and lean and strong and no one could stop her. She jumped and caught her own ball and then she took her ball from the edge of the court and threw it in a perfect arc and put it in a hoop that some people standing close to her could not even see.

She was an athletic goddess. The Queen of the court. And what she did changed everything—and nothing.

Mr. Stevenson went wild. He had never even seen one of his own boys play like that, and he was pissed as hell. His own daughter, who would grow to be six feet two inches tall and who possessed the ability to play in the professional leagues, would never touch a ball when she heard about what happened that day in the gym. She never spoke to her father after her mother finally kicked him out, but her own daughters are now on full-ride scholarships at major universities and they sign autographs after every game. His daughter heard the story about that day in the gym when a little girl learned she could take a ball and turn it into a glass slipper, and now her own daughters wear the slippers very proudly.

Meggie saw it coming, and she moved behind the bleachers close to the door. Mr. Stevenson called the security guard, who came down to the gym with his big feet and a voice that could make a train stop and informed every single girl she would be suspended for a week if she did not leave.

They would not leave. They bounced their balls.

"Call," Kaye said, with her ball bouncing the loudest. "Call."

The security guard looked at the girls, and he could not call. He thought of his sister, who played tennis against the garage door for twelve hours one day but who could never be on a team, and he could not call. But he did step forward.

"You are right," he told the girls, and Mr. Stevenson dropped his jaw into the top of his blue-striped boxer shorts. "It isn't fair."

The security guard did a very brave thing, which came back to him so many times in so many wonderful ways after that moment that he wondered if an angel had not moved into his body.

He let them play.

The guard ordered the boys to watch, and for thirty minutes he let the girls play while he stood with his arms folded under the north basket.

Mr. Stevenson stood there too, and he memorized each one of the girls and he filed a report with the office, which mysteriously disappeared the next night when the security guard had access to the files.

Meggie stood back. She always stood back, and although she could feel the round hardness of the ball in her hand and the sweat that poured into her face as she came down the line, she could not move.

Nothing changed and everything changed because of that

afternoon. It would be years before girls moved into the arena with the boys and were guaranteed equal time, but surely, even to this day, not equal pay. Kaye and Pam were too old to play ball in college, but they joined local leagues and saw the sports world change because of what they did that afternoon, and they both remain as coaches of two highly successful high school girls' teams, and their own children—both boys and girls—treat the world and everyone in it with the same feelings of grace and respect.

Meggie turned to leave the gym that afternoon when the boys got the gym back after Pam and Kaye left together with their arms wrapped around each other, and she walked right into three of the biggest asshole boys in the entire county.

"What a joke," they sneered at her as she turned to walk in the opposite direction. "Girls will never be able to play with the boys."

Meggie stopped. She was not scared, but a tiny part and then a larger part of her believed them, because her world was full of men who crossed their arms and stood at the door so that the women and girls could not leave to go out into the garage and get their balls.

Down in a place that was so new and so frightened, there was a voice that had not yet learned how to speak. Her mouth opened just a bit and the voice went dead. Meggie could feel her throat scratch and then she swallowed hard and that feeling, that sensation that you are about to choke unless you do something—anything—vanished.

Meggie began to run then, and she never heard another word the three boys said, but the echoes of their laughter filled her soul so tightly that she felt as if someone or something had wrapped itself around her neck and was trying desperately to wrestle her to the ground.

10

I think I hear the doggies, but they are so far away that I am certain there are hours and hours yet to drive.

It must be close to dawn, and I am swaying in a hammock that has been wrapped with colors so bold and brave, I am wishing they will sink into my skin and color me, tattoo my white flesh, so that when I awaken I will be someone entirely new. Someone who will not mind that there are no doors and windows and that below me on the floor a family of seven or maybe eight sleeps on mats and wears clothes that I probably gave away nine years ago. There are suddenly no borders around the edges of my life, and for the first time since I was a little girl I actually decide to think about that and to wonder if I want the edges or I do not want the edges to keep me locked secure in a place that is routine and familiar.

There are thousands of miles between me and my real life—or maybe my old life. Miles that have feathered themselves into my mind in such a way now that it would be difficult for me to remember the size of the kitchen sink, how many steps there are on the front walk, the color of the bedroom walls that I stared at for all those long years. The familiar parts of my life suddenly do not seem to matter. Swaying in this hammock, sharing the simple and single thread of air that moves through the open windows and doors with people who cannot communicate with me in words, seems essential to everything that I am and will be—if I could only know why. If I could only grab on to a moment just like this and hold it in a place that might give me direction for what is next and then next after that.

What this change in life has done is to separate everything. My life back there is back there. I do not have to focus on the probability that I may run into Bob in the hall or that he may find me in the kitchen at two A.M. drinking white wine while I look out into the night. My daughter is off running through her own bushes, pretending that everything is fine because it's much easier to deal with your last year of adolescence—or any year, for that matter—if you can focus on just yourself. Work is just work—they might not even know I am gone, because a good deal of what I do is research where I am locked away in libraries and talking to people on the telephone who I will never see or touch. So I have this space of time to focus on a horizon that is not visible but which is calling to me in a manner so seductive that I feel a bit boozy.

And Jane. In a strange, almost inexplicable way, Jane has given me this sweet level of hope and encouragement, because she herself is so desperate for help, for one kind word. I admire her simplistic reasonings. She decided to stay in Illinois, find a job, sell her house and create a life she has never had but has always wanted—she just has no clue how to do that.

We drove almost all day over roads that were littered with holes and rocks the size of basketballs. Sometimes we drove so slowly that Elizabeth and I jumped from the car and walked, while Linda drove in gears so unimaginably low that we could cling to the back end as we leapt over rainwashed craters.

"Fucking shit," Linda said more than once and pretty close to a million times. This woman had a way with words.

"When was the last time you drove this road?" I asked her.

"Two weeks ago. Brought in a doctor when a woman needed help with a breech baby."

"How did they call you?"

She showed me, once we got there. A small, older-than-forever radio, which looked vaguely like the one my grandpa used on the back porch in Michigan when he was trying to contact someone from Russia or Amsterdam or one town over or from a place he dreamed about when he had had way too much whiskey.

Jane kept looking from me to Elizabeth and back again with eyes that seemed to get larger as the day progressed. When we asked her, she said only, "I'm good." She said it softly but surely and then she would grow silent and look off as if she were watching something that was totally visible to her and totally invisible to us. "Thinking," she would add. And we let her do that. We did.

And Linda? Where the hell did this woman come from? The simple and strong elegance of her physical beauty alarmed me. I couldn't imagine anyone in the world or their right mind not wanting to make love to this woman, and I had never even wanted to do more than hold the hands of my girlfriends as we walked up the hill toward the local bar. I asked her fourteen thousand questions.

Do you have a lover?

Several.

Men or women?

Are you propositioning me, Meg?

My heart flutters. No. Just asking... I want to say *"but."* There is no way in hell I can say what I want to after that *but.* "One step at a time," I tell myself. Jesus, Meg. *But* what I want to say is "I want to lie down next to you and put my lips on that spot right there on your forehead and then have you run your fingers up and down my arms, and feel what it is like to have a woman who takes my breath away kiss me." *But*... I do not say that. "One step at a time," I tell myself. Jesus.

It's my background, I say, lying while Elizabeth pokes me from behind so hard with her left hand that I could almost cry.

Mae West, Linda says.

I know Mae West, and I laugh.

Mae West, I finally say, did not want to exclude 50 percent of the population, so she slept with everyone, anyone, lots of men and women.

But. I push my question. Is there someone?

There is always someone, Linda says. At the moment it is another archaeologist, who flies in and out of this country inside of a plane so small, I could hold it in my hand, and he is kind and fun, so damn much fun. But, she adds—raising her voice just a bit so that I know something serious is coming—there is also always just me, and that is most important.

Just you? I question her but I am really questioning myself and she reaches over to touch my hand and then says, Just me, and I let it ride inside of me, tuck it away so that I can bring it out later when I am alone and can think about what that might really mean to a woman like me who does not even urinate alone half of the time. I have been alone so rarely during the past twenty-five years, I cannot even bring to mind one stretch of time when there was not a child, a husband, a mother, some relative or neighbor or someone from work propped up in my life. My head could explode simply trying to remember all the faces.

Our conversation has made Elizabeth very happy. She is laughing and pounding her knees and of course I think she and

Linda have slept together and have been lovers, but these days I think that of everyone. I think that the pilot slept with the baggage woman and I think that the bus driver slept with the woman at the front desk and then it dawns on me that I have not had decent sex in so long that I think the birds are mating and that every creature in the world is ready to copulate. My hormones must be off the chart after all these years of languishing in hibernation while apparently the entire world carried on in glorious sexual delight. And Linda reeked of sexiness, something I may be trying to catch, hoping to catch, and what a beautiful disease it might prove to be.

What do I know when I am done with my interview? Not much and everything and I hear a tiny door, about the size of a simple matchbook cover, spring open. Possibilities. There are so many possibilities? What have I been thinking? Have I been thinking?

There are pauses in these hours to do that—think, about sex, life and being alone and which direction I am really headed toward but there is also the following of the basic commandments. Commandments such as—Thou Shalt Find a Road Where Gas Is Available—and Who Shall Let Us Spend the Night? And How Will We Get There?

As these questions pound through my mind, it suddenly dawns on me that I trust this woman-driver-sexy-thing Linda more than I have ever trusted anyone, except Elizabeth, who has ushered me into this place, and oh, yes, my Auntie Marcia, who I continue to think is the reason we are here—I am here. I am here. Right here in the heart of a Mayan village where nothing seems familiar and where everything is simple and pure and basic.

Linda showed us everything in this little—what?—village, settlement, place of several huts—where families have carved out spaces for their no-door-or-window homes and put in a pump and turned their few animals loose and then began the te- dious and eternal task of making a living. A living for them does not go beyond the basic elements of food and shelter and appar- ently being able to reach over on this tiny, cold, earthen floor to make certain that there is someone next to you.

Tourist is not a word I would call myself, but that is what I am, and it embarrasses me more than watching my husband make love, which is really, when I pause to think about it, not embar- rassing at all. So I choose to call myself a "visitor." Someone just peeking in through the cracks, invited, of course, who will not be obtrusive or take photos of someone while they are indisposed.

Linda has instructed me to just be. Like I know what that is. Do not offer them anything, she says. Be gracious. Just be. The educator in me parades out to the center of the ravaged highway as if it were the Fourth of July.

"Have they been inoculated?"

"Yes. Your aunt took care of that."

"What?"

"Later," Elizabeth bellows from the backseat.

Jane continues to look startled and slightly amazed by the fact that she is even with us. "No one, no one who has ever touched my world even knows I am here," she tells us proudly. She dips into our conversations as if she is not even listening to where they are going.

"School?" I ask Linda.

"Some of them travel to Quinchinita. They have no need for school."

"Quinchinita?" I ask.

"Next stop."

"Water?"

"A well, but it's not safe by our standards. It's the only source of water for this entire village."

My mind is a machine gun. Their lives. Marriage? Death? Where did they get the tennis shoes? Who the hell gives them candy? Who built this road? What did they wear before we showed up with our T-shirts and hand-me-down dresses? Tell me—tell me everything.

Linda tries, but we reach the village before everything can be answered, and suddenly my hands are moving across the back of a dog that is crawling with fleas and ticks and has tits the size of golf balls and I am standing in a yard where a pig is the family pet and this dog, which I have touched for ten minutes, is considered wild and ugly.

Oh, Meg. Oh.

Oh a hundred thousand times over, and oh when Linda passes me water from her bottle and puts her finger to her lips, and oh when Elizabeth disappears, just walks off with people who come to greet her as if she were their favorite sister and Jane goes along. How about that? Jane goes along.

It is easy to forget why I have come. It is easy to get lost in watching and letting my mind hang its hat in this place that seems simple and at the same time mysteriously complicated.

As we settle in with the family, who Linda tells us have never before had overnight guests and who have skin the color of the early-evening clouds, I cannot stop thinking about my aunt and what she was doing here and how she found this part of a country that was so far removed from the rest of her life. Beyond that, why did she want me to come here and what does my trembling heart need to learn beyond everything—every single thing?

We are asleep just after dusk and I sway myself into sleep with Elizabeth on one side of me, Linda on another and Jane next to her, bodies scattered on mats around the dusty floor that must have seen the bottoms of many brown feet but never the swaying forms of four white women who sleep in shorts and T-shirts, with their eyes watching the last corner of light that disappears beyond the trees.

The day I married Bob, it rained. It was not a gentle, welcome-to-married-life-which-will-be-absolutely-beautiful-and-like-page-37-in-*Modern-Bride*-magazine kind of rain. It was a hurricane rain. Wind swept off the fields, and the tops of the old pines touched the midsections of trees planted fifteen feet away. The sewers were clogged full of cardboard boxes, roots the size of bicycles and small animals—including the neighbors' white poodle, who probably yipped all the way down that dark ride to the bowels of our city.

My mother wept when she woke on April 23, 1977, and saw clouds as dark as midnight instead of the bright blue heavens that she had imagined would produce streams of sunlight coming through the stained-glass windows at St. Agnes Church, where she would stand and watch me walk up the aisle and into a bride's magazine world that left me dazed and confused.

I woke to her sobs early the morning of my wedding after a night of tormented dreams, which were of my unfinished dissertation and a feeling that I may be making the greatest mistake of my life.

"Margaret," she screamed from the living room. "Margaret."

Apparently the rain was my fault along with everything else that went wrong that day. Dresses were torn, the cake was late, my dad's brother—Drunken Eddie, as we called him—bashed his car into the head usher's new Chevrolet and it never stopped raining all day long, not even for five minutes.

Later, years and years later, when I gave up, I remembered something from my wedding that I must have buried in a very deep spot. There is screaming in the car and my friend Susan is holding my hand and telling me everything is going to be okay, and closed streets and a mad dash by everyone when the car pulls up behind the church. I get out last and do it very slowly. The rain is pounding—there is no other way to describe it—and when I get to the door of the church, one hand there, the other dangling by my side, I realize that I am crying.

The rain splashes against my face, mixes with my tears and onto the black raincoat that I found hanging in the basement from Girl Scout camp days, and I say, "Thank you" out loud to God or some saint or anyone who might have been responsible for letting me hide behind the walls of water.

That is what I think about when I wake up in the middle of the night from my hammock in Mexico, because I hear rain pounding into the ground outside of the hut. If anyone else is awake, I do not know it, and the rain slows until the slice of sky I see from the open door lightens and the stars blink back on. I do not want to be thinking about the rain at my wedding, but I let my mind pause there for a moment and dip into the swell of what happened after I went into the church and dressed and walked up the aisle and then drove off again, still crying, into a rain that lasted four solid days.

When I wake again, just after dawn, I shake my head to clear it of my midnight dreams. Before I have time to blink, Linda has us on our feet and we are back on the highway, which is really not a highway at all but a large path chopped between the trees.

"How far to Quinchinita?" I want to know.

"Maybe seventy-five miles, but I'm not sure about the road after that rain last night. Sometimes it's worse the closer we get to the ocean, where the storms blow in."

"Then what?" Jane asks.

"Last night I asked about the man who knew your aunt, Meg, and I mentioned those damn dancing dogs, and I have an idea, not very clear but an idea, where we might find your doggies and any trace of your aunt. People in this village remember her."

"What do they remember?"

"Mostly that your aunt was just here and that when she was here she brought medicine and that she laughed."

"That would be her," Elizabeth says. "If I remember anything about your Aunt Marcia, it was that laugh."

I remember it too, almost as well as I remember my own laugh, and in a second, in the time it takes to say a name, I can pull the way she tilted her head and sucked air into her lungs fiercely and then let it blow through her throat and nose and mouth, I can pull that memory right out of my heart because I have carried it with me for my entire life. I think of it and my aunt with a kind of wild and free grace that tastes a bit like the dirt on the Mexico highway, and for so many years now it has been the only place I can touch that actually feels free. My aunt's stored laugh, tucked halfway between my stomach and my waist—like rolling thunder—always makes me feel free. The wild part, well, apparently I am working on that at this very moment. There are miles to go before I sleep and become Aunt Marcia-like wild—miles and miles.

So we drive, and it is slow and then fast, and I do not focus on the fact that my back is killing me or that I would commit a crime for an ice-cold beer, which I have been promised if we ever get to the other side of the world.

"Lots of beer, baby," Elizabeth says, "and there will be rum to set the lining of your stomach on fire, and the *views…*"

She closes her eyes when she talks about the views from small hills that are not blotted by condos and hotels and signs offering parasailing and men who cannot play the guitar singing next to a palm tree at midnight.

"You have been there?" I ask.

"Not this spot, but farther down the coast, and I imagine it as being almost the same."

"It is," Linda says. "It's quiet and beautiful and if I could pick one reason why I stay in this country, it would be because of Quinchinita."

"Wow" is all I can think of saying, because it is hard for me to imagine anything more beautiful than the other side of the peninsula.

We stop once to eat fruit and granola bars, and when I peer into the thick jungle I wonder how far I would have to walk before I actually saw another person. It took three hours to get here in an airplane and it is a million miles away from where I live.

By four P.M. we have crossed some kind of imaginary line and we begin to see huts, a few live human beings, and Linda tells us that within ten miles we will be in the town. "Town," she adds quickly, "meaning streets and a few businesses and stores and the most wonderful market you will ever see in your life, and yes, before you ask, there will be cold beer, and that is where we stop first."

Once when I was in high school I read a book about a young woman whose mother had died when she was a little girl. She had no real memories to hang on to: thoughts of what her mother must have been like, how she sat on her mother's lap, touched her hair, whispered in her ear and smelled her skin almost drove her insane. One day the girl fell into a deep sleep, no one could wake her, and in her dream her mother came to her and answered every question. The girl slept for days and when she woke up it was as if she had lived with her mother every day she had been alive. She knew everything she had always wanted to know.

That story rode with me and I wondered if it was possible for me to close my eyes after this adventure and feel as if the missing answers to all my questions would be lined up on the bathroom sink the first morning after I returned home. Aunt Marcia tried to show me how life could be, how my life could have been, and I was trying hard to remember events, people, things she'd said were part of my lost set of life directions.

My deep thoughts vanish as we breeze past a row of houses, maybe seven or eight, hardly enough to be called a congested block, and Linda pulls the Jeep in front of a tiny store that looks as if it has been standing since the beginning of time. Small sticks for the sides, no windows; from what I could see from the highway, there are dirt floors, colorful hammocks woven in reds, greens, oranges, pinks and blues hanging outside of each door and then the one glorious item we had been looking for, waiting for, hoping for since we hit the dusty road two days ago—a small rusted sign in the shape of a beer bottle.

"Is this what I think it is?" I ask, leaning forward.

Linda smiles, pushes back her hair as if she were in a movie and says, "Get your ass out of the Jeep and drink."

The cold beer can not dislodge the thoughts of Aunt Marcia's lost lessons and I wonder if my auntie drank beer here, did she in front of this old building, did she know the shopkeeper, what did she want me to see as I stood in this hot Mexican sun?

Jane interrupts my quiet drinking with a question.

"You okay?" she asks as we lean against the back of the Jeep.

"Thinking about my aunt, life, this trip."

"I can't stop thinking, either. I've been terrified of being alone all these months," she says, quietly at first and then with her voice rising. "All these months I've felt that unless I was with someone that life was worthless. Being alone shouldn't feel like that."

My hand moves to her arm without thinking. I want her to know that I am listening, that I understand, that it's okay to tell me what is on the very top layer of her heart.

She goes on a bit louder as if the first sips of beer have kick-started something that needed just a bit of oil.

"I'm pissed off. Angry that I lingered so long in a place that now seems a bit disgusting to me."

"It's part of the process I think," as I try to convince myself as well. "Maybe what Aunt Marcia was trying to tell me is that there are no 'right' set of rules and directions and guidelines. Maybe it didn't matter if I came to Mexico now or twenty years ago. Maybe it's just right if your process of discovering that being alone is just a fine way to be took you over a few backroads."

Maybe.

Maybe is what we decide to hold on to in our left hands as we drink our beer with our right hands and lean into each other and then into the rest of the day and the possibility that we may know exactly what we are talking about.

11

When Katie was born, the very second, I felt as if something moved through my entire body. This sensation overwhelmed me. It was beyond the physical pain of having something the size of an enormous watermelon pass through a hole the size of a grapefruit. It was beyond the very real knowledge that a baby was moving from inside of me and out into a world that I was certain neither of them were ready for. It was a sensation that some powerful force was cleansing me with some kind of invisible potion so that my daughter could leave me and begin her own life.

I felt a set of hands push down, gently, so gently, from inside of my head. If I could have focused, if anyone would have asked me during those moments and I had explained it like this, they may have never let me leave the hospital. But they did not ask, and with my eyes closed I reached up to take the hands and help them move through the inside of my body.

There was someone very far away ordering me to push and incredible pressure that made it difficult for me to breathe centered just below my waist and this sweet sound of the hands moving like wind and my fingers gliding on top of them, touching silk and then rumbling past my throat and lingering around the edges of my heart, and me thinking just then that no matter where these hands swept, the scent and feel and taste of this baby would never leave me.

When this force reached the very top of the curve of my stomach, just where I imagined the tips of the baby's feet might be resting, it stopped, and I did also. When I opened my eyes there was a mass of heads hovering below me and looking into that place of finesses, into me, into my vagina, where the round ball of my baby's head was jamming up the process, and I calmly said, "She's coming," because at that moment I knew that the baby was a girl and who she was and that the hands were really there inside of me.

She came then, screaming before anyone but me could hear her, and I felt the hands glide and pull and push the baby girl into place, and then my hands boldly stopped everything because I knew I would never, ever have another baby and I wanted to feel this last moment, the moment when pain shutters everything so tightly that there is room for nothing but the simple hope that you might live beyond that very moment. The moment when you can imagine the welcoming arms of death and when you can feel your bones stretching and the songs of birds flying to peck out your eyes and the roll of drums as objects draped in black come to seize what is left of your flesh.

I held on to that moment for one and then two and then ten seconds and then I screamed from a place I had never been to before or since. I screamed and I felt the edges of something filled with fire and then I grabbed the top of the hands and I pushed them out of me behind the baby girl, and even then this force lingered in the room. Lingered because the baby had grown so quiet. Quiet, we quickly discovered, because she had been removed from my dark and safe uterus and thrown into the cold and rather bright world of the hospital delivery room.

When I closed and then opened my eyes, whomever or whatever had entered the room was gone.

Katie, some would say, came to me possessed. She was a kindred spirit filled with all intentions good and wonderful, because Katie was an independent gem from the moment she was born.

She is always in my heart, but when she plows into my mind and sits there hour after hour, there is something she needs from me. I know this just as I know my need to drink water or to lie down when I can no longer stand. That is why I ask Linda to help me hunt for a phone right after we inhale our second beer.

"A phone?" Elizabeth asks as if I said I needed to quickly rent *Gone With the Wind* or order a taco to go. I can tell she wants to argue, so I don't even bother to say anything. Sometimes she gets like this.

"Whatever it is will have to wait, Meg. Are you crazy? Who do you want to call?"

We are hanging on to the Jeep, and all I know is that I need to hear my daughter's voice and to know what she needs.

"Katie," I say. "She needs to ask me a question."

Before I can say another word, Linda hands me a cell phone. This is the first time I have seen it. She must keep it zipped up inside the white vest she never takes off.

"I have a daughter," she tells me, holding her hand against mine while she puts the phone inside of it. "I was in high school when she was born. She's twenty-two now. In graduate school. She's the only one who has this number. Call your daughter."

Has life always been like this? I want to ask someone this question, but it will only make me look more foolish than I already feel. I want to know how much I have been missing, how many things I could have had if only I had bothered to ask. What was the whole world doing while I folded socks, studied for anthropology exams and stared blankly out of the kitchen window? Where the hell have I been?

Katie is not at home, but I call her own blessed and lovely cell phone, and when she answers, when I hear the sweet sound of her voice saying, "Hello," and then lifting two hundred degrees when she hears me say, "It's your mother," I start to cry.

"Mom, are you okay?"

"I'm fine, baby. What do you need?"

"You."

"What?"

"You forgot to leave any phone numbers and I was worried about you, Mom. I knew if I thought about you long enough that you would call me."

"Jesus," I think. In a flash, a blink, my daughter has become my mother. Then I realize that I am no longer someone she knows very well. I have never left her like this. I have never traveled off in search of the source of my silver rings in the land where dogs dance and mysteries of the past are hidden under brightly colored blankets. I have always been around the corner or over at Grandma's house or in the library or out waiting in the car.

"I'm in a small city that is not on a map. It's on the east coast of the Yucatán Peninsula. Between Campeche and Celestun. We're looking for those dancing dogs I told you about."

"Mom, are you smoking dope? You know what that will do to you."

She is half joking and half serious, which gets me half concerned. If I find out she has volunteered to cook a meal or walk the dog, I'm flying home as soon as I can get back to the airport.

"Not yet, it's too early. We're sticking with the Mexican beer until we find something better. I love you, Katie."

Jane whispers to me as I disconnect and hand the phone back to Linda. Jane tells me about the baby she lost. The baby lived for three months, she tells me while Elizabeth and Linda huddle near the front tires. Three months and then this sudden rush between her legs and wailing that seemed to come from a place so far away, which turned out to be her own voice.

"That was it," she says, even more softly. "No more babies, and he wouldn't adopt, and I kept padding through all those days and nights, wondering about motherhood."

She tells me that during the first days alone, in that nice house where some lights are never turned off, she dreamed her lost baby back to life for a while. Crawling, walking, talking, graduating from high school, coming in to sit and talk with her after a date or a game.

"Some things you never get over," Jane explains. "I accept that, but I wonder—now, more than ever—if I couldn't have filled up the empty space with someone else."

Wow, Jane. Wow.

Linda brushes off my thank you with a wave of her hand and we manage to pull Elizabeth out of the shade, where she is conversing in her interesting version of the Spanish language with two men who both look terribly confused. Elizabeth could probably get elected mayor of this village in two weeks if we left her here alone. Me? I like to keep one hand on the Jeep at all times.

Three hours later I find myself sitting at the edge of the ocean, fairly oblivious to anything that exists beyond what I can see when I turn my head from side to side, and what I see is enough. I am immersed in a world of blue—sky, water and roofs. The brightness has me cornered in a way that makes me think of nothing but what I see and I know this is a good thing for just a little while because what I need to think about is big stuff, really big stuff. I like to believe that I know what I am doing here on this beach, but if I move even an inch I can hear myself shift in the wind. My life is a question right now—one huge question.

Linda has deposited us at a cottage just north of the city, and from what I can see in the first five minutes, I know this is what the entrance to Heaven must look like. Everything is simple and clean, and Elizabeth, who claims to never have been here before, seems speechless with happiness for a good five minutes, which is a very long time for her. Jane is quiet, looking everywhere, exploring her temporary landscape like someone who has just had her sight restored.

Linda barely stopped the Jeep before she whirled back in the direction from which we'd come, shouting that she was off to find the dogs and that Angelica would take care of us. Angelica finds us with our bags in our hands, staring out at the endless sea as if we are waiting for a lost lover to walk right out of the water. When she speaks we are all startled.

"¡Ay, mujeres bonitas! ¡Bienvenido a Fiesta Harbor!"

I say "Hello" because fake Spanish is worse than anything I can think of during that moment and I can barely order a beer in the native tongue. But Elizabeth launches into a conversation that Angelica must be able to understand, because she answers back.

She asks her about the resort where we are staying first in Spanish and then as an aside to me in English. Elizabeth tells me the piece of land and small rental business have been in Angelica's family for a very long time.

We are both dying to know if Angelica knows Linda.

A frequent visitor when she comes to this part of the peninsula, Elizabeth relates in Spanish.

And what about the mysterious Pancho who is somehow tied to my dead aunt and may be the internal director of the Mexican mafia?

Apparently everyone knows this man and my aunt; I am tugging at the edge of Elizabeth's blouse. And she finally asks.

"*¿Conoce usted a la Americana que se llama Marcia?*"

Angelica's face suddenly moves in a wide and beautiful smile. Before she says, "*Que mujer mas bonita,*" I know that she has seen and met Aunt Marcia and I want to know, but Elizabeth is already stumbling over her Spanish as if she has on shoes two sizes too big.

"*¡Basta! Tendra la informacion mas tarde. Ahorita trate de gozar.*"

Elizabeth has said enough. Damn. Elizabeth explains that this way of speaking is simply part of the respectful Mexican culture. You don't say what someone else is supposed to say, and my mind jumps to two places at once. Either something horrible and sinister happened to my Aunt Marcia and her glorious companions or the story is not tragic but beautiful and quiet.

I stand by like an overanxious American as Elizabeth finishes her conversation with Angelica, but Elizabeth tells me everything when she is finished and then Angelica walks us to our sleeping quarters and tells us her son will come to find us so that we can share dinner with Angelica and her family.

Simple. Everything seems simple.

"Elizabeth," I say as I throw my bag on the sandy floor and take her hand. "Elizabeth, this quiet is light and perfect and I feel so far away."

"So far away from what, sweetheart?"

"Everything."

"What does *everything* mean to you right now, this second, while you are looking out at an ocean of possibility?"

"Everything hard and routine and things, everything that I don't want to do."

"What don't you want to do?"

"Every single thing I ever did before this moment, before right now, before here..."

Elizabeth smiles, but she sees me hesitate.

"... What I want to keep are my kids, some parts of my work, and a few simple routines."

"And?"

"Maybe I don't really miss anything. Maybe I am just a maybe."

"Maybe is okay, Meg. It's okay to just be a maybe right now. Maybe you will want to go back and embrace your life. Maybe not. How long did it take you to get here?"

"Don't make me say it."

"Well, Jesus, Meg, you don't have to build the entire tower in one day. Let it happen. Let it happen how it will happen."

The next few hours prove to me that I have forgotten the simple joys of doing just that. Just letting it happen. Elizabeth and Jane decide to walk, and I just want to sit and stare out at the water. The overwhelming tiredness that I felt in Dr. C's office has not totally left me, and that coupled with the trip and the weight of the world that keeps shifting its spot from shoulder to shoulder makes me want to lie down for a very long time. When I find my place in the sand, it feels like the warm part of Heaven. I cover my eyes with my bandanna, spread my legs, push my arms out to form the universal angel and, before I can take another breath, fall asleep.

I wake up with a grumbling volcano-like semi-empty stomach and to the dark eyes of a little boy who is pushing my shoulder and saying, "*¡Mujer! ¡Levantese! Venga y conya mi madre ha prepardo la cena.*" This, I think, means get up and eat or his mom will kick my butt.

It takes me a minute to remember where I am and then another minute to realize I have fried my face and legs and arms in the Mexican sun. I want to jump in the ocean and have the salty water sting me back to consciousness, but dinner is waiting, and my stomach cannot wait.

We feast on rice, beans and tacos, while Elizabeth carries on a conversation—well, sort of a conversation—with Angelica and her family. I imagine she is ordering geese and asking them about their sex lives when she really wants to know about the winter weather and how they manage to prepare food in a kitchen the size of her bathroom closet.

We decide not to worry about Linda. "I'm pretty certain she can take care of herself," Jane laughs, and when it gets dark outside I convince her and Elizabeth to go for a swim with me, because my lobster-red skin is screaming so loud, I cannot bear to listen to it any longer. There is a torch outside of our hut, which we light and take with us to push into the sand at the edge of the water. It should not surprise me that Elizabeth wants to swim naked and insists that we join her.

"What about the family?" Jane asks.

"They won't watch. The people here are very respectful."

"Well, shouldn't we be?"

"I am not swimming nude to offend them, Jane. It's part of who I am. I'm certain they won't look. Meggie, my gray-eyed beauty, when was the last time you went skinny-dipping?"

Have I ever gone skinny-dipping?

"Well?" she asks as she slips out of her shirt and shorts and stands with one foot in the sand and the other in the water.

"I'm thinking. . . . There was a night in Chicago, but there has to be a time after that."

"Was there?"

"Well, when I was a little girl, Aunt Marcia used to take me swimming at her friend's cottage in northern Wisconsin, and she said that if we swam naked during a full moon and exposed our breasts to the evening sky that we would have good luck until we swam under the full moon again."

"Really? How wonderful."

"She also told me that if I swam under a full moon I would become a virgin again, which I thought was cool and I actually believed that lovely story for a number of years. It was sort of like money in the bank, even though I never did anything about it."

Elizabeth hollers with glee at that story and I tell her how I tried to carry on the ceremony with my own daughter, but just like everything else significant in my life, I got to the edge of the water and then chickened out.

"It's never too late," she tells me as she backs into the water and then falls over as if she were a tree hacked off by a wicked chain saw.

"Why," I wonder to myself as I stand there alone, "is something like this so damned *hard* for me? Why is a seemingly simple act, something that could be beautiful and gracious and new and lively—why is it so *hard*?"

Jane tells us she doesn't even know how to swim, and laughs at the idea of taking anything off—even her shoes. "You are way ahead of me, Elizabeth," she says, sitting at the water's edge, fully clothed and with her tennis shoes on. "I'm just going to *look* at the water. You two do whatever you want to. I'm going to float on the *beach*."

I enter the water with my swimming suit zipped and tucked and totally on. The one with the flowered bottoms and black top that seemed perfect for a mother with two teenagers just a few years ago and now seems just a bit on the conservative side. Elizabeth and I bounce very close to shore and then I slide all the way under the water and then pop up through a delicious spray of waves. Simply delicious.

I lie back then so that the waves can carry me right into the beach, and I let go and make myself feel as if I am the ocean— moving in a patterned direction yet free enough to curl and shift if the wind touches me in the right spot. Then I ride the wave into shore and go back out and ride another wave back in. I cannot take off my bathing suit, not yet. Maybe on the next trip or at the end of summer or in a year, but not yet. I already feel too naked, even in the darkness.

Elizabeth has propped herself up on the beach next to Jane and she is watching me. When I catch a glimpse of her, I see her white teeth flashing and I think that this is one of the most intimate moments of my life. Me flying through the waves, and two women who would fling themselves in front of a train for me, women who have shared moments of personal anguish and who love me, truly love me, watching me surf through a moment that can only be described as totally fabulously wonderful.

I cry then, and my tears mingle with the waves and the moon, a sliver of golden lightness that smiles at us over the horizon. When I lie next to Elizabeth in the sand, there is absolutely no need for me to say thank you, because she knows. She knows.

"You know, Elizabeth," I finally say. "I wanted to go skinny-dipping all those years ago. I stood there on the edge of Silver Lake with Katie's hand in mine and my other hand on the towel and I worried about everything. What would people think, what if someone saw me—"

She cuts me off.

"They'd be lucky. We grew up, Meggie, thinking that nakedness was wrong. We were supposed to be chaste and only the boys could go down to the strip joints and watch women take off their clothes. You were formed by the voices you heard all your life. In many ways you didn't have a choice and in many ways the people uttering what you heard had no choice. You really didn't have a choice."

"How about you?" I ask her, imagining that she was raised by hippies—or wolves in some cave just inside of the city before the stop signs gave way to deep forests and long rivers.

Her story is similar to others I have heard from my university friends and educated women who stepped out-of-bounds and never ever thought of going back inside those heavy lines. Strict parents. Way-strict parents who demanded and pushed and pulled, so that their daughters decided to try to be and do everything that seemed evil and horrid, because they needed to try—just try.

"I just became comfortable with who I was and how I wanted to live my life," Elizabeth tells me. "It's not for everyone, but it works for me."

Jane goes next. Large Christian family. The burdens of religion. Guards at the door day and night, and always wondering what it might be like to fly and then pass over the top of her real life and see what she looked like from a new angle.

"I'm getting ready to get my pilot's license," she says. "Meg and I will take off our bathing suits as soon as I can get my entire body into the water, so no one can see me."

We talk and laugh for a long time, lying in the sand practicing "being naked," until I hear the shriek of the Jeep brakes and Linda's wild voice calling our names.

"Down here," Elizabeth yells.

"You—" Linda starts, but the sight of us cuts her off.

"Did you swim?" she asks, standing above us with her hands on her hips.

"Yes." I answer. "It's wonderful."

Without hesitating, she announces that she has fabulous news and that she is going to swim too. Her words get cut off as she whips off her blouse and vest and pants... "Hot... damn... found him... wait till you hear... exhausted... hot..." And then she is in the water, her white ass waving to us and me plunging in one more time to get the sand off my own white ass, which is still covered by a bathing suit.

"Little by little," I tell myself.

Linda swims for a long time. Elizabeth stays down by the beach to watch her, and I walk back to the hut to grab some beer from the cooler our hosts have graciously left for us and then I rejoin them at the edge of the water, where Linda launches into her daylong adventure with such gusto, we could be filming a Miller Lite commercial that features middle-aged women who leave Chicago to find themselves after years of bad relationships and hard times.

"I found him," she tells us. "Pancho Gonzales Quintana is a very old man and he thought I was you," she says, putting her hand on my arm. "He said he has been waiting a long time and that your aunt said you could come when you were much younger but you never came. His story and your aunt's story . . . they are remarkable."

"Tell me," I beg. "Tell me."

Linda laughs at the very moment she is taking a sip of her beer, and wisps of foam fly into the air like an out-of-control water fountain.

"He said you will know what to wear and that he will recognize your eyes because your auntie told him about your eyes and the power of your heart."

"They must know something I do not know," I say, looking off into the dark that now hovers where the moon had danced just a short while ago.

"Forget her heart," Elizabeth says. "What about the dancing dogs?"

"I'm pretty sure we will see the dancing dogs, especially if Pancho knows it is you. Do you know what to wear, Meg?"

"Yes, but we need to find it."

My three friends look at me as if they have never seen me before and want quite suddenly to know my first name, where I live, anything about me.

"A purple skirt," I tell them. "I need to wear a purple skirt."

"Can we find one?" Elizabeth asks, never even bothering to find out why it has to be a purple skirt.

"We can find anything. Are you kidding me? I found Pancho, don't you think I can get a purple skirt?"

I think that Linda can do anything. Anything at all. And that locating a purple skirt may very well be the easiest part of her day.

I sleep that night wrapped in blankets the color of the rainbow, with the sound of the waves rolling up the sand, slipping into my hair and then my eyes and face. My dreams are filled with wild beer-induced messages from the ancient spirits who wandered these beaches long before the feet of white women touched down on them.

In my dreams, I am naked and no one seems to notice and I put on clothes only when I am alone. I can hear what people are going to say before they say it and every night that I wish for a full moon, one appears and glides across the horizon left to right and then back again until the sun kicks it out of the sky.

Everything is real inside my dream, everything I want is right there within reach, and the first thing I think of when I roll out of the hut at two A.M. to use the bathroom is that I need to find out who makes the beer and where I can find it near Chicago or Minneapolis or Milwaukee. I will drive a great distance to buy this beer, and then I will take it to a beach when there is a full moon, and when I do, I will finally take Katie and Jane for the swim of their lives.

12

1973

It is a night of surprises. Margaret's brother Michael has graduated from college and his party, in the backyard, under the towering maple trees that were tiny buds when he was a baby, has slowed to a crawl. Three of his friends are sleeping on the floor of his old bedroom and everyone but one uncle, who is loud and loves to touch all the pretty ladies, and his silent wife, who smokes endlessly and picks at her nails, has left. It is past midnight and upstairs in her bedroom Meggie can hear the muffled sounds of her father and uncle talking and the women picking up glasses as they move in and out of the kitchen.

"Can I come in?" Michael asks her, pushing her bedroom door open just wide enough so she can see that he has two beers in each hand.

"Oh, please," Meggie says through a laugh, and stretches out her hand for the beer she is usually forbidden to taste. "Will we get in trouble?"

"They'll be talking another hour and they think I'm passed out with the boys. Don't worry, baby, I'm twenty-one now, so I can corrupt anyone I want to. See?"

Michael, her brother with the gentle eyes and soft heart who rarely raises his voice above a whisper and who now has an engineering degree, pulls out a small bottle of whiskey and says, "Now I can celebrate with my favorite sister."

"I'm your only sister, goofy."

Meggie has tasted beer and wine and everything else her parents keep in the old ice chest behind the couch. She has had two cigarettes with her girlfriend Marcy and she has allowed Jeffrey Jablonski to slip his hands under her blouse, but Meggie is so terrified of her father's rules and her mother's enforcement of them that she has never broken them. Occasionally, she slips her foot just over the edge of the line and laughs into the wind for about fifteen seconds, but then she quickly goes right back to stand in the designated areas.

Michael tugs her out of bed and grabs her quilt off of the pillows and they circle it around themselves and sit with their backs against Meggie's bed. Then they begin their party.

"Will you get in trouble?" Meggie asks Michael as she takes a huge sip of the whiskey and washes it down with her beer.

"Oh, my baby, I am going to get in trouble, but it's not because of this."

Meggie watches her brother move his long legs out so he can cross them at the ankles, and she cannot remember a time when she has not been able to count on him. When he left for college four years ago, just before she started high school, she was devastated and had to leave the house so she would not see the car when it turned the corner to take him away from her.

But those hundreds of miles did not make a difference and he called her and sent her photographs of his friends, and on long holiday weekends when their brother Grant was racing through town with his girlfriends, she and Michael would go to the movies and talk, just like this, about everything, or so Meggie thought.

"I'm in trouble, baby sister," he says, dipping his head and slouching his long body into a tiny ball. He rises just a bit and adds, "But it's not totally bad trouble."

Over the years they have talked about everything and when Meggie's girlfriends had crushes on handsome Michael, he was always gracious, and when Meggie talked about her dreams and about how she wanted so many things that her parents did not want, Michael would hold her against his chest while she cried and tried to figure out who she was and what she wanted to be when she grew up. "Oh, my Michael," she would say over and over again, "Oh, my Michael."

Meggie cannot imagine steady, wise, gentle Michael even knowing what trouble might feel or look or smell like. When she closes her eyes, she sees him with a long sword in one hand, his arm around her terribly slender waist and an olive branch tied up in his brown curly hair. He is her friend, her guardian, the one she has always gone to.

They are getting just a little tipsy and Michael says he has things he needs to tell her so he can practice telling their parents in the morning before he leaves.

"You're leaving?"

"Oh, yes, my Meggie, I am going far away."

There is a hot knife burning a hole in the pit of Meggie's stomach, and she can barely speak. "What are you talking about?"

"Oh, Meggie," he says gently. "Don't cry, baby. Please don't cry."

"Tell me, Michael, just tell me. Get it over with. Just tell me."

Michael wraps his arms around his little sister, holding her while he wipes her face with the edge of the blanket, and then he begins his story. Meggie cannot move. She is horrified and at the same time terribly happy. Michael's story is as old as he is and

Meggie understands some of the pieces of his tale, because it is her story too.

Michael did not want to go to engineering school. He did not want to go to school at all. He did not want to spend four years studying something he never intended to practice. Michael wanted to travel and paint and lie on his back near the ocean so he could see what happens to the clouds when they pass across the sea and then bump up against a mass of solid earth. He wanted to have his own life and his own friends and he wanted to love who he wanted to love.

"I was in love with this woman," Michael tells his sister, beginning to cry himself. "Oh, Meggie, I loved her so much. I will always love her."

Meggie can't move. She is astounded, because she has never heard this story and she never knew. She never knew. Michael cries in her arms now as huge waves of tears, like the clouds he has never seen, roll through him.

"Tell me," Meggie whispers gently into his ear, wiping his tears the way he has always wiped hers.

"She lived in my dorm and she was an artist and I loved her the first time I saw her. I love her now. I do."

"What happened, Michael? Where is she?"

"She is black, Meggie, and when I told Mom, when I wanted to bring her home, when I said that I was in love with her, she told me I had to choose."

"Mom said that?"

"Yes. She said I could have the woman I loved or the family I have known and loved forever, but I could never bring her home, and if I did they would never speak to me again."

Meggie has to focus so she will not throw up. The beer and the whiskey have her head spinning and she is imagining what the conversation must have been like as Michael sat with his head in his hands and their mother broke his heart.

"Oh, Michael, I am so sorry."

"It was my choice. It was the biggest mistake of my life and a mistake I will never make again."

"Where is she, Michael? What happened?"

Michael's girlfriend, wise and beautiful, was used to the searing eyes of discrimination. She was used to the mothers and fathers of the world looking at her, seeing only one thing and dismissing her as other mothers and fathers and sons and daughters had done for more than a hundred years.

"She left me. When I got back from Thanksgiving break she knew what had happened without me ever saying a word. Oh, Meggie, don't ever let this happen to you."

Michael cries then like Meggie imagines he has never cried before and she holds his head against her heart and runs her fingers through his beautiful hair and lets him cry out his anguish and his anger and his regret—his burning, horrid regret.

"Where is she, Michael? Why can't you get her back?"

"I don't deserve to have her back, baby. She is who I want to be. Strong and true and living a life that is honest. She finished school and moved to New York."

"You could find her again, Michael. Go find her."

Michael cries harder, imagining what his life could have been like with a beautiful and brilliant woman who wore her passion every moment of her life. He is ashamed, he tells his sister, so damned ashamed.

"Go to her," young Meggie says.

"I have to find my passion first. I have to become a man, Meggie. I need to find my own life before I can dare to assume someone like that will even want to be in the same room with me."

It is almost too much for Meggie. Meggie, who at seventeen

dreams of love and romance as if it is all pouring out of a novel. She does not know the complicated entanglements of life. It will be a very long while before she understands the importance of passion as a grounding stone, a way of life, a place that you can never back away from.

"Someday, then, you can find her again," Meggie tells him.

Michael desperately wants his sister to know that women and men with passion in their lives must not wait. He wants to grab Meggie by the shoulders and tell her to run from these last few years of her life in this town and with this family. He wants his sister to love and live wildly and to know that she can design every moment of her life and then live it exactly like that design she created. He wants to put her on a cloud and have her see what he has already seen.

But he can't. He knows that Meggie must find her own passion in her own time and in her own style, and his wish that night—the night before his leaving—is that he has planted a seed, a thought, a place for her to begin.

"There's more," he says, sitting up and turning to face her. The quilt falls away from their shoulders and for a few seconds there is a silence that goes from warm to cold.

"Meggie, I joined the Peace Corps. I leave in the morning. Mom and Dad don't know, and I don't know when or if I will ever come back."

Meggie cannot breathe. Something has clamped its hands around her throat, and she wants to scream and lie down and never get up. Michael. Her Michael. The rock in her life. The one she calls at midnight.

"Listen," he tells her, knowing that she now thinks she cannot go on, that without him she cannot make it through the week.

"Where?" she manages to say.

"Tonga."

Meggie can barely imagine it. Tonga. Tonga. Tonga. She can't even remember where it is.

"It's a place for me to start," Michael explains. "I'll be doing engineering work, which I hate, but this is my choice and the place I want to be. And where it will take me is beyond anything I need to know tonight or tomorrow or the next day."

Meggie wants to be glad for him. She wants to understand this huge change in his life.

"Michael, I know this is good. Will it make you happy?"

"It's already made me happy."

"How will you tell them?"

Michael smiles. "I'm leaving them a note on the table and I'm running away."

Meggie cannot believe it. "Really?"

"Yes, my bags are at my friend Mark's house. He's taking me to the airport in three hours, and I'm out of here."

Meggie thinks for a second. "Isn't that kind of like being a coward?"

"I don't care. It's how I want to do it and it's what I need to do. By the time they get up, I'll be boarding the next airplane in Los Angeles."

"Wow."

Michael has other things to tell her. How to reach him, what she should do her senior year of high school, how she should act in the morning when all hell breaks loose, but Meggie has already slipped away. She cannot focus on anything but on the fact that something delicious and solid is leaving her life.

Meggie does not know that Michael has settled so deep inside of her heart that he could never, ever leave her. She did not know that long night that her brother would find his passion, not in Tonga, but in being true to the callings of his own beautiful heart. One day, years later, she will learn that his first great love was miles ahead of him and that when Michael finally caught up to her, she had passed her heart on to another man. Michael tried desperately to tell Meggie that every moment counts and that she should not waste even one of those moments. He sent her letters from Tonga, messages that he thought would help her glide to her own passion. When he moved to Seattle and began to paint and went back to school to become a grade school art teacher, she understood what was happening but she did not realize it also had something to do with her.

That night, with Michael holding her hand and pouring out his longings and realizations, there was the soft beating of a Tongan drum in his head. But Meggie heard nothing. There was an ocean right outside her window and there were strange but beautiful birds calling her name and the whispers of ancient souls pointing her in the proper direction, but she was not ready, would not be ready for a very long time.

Margaret Joan Callie dreamed, but she did not know how to dream. Margaret Joan Callie loved, but she did not know how to love.

When Michael left, she was brave enough to stand in the yard and hold him one last time before he slipped into Mark's car and disappeared down Washington Avenue and toward the swaying palms of the South Pacific. She thought she heard someone whisper her name before she snuck in the back door and quietly slipped into bed, wrapping the quilt around her shoulders to savor the final scents of Michael's aftershave and the beer and maybe the lingering echo of one more laugh.

She thought it was the beer when she heard the whisper again, or maybe the whiskey, and so she did not listen. She did not listen to the whispers of her life, and while Michael winged his way west she embraced her old dreams, the ones with ponies and bright morning light and girls dancing in tights. She did not hear the whispers that spoke to her of mountain passes where the birds' wings touched the tips of the trees and all the good men in places with names she could not pronounce who would hold her hand but never hold her down and the way everything that touched her lips never tasted bitter, but sweet and fine.

She did not hear the whispers.

13

There is a golden unwritten rule in Mexico. It is the rule called "Never hurry up when you could go slower." This rule has me totally messed up. I do not like to wait; I do not know how to wait. But in the morning when everyone in this part of the universe is still asleep, I want them all to be awake. We should be driving and galloping and running at full throttle toward this momentous life occasion that will show me whatever in the hell it is I missed and should have come searching for years and years ago.

Elizabeth is asleep.

Linda is asleep.

Jane is asleep.

No one in the very dark and quiet home of our lovely hosts is moving, and here I am all dressed up in my purple skirt, with nowhere to go.

"Damn it," I say to myself as I kick sand all the way to the beach. "Damn it."

I decide to walk the beach and air out the purple skirt. It could be hours before anyone wakes up, and I am far too restless to sleep. The sun is not close to blinking awake yet either, and I have no idea what time it might be, so I walk into the beginning of the beautiful Mexican day alone and waiting—two items that seem to be appearing at the top of my list quite a lot lately.

The light here is exotic to me, dancing colors that seem more vivid than the colors of the world I am used to. The sky this early in the morning is just now beginning to turn into a flame of orange. The ocean is not just aqua, it is a shimmering wedge of turquoise that slaps my eyes in a way that feels addictive. I cannot stop looking at the water. Even the air has the scent and feel of something earthy, foreign, new. When my feet kick up the sand, I cannot help but think of the mix of men, women and children who have walked in this very same direction. There is a feeling of foreign grace in every movement. With each step, I wonder whose footfall I have replaced, what great woman has walked this same path, what ancient ship passed on the horizon a hundred years ago right in front of where I am standing. The past, I think with a laugh, is not so far behind me.

Direction has not been my strong suit for quite some time now, but I head—what, east?—along the water's edge and past low bushes, where the scent of something sweet—an unknown flower—drifts across the surface of my skin and makes me smile. I think in that moment that this is the first time in weeks and weeks that I have felt great, just simply great. The confusion of my direction does not matter right now; I know my daughter is all right, I am with three of the most wonderful women I have ever known and I am wearing a purple skirt. There is something in the air, in the simple joy of movement, that delights me, and I consciously choose to be happy, and hope to God I can make this happiness last for a very long time.

It is fifteen minutes before I see a building or any signs of life, and then another forty-five minutes before a group of old, battered tables appear on a small hill just at the edge of the water. A café? Maybe some kind of gathering spot. I cannot see over the top of the hill, but I decide to stop and sit in one of the chairs. It looks as if this was at one time a popular place to stop, and when I close my eyes, for just a few seconds, I imagine it is 1959 and that people from all over the peninsula have come to spend a day or two here and that the beach is littered with wealthy Americans and everyone is happy and having a great time. There is no way I could not stop and rest in this terribly important place.

I suppose I should not be startled when a man comes over the rise with a cup of what I presume is coffee, but I am. "*Café solo, señorita,*" he says, startling the living bejesus out of me and causing me to rise right up out of my chair as he passes me the small cup, tilts his head and smiles. He has beautiful teeth, white and straight, and I stammer, "I'm so sorry, I just stopped for a moment to rest, and I have no money."

I should have kept up on my Spanish. "Damn it," I think to myself, as I stand there desperately wanting the coffee and totally penniless and unable to say anything that I think will make sense to this man with the fine set of teeth, but he startles me again by answering in perfect English.

"Someone has already taken care of this, señorita," he says. "A gentleman who said to watch for the woman in the purple skirt who might pass this way early this morning. I have been looking for you. We open very early, but business is slow in this sleepy Mexican village in the mornings."

My heart begins to race as if it has been suddenly shoved off a cliff. A man? My aunt's friend? I turn quickly, to see a tall man with a short-brimmed hat move to the edge of the hill. He tips his hat and walks away just as a large bird, the size of a small dresser, takes flight from a far side of the tables. I lose my balance in the cosmic moment and the waiter reaches out to take my arm, and the simple touch of his hand there, just above my elbow, unsettles me even more. It is so warm where he touches me, and when I turn to look at him and his beautiful smile and then back up the hill, the man with the hat has disappeared.

"Wait!" I yell, still unsettled.

"It is okay," the waiter says. "He cannot stay. He said to tell you he will see you very soon."

"Who is he?"

"He will tell you that."

My hands are shaking. I want the beautiful man with the even teeth to stay with me. I suddenly become bold. This is definitely something unusual.

"Will you please sit with me and drink coffee?"

The waiter nods, still holding on to my arm, and then lets go so he can move up the hill to get more coffee. Before he leaves, he gently places me in the chair and tells me not to go. He is back in moments with more coffee and a plate of rolls.

"You are too kind," I say.

"It is nothing. Your friend on the hill left this note for you."

The waiter sits while I fold back the single white sheet and read what the mystery man has written.

> *A beautiful morning.*
> *The beach is also what she loved, and often, so often, she came to sit in the very chair where you are now drinking coffee with my son, Tomas. Tomas has a heart lined with simple kindness. Let him take your hand. He will bring you to me, and many other places, if you let him.*

I am stunned and thinking that I may be in a movie. I look around, turning my head to make certain that everything is real, to make certain that I am real.

"Are you okay?" Tomas asks me, concerned.

"Yes. I'm a bit scared. Was this all planned?"

"Yes. And no."

"Please tell me where you learned to speak such perfect English, Tomas."

"I attended a boarding school in Boulder, Colorado, for my high school years and then graduated from the University of Chicago."

"Chicago?"

"Yes," he answers, and then I get it.

"Aunt Marcia!"

"Yes," he says, smiling as he sips his coffee.

"Me this morning and the coffee and you coming to meet me. How did you know?"

"My father knew that you would be like your aunt because she loved you so much. He said that your aunt gave you part of her spirit when you were not working and that she worried you would never realize it, because you, well . . ."

"What?" I demand to know.

"Because there were many things in your life that you did that drove her half crazy and she did not understand why you never followed your heart."

"My God."

"When we found out you were coming, when Linda came to find my father, he knew that you would travel the same path."

"The same path?" I ask, confused and on the brink of tears.

"The path by the beach, for one thing. You are following her path, which has been your path all along. Same path, different direction."

I do not even know this man who appears to be reading my palm. He has a singular energy that makes me want to fall into his arms. Strong. Kind. Slow and gentle. Wise. How could he be so wise?

"It is a lot. I know it is a lot," he tells me, reaching out again with his hand to touch me.

I want to know everything, every single thing about him and his father and my aunt, but Tomas will only tell me about his life, and it does not strike me as odd or strange or anything but wonderfully cosmic that I am sitting at this old table, on a beach in Mexico, with a man who makes my body tremble when he touches me and who begins to tell me a story, a small part of the whole story, that I swallow as if I have not eaten for days and days.

"My father will tell you more later today," Tomas says. "But I owe you my story now while we drink our coffee and watch the sun. This is my favorite spot. It has always been my favorite spot."

It has been a long time since I have enjoyed the company of a man. A very long time since a touch has ignited a spot anywhere on my body, and as his story unwinds and our unlikely worlds begin to merge and touch here and there, I wonder what it would be like to know a man again. This man, any man. I push the thought away hastily because it does not seem appropriate, and I dig my elbows into the table and savor every word of his life story.

Tomas is a computer engineer who has come home to help his father, Pancho Gonzales Quintana, die. When he tells me this part of the story, I keep the news in a place of reserve because I cannot deal with it now. I do not know his father or love him, but I know I will come to that place, and when I do the grieving and invent my own new story, the places I am about to discover, will be extraordinary.

He tells me his story—divorced, a bit of a wandering heart, a world traveler who has spent a great deal of his life close to me in the Chicago area. I tell him how strange it seems now to think that we may have passed on the loop or walked next to each other along the lakefront or eaten at the same downtown restaurant.

"Life is more of a mystery to me every day," he says. "Yesterday, I wondered how long it would be that I had to live here and how I could deal with my father's death, and then I look up and a beautiful woman in a purple skirt is walking across the beach and into my life."

"Am I walking into your life?"

"Here you are. That says it all."

"Thank you for dropping out of the clouds for a bit," I say not as shyly as I should have.

I ask him to tell me more. His father owns many properties, and Tomas manages this small restaurant while he is here, juggling through paperwork and accounting files to settle his father's estate before his father can no longer communicate his wishes and hopes. He is an only son. There is no one else.

The prostate cancer, he tells me, has moved from this part of the body to the next until there is no place else for it to go but back around again. There is maybe six months at the most, and Tomas, who readily admits that he loves working in the restaurant, says he has no idea what he will do or where he will go after his father's death.

"I am a wandering heart now," he says, quietly, softly, and then asks for my story.

"What do you know about me?"

Very little, it seems, and I tell him as much as I can, as much as I know, and then for the first time I say something out loud that I did not even know myself.

"I have to leave for good and divorce him. I have not loved

him for a very long time..." My voice trails off. It is a broken vibration. I have been holding this thought, and now, as I release it, I want to slump onto the table and rest.

Tomas touches me again, damn, and finishes my sentence for me.

"And you are terribly unhappy and walking this beach and finally coming to the heart of the world, this Mexico, as your aunt requested so many years ago."

"Yes," I say firmly and with the knowledge that now something new will happen, is about to happen, is happening.

We talk for two hours and drink so much coffee, I feel a bit stoned. I have shared stories of my children and my work, which he senses do not "fill me up," and of my three friends, dead asleep miles behind me. Tomas invites me for a larger breakfast inside his restaurant, but I tell him my friends and I have a date with a mysterious man who likes to stand on the hill and flag in women off the beach.

We laugh together and he reminds me that he is more American than Mexican.

"What does this mean?" I ask him.

"It means I am bold enough to ask you to join me for a drink and dinner after you meet with my father this afternoon."

"Like a date?"

"It would be a date in America, but here, because you are still a married woman, it will be a meeting. A meeting where you will offer me help with my father's estate and offer me advice on what to do with the rest of my life."

"How could I say no? Especially because I am so good at figuring out everyone else's life and not my own?"

"It is impossible to refuse me. Because I am Tomas, the son of Pancho Gonzales Quintana, and I am a handsome computer nerd turned waiter."

We laugh, and before I hurry back so that my friends will not think I have run off into the jungle, I ask him about my aunt.

"Did you know her?"

"Yes, but I cannot tell you more. The story is tragically beautiful. Prepare yourself, Ms. Meg. Your heart will ache."

"We leave you alone for a few hours and you get a date, have coffee with a mysterious stranger and decide to file for divorce?"

This is the chorus that greets me when I find my friends pacing outside our temporary home. All I can do is roar with laughter, because they are semi-serious. I had no idea, I tell them, that so many life-changing moments would occur while they were sleeping off last night's festivities. Now they want to hurry. They want to see how this story plays out; they want to watch as I make another life-altering decision.

A part of me wants to know what will happen, where I will live, what I will do with the rest of my life, but another part of me, the part that I am just beginning to know for the first time, wants not to rush blindly into a present that excludes the now. I want to savor the moments, but I also want to think.

"My mind is flying," I admit. "I want a hundred years to figure things out and to remember and to understand."

"You can't have it," Elizabeth says as if she knows something that I do not. "You have already wasted too goddamned much time, and what you need to know and learn will not take that long to swallow anyway. You too, Jane. Snap to it."

"You're cruel," I tell Elizabeth.

"Honesty always has a hint of cruelty," she replies. "You get there, we all get there in our own time, but you are so close. Sometimes it drives me crazy."

"Especially if you have a bit of a hangover," adds Linda.

We head first inland and then out past a long stretch of jungle. It takes us close to two hours to get where we are going and I am wondering how my ill friend Pancho could make this trip twice in one day. We pass fields of sugarcane and Linda finally pulls into a dirt driveway that is partially blocked by a steel gate. When my hands touch the steel bar and push it open, my heart races. Was my aunt here? What happened? Will I hear her story and will it somehow blend into mine? This is the unsureness of my existence. One minute making a huge decision and the next ready to pee in my pants because I cannot decide which of the three thousand trees I should go to the bathroom behind.

I expect nothing as we glide for a good mile down a well-traveled path. There are groomed bushes with wide pink flowers, and paths that wend away into clumps of trees. We see no one, but when we pass through a simple clearing, here is what I see: a grand house with adobe walls and a porch that flows from roof to earth like a solid hammock. Gardens everywhere, and one, two, at least five men working in the yard, and then we park and I see that the front of the house slopes gently into that aqua ocean. It all takes my breath away.

"Beautiful," Jane says for us all.

A woman, perhaps a maid, is waiting for us, and she greets us with kind words in Spanish and takes us to a room that is wide with unusual windows for an adobe building. They are huge windows shaped like pears, and of course there is no glass in this climate and each window has a built-in chair that is wrapped along its edge, and at the base of each window are fresh flowers. Every window in this enormous room has a view of the ocean. The last time I saw something like this I was in a waiting room at my dentist's office reading *Islands* magazine. Everything is spectacularly beautiful. Clean. Quiet. I feel a sense of great comfort and calmness just being in the room.

When we sit in three chairs that are facing the windows, the kind woman brings in four glasses and a huge crystal pitcher filled with red wine. She tells us that our host will be here soon. As we know, she announces, he is not well, and so everything takes a bit longer.

While I sip my wine and imagine what I am about to hear, I let my hand drop to my skirt and finger it with my thumb and forefinger just as I still sometimes finger the silk on top of the old green blanket in the house where I used to live. I do not expect to hear anything terrible, just a story about my aunt and a portion of her life that has been stored away for me until this moment.

We are each well into our second glass of wine when Pancho Gonzales Quintana comes into the room. I notice immediately how pale he is. When he pauses in front of the window, I swear I can see his bones, the ragged edges of his veins. But even in what is left of his shell, he remains handsome. Tall, elegant, with dark, intelligent eyes, and hands that move when he speaks.

We have all risen, and he comes first to Linda, whom he kisses on the cheek, and then to Elizabeth, whom he also kisses and embraces, then Jane and finally to me. He stands with his arms outstretched and looks at me closely with those dark eyes, and the hint of sadness in them makes me wonder if he is going to cry. He whispers my name, and then pulls me into his chest and murmurs, "Marcia's girl. How wonderful to meet you." He uses the same blend of English and Spanish as his son, Tomas, when he speaks.

Pancho thanks us for coming and lets me know that he will share the story with all of us, because he knows these women are my friends and that they are now part of whatever it is that is happening.

"I may cry," he warns us as he sits in the chair across from me. "Everything makes me cry these days, and especially this, the story of your Aunt Marcia and Mexico. It is also the story of me, because I loved her very much. I want to tell you this story and it will be all I can do today, because of the trip I took into town this morning. Then, Margaret, would you please walk me to my room, because I would like to speak to you privately."

Pancho pours us all more wine and closes his eyes for a moment as if he is gathering strength, and then he tells us:

"Your Aunt Marcia, she thought of you as the daughter she never had and she worried about you until the day she died, as if she were your real mother."

"I know," I say quietly. "She was and remains a very fierce and important part of my life."

The fall my aunt drove to Mexico with her car filled with her girlfriends was the fall everything changed, Pancho begins. The girls took the trip not so much because of their sense of adventure, but because one of the travelers, Gretchen, was pregnant, and because Marcia had been given the name of a doctor who was trained in the United States and who would help them. Things, of course, were different back then, when pre-marital sex was a horrendous act, and because the girls had already planned a great adventure, this aspect simply added one more element to the suspense. It also added a hint of survival. No one was supposed to know. The doctor was Pancho's brother, and it took them almost seven weeks to find him and his clinic in the town where we are staying.

"Your aunt fell in love with Mexico and she fell in love with me," Pancho says, shifting as the pain coursed its way through his body. "But I was married."

The four of us are not moving. We want to hear every word. I want to take Pancho's hand, but mostly I want him to take my hand.

"The women stayed at one of the cabins my family owned,

and immediately the entire village fell in love with them and they with the village," he tells us. "My brother performed the abortion, but it was not a perfect procedure and the girl became very ill. This is how your aunt discovered how primitive the medical conditions were here and why she made helping our people, especially our women, a huge priority in her life."

I am astounded. For years and years, and even now because of a foundation she established, Pancho tells us, my aunt and the women who came to Mexico with her raised thousands and thousands of dollars for medical clinics and supplies and to quietly, and often secretly, teach the women about birth control. What they did was brave and risky because it went against everything taught by the Catholic Church and the Mexican culture.

"But they were fearless, these American women, and our women supported them and so did my family, my powerful family," he says. "The same family that arranged my marriage to a woman I never loved."

My aunt began her life's mission and her love affair with Pancho with nothing but her lovely heart and her own passion for life. "I helped Marcia from the first day, when she came into town in her pants, women never wore pants in those days here. Because I had been educated in America, I knew what she needed and I knew too that nothing I could ever do or say would stop her."

Pancho smiles when he tells this part of the story. He recalls her spirit and how she would not listen when he told the American women they would be in grave danger if people knew what they planned to do.

"I took her into the jungles and we carried vaccinations in tiny boxes and we slept under canvas tarps and went days without sleeping, and then she would go away from me, raise her money and come back to me, and we would do it all over again."

She never asked, not once, for anything to be different. She knew that he would never leave his wife and at the same time she knew that he would never love anyone else but her.

"People knew, you cannot see two lovers together and not know," he says. "Loving your aunt was the hardest and the most wonderful thing I have ever done in my life. It is beyond anything I imagined I could feel. And what she did for the people here was almost as remarkable."

There is more.

"The woman who was pregnant when they left Chicago never went back," he says. "It was some group of women, these American friends. Imagine, if you will, a cross between Jane Fonda, Gloria Steinem, Mae West, Gertrude Stein—and who is that actress, Susan Sarandon—yes, and that is what you got in each one of these women."

The pregnant woman stayed and married Pancho's brother Juan, the doctor.

I have to stop him now.

"How come I never knew this?" I ask.

"Your aunt felt that when you were ready to know, maybe ready to carry on her work, that you would come find out where she spent all of the time when she was away. But your mother knew. Your mother helped and she still helps."

I think I cannot bear to take another ounce of truth. My mother? The same woman who ran off my brother's black lover and who shouted at my wedding and who tried to make me live the life she wanted—helped?

"She is now the executive director of your aunt's foundation."

"My God. My God."

Elizabeth, Linda and Jane have not moved.

"Your aunt talked all the time about simply stealing you and bringing you here to live," he says, laughing for the first time. "I would not let her do it. You needed your mother, your connection, your time to find out whatever it is in your life you need to find out."

"And your wife?"

"She died ten years ago."

The year my aunt told us she was going away for six months.

"She came then, after your wife died? My aunt came for six months?"

Pancho is so quiet, I wonder if he has stopped breathing. His eyes close and he goes away to a place that must be either terribly painful or totally wonderful.

"I built a house for her. Tomas will take you there, because the house is yours now, Margaret. It was the only time we ever lived together as a man and a woman would live together as a couple. Marcia was planning to stay here. But when she went back to the United States, she fell ill. I went to her. I stayed in Chicago for two months. I was with her the night she died."

Can there possibly be more? I can no longer hold myself back and I go to Pancho, kneel at his feet and place my arms around his waist. "I am so sorry," I sob.

"But, my dear girl, I was never sorry. I never wasted one second of time that I was with her. We danced and sang and we made love on every beach on this entire peninsula. I miss her every second that I breathe, but soon I will be with her again."

When I walk Pancho to his room and he leans against me, I realize that soon means very soon. There is nothing left to him but bones and air, and I think that his heart must be taking up most of his entire body. He is a feather, and as I walk him to the edge of his bed and lift his feet and place a blanket over his legs, he asks me to sit for just a moment.

What he gives me next is the world. The deed to the small house that Tomas will show me, a package of letters, old photographs—not the ones by his bedside—and a silver bracelet laced with turquoise that he said was a sign of their love.

"You must always wear this when you are in Mexico," he tells me, folding it into my hands. "If you can, you should wear it all the time. It would match the beautiful silver bracelet you are constantly playing with."

"Is it that obvious?" I ask him.

"Yes, dear, it is time for you to choose to be happy. Can you do that?"

"I am trying, I am trying very hard."

I may never see this man again. Maybe in a week Tomas will call me and I will hear cracking over the wires and he will let me know that his father has died. Maybe I will fly back and stay at the little house while they scatter the ashes. Maybe Tomas will kiss me by the ocean and we will hold hands like his father and my aunt did.

For now I can only say "Thank you" through a stream of tears, which spatters my purple skirt. This reminds me to ask a most important question.

"Why the purple skirt, and where are those damn dancing dogs?"

He laughs, but then stops because the simple action appears to bring him to the edge of terrible pain. He waits a few moments and then begins speaking again.

"Marcia said you were born to wear purple but that you had spent your life clinging to yellow. Tonight, when you meet Tomas, you must also take your friends. It is the night of the dancing dogs. You will see."

When I leave this gracious man, I kiss him gently on the lips and I slip the bracelet on my left wrist, just above the narrow bones, where I will always be able to feel it pressing against my skin. I tuck the precious key to my new Mexican house into my purse next to the papers that will surely change many things about my life. It is impossible now to even think of what most of this means. It is impossible to imagine that I have a piece of this intoxicating land in my pocket. One step at a time. That's what Auntie Marcia would have said. That's what she did say. If only I had listened.

When I bend down one last time, Pancho smiles, and I can think to say only one thing. "When you see her," I say, "please tell Auntie Marcia that I am finally listening."

14

Who would have thought that the possibility of discovering dancing dogs would be so intoxicating? Who knew such things existed? Who knew that the way I think and live and how I consider the world could change so drastically in twenty-four hours?

The girls are a buzz of activity in our small hacienda. We have discussed everything from the new house, which we hope to see sometime in the next three days before we drive back through the jungle; the great love affair between Aunt Marcia and Pancho, and my date with Tomas—which I continue to explain is not a date at all. Life, love, the perils and perks of dating someone in a foreign country, the foundation to help Mexican women—and most important at this very moment—what does one wear to the dancing dogs show?

Skirts, of course, and a white blouse looped with the colors of the rainbow. Mexican sandals and silver bracelets, whispers of the early-night air, a flower above the left ear, a happy heart and the all important, open and willing thoughts. No excessive baggage allowed.

"You are quiet," Elizabeth tells me as we pause outside of the hut to drink a beer and settle our thoughts. "Where is your mind?"

"It's almost too much. My aunt and the way she lived and what she must have sacrificed to love him."

Elizabeth does not hesitate. Clearly what she says next is something she does not have to think about but something she embraces and knows as the truth.

"You're wrong. She didn't sacrifice anything. She had exactly what she wanted."

"Do you think so?"

"Your aunt and I are very similar. We know what we want and then we go to that place."

"But the possibility of a life with someone you love. A life that doesn't seem quite—what? I don't know—quite whole."

Elizabeth sets her beer down and shifts in her chair so that she is no longer facing the water but looking directly at me. She could almost be angry.

"You have read too many *Good Housekeeping* magazines, darling. There is great joy in sometimes being alone. Being alone and loving someone is not a horrific choice. It's a wonderful choice. Have you actually thought about how you have lived for the past ten or so years? You've been alone but you just haven't been able to enjoy it."

I'm a bit stunned. I have never imagined my life as being one of aloneness. The job. Marriage. Kids. Family obligations. Surely I have never been alone.

"How often did you feel alone?" Elizabeth asks.

"I never thought about it," I reply honestly. "There were always too many people around."

We both laugh at that thought, but she goes on to explain the difference between being alone and loneliness. Being alone, she thinks, does not mean you are automatically lonely.

"Did you feel lonely when all those people were around you?"

Just when I think I am finished crying and hours after I have

held the hands of a man who is dying and days after I have unlocked some long-held passions and notions and thoughts so
that I took them into my heart without actually claiming them
as my own, there is yet something else to address.

Elizabeth reaches out to take my hand and then raises my face
with her other hand so that I must look into her eyes.

"I was terribly lonely," I admit. "It wasn't so bad when the kids
were small, because they needed me, but the moment high
school started it was as if there had been a mass exodus from my
life. And Bob—Bob was never really part of anything except for
the first few years we were married. He would come to the soccer
games and we wouldn't even talk. He dropped Shaun off at practice but he never really did anything. Do you know what I mean?"

Elizabeth doesn't reply. She wants me to see this myself, to circle around and around until I spot the perfect angle and come in
for the kill myself, unaided, with my head held high.

"I was terribly lonely."

"Tell me, say it to me again. Tell me one story."

I suddenly want to apologize to Elizabeth. I feel as if I am one
thing after another, the gift of confusion that keeps on giving,
and that since the night I called to have her rescue me from
Kmart, it has been a nonstop crisis.

"We should be drinking beer and just enjoying these moments," I say. "I'm feeling bad. This is like constant therapy."

"Listen, it's all coming fast to you now. It would be one thing
if you were not here and if you had not watched your husband
making love and if you had not discovered the secrets your
Auntie Marcia had been holding for you. But you have all those
things now and you're not backing away. This is important stuff
and you give me so much, Meg, your friendship is a treasure to
me. Watching you discover who you are, where you are going is
really a gift to me."

"Okay, Elizabeth, I've still got that Catholic guilt thing going on," I say as if I have been discovered eating a candy bar in the church vestibule. "What do you want?"

"Tell me a story of loneliness. Tell me one right now, and then we'll finish this beer. And the rest of the night, which may become endless, we will savor the joy of what we have."

There are dozens, maybe hundreds of moments of loneliness to pick from. A flood of memories that have me paralyzed, frozen in place, despondent. I reach in and pick a quiet moment where the world of others is swirling around me and where my own world has all but disappeared. It is very early in the morning. Fall. School has started again and the smell of exhaustion already hangs like invisible cotton in every room of the house. When I wake, suddenly, at 4:15 A.M., I realize that Bob has not come home or maybe he left early. Maybe I will never know. I often sleep alone.

I slip out of bed and bundle myself inside the frayed blue terry robe that I drop next to the bed each night. I dare not look in the mirror and I have no idea why I am awake. Shaun, who I check first, has fallen asleep fully clothed with a math book on his pillow. I quietly cover him up with the Notre Dame blanket that he has been sleeping with since second grade. I want so desperately to touch him on his arms and neck and face. I want to whisper into his ear that I love him and that I want him to come back to me. I cannot do this. If he saw me standing there, if he knew that I had touched my lips to his, I think that something would change. Maybe I am wrong. Maybe it would make everything better. My son does not move or turn when I run my fingers over the pages of his math book where I suspect his fingers were resting before he fell asleep.

Katie is a dream. I could lie next to her and hold her and she would move against me and call me "Mommie." I do kiss her, my lips brushing the skin of an angel, and I can see her eyes moving back and forth under her pale eyelids. She must be dreaming of wild horses and middle school boys who might some day grow tall enough to bend down and kiss her. This girl still sleeps in pink sheets and I can see the faint hint of her blossoming breasts underneath the cotton blankets and a part of me wants to hold her down in this exact position so that she will never change or grow or move and so that I can always tiptoe into this room and watch her sleep.

Downstairs it is dark. The hall light has died again and I have to feel my way down the steps, where my foot bumps into Bob's briefcase. Home and then gone again. I cannot even bother to think where he might be. I can't even bother to care.

It is the kitchen that throws me over the edge. I see that some-one has made a pizza and that Katie has had another bowl of ce-real. There are socks on the floor, a note to sign for a field trip to the theater and on the counter—and table and on the floor—there is not one single sign of my life. Not one thing. The dishes were Bob's mother's. There are no letters from old friends stacked next to the phone. The old table was a hand-me-down gift from a distant cousin. My mother picked out the kitchen wallpaper. There's no note tacked up on the refrigerator remind-ing me to show up for a book club or a walk with the dogs. It is as if I do not exist in my own home, and I am gripped by such a sudden and painful feeling of loneliness that I drop to the floor and hold the socks against my face and cry. This is not my world, but theirs. Their plans and friends and food and clothes. Where they need to be and where they are going. I am a kiss on the cheek and the ride to school. I am the one who waves good-bye and fills the refrigerator and waits. I am the one who waits.

"I cried for a very long time, Elizabeth. The house was filled with my two kids and their lives and by then it was essentially a place for Bob to store his things and I felt like a stranger, as if I were a guest who didn't know anything about the people I was visiting except their names and what they liked to put on top of their ice cream," I tell her. "I was not alone but I was terribly lonely."

"Do you see the difference?"

"I see the difference. I understand."

"Your aunt was occasionally lonely. She loved this man. Fiercely. Her love was powerful and true. But she also realized that she knew him in ways that few men and women ever know their lovers. Everything we have and know and feel is a choice, Meg. We always have a choice."

"Maybe it would not have worked in the traditional way," I suggest. "Maybe it was what it was, and maybe, like Pancho said, it was every second that they treasured because the seconds were so rare."

"Ah, Meggie, you are getting it. Most people live in a place of past and future. They lose this moment because they are worried about what happened ten years ago or where they might be with this lover when the children are gone. But when they do that, they lose the now. Jane knows. Ask her. She's finding out the same things you are."

"Are you ever lonely, Elizabeth?"

"Sometimes. But I relish even those feelings because they take me to places that can often be astounding. I am a grown woman, sweetheart, a woman in full, a woman who has almost always known who she is, and yet there are times—always when I am alone and embracing my loneliness—when I discover something new about myself. And then I marvel at how I could have missed it."

"Do you ever regret not being with someone all the time?"

"Oh," she says, laughing very hard and slapping my face in a playful manner. "I am always with several people all of the time."

And then, without thinking, I ask her if she will save a dance for me at the dog and pony show.

"Why wait?" she says, and grabs me by the waist so that we can move together across the entrance to our hut.

And so we dance, dipping and swaying and laughing, neither of us wondering what will happen in the next three hours or on the plane ride home but simply dancing in the moment, which is as sweet as it could ever get.

We can hear the dogs even before we get to Tomas's restaurant. Elizabeth has asked to drive the Jeep and we have bounced sideways the few miles to the restaurant, laughing as she tries to recall how to drive a stick shift. I can already see her banging down the freeway in Chicago with the top down, wearing her pink jogging bra and not much else. What have we done? I ask this question to Linda and Jane about every three or four minutes and Elizabeth is absolutely no help at all. My Elizabeth has decided that this is going to be the night she drinks lots of tequila and never goes home. Jane keeps laughing and then says that maybe she'll be getting the pink bra. What have I done?

And me? I am excited about the doggies but more excited to see Tomas and find out what he knows and remembers about my aunt and his father. Excited to be in whatever moments happen to arise, just as Elizabeth has commanded, and just a bit uncomfortable about the possibilities that may arise from anything and everything. Hopeful also that there is no oncoming traffic between our hacienda and the restaurant and that no one hands the Jeep keys to Jane.

Just a block or so before the entrance to the restaurant we begin to see candles inside of small pottery vases lighting the way to the doggie party. The candles look like tiny hands waving us into a party we have always dreamed of attending. There are more than a few cars parked along the side of the highway, and the unmistakable yelping of dogs. Lots of dogs.

Tomas, dressed not in his waiter's uniform but in a soft dark peasant shirt and loose cotton pants tied up with a black cord, greets us as we jump out of the Jeep. He embraces me first and then I introduce him to his other three dates.

"Before we go in, let me explain this or you will think that the entire village has gone crazy," he tells us.

"Tell us, Tomas," we beg. "Please." Jane is jumping up and down with anticipation. She is ready for whatever the night brings to her.

In many parts of Mexico, Tomas tells us, dogs are wild and it is more likely that a family would have a pet pig or chicken than a tame dog. But in this village, a long time ago a barking dog saved a family.

"It is a long story that has lost its power and most of its truth, but what I know is that there was a fire and the family got out of their burning hut in time because of the dog," Tomas tells us and I am wondering how many times he has had to tell this exact story. "After that, people looked at dogs differently and they started to keep track of what they call 'the Dog Miracles.' Lost children being found by a dog. The old man who fell and was rescued by a dog. A dog recovering a lost ring. Well, it goes on and on, and so the villagers began to celebrate once a year, kind of a Day of the Dog, and because you are here and because of your aunt, we are having a special Day of the Dog tonight. It's really an encore performance for you, our special guests, and to honor the memory of Marcia Sinclair."

I ask if this is because of her work with the women and the foundation, and Tomas begins to laugh. It is a deep and bold laugh that I can actually see rise up from his chest. "Oh, that is part of it, but what she did was to put clothes on the dogs."

"What?" all of us say at once.

Tomas cannot stop laughing.

We press in against him.

"Your aunt felt that the dogs had ancient souls. She thought that there was a good chance that the dogs had been sent back to earth to watch over humans in special ways with special powers and that a tribute to them would be to consider them equals. That is why we dress up our dogs and dance with them. Before she came, we danced with them just as dogs without any clothes. Now... well, you are about to see."

It is impossible not to laugh as we imagine the scene we are about to witness, but when we walk around the side of the building and into an adobe-lined walkway that leads to a huge outdoor patio, we see what no human could really imagine. Ten, fifteen, maybe twenty dogs dressed up in coats and hats and dresses and young boys and girls and grown men and women tossing back drinks and dancing with the dogs in their arms and on their hind feet and the dogs, every single one of them, looking as if this is a perfectly normal occurrence.

"My God," says Elizabeth, who I know for a fact does not believe in God. "This is brilliant."

Linda has already moved away from us, and as far as I can see is searching for the perfect dance mate. Jane has been struck dumb. I can only stare. It is an amazing sight. A swirl of fur and lights. Men tossing dogs as big as themselves from arm to arm. Women kissing shiny black dogs who look like young kings. Little girls combing the fur of yellow labs with brushes the color of a beautiful sunset. One little boy lying at the edge of the floor and trying with all his might to get a dog the size of a cooler onto his back.

"It's for fun," Tomas tells me, understanding my incredulous gaze. "It is a wonderful break from the realities of the day and a great excuse to have a party. See, in many ways Mexicans are no different than Americans."

"I know of some people who have tried to marry their pets. This seems perfectly normal to me," I shout at him as we find a table and I try to sit.

"Oh, no," Tomas insists. "You cannot sit until you dance first with me and then with a dog. At least one dog."

Which is exactly what we do, and within the first five minutes I realize that I have never had this much fun in my entire life.

My friends become lost in the evening and we drink tequila and beer and my first dance with a dog proves to be very successful. I assume my dog is female because she has on a dress, which is terribly sexist of me, and I take her front paws, which she willingly gives to me, and we move very slowly and very carefully about three inches at a time. I feel just a bit absurd, but it looks as if my doggie partner is having a good time and I see that the other dogs are being fed tiny pieces of meat and that the children are petting them and that the dogs bark only when they are excited, and they look happy. I would do the exact same thing.

Jane waltzes past me with a tiny Chihuahua in her arms and then comes back to tap me on the shoulder.

"Switch partners?" she asks as she gently places her dog, which has a tiny sombrero on its head and a little cape, into my arms. I am laughing so hard, I almost drop both of the dogs. Jane steadies me and we both put our faces together and laugh like we are the first two women in the world who have discovered such a sound. The dogs—mine's a cross between a small black dog and a large brown dog—lick our faces.

"I cannot believe we are doing this," Jane tells me. "Will anyone believe we danced with dogs? I read lots of books and I've never heard of this."

"There's probably a good reason for that," I shout into her ear. "People would think you are nuts if you told them. Who the hell is going to believe this?"

"From what I hear of your auntie, this gig has her name written all over it."

"She never had a dog."

"They were probably terrified. You know, dogs communicate. The Mexican dogs probably sent the Chicago dogs a telegram and warned them. 'Hey, watch out for the crazy woman who likes to put clothes on dogs.'"

The dancing seems endless. I dance with at least six dogs, five women, three men and more children than I can count. Finally, Tomas comes to find me and asks if I would like to walk to the tables by the beach. I say, "Yes, I'm dog tired," laughing like the wildest dog on the block, and we hold hands and walk to the very same table where we shared our morning coffee.

There is a light mist blowing across the ocean. I can only see it because of the bouncing lights from the party and it makes me wonder what else I miss because I don't have the perfect light. The ocean is a gentle whisper, waves rolling in, the wind at rest, night standing guard over its allotted hours. Everything is lovely.

Tomas, it seems, remembers very little of my aunt. He was away for many years when his father met my aunt and it was not until after his mother died and because of the respect his father had for that relationship that his father told him the true nature of his relationship with Marcia.

"I knew," Tomas admits to me. "I did not know when I was a young man and consumed with just myself, but as I grew older and understood the powers of love, I realized that this was more than a mere friendship."

I want to know what he remembers and if he spent time alone with her and what she was like in this country.

Tomas remembers having a crush on Auntie Marcia when he was a teenager. She would sometimes be in Mexico when he had school breaks and although she was quite appropriate, she was also very much fun.

"She would sneak beer out of her little house for me and we would sit by the water, I will show you where, and we would drink and talk about everything from the stars to what my life would be like when I was a man."

Her laugh. He remembers her laugh and pauses to tell me that there are many things about me that remind him of her.

"Me?"

"Oh, yes. You are fun and beautiful."

It has been a very long time since anyone has said anything about me that didn't have something to do with work or my children. No man has ever called me beautiful that I can recall, and besides my small pack of female friends I cannot remember anyone focusing in on anything about me—mostly because there has never seemed to be anything remarkable about me.

I can only think to say, "That is lovely," and ask him when he can take me to see her house—my house—the house.

Not tomorrow, but the next day. He imagines that I will need tomorrow to recover from the dancing dog evening and he has business. We finalize the plan, he rises, kisses my hand, and then we walk back up for the last round of dog dances and enough tequila to get us all barking. Tomas insists that we dance with a doggie to celebrate the event—which has never before happened twice in one year and to honor the very woman who is my reason for being in his arms.

He is sweet and kind and holds his cheek against mine, and I focus hard to let my mind stay there, just there, and to not wander to any other place or time or person. This is not as easy as it sounds for someone whose life has been ruled by a Palm Pilot and who has tried her whole life to stay on this side of the line. But I do it. I think of this simple moment and how fine Tomas's hands feel against mine and how wonderful it is to come this close to a man's beating heart and to know that the heart finds you beautiful.

I think of nothing then but the color of the dark sky with the *lumeneros* dancing against it and how my aunt must have done this exact same thing with Pancho and how I hope that I can come back again and again to this place and dance with the doggies. My feet move like middle-sized bricks against the sandy floor, I can surely feel the tequila and once when I close my eyes very tightly I can see myself and for just a second I think I just may be beautiful. I may be beautiful.

When we leave, I am the one who has to drive. Tomas walks us to the Jeep and offers to bring us home, but I know I can manage the Jeep and the girls, who are already a pile of giggles in the backseat, and when Tomas makes certain I am pointed in the proper direction he tells me he will pick me up the day after tomorrow at ten A.M. to see Aunt Marcia's Mexican home.

I put my hand on his face just before we leave and say one simple thank you. He smiles, with those damned white teeth blazing under the Mexican moon, and I drive home slowly—my passengers do not even notice we are moving—so that I can feel the night air brush against my face, memorize the color of the sky and smell the first blush of morning as it rushes up from behind the dark arms of night to claim its place in the divine rotation of life.

Tomas is a mixture of meditation and gladness when he comes to get me. I know enough of him already to realize that something must be roaming through his head, that he is hesitant, anxious, excited.

"Tomas," I say as we head south, and not north, in the direction of his father's home and where I expected we would travel. "You are sad."

His eyes are as big as the hound's that I could not lift off the ground a day ago at the dance. I suspect he has been crying. The sadness balancing on the edge of his heart is a weight that drifts over toward me.

"My father," he tells me. "I think the time is coming fast. He will not go to the hospital. He wants to sit in the place he loves. We have brought in a nurse."

"Tomas, I am so sorry."

"It could be months, weeks, days, but it will be before the seasons change and . . ."

His words trail off. He wants to tell me something. Boldly, I reach over and bring his face toward mine.

"Can I tell you?" he asks.

"Yes."

"I think he is relieved that you came, that he saw you, that you have the house and know about everything. I think it has helped him let go."

Sweet Jesus God Shit.

Tomas pulls the Jeep to a stop right in the center of the highway, which doesn't matter because there is absolutely no traffic.

"Was it wrong to tell you?" he asks, moving one hand to his

chest as if he is holding back something that is lodged very close to the edge of his skin.

"Oh, no, Tomas! It was right to tell me, it just—well, it needs to settle. One part of me thinks that I am now going to be responsible for a man's death and the other part of me is very happy that someone who is obviously very wonderful can die in peace."

Tomas lets out a sigh.

"You know," he tells me quietly like you would after all the bad news has been spoken out loud, "it is a relief for me to talk to you also. This is not something I can share with anyone and it is not good to grieve alone, I think, not good."

"I think I can handle anything. Tell me what you need, Tomas. My world has flipped over about fifteen times the past few months. I am a mother, daughter, friend—I cannot think of anything that would be impossible for me to handle."

"Well..." He laughs to help break the spell. "This is a bit much. Death and life and love and what might seem to many others as infidelity. I am glad you have come into my life, Ms. Meg. But promise you will let me know if it is too much."

"Okay," I say, and then we drive and hold on to each other's hands, which I take as a simple sign of acceptance of this wonderful deal that we have just completed.

I have tried hard not to imagine what this house must look like. I have tried not to think of my aunt walking up this road and of her heart racing to think that Pancho would be waiting for her. I have tried not to imagine the scent of the sea at dusk at this very spot and the sight of birds dipping and swaying in the morning wind when they spy a place to land. I have tried not to imagine the bed, the chairs, what she kept on the windowsill. I have tried and failed miserably.

It is a simple, beautiful cottage. Small from the outside, with gardens that look as if they need little or no tending at all. This makes me laugh and I quickly explain to Tomas that Marcia hated to garden. She would rather be writing or reading or swimming naked in the surf. "I know," he says, laughing too. "I watched her doing exactly that many, many times."

Tomas goes first, walking slowly to let me take it all in, and then I get an idea, and immediately think that my aunt's spirit is already working its magic.

"Tomas, stop, please."

"What?"

"Did you bring any food?"

"Enough for lunch, and I know there is more wine in the house and a few things that my father could not throw away."

"I want to ask you something that may be difficult for you."

"Anything, just ask, please."

"Could you leave me here alone tonight? Just right here, go no farther, leave me the lunch and then come back in the morning?"

He thinks for a moment, smiles, then he raises his hand and asks, "You need this?"

"Very much so. Not just for her and your father, but for me. Just the moments for me to be in this space alone and see where it takes me."

"Perfect," he says, and with that one word I imagine all the thousands of women who have fallen in love very quickly with the first man who touched their hearts with the soft feather of a word like *perfect*.

He leaves me with a basket of food and directions on how to light the lamps and how to latch the door when I want to go to sleep. "Your aunt," he adds, "she never locked a thing or closed a window, but I don't suppose this is news for you."

When he leaves me there, I am suddenly astounded by what I am about to do. It makes me laugh at first but then the laugh catches in my throat and I have to fight back a sudden ripple of fear. It is that precious moment when I can go either way—laugh or cry—run with the wind or lie down and pray to God the storm does not eat me alive. Jesus. I am alone in Mexico in a place that is miles from what anyone would barely consider a town, but then I hear the tip of a wave pounding against the beach and I stop in my tracks to bend down and run some sand through my fingers.

"Her feet passed through these grains of sand," I say aloud, and in the same moment file through the thousands of pages of letters and documents I have read as part of my work that proves, at least to me, how one person's first step can change the world for so many of the rest of us. I decide not to be scared. I decide to bury every single goddamn fear that I have right in this sand, and I really get into it.

I bury my fear of being at this spot alone.

I bury my schedules and my notebooks.

I bury cleaning the house and living with a man whom I have not loved in a long time.

I do not bury my sexual desire, which I must eventually pull up from under the sand, deep, way down there, far below anything I decide to bury.

I bury my deepest fears about my skills as a mother—especially my skills as a mother to a son whom I have all but lost.

I bury all the hundreds of things I did because someone else wanted me to.

I bury the sorrow in my mother's eyes that haunts me even now.

I bury that one day when I could have turned and run from my marriage, my job, any part of my life and I chose instead to stay.

Without noticing it, my hole in the sand is getting rather

deep, and I pause, for just a second or two, to make certain I am truly alone. I kick off my shoes and I keep digging. I have not moved from the spot where I stood when Tomas drove off. I apparently must do this and I must do this now.

There is way too much to bury, I think suddenly. I could dig a hole to China and work my way through the jungle and back to the village. I could dig for days and nights and weeks and fill up this entire peninsula. Then there is the realization that on a windy day all my shit will come blowing out of the holes and float back to find me. Is any hole deep enough?

"Enough," I tell myself as I stand and wipe the sand from my hands and knees and elbows. "That's one hell of a start."

I leave my shoes right there and boldly move to the front of the house. The view is even more glorious than I thought it would be from my sand pile. Aunt Marcia has spared as many trees as possible and she has left the front of the beach alive with natural vegetation—ferns and rocks and large bushes. The low branches of all the trees close to the house are loaded with hanging chimes, clay figures and bits of cloth. Scattered throughout the yard are huge, brightly colored pots that are filled with flowers that look as if they are tended on a regular basis. Close to the beach there is a table and two chairs exactly like the table at the restaurant where I met Tomas—two days ago, but it seems like twenty years ago now. It is breathtakingly beautiful and everywhere I look I see the touch of my aunt's artistic hand.

The door to the house pushes open easily, there is not even a doorknob or lock. Inside, I set down the basket on a small table that sits in the middle of the only room I can see. The living room, kitchen, dining room—three rooms in one—is small, sparsely decorated but warm. There are rugs strewn about the wooden floor, and the walls in this room are white but streaked with the colors of the rainbow. It looks as if my aunt took all the brushes in her hand at once and ran through the room jumping here, sitting there, reaching toward the ceiling there. The effect is glorious and wild. There are small shelves with figurines, and oil lamps hanging from wrought-iron fixtures. Candles are everywhere, and at the far end of the room there is a fireplace with a mantel filled with beach stones, and a mixture of long and short pieces of driftwood are placed in no particular fashion under a chair, next to the window, across the window ledge. I am thinking that if Pancho built this house as a gift or a surprise, he knew my aunt like no one else ever knew my aunt. This house is hers everywhere I look.

To the right there is a tiny hall. There is no electricity here, but somehow Pancho has managed to bring water into the house. A bathroom. Tile floors. Plants, all about to perish, a mirror the size of Cincinnati covering the wall on the opposite side of the huge bathtub—and touches of Marcia everywhere, rocks and dried flowers and poems tacked to the edges of the sink. This must be exactly how he found it after she died. The fingerprints of her life are everywhere here.

There is one room left in this three-room house. Before I pass through the wide, doorless entryway to the bedroom, I stop and gather my energy into a tiny pile that I will use to help me get through the next few minutes. It is a good thing I have this energy, because when I take two steps forward I instantly lose my balance and my breath.

"Oh my God," I say to myself and to any living thing within a mile from where I am standing. "Oh my God."

I have never seen a more beautiful room. Pancho must have built this from the center of his heart, and my aunt surely decorated it from the center of hers. I drop to my knees in the doorway because the scent of my aunt lingers here and it is all so real I can feel her, I can feel her in this very room. I smell sage and patchouli and the wild roots of every season I have ever known. The bed, a huge antique wooden piece of furniture, is standing guard against the far left wall. Its massive headboard is carved with the figures of naked women. Oh, Auntie Marcia. There is no footboard and no sides and the bed is extremely low to the ground and thus to the window. The entire wall facing the ocean is glass, and it is the only glass in this home, which looks as if it is normally simply shuttered closed if someone is not living inside of it.

There are photographs of Marcia and Pancho everywhere. Holding babies. Walking on a beach. Skipping stones in a river. Sitting with drinks in their hands. Two entire walls tell the stories of their life together. The very brief moments of their lives together. The tile floor is dusted with one large rug the color of a fall sunset, burnt orange with a tinge of red—the beast of summer unafraid to fight for one last day of the season. What draws my eyes are pegs against the far wall hung with what I can only assume are her clothes. I want to touch them and hold them to my face but I dare not do that yet. I imagine she wore little here in her isolated retreat, but I also imagine what she looked like standing guard over the ocean with her purple dress and her straw hat and nothing else between her and the world but all this beautiful space and time.

There are so few distractions in the room. The view, the bed, a wooden table with a now-empty vase and two water glasses. The simple elegance of the room tears at me. That someone could love another so much as to build a place like this, a room where whispers vanished into the walls, where lovemaking was a spontaneous extension of true affection, where the sounds of water could wash away the realities of what was waiting down the road—well, it makes me angry and envious and grateful, just to know that such a possibility exists.

It takes me a while to move, and when I do it is to the window, which I discover has a set of hinges at the bottom so it can be pushed open. This makes me laugh, because all the times I spent at her house in Chicago my aunt kept as many windows open as possible. It did not matter if it was summer or the middle of winter. Once, snow actually blew across the top of the sheets and in the morning we had to put a pile of it in the bathtub—but only after we dabbed our faces with it because it was "pure" and we would be too, she said, after this morning ceremony. She had to have air, and here, I imagine, she had to hear the waves and feel the touch of sea spray on her face as often as possible, and when she lay in bed watching the sky in Pancho's arms, she wanted it all. Every single thing—she wanted it all.

I move, just a few inches, and am tunneled back many years ago. When I was in eighth grade my parents took us to Florida during Easter break, because everyone from the Midwest goes to Florida during Easter break. I remember pieces of the trip— many, many arguments and my mother locking the keys in the trunk at a wayside and the fierce intensity of the sun, but what I remember more than anything is a visit to Thomas Edison's home.

When I close my eyes, there in front of the sea and fingering through the last days of my aunt's life, I feel just as I did the day I walked through Edison's home and his workshop. Sarasota. As a budding sociologist I was astounded to learn during the orientation that every single thing we were about to see was left exactly how it was when the inventor was alive. "The day he died," I remember telling myself, "this room looked just like this." For the rest of the tour I was spellbound. *Spellbound*—to be lost in a world that captures every part of you. *Spellbound*—to be transported back to a time and place where everything you see and feel and touch belongs to another world and dimension, and for moments, brief moments, you are allowed inside of that world. *Spellbound*—to see the test tubes and beakers and the old rags and pieces of tubing that Edison used when he worked and to sneak over when the tour guide is preoccupied with his own voice so that you can touch the edge of a glass and know what was inside of his heart the last time, any time, every time he touched that glass. *Spellbound*—to be so close to greatness and wonder that you cannot think to breathe or move beyond that precious moment when you touched the hand of a genius.

I could not speak for hours after that visit and my mother put me to bed in the hotel room with aspirins and water and the wrong notion that I had eaten something terrible at lunch from the cafeteria that my father wanted us to eat at because it was so "damn cheap." That is all I remember before I drifted off to sleep and saw the very hands and face of Edison working for hours and hours, with that huge eucalyptus tree outside of his window while the rest of the world was at a total standstill because he was in his zone, and I was—spellbound.

My aunt's room was just like Edison's Florida space. I worked my way from the dresser to her hair bands to the robes and hats on the wall. I let my fingers glide across the top of the bed and I bent down to feel the cool tiles and the soft fibers of the rug. There is something here for me. Something I need to remember or forge in my soul. I am definitely *spellbound* and I pray that the spell will last a very long time so I can figure out what in the hell to do next.

15

1976

The second floor of the Haight girls' dormitory has erupted into a somewhat spontaneous and terribly wild celebration. Amanda Jane McCafrey has just announced her engagement. Half the girls do not know Amanda. Half have never bothered to ask about the boyfriend. Half cannot be bothered to worry about an engagement announcement, and part of that half, at least three women—all members of the campus chapter of the National Organization for Women—are so disgusted they are sitting out on the top of the roof under the last rung of the fire escape and are smoking a joint.

The other half are swigging Mountain Dew laced with a fifth of vodka that one of the women on the fire escape gave them. Amanda has called her mother, six of her aunts, her cousin in Cincinnati, thirteen high school friends and the last guy she dated, who thankfully was not home.

Amanda is twenty years old and a sophomore majoring in education from a small city in southern Illinois. Her roommate and best friend is Margaret Joan Callie. Meg is suddenly in charge of her first wedding shower, which could not have come at a worse time. It's spring semester and she has five major finals, undecided plans for the summer and not even the slimmest prospect of a date, let alone an engagement ring. And every week she hears about it from her mother during their Thursday night phone calls.

"Have you met anyone yet?"

"Mom, I meet lots of people. I have tons of new friends."

"I mean an m-a-l-e." Her mother spells it out as if she was in the middle of some kind of contest.

"Mom, there's no one special."

"I heard Judy Wharton is getting married on the Fourth of July."

Meg longs to put her hand through the phone and wrap it very firmly around her mother's throat, but she is her mother's daughter.

"That's nice."

"Yes, it is," her mother answers slowly. "Yes, it is."

The Haight dorm celebration may as well have a line drawn down the center of it, with Amanda's friends on one side of the line and the feminist circle and those who simply don't give a rat's ass on the other.

Meg has managed to scrounge up chips and popcorn and forty dollars to order pizza. On her way to the bathroom she gets a whiff of the marijuana smoke and edges past the bathroom door so she can see who is out on the roof.

"Hey," she says as she sticks her head out of the open window.

"Hey," the women say back. "Come on out."

It's Anne, Maureen, Kaye, a woman who calls herself Brilliant, and Marci Dugan, who announced her intentions weeks ago to spend the rest of her life celibate because she was sick to death "of stupid-ass men."

Meg looks at the roof gatherers, turns her head to hear

another wave of laughter and doesn't hesitate again. She's tried marijuana before and sat in on a few of the radical discussions this group seems to have constantly, but tonight she's more interested in getting a break from talk about honeymoons and shopping for bridesmaid dresses.

"You defecting?" Marci asks.

"For a while. Jesus. Are they laughing enough?"

"We think it's funny, but also sad," Maureen says.

They pass the joint to her and Meg suddenly wants to eat it. She thinks, for a tiny second, about wetting the end with her tongue and then swallowing it whole. "Maybe," she thinks, "my entire body will go numb."

"Sad," Meg responds not as a question but just repeating the word, which is what she chooses to swallow instead of the dope.

"Yeah. Come on. She's, what—Christ—twenty or something and it's 1976, for God's sake. Who gives a flying fuck about engagements and weddings?" This from Marci.

"Well," Meg starts out slowly because her lips are moist and hot from smoking, "She seems happy...."

Groan.

"Shit, Meg, how can you go along with this patriarchal bullshit? The guy asks the girl. It's traditional, heterosexual bullshit. She gets a ring. It's bullshit. She'll probably wear some stupid-ass white dress and have a reception and end up in an apartment, quit school so she can put him through school, and then he'll get pissed off one night, slap her, and she'll be in that apartment working as a secretary while he goes off and fucks the world and gets a great job."

"You don't know that," Meg protests.

"Yes, we do."

Meg is quiet. She takes another hit and pushes her head against the hard brick wall.

"Have her do the game," Anne says.

They all look at her and Meg opens her eyes and smiles.

"Spin the bottle?" she asks.

They laugh.

"No," Brilliant says. "It's the Five Second game."

Meg's head is bouncing a little. Her knees have slid down so they can touch the roof floor and every part of her body suddenly feels soft and smooth.

"I'll play."

"It's easy and rarely takes more than one second, really," Anne explains.

Everyone thinks Anne has a crush on Brilliant and this is all Meg can think about. She wonders if they have kissed.

"Ready?"

"Yes."

"In five seconds, name three happily married couples."

Meg is stunned. Her mind is clouded in smoke from a plant that was grown in a basement sixteen blocks away.

"Happily married couples?"

"Yep."

"Shit."

"Four seconds left."

"Damn."

"Three..."

"My grandparents."

"Two."

"Damn."

"Anyone?"

"Shit."

The women are quiet. There is a ribbon of kindness—even when they sound harsh—wrapped around them that they have extended to Meg with their silence. A hundred images have flashed like a fast slide show behind Meg's closed eyes. Parents. Arguing. Neighbors. Divorced. English teacher. Single. Aunt Marcia. Single.

"Wait . . ."

"Too late."

"Who was it?"

"Some people from my parents' church."

"How do you know they were happily married?"

"Well, they looked happy."

"So do you."

Meg opens her eyes to look at Kaye. Kaye the quiet one. The last one who speaks but obviously the one who sees the most.

"Wow," she says into Kaye's face, just inches away. "Do you think I'm unhappy?"

Kaye touches Meg's arm and holds on to it as if she is trying to steady herself. "You haven't thought about it much but when you do you will realize you are unhappy."

"Wow."

"Is it because I'm not engaged?"

Everyone laughs. Kaye laughs too, but not very much. She knows something Meg doesn't know or doesn't want to know.

"Can you see through me?" Meg asks.

"I can see into you," Kaye tells her.

Meg suddenly wants to talk all night. She wants to find out why these women are on the roof talking about women's rights and why the other women are inside worried about the color of dresses. Meg is in the midst of her first women's studies class and she gets to the class early every single day. The discussions and questions tantalize her, but she has yet to speak in class.

While everyone laughs and Anne goes out to steal back the food Meg has already stolen, another joint makes the rounds, and Meg cannot remember ever feeling more light or more free or more able to say things she would never dare to say to her roommate or anyone else she may have to see when the sun rises and the lights go back on again.

"Aren't you ever scared?" she asks all of them.

"Of what?"

"Missing whatever everyone else has. You know—a house and all that stuff."

Brilliant puts her face into her hands and it is Kaye, again, who straightens the path.

"Are your parents happy, Meg?"

"No. They fight; my mother is miserable and has never done one thing she has wanted to do. But, this way of relating is what I see everywhere."

"Exactly!" Brilliant shouts. "If you had a choice, would you choose what they have or a wild, wonderful, free relationship— or better yet, how about being and staying *alone*?"

Meg tries to move her lips but they are frozen in place. She is totally blasted, but in her mind the world and the answer is clear and straight. She has always felt alone except when her brother lived at home or when her Auntie Marcia came to find her.

"Being alone," she manages to say, "isn't all it's cracked up to be."

"It is if it's a *choice*," Brilliant tells her.

Everyone is quiet. Meg looks around the circle. She sees that these women have already traveled to places she has barely imagined visiting. She is jealous and tells them just that.

"It's all I've known," she says. "I've never had a real conversation with my father. My mother calls me and all she cares about is if I've found someone to marry. I feel like I'm supposed to do what they think I'm supposed to do but I don't think I've ever been happy or thought about the possibility."

"Oh, baby," Maureen croons. "Poor baby."

Brilliant is pissed. Impatience and anger rise off her face like the heat from a summer sidewalk. Her anger feels old to Meg. Something deep that will take a long time to go away. She tells everyone it is hard for her not to slap Meg across the face and say, "Wake up, goddamn it, wake up."

"I like you very much," Brilliant tells her, leaning into their circle and touching Meg's leg. "You seem so smart. I bet you out-GPA everyone in this entire building, but I also think you are fucking stupid about the choices women have, and that part is hard for me."

"Hey," Marci interrupts. "Give her a chance. You've been flying like this a long time. Okay, Brilliant?"

Brilliant does not want to stop. She clearly wants to take Meg by the shoulders and whirl her around so that she can see what it is going to be like to be in her roommate's wedding now that she has been on the roof.

"Can you see?" Brilliant asks her.

Meg wishes that she would go blind. If she sees any more, she thinks, she may never be able to get up, breathe, live, swallow a drop of water.

She cannot answer, and Brilliant sees the uncertainty and vanishes back into the building in disgust.

"She's hard," Marci leans in to tell Meg. "It's a lot, and she's, well, she's impatient because she wants it all now."

Meg drifts back into the dorm, where she lingers near the bride's room, her room, and listens to a conversation that she cannot comprehend. Rings and the church hall and the honeymoon filter through her stoned façade, and she cannot bring herself to go back into the room.

Becky Smith captures her as she is about to leave and spins her into the room, where the bride-to-be asks her in front of everyone if she will please, please, please be her maid of honor.

Meg does everything she can not to be sick to her stomach. She looks into Amanda Jane's eyes through her haze of nausea, and through something new that she cannot name. Before she answers, she turns to see the backside of Brilliant's jeans and her long, dark hair. Then she turns to Amanda and she says, "Yes." Then she says it one more time, "Yes," and again, "Yes, I will," and Brilliant is gone and she hears the roof window slam shut and someone needs another drink.

16

Vickie Burnette has not stopped talking since 8:02 A.M., when I saw her clock in and waltz on over to her desk, plug in her headset, set down her gigantic cup of Starbucks and act as if she was going to do a full day's work.

Since I have returned from Mexico, even the smallest of things piss me off. I want Vickie to answer my calls, write down a message, copy my papers, act somewhat professional and especially tell me if someone named Tomas calls me. I must be nuts. It has taken me eight years to realize that I have missed everything from the last six University President's conference planning sessions to a call alerting me that my credit card was overdrawn, and just recently a notice from my attorney reminding me that I have an appointment on Friday to discuss what Ms. Vickie finally remembers to tell me is "some kind of new divorce thing where it's cheapo and fast because everyone gets along."

"Are you getting divorced?" she asks me just after she admits, without hesitation, that the message is a week old and the appointment is for this afternoon.

"What the hell, Vickie," I shout, but it's not really a shout like other people might shout. It's more of a loud form of talking, which I suppose would be a shout.

Vickie almost drops her coffee and stares at me as if I have just confessed to six murders and sleeping with a Republican.

"Wow," she shouts back. "This little trip to Mexico has unleashed some old toxins. Divorce. Late for work. Checking up on the secretary. Now shouting. I suppose if I tell you a man named Tomas left a call on the answering machine, you would want to know about it right away."

It's best not to speak. That is what I decide. A machine gun could pop out of my mouth. Spear guns. A hand-to-mouth grenade. Vickie does not move and neither do I. She has her hair tied up and moves her hand very slowly to make certain that the back of her head has not fallen apart. I do not have to check. The back of my head has exploded. I have been home from Mexico for four long weeks and I cannot seem to focus on anything but basic movements, making certain I take in enough nourishment and that the one child of mine who still speaks to me is fed and clothed and not doing anything illegal.

The days and nights since I left Mexico have branded me a changed woman. I know as soon as I really wake up that I will see more than Vickie, who is actually assertive and regular and mostly okay when she remembers to do her job, for the truth of who and what they are. Now everything is a bit cloudy. Just a bit. Everything seems the same and I recognize nothing. Damn it. Just damn it.

My office, my work, the dreaded moments I spend driving back to my home each night have all combined to make me feel worthless, undestined, depressed. Dr. C has moved me forward about half an inch during the three sessions we've had since my return and what I do find is that now I am impatient and long for the sound of the ocean hitting the sand on my beach— *my beach*. When I say those words, my mouth turns up in a smile and I leave Ms. Vickie in the dust of her own words to go to my office to stare at the photos I took the day I left the beach house.

I did not sleep that night. For hours I moved through the tiny cottage looking at everything, opening the kitchen drawers, picking up each book, rising to look at the door each time I heard a chime clang against the side of a tree or a wave drop hard against the sand. Every new noise made me look up as if some-one were knocking at the door, as if there was an invisible person trying hard to get my attention.

In the kitchen I found a book of notes my aunt had kept. They looked at first as if they were random thoughts that she had written at odd moments, beginning with the day she moved into the "cottage," as she called it.

"Tuesday—June 8—The noise of the workmen is driving me mad. Last night I slept on a blanket on the beach. Sky on fire. Midnight—the crossing of the turtles."

"July 12—P. arrives. The world circles in. Every second—tomorrow does not exist."

"August 5—Bedroom done. Quiet storm last night. I will never leave."

"August 10—Trip to the clinic. Desperate for miracles. Five young girls all pregnant. Exhausted. I want to lie down. Lie down."

Tons of notes like this, and I find the wine from Tomas's lunch basket and go to the beach, fanning through the pages, absorb-ing every word and then making believe that I know everything there is to know about the cottage and my aunt and the years she spent pacing this spot where the sea meets land. There are pages of notes that need translation—*"Damn it. Birds in the kitchen. Juan did it again."* And I imagine somewhere that there is someone who could tell me a story, that story, any story about what it all means. But I cannot wait. I drink the wine, every drop of it myself, and I make up stories as I fry in the sun and turn occasionally to see if the cottage is still standing and I am really sitting in such a paradise. When I lie still and close my eyes, my aunt and her friends, her lover, they all come to life and I see them running through the pages I have just read and they are as real as my own skin lying on sand that has been touched by their very feet.

I walk the beach a good mile one way and see not one person, not one house, then I turn around and walk the same distance. Light is fading by then and half a mile from the cottage I see a break in the stand of trees. Piles of stones, placed in a long oval circle with dried flowers scattered about its center, protected from the wind, huddled in piles several inches thick. I bend down and smell them—a rich scent of orange sweetness that makes my limbs weak with delight. I barely fit inside the circle, but when I get inside of it, the smell, the heat from the sun-warmed rocks and an occasional breeze from the jungle all combine to make me feel as if I am being cradled by the very arms of Earth herself. Then I laugh.

I laugh long and hard and I push my face against the flowers and drop them on my head and across my legs, and I know that this is exactly what my aunt did in this spot and this is why she built it. She built it so she could just be here and do this. Feel the rivers of jungle air washing over her. Feel the scent of the flowers moving into her hair, under her skin, in and out of her fingers. Feel the rhythms of the waves circling in to land at her feet. Be silent and touch her self, her soul, her own rushing waves. Feel. Just feel.

There is no secret note hidden under a rock or buried under the flowers and there doesn't need to be. Being in the circle made me happy—the wine helped too—and that was the message. "Staying in the circle," I remember saying to myself, "that's going to be the hard part." and centering myself on that occasional breeze from the jungle I need to wrap around me and hold me and keep me centered. It is the feeling of being inside my aunt's beach cocoon that I seal into my heart and take with me when I finally get up, brush the flowers from my skin and step back outside the circle.

I spent that night wrapped up in a blanket, sitting on the beach. I could not bring myself to sleep in my aunt and her lover's bed and as I dozed with my face dusted in sand, I wondered how long it would take me to make the house my own, wondered also if I could possibly keep it, spend months there, in my own circle of laughter, just as my aunt did and keep the light tilted just the way she had seen it on her life.

I wondered if I would have the courage to actually file for divorce, to move out or ask him to move out, to...what else? That entire night, all those hours, my life paraded in front of me and I was the lone spectator and the theme of the parade— "Margaret's Missed Life" was much longer than I had expected. In spite of the circle of laughter, I was totally missing the point.

I know this now, sitting in my office with two of the rocks stolen from that beach resting on my desk. I know it and pray to God that it isn't too late to do something about it.

If I had a sister I wonder if we would be as opposite as my mother and her sister were. My mother's new condo kitchen, where I am standing and where Dr. C has strongly suggested that I visit, is totally humorless. There are no dishes in the sink, no tipped-over wineglasses on the counter, the garbage is empty, there are fresh flowers on the table and not one aging note is tacked up on the refrigerator. My mother has just made us tea and we are moving onto the porch to have what she calls "a little chat."

I watch her pour the tea and wipe up what she spills on the white Corian counter with the edge of an exquisite cotton cloth, and my heart fans out just to see that. I always knew that my mother loved me and that she struggled with many things. I knew that she had piled her dreams into a paper bag and thrown them out the back door—well, actually she'd placed them gently into the bottom of the stainless-steel can under the sink, but throw them away she did. We talked, my mother and I, but we rarely shared. If I were younger, I might rage and ask her why. If I did not know that she loved me and that she had tried to move her corner of the world for me at least once, I might be angry, but somewhere along the road leading up to this moment I decided to embrace her, just embrace her, even if that meant holding her at a slight distance while I did it.

"So," she says as a way to kick-start whatever it is she thinks I need to say, and as she says it and turns her head, I notice that the lines along her eyes match mine and that she has developed a nervous twitch above the left line of her lip. I wonder in those few seconds as she sets down her cup and looks out across the courtyard if she misses my father. Could she miss my father?

"Mom," I say suddenly, changing the direction of a conversation I had totally planned. "Do you miss Daddy?"

She pauses, closes her eyes and says without looking at me, "No one has ever asked me that question."

Oh, Mom. Oh, Mom.

When she turns, I see little emotion in her eyes. No tears.

"I'll tell you, Margaret, because I know you have come to tell me some things that are hard. I may be old but I am not stupid. You have been unhappy most of your life."

Oh, Mom. I am the one who starts to cry.

"A part of me was glad when your father died, which is a horrid thing to say. But it is true. A part of me will also grieve and ache for the familiarness that grew between us, for knowing what time he would come home, for being able to fix his dinner just the way he liked it . . . for many, many things."

"But—"

"Let me finish and then you can talk."

My mother turns to face me and it is all I can do to sit still and not sweep her off her feet and hold her like a baby.

"We should have had this conversation twenty years ago. I'm sorry for that, Margaret."

"But—"

"No," she says louder. "Let me say this.

"I made mistakes. I could never stand up to him, never step out of the role someone else had designed for me, and because I couldn't, I did not have the courage to let you create your own role and place in life. Me not going to college and putting up with his temper and allowing him to dictate . . . well, I will hate myself until I die for that."

She has stunned me into silence. The tea will never do it. I'll need Irish whiskey. I cannot move.

"But the terrible irony is that I loved him, honey," she says. "I thought of leaving, but I couldn't imagine myself without him. Do you know that he used to sing to me?"

"What?" I manage to squeak out.

"Your father sang to me. Not a lot, just once in a while, but it was enough."

"Mom . . ."

"But I wonder, I will always wonder, what my life could have been. He was a jackass. He was a goddamn jackass."

She still does not cry and I know she must have had this conversation with herself a hundred times, maybe a thousand times.

"That's it," she says, moving her hands off my knees. "I don't need you to say anything now, except what you came to say. We'll see how that goes."

Before I share my glad tidings, I tell her I must go to the bathroom first and I ask if there is whiskey for the tea. My mother laughs and says that part of me has always reminded her of my father and her sister. "God, how you two loved each other," she says with pure pleasure of my relationship with Aunt Marcia.

While she gets the whiskey I stand in the bathroom without turning on the light, without actually using the toilet, and I feel like a fool. I feel as if everyone in the entire world has known some huge secret about life and I am, once again, the last to know. It is hard not to hate myself. Not to waltz over the edge of that place where you want to slap your own face in disgust and embarrassment. I am so goddamned stupid, I never even imagined having the conversation I have just had with my mother.

When I go back out to the porch, she is sitting with her back to me and I move in behind and place my hands on her shoulders. It has been a long time since we have touched on purpose beyond those random acts of passing in the hall and hugging good-bye. My mother brings both of her hands to mine and I sense in that moment the patience that kept her with my father, that helped her raise three children, that got her through what I can only now imagine as days and nights darker, much, much darker than my own.

"Sit," she finally tells me.

When I begin to talk, nothing seems to make sense at first, and then she touches me again and I feel something smooth and lovely move between us and I embrace the importance of touch and holding as the one solid thing that I have ever known as true. My mother's hand on my back as I walk into the hospital to give birth to my first child. Her fingers in my hair when I am a teenager and sobbing in her lap because of some now long-forgotten adolescent crisis. Her gracious shove the day of my wedding when I was panicked about making it up the aisle. All those nights she slipped into my bed after I'd heard the yelling, and her legs warm and firm against mine and her hands moving to rub my back and arms when she knew I was worried about her and him and us, as she cried quietly. The one day, many years ago, when I fell out of the car, my arm pushing down the lever in the new red Ford, and me rolling and rolling and rolling and my leg bent sideways and the gravel that dropped from under my skin and my mother's hands there again in my hair and touching the top of my chest and moving in circles on the side of my face that was not bleeding. The touch. Always the touch and the fine flow of energy from her skin to mine and the firm feeling of strength that I could feel rising from her—through her—to me. Her touch now gives me the courage to begin again.

"Mom, you are right, I am so unhappy. I can't remember being happy, really happy, for a very long time."

"Tell me, baby, just tell me."

And the circles of her fingers keep moving and I tell her everything. I tell her about the wanting to watch and leaving and then coming back. I tell her about Mexico and about following the trail that had been laid together piece by piece by her sister until I ended up on the edge of a sea wider than anything I had ever seen or felt and the circle of solid stones that sifted in an occasional breeze from the jungle, and I tell her that I know about my aunt's foundation, and then I pause and wait for her hand to stop moving on my arm, for her to walk away or to simply be quiet, and she does none of those things.

"Meg, you should have been my sister's daughter. Something got screwed up along the way and I ended up with you, such a great prize, one that I never felt I quite deserved."

Mom. Oh, Mom.

She doesn't stop. I lean into her even more but she doesn't stop. She may explode, I think, if she doesn't get this out.

"You always seemed perfect to me, Meg. You did, really. I've wanted to tell you your entire life how sorry I am for all the times when you needed me to push through the door first and I couldn't do it. I just could not do it, and I apologize now, but I just could not do it."

Mom. Oh, Mom.

She goes on for what I am sure to her seems like an eternity, when I realize that she must be doing this for a reason that is about to make itself known in a big way because we have had portions, in very small doses, of this conversation several times during the past three years. A weepy session at the hospital the night my father died. The funeral. Selling the house. A month alone in Arizona and dozens of late-night phone calls. One afternoon of wine and remembering things that would have been better not remembered. A lost card from Marcia arriving in a tattered envelope from the post office.

So this, some of this, most of this, is old, maneuvered back into place by my rotting life. Or is it something else?

I start talking again when she finishes, reassuring her that I understand the place and time, and then forgetting my premonition to ask her what the hell I should do next. It must be the whiskey and tea.

"What do you want to do, Margaret?"

"Start over."

"Well, then, why do you ask me what to do?"

"I feel bad."

"Oh, screw feeling bad."

"Mom."

"You would say 'fuck it,' but I can only say 'screw it.' That's all you are getting."

We laugh, which seems to be the thread of who we are, have been, will probably always be—and without realizing it, I am holding her hand and kneading my fingers in between hers so that she can relax and let go of whatever it is she has left to say.

"So?" she asks me.

"I'm still exhausted, even after that trip."

"You've got years of unburdening to do. I'm surprised you can walk, for heaven's sake."

We pause again, take a sip of the whiskey tea and watch as three sets of golfers jockey for a place on the third tee that she can see from her porch. A breeze kicks up that ripples through the trees just below us, and it is as if something or someone is whispering in a quiet concert designed for us.

"Did you hear it?" I ask her.

"You think it's a voice from the dead?"

"Maybe just the cranky neighbors who heard us talking about sex."

She laughs and then turns toward me quickly. A sharp turn. Fast. My head aches from the whiplash.

"Tell me what you want, Meg."

My heart pounds. I cannot breathe, but I know. I suddenly know what I want.

"Something simple. An apartment," I say, and then it is as if a dam has burst open, as if someone has plowed through an ice field that is a thousand years old, as if a dried-up spring has begun to flow, as if the blind can see and women are ruling the world.

"I want to live how I want to live and quit my job and spend lots of time in Mexico and make certain that Katie does not end up in prison and..." There's so much. I'm afraid that if I keep going I will never stop.

"What?"

"Well..."

"Baby, say it. If you say it, you make it real."

"I want to be alone. I think I just want to be alone for a while, maybe for a long time. But I'm scared. I'm so scared."

She laughs again and I know that she's not laughing at me but for some other old and ridiculous reason that I don't need to hear about.

"That's it?" she asks.

"Well, part of it."

"That's enough. It's huge and perfect and you'll do it. Soon."

"Really?"

"Oh, come on. Look what you've done in the past few months. I was beginning to think you were going to start selling Tupperware or those baskets at home parties, for crying out loud."

Who is this woman? Where the hell did my mother go?

"Really?"

"Really."

"Why didn't you say something?"

"You had to come into it on your own. It wasn't right. Timing, you know. It's important that it be your choice and your life and not mine. Never mine or anyone else's."

Mom. Oh, Mom.

I think we are done then. I think that when I get up and drive home that there will be a little book of instructions on the kitchen counter to tell me what to do next. Everything will be outlined and the important stuff will be boldfaced and there will be a choir of naked male angels singing in the backyard to help me when I get low and lonely as I cross out one task after another.

This is when I realize the whiskey has taken its toll on my afternoon heart. I'm tipsy. Not drunk, but woozy enough to want to lie down on the porch and pull my shirt off over my head. Bad enough to know I should not leave my mother's wonderfully decorated condo.

"There's no way in hell I can drive home, Mom."

She laughs again.

"This is like college or that last week of high school," she tells me, moving already to get the pillows fluffed and pull back the covers. It's what? Jesus, not even eight P.M., and I'm sauced.

In bed, she tucks me in like she must have hundreds of times when I was a little girl, and her fingers, just like then, linger on my face. When I open my eyes, I see that she is crying. My hand goes to hers and I rise up from the pillow. I cannot seem to speak.

"Meggie, this is something, isn't it?"

"Yes, yes it is," I say through tears as thick as the wall we have just tumbled through.

"Meggie, just saying this has made us stronger, but..."

She pauses, and my heart, already flat and exhausted, stops.

"There is one more thing. It's a tough one, honey. Pretty damn tough."

My mother never swears. She's done it several times in the last few hours.

"What?" I ask as I leap outside of my body and watch us, hands together, hearts beating from the same origin. "What?"

She takes a breath and even in my boozy state I can see that she has the words in her mouth but she is having trouble getting them to the next step.

"Honey, I have a lump. They found a lump. This is the worst

possible time for you. But I need you. Auntie Marcia is gone. I need you."

My mind is frozen and then dips suddenly to the warm beach and to the scented circle of laughter. I will myself to feel the breeze that shifts through the long green leaves, past the rows of grass at the edge of the beach and through the tiny cracks of the rock wall, and then I take my mother in my arms and say the only word that I can remember. The only word that seems finally perfect.

"Yes," I say to her. "Yes."

17

The mirror in front of the bathroom sink extends just far enough so that when I stand back I can see my body from the waist up. Once I lock the door, I turn on the lights and then look into my own eyes. I want to see myself as if I am a stranger, someone walking down the street who looks up and is suddenly greeted by my eyes, my smile, the color of my hair.

"Hello," I say, and what I see are fading dark circles around eyes that are the color of a November afternoon, hair tousled by a sleepless night on the chair, couch, that goddamn twin bed.

"Hi," I say back, wondering why this woman looks so tired and why when she smiles only the left half of her face moves up. What secrets are behind there? Who is she? Where is she going?

I have come to the bathroom alone at 4:30 A.M. to look at my breasts. I have never looked at my breasts. Well, I have looked at them in passing but I have never saluted them, paid attention to their importance, lit a candle in thanksgiving for having them attached to my body. It is time. Katie is asleep. Bob rarely comes home, but I lock the bathroom anyway. It would be just my luck that someone three blocks over would pick this morning to sleepwalk and climb her way up the stairs to this particular room.

I take two steps back and then move in a few more inches. My long shirt falls easily off one shoulder and then the next and drops to the floor with a nearly soundless whoosh. I do not have on underwear, and a simple silver chain that I bought in Mexico balances at the edge of the bone below my throat. When I push my hair behind my ears it slopes behind me and I imagine exposes my breasts even more, but I cannot bring myself to look yet.

"What would happen if I lost one?" I ask myself. "Or both? Or the muscles under my arm and from the top half of my shoulder?"

I close my eyes and bring my hands up to cup my own breasts, remembering the first time I saw them budding out when I was eleven years old. It was as if I had gone to bed in my tiger pajamas and woken up in a silk nightie. There they were, tiny caps of flesh mounded around my nipples. I wanted to die. I wanted them to go away, and then, within weeks, was wishing I could water them at night with special breast-growing medicine so that they would get larger. Every girl I ever knew wanted Barbie doll breasts. How sad is that?

Now they have been pressed and sucked and stretched. They are close to fifty years old. Two babies have touched them with tiny fingers balled into fists as they filled their stomachs. They are definitely starting to head south, no matter how tight my jogging bras remain.

For years and years now I have done breast exams. At night, sleepless for what seemed like the forty-fifth night in a row, I would roll to one side and then the next and push my fingers in the obligatory circles, searching for a grain of sand, a pea stuck below the surface of my skin, and always I would fall asleep knowing it was okay, my breasts were okay.

I finally drop my hands. The great Breast Goddess has inspired me. I am ready.

This morning when I look at them, I see two mounds of possibility. At this exact moment, there could be cancer cells climbing their way through my skin and into the very tissue that supports my nipples. I could go to my next mammogram, just as my mother did, and see the dark swirls of evil smiling at me from the X-rays. Everything I have and am could change in a second, this second. This very second.

I move first one hand and then the next around the edge of each breast. My skin moves slightly and I focus on feeling, just feeling, each one. Sides, nipples, round top to rounder bottom. I don't remember them as being quite this large, but today they feel huge. Half of the world rests in one hand and half in the other.

I want my breasts to know that I love them and that I like them very much and I want them to know that I realize breast disease is often hereditary but that it does not have to be. My mother's cysts could become my cysts. Her lump could grow into mine. I promise them that I will guard them and protect them and if I ever get the chance again, I will allow them to become the focus of some wonderful physical pleasure.

I want them to know that I appreciate everything they have ever done for me. Fed my babies, held up my sweaters, in the heat of passion made me feel lovely, pointed toward the next direction every time I turned a corner, connected all my female vessels. Their wonderful duties have been endless.

When I drop my hands after my exam and breast honoring, which I promise to do on a very regular basis, I lift my shirt back around my shoulders, but I do not button the edges. I want my breasts to feel the air and see the light and travel with me back to the spare bedroom, where I will gather my clothes before my early-morning shower.

My mother is in bed this very moment, while I am worship-

ping my breasts, sleepless, I assume, waiting for her trip to the
hospital for the biopsy. I am the driver, the support system,
pretty much her everything. Bianna and Elizabeth have both
given me chants and spiritual paths and special incense and I
have used every single thing they have given me, but this morning I also decide to pray. A Hail Mary flies from my lips, a memorized litany that remains meaningless except for the female
connection I feel toward Mary—woman, mother, wife—posses-
sor of breasts—and then as I am leaving in the morning darkness, I whisper, "Please, please, please" to anyone or anything
who cares to listen. Then I drive.

My mother is actually cheerful when I pick her up. She
is waiting and dressed to kill with her long, leather trench
coat, black sandals and her hair—which she still wears to the
edge of her shoulders and today is turned up in a rather sexy-
looking bun.

"Hey you," she murmurs as she climbs in and kisses me,
touching my arm. "Let's get this over with."

"No shit," I say to get us laughing, and I move my hand
against the bottom of my right breast in a final salute to my
mother's breasts and all the fine breasts of women everywhere,
and we are off.

At the hospital, my mother is gracious and kind. I would be
crawling on all fours if I could, but I hide my trepidation as we
pass through the "Hello, Mrs. Callie"s and the first round of instructions and my mother deciding she wants me in the white-
as-snow room to watch the procedure. This was not something I
have thought about, but I do not hesitate. The Breast Goddess is
smiling on me. In I shall go without hesitation—mostly without
hesitation.

While my mother undresses, I file through all the hospital
scenes that have filled up my life. Births, my son's bursting

appendix, the night my college friend Kaye slammed her car into a bridge and she told the nurse to call me first and the night, which I suddenly remember as if it were yesterday, when my brother Grant flipped his bike into a ditch and a steel rod went through his left leg. When I remember it now, while my mother is prepped for surgery, I see something I would never have seen as a young girl.

My father could not go into the room where my brother was screaming for help. I was sitting on an orange plastic chair that had a scooped-out section for my butt, when I looked up to see my father leaning against the wall, his face white.

"I can't," I heard him whisper.

"You can't."

My mother said it to him like a fact, like something she already knew, and not a question.

"I can't," he repeated, even softer and slower.

My mother went into that room and did not come out for a very long time. When she did, hours later, or a hundred days for a little girl, I saw speckles of blood on her arms and down the sides of her skirt. Her hair had fallen out of its sideways loopy holder and hung in tangled locks around her face. My father was in the car. He sat in our car alone the entire time until my mother brought us out and told him that my brother was in surgery and that she would call when she could.

He never looked at her. They never touched. He told us to get in the car, and we drove off and I rolled down the window, stretched out my hands and said, "Mommie." Just "Mommie" as she walked back into the hospital alone.

My brother still has a limp from that ill-fated bike accident, and I now have a resurrected memory of my mother as the woman in charge and my father as a stereotypical pay-the-bills man who tricked me into believing that he was strong and tough.

I choose quickly—if I can convince anyone that forty-eight years is quickly. I choose my mother. I choose to be like her, just the way I know her this moment: strong, wise, kind, generous and loving. I choose, and then I take a step into the procedure room, where my mother smiles at me and holds out her hand.

During the days we wait for the results, Tomas calls me twice to see how I am doing. He also tells me that his father saw more than a hint of his Marcia in my eyes and wonders if there is any chance that I will come back to Mexico in the next few months.

I stumble in reply. A few months? I am trying to waltz through the next few minutes, three long seconds, a long afternoon. But I tell him I will try, and Tomas, such a gentleman, tells me he is in a position to come to me if there is anything I need. What I need is a U-Haul and a pickup truck to carry my life in a new direction. But I keep this news to myself. Tomas has already done enough. More than enough.

"I will try," I tell him again, deciding on the spot to omit the latest news about my mother's breast. "If I can, I will come."

Tomas accepts my promise, lets me know that the sands are shifting on my beach but that all else remains as it was, and I think that there must be a double meaning in what he is saying. Shifting sands is just a small portion of it all. There's a tornado brewing on the edge of my left shoulder that is about to move to the next limb. The sand, I think, is about to turn itself into dozens of intricate castles that can sit up and speak in foreign tongues.

My mother passes this time doing what she has always done.

She gets lost in a few games of bridge, cleans, goes shopping for clothes and trinkets that she will most likely take back to the store the next day, reads cookbooks and decides to take a yoga class.

"Yoga?" I ask her from my office phone as I check in on the third morning in a row to see how she is handling the long breast wait.

"I've tried tai chi and a stretching class but I think yoga will help me put my mind on pause occasionally."

"Mom," I say impulsively, "are you okay?"

She pauses and I imagine she is standing by the kitchen sink, where she can look out through the side window and across her driveway lined with her beloved yellow flowers.

"I'm terrified. But I can ride it a little bit so it doesn't run over me."

"Do you want me to come and stay with you?"

She laughs. "And ruin my glorious solitude?"

"Does this mean you are okay?"

"Terribly okay. I've been doing this for quite a while, sweetheart, and I love every moment of being in my own space."

"Mom, tell me about Aunt Marcia's foundation."

She takes in a huge amount of air and tells me she has a stable of steady donors who keep the coffers filled and the clinics open.

"We have a network of volunteers throughout Mexico who help do all the work down there, and there is a board of directors that meets once a year, mostly women and some men, from all over the country."

"Why didn't you ever talk about it? Were you waiting until I was old enough?"

"Don't be sassy. This isn't my foundation; it's your aunt's. I did what I was told. Depending on what happens with this damn breast, you'll be in charge sooner or later anyway."

"What?" I have jumped up from my chair and my left hand is moving around as if I am conducting an orchestra.

"Well, who did you think was going to do it? You are perfectly capable; it's not difficult. It's terribly important, and if I can do it, a smart woman with two master's degrees can surely steer the ship."

"She's probably right," I think to myself; it's just that the news is a bit startling.

"How much?"

"How much what? You sound like your aunt when you talk like that. I swear to God I had her baby for her and that baby was you."

"Don't be sassy yourself. Money. How much is in the foundation?"

"Close to a million dollars."

Jesus.

"Meg, we run clinics and pay for doctors and support women with young children. The money has been invested wisely. The next meeting is in November. You'll find out."

I don't even consider saying no. When I put the phone down, expecting to have a few moments to still my heart, it rings instantly. It's Jane. She's breathless.

"Can I come over? I'm about to explode."

"Hurry," I say, and hang up before she says another word.

Jane. Oh, Jane.

She has been on Meg's Let's Move Forward With Our Life Plan A. I have been fast-tracking her since the night I met her at the bar. She calls it "The Life Emersion Program" or "How Meg and Her Friends Taught Me to Breathe." It's really nothing more than jump-starting what has been idling for a very long time, but for the first couple of weeks Jane needed heavy deprogramming. Bianna has her chanting.

"I am wise. I am wonderful. I can do anything. I can take care of myself. I am beautiful. I have power over every single thing that happens in my life."

The chanting has become a nice addition to my life as well, and Jane thinks I have saved her, which is terribly ironic considering I have been swept out to sea myself, but Jane just says, "That's what women do."

That's what women do, if someone needs help, a shoulder, a place to live—we do it.

Jane's news is wonderful. She has found a job.

"It's something," she tells me, bouncing from one foot to the next. "It's a start, and I will meet people and keep looking and put the house up for sale and move closer to the city and change my name."

She is talking so fast, I can barely keep up.

"Change your name? Do you want to be Madonna... or _____?"

She laughs, which is a glorious thing to hear. A wide chorus that comes from a place fresh, deep, never before touched.

"My last name. I'm taking back my maiden name. It's a statement. A step. Starting over."

Jane has talked the managing editor of the community newspaper into a job as a reporter. The pay is less than half of what I make, but Jane, for the first time in twenty-one years, will be doing what she has always wanted to do.

"I'm really brave about this now, but I may throw up the first day and pretty much the entire time I am there."

"I hear it's like riding a bicycle," I assure her.

We end back at the café where we met, and I listen to her for three hours. I listen and I watch. It is like seeing someone rise from the dead. Jane is back.

"I think you saved my life," she tells me, taking my hand.

"You did it."

"I needed help and you helped me. I'm not done, I know that, and I may slip backward again, but, Meg, I owe you, I thank you . . . I haven't had a friend like you in such a very long time. I love you."

I tell Jane through my own tears that she has also become a great gift to me and that all the things I have told her have bounced right back into my own arms.

"I needed you too, baby," I say.

18

1983

Mrs. Jeske was in the living room. The bright red curtains, flaming segments of the rainbow that had stood guard for at least twenty years, were piled in a faded heap outside the open window.

Meggie saw her bobbing from box to box, the forbidden divorced woman on the block where she grew up, and impulsively walked up to the window.

"Hi, Mrs. J."

"Margaret, darling, come in. Come around the back. I have shit piled to the sky against that front door."

Mrs. J has been the street-, the block-, the subdivision-harlot for the past twenty-one years. In 1962, years before the unhappy husbands and wives of the world discovered they could divorce without immediately being sucked into the palm of Hell, Mrs. J was the talk of the town.

She kicked out her husband.

Meggie would never forget it. Past midnight in summer. July, maybe it was July. She hears the yelling much like she will hear the yelling in 1963 and for many years after that when the echoes of her parents' late-night arguments roll up the carpeted stairs and float under her closed bedroom door.

It was not the sound that drew Meggie to the window that summer night but the way the breeze would move across the windowsill and dart in to touch her face. But when she got to the window, what she heard made her forget about the gentle wind.

Every light was on in the Jeske house across the street. In the middle of a dark summer night with no stars and low clouds, the house looked like Christmas. Porch light blazing. Bedroom and living room lights on. There was a car in the driveway, parked, engine running, and the driver's door was flung open as if someone had forgotten something and had run into the house to find it.

And the yelling.

Meggie leaned out of her bedroom window farther than she ever had. She pushed her elbows against the sides of the window and stretched her neck so she could see what in the heck was going on.

"Wow," she said quietly. "It's a fight."

It was a fight and she wanted to run from the window to tell her parents, but she couldn't move. She tried moving, but she was stuck right there with her head and arms and chest hanging out of her bedroom window, waiting, just waiting.

The sounds coming from somewhere inside the Jeskes' house got louder, voices slamming over each other, someone yelling, then a collision of sound. She wondered where Jill and Stacey were hiding. Were they safe? Could they hear? Oh man, oh man, oh man.

Mr. Jeske came out of the house first. He had a box in one hand and a suitcase between his legs as he stopped by the door.

"You are a fucking whore," he yelled.

Meggie could only imagine what that was. Something terrible. Something bad enough to make Mr. Jeske want to leave in his car past midnight and yell really loud so that the neighbors could hear what he was saying.

"Everyone will know. Everyone will know who you really are. I'll tell the world. Goddamn you. You whore."

Meggie heard Mrs. Jeske yelling back, but she was too far into the house for Meg to make out a full sentence, just words, "Wait...sick...laugh...moving..." Nothing that made sense.

Meggie held her breath. Mr. Jeske was striding toward the car and Mrs. Jeske stood on the tiny concrete porch, throwing what? Clothes and books and his cigar box. It was too dark to see, but in the morning the lawn would be littered with so much stuff that the grass had disappeared. It looked like a tornado had touched down on just that tiny square spot split by a once-tidy sidewalk, now the scene of an incredible battle.

Before her parents woke or anyone in the neighborhood bothered to grab their newspaper off the front lawn, Meggie took a handful of garbage bags from the kitchen and slipped out the back door, around the side yard and across the street.

She packed socks and deodorant and tennis shoes and pants into the bags. It was an amazing adventure. An old belt. A packet of letters wrapped inside of a paper towel. Some screwdrivers. Meggie imagined that Mr. J's entire life was just lying there for the world to see the moment it woke up. Near the bushes along the front window she found a Rolex watch and a gold ring.

"Holy crap," she whispered. "His wedding ring."

Meggie didn't want to drop the ring in the bag. She looked around the yard, and then saw the tiny metal hanger below the front windowsill that cranked open the winter storm windows when it was time to put on the summer screens. She slipped the ring over the end and pushed it to the bottom. The ring disappeared like magic into the handle.

Meggie carried all the bags around to the back of the house and set them down near the garage door. She never told Mrs. J who picked up the yard, but she watched like a spy as men came and went, as Mr. J showed up and tried to break down the door, as a parade of not-so-nice neighbor kids egged the windows, left piles of dog poop in burning bags on the doorstep, as all the women in the subdivision stayed away and never invited Mrs. J to parties and meetings.

This is what Meggie remembers now as she walks to the back door more than twenty years later and climbs over boxes and chairs and finds Mrs. J, hands on hips, drinking wine in what's left of her bedroom at 11:05 A.M. the day before Thanksgiving.

"Meggie, you sweet thing, how nice to see you."

They hug, and without asking Mrs. J pours her a glass of wine and they sit, shoulder to shoulder against the bare wall, feet pointing toward the house where Meggie spied on her all those years ago.

"My mother didn't tell me you were moving," Meggie says, glad to sit and talk to someone who she liked, no matter what her mother had told her. Mrs. J always gave her a ride when she saw her walking and laughed at her jokes and told her she was going to knock the socks off the world.

They rush past the "stuff"—Meggie's still-fresh marriage, graduate school, where Stacey and Jill are living—and then the leap, with the second glass of wine, into the present, which is a place Mrs. J has always loved to embrace.

"My mother didn't tell me you were moving."

"Jesus, honey, your mother still thinks it's 1958 and that I should have stayed with a man who hit me, slept around and then got pissed when I started to sleep around."

"So all those horrid rumors are true?"

Mrs. J laughs from a place wild and free. A place that makes Meg just a bit jealous.

"Hell, yes."

"Remember the night he left?"

"Which time?"

"Summer, July . . . I think I was in first grade or something."

"The night he came in the front door and Jack Blakely went out the back door?" Mrs. J laughs.

"You are so wicked, Mrs. J."

"That's the nicest thing you've ever said to me, honey."

They both sip their wine, and Meggie reaches back and remembers the garbage bags and the ring.

"Good God, did you ever find the ring?"

"What? What ring?"

Meg tells her the story. The soft breeze, the yelling, the garbage bags, and Mrs. J almost drops her wineglass into her lap.

"You did the garbage bags?"

"Yep. It was me."

"My God. I had no idea. I had no idea. Do you know what that meant to me? It gave me a hint of hope that someone else knew me and my life and wanted to help. It was you? Wow. It was you."

"The ring."

"John's wedding ring?"

"Did you ever take it off the window?"

"Meggie, I thought it got sucked up in the power mower. I never found it."

Meggie rises as if she has been shot, grabs Mrs. J by the hand and rushes with her over the top of the boxes and into the front yard.

The untrimmed bushes have taken over the front of the house. They have formed a protective fort around the windows.

Meggie goes right to the window, pushing past the tangled bushes and moving her hand without even looking to the edge of the handle. The ring is there, but it has molded itself between the handle and the window through many cold winters and hot summers. Meggie looks around, finds a rock that will fit in the palm of her hand and she pounds the ring until it comes loose.

"Here it is," she exclaims, holding it up like a treasure.

"Sweet Jesus," Mrs. J manages to say, laughing.

They sit on the doorstep then, not caring who will see them drinking wine and fondling an old wedding ring before noon. Meggie waves once to her mother, who spies them sitting there, and Meggie knows there will be hell to pay before she helps get the turkey into the oven.

"So, where are you going?" Meggie asks, tipping her glass toward the boxes and leaning in toward Mrs. J.

"I'm moving to Hawaii."

"Serious?"

"Serious as death. I've been planning this for a long time. I have a job, a few friends over there, and I doubt if I'll ever come back."

"Wow."

Meggie is thinking how Bob would never let her go to Hawaii. She is thinking about how tied she suddenly feels to a life that seems to be telling her everything and never listening.

"All those years ago, the way people treated you, how did you manage to keep your sanity?"

Mrs. J puts her arm around Meggie, her fingers dropping gently against her shoulder, and Meggie leans in under the circle and stops breathing.

"I didn't care what people thought, honey. Everyone wanted to do what I did. Everyone wanted to live how I lived. No one had the courage to do it."

"Really?"

"Of course really. Sweetheart, look at your own parents. They never were and they're still not happy. Mrs. Swobada is on medication, and half this block of finger-pointers is sleeping with someone they are not married to. There are so damn many lost dreams on this street, it's a frigging wonder anyone can get out of the driveway."

"Am I blind?"

"We see what we want to see."

"That makes me pretty blind."

"Meg, why did you get married?"

Meggie wants to breathe again, but she cannot. There is a weight pushing against her chest that feels as if it is going to crush her lungs.

"I know what I am supposed to say," she whispers. "But I can't say it. I can't."

"Oh, sweetheart, listen to me. Please listen."

Mrs. J puts her hands on Meggie's face and draws her within an inch of her own face. Meggie smells the sweet scent of wine and something strong and powerful, something that could push back a train.

"Anything is possible," Mrs. J says. "Anything at all. You don't have to be like everyone else and you don't have to listen to anyone else and you can be your own person and live how you want to live. People will always try to say things about you when you do something like I did, because you make them think."

"What do you mean?"

"It's frightening when someone else does something you

know you should do and you cannot do it. Change scares the living hell out of people."

"Like you kicking out your husband and staying in the house and getting a job?"

"That and moving away, saying no. Not marrying. Being alone. Everyone is so goddamn afraid of being alone. What they don't get is that we are alone no matter who we are with."

Meggie starts crying without realizing it. Tears drip from her eyes and across her face and drop onto Mrs. J's fingers.

"Why are you crying, baby?"

"I'm scared."

"Scared of what?"

"I think I've already made a ton of wrong decisions. I don't know if I can be like you."

Mrs. J has pulled Meggie onto her lap and she is running her fingers through the hair that has fallen across her face.

"The world is a mess. It isn't easy to be different and to do what you feel is right for you, just you, and not for your mother or for the minister or for all the people who think they control our morality."

Cars pass, someone waves, Meggie imagines her mother across the street peering from the side bedroom, and she wants to get up and go home but she cannot move.

"Was it hard?" Meggie asks.

"Oh yes. Imagine living how I did with all those eyes on me. I was always on display. But I think it would have been much harder to live the other way. I just couldn't do it anymore. I needed to be truthful."

They talk about hopes and dreams and what it means to be a woman in a world where you have choices but the men are still in control. Meggie hears about how Mrs. J worked for so much less at the bank than the men who did the same job and how she had to fight to get Mr. J to help her pay for the girls' college and how even in a world where 50 percent of couples were eventually getting divorced, her community looked at her as if she had a disease they might catch if they got too close to her.

Meggie stays a long time. She hauls some boxes and gets the Hawaii address, and when she leaves, Mrs. J presses the gold ring, tarnished with years of weathered waiting, into her hand.

"Keep this and remember that you can always choose, you can always start over. You can always put the ring wherever you want to put it."

Meggie kisses Mrs. J and then she puts the ring into her jeans pocket and she rushes across the street without looking back, because she knows her mother is waiting. She knows.

19

Bob has disappeared.

Pieces of his life have been removing themselves one by one from our house for weeks now. Shoes, golf clubs, entire sections of his closet, piles of junk I may never have noticed until I went looking for him have vanished, fallen through the ice into the depths of a lake the size of the moon.

Maybe Katie knows. I catch her flying through the kitchen on the way to who knows where. She has that "I'm always late" look oozing from every ounce of her flesh and from one end of the house to the other—grabbing cookies, changing socks, checking her phone messages, throwing me a kiss.

"Honey, when was the last time you saw your father?"

She has to stop and think, which is a good thing, because she may not have stopped for anything else in a very long time for more than five seconds.

"What day is it?"

"Monday."

She's thinking, moving her foot, afraid to stand still, it seems, and what comes to her mind makes her stop everything, which is a rare occurrence.

"Shit, Mom, it's been days."

"How many days, do you think?"

She thinks again.

"Saturday, maybe. Mom, don't you speak to him?"

A million memories flash in front of my eyes. Don't I speak to my husband? Did I ever speak to my husband? Years ago, when we lay awake all night on a bed the size of an air mattress, did we speak or did I just listen? Did I speak to him when I wanted to quit teaching and when the kids were little and I thought I should stay home more? Did I speak to him when I wanted sex and he didn't? Did I speak to him when I noticed he never came home anymore? Did I speak to him when I felt as if the center of who I was supposed to be had been stolen? Did I speak to him when I felt such a surge of sorrow after my aunt died that I could barely walk? Did I speak to him when our son fled from this house because he was being suffocated by all the unsaid words? Did I ever *really* speak to my husband?

Katie stops me by grabbing my hands and shaking them.

"Mom, where did you go?"

"Thinking."

"About?"

"Speaking to your father."

"How long has it been?"

When I look at Katie, really look at her, I see that she is no longer a girl. This is no news, but this time it registers in a place in my brain that makes my heart start-stop for just a second. Behind her wild eye makeup, shades of orange and black, I see the hint of my baby girl, but beyond that, everything else I see—full lips, the way she carries herself, the swaggering lilt of young beauty, her self-assurance, smell, the way she holds my hands, the fullness of her breasts and the glow of strength pouring out from her skin—she reeks of womanhood. My daughter takes my breath away, and in that same breathless instant I know I cannot lose her like I lost her brother. I cannot go through the wondering and the missing and the guilt and the loss, and so in one second, the second when I remember how I promised myself I would never hold on to my children when they were ready to fly, I decide to tell her something I have rarely told anyone. I must tell her the truth, and then I can let her go. I cannot at that moment think of anything more courageous that I have ever done in my entire life.

"Katie, we have to talk."

I grip her hands so tight, she lets out a small moan. If I let up she may move away. I cannot let her go. Not just yet.

"Mom?"

"Where are you going right now?"

"Just to pick up Colleen."

"Stay, okay? I have to tell you something really important. Can you stay with me?"

Katie does not hesitate, which brings me to the edge of a place that I see as a valley so wide and beautiful that I wonder if I can ever walk through it with my eyes open and not faint. I need her. She sees it and she puts her arm around my shoulder and walks me to the saggy couch out on the back porch. She knows this is my favorite place in the house because from there I can see the unbroken line of the horizon to the west and I can place my mind right there on that thin line and rest in silence. I have been unable to do that anywhere else in the entire world.

"Mom, I'm here. Tell me."

She sits on an old wooden box, feet placed alongside mine, her beautiful hair pushed behind ears that are delicate anchors on each side of her head, and she stops her world—like a friend, like a woman—and enters mine.

And I begin.

I tell her everything. Mexico. Aunt Marcia. How unhappy I

am. How this desire to be alone, maybe live alone, has risen up inside of me in such a fierce manner that I cannot stop it. I tell her I am afraid and I talk on through my embarrassment about how I have always—almost always—done whatever everyone else wanted me to do.

"Why, Mom? Why did you do it?"

"I guess I was scared. I never wanted to disappoint anyone. My mother. Your grandfather. The people at school who took a chance on me. Your father. It was one thing after another, and I never bothered to get out of the stream long enough to decide if I even wanted to be in the water."

"So why now? What happened?"

I tell her even that. I tell her how I came home and how I heard a rolling thunder from the bedroom and how I watched her father and the flower woman. And she smiles.

"Awesome."

"Awesome?"

"Well," she says, quickly patting my hand, "sad but awesome that it was the moment that took you to where you needed to go."

Is this my daughter? Is this the brat who pounded through the house five years ago and who told me she hated me when I wouldn't let her have a sleepover homecoming night with boys? Is this the girl who begged me to let her drop out of school in eighth grade so she could ride her bike to California? The teenager who threw the telephone down the hall and whacked her brother upside the head when he looked at her—simply looked at her? Who is this grown woman who has my nose and hips and shining eyes and long, tapered fingers? Who is she?

"It's your father. *Your* father who was screwing around! How does this make you feel?"

"Mom, it's okay. He's been kind of a jerk for a long time. He's never here. Heck, we can't even find him today, and neither one of us has seen him since—what did we decide—last Saturday? He's just, well, Bob, my dad."

She's thinking serious thoughts again. When did this happen?

"Mom, he's obviously been unhappy too. Shit—people, even my parents, they shouldn't be miserable. And I can't stop seeing you sneaking up the steps and them making love and that old bed squeaking and . . . well, it's not a pretty picture."

I feel a pang of guilt. "Is this too much for you?"

"Mom, I'm almost eighteen. I know stuff, you know?"

That sounds better. I feel like I did when her brother called everyone "hey dude."

"Katie, don't do things just for me."

"Like what?"

"College, although that's kind of important, marriage . . ."

"Mom, that was your life. I know your marriage was a mess—I watched it, for crying out loud—but you've done things. Look at your research and what you've done with your students. You've done things other moms haven't. This other junk, it's just taken you a while to get it out of the way."

I say it so fast, I don't even realize it's coming. "I was trying to find your father so I could let him know I'm going to file divorce papers tomorrow."

"No shit, Mom."

"I hate it when you talk like that."

She laughs. Where have I heard that laugh? It's a mixture of lovely, honest-to-goodness hilarity and something deeper—like she knows more than I do.

"Katie."

"What?"

"You laugh like your Aunt Marcia. Oh my God. That's it. It must have skipped a generation."

"What skipped?"

"That, well, that ability to live like she did."

"It hasn't skipped, Mom. You are just one slow-ass learner."

I can't stop now.

"So you don't mind?"

"That it took you almost fifty years to figure out who you wanted to be when you grew up?"

"Katie . . . No, that I am getting a divorce."

"It's a pisser, but it's not like I need a mommie and daddie anymore. Dad will help me if I need it. He's just a little bit of a jerk. Besides, I won't even be around much longer."

"What?"

"You have been *gone.*"

She says it as if she is drawing out a journey on paper. *Gone* as in a very long journey that has finally come to an end.

I remember. I suddenly remember. She's going to Mexico.

"Katie."

Mexico.

Something snaps. There can't be much left to unsnap. I completely forgot. Six months in Mexico before she starts college in early winter.

Mexico.

She gets it faster than I do. The house on the beach. Aunt Marcia. Some kind of cosmic, fairly bizarre moment has just passed the test of time, and my daughter falls into my arms as if a gentle wave has crashed against her back. She is crying so softly, it takes me a while to notice, and I rub my hands across her shoulders, remembering, the way mothers do, how tiny she was when she was a baby, white as snow, how I kissed her over and over, never quite believing that a part of me had made her.

"Oh, Katie." I cry myself into her right shoulder, the one I kissed the most when she nestled against my breasts and reached her hand toward my face to play with my hair. "Everything is changing. Everything. I don't want you to hate me or feel bad, I just don't think I could stand it now."

Katie pulls away. She holds me at arm's length and she moves her hand through my hair. Her fingers are a massage of total love.

"Oh, Mommie," she says, she calls me "Mommie" and I cannot stop my tears. "I have a terrific life. I do. It could have been easier, especially when I figured out that you were so unhappy, but hell, I've been wrapped up in my own stuff—you know, school and friends—and, well, I've actually felt bad that I couldn't help you more."

"I'm not sure what you mean."

"You know, like this, told you it was okay to leave him and let you know I wouldn't die if it happened."

Oh, Katie. Oh.

"Your brother...was it all this stuff? Is that part of it?"

"Mom, don't you know?"

She can tell then by looking at me, my eyes as colorless as a February morning, that I have no clue.

"Tell me. Please."

"Mom, Shaun's gay. You know, GAY."

I'm so relieved, I could fall to the floor. Katie must feel me slip a bit and she pushes against me.

"Mom, are you okay?"

"I thought it was because he knew I was living this lie, this here-we-are-all-one-big-happy-family bullshit and he hated me for it."

She laughs richly and again I hear Aunt Marcia's laughter in it. An echo of my eternity.

"No, no, no. He thought Dad would kill him and he didn't want to bother you. He knew you were really unhappy but he just didn't know what to do about it. Oh, Mom, Shaun loves you so much. When you get through this, go to him. Everything will be fine."

I am torn between being pissed at being so stupid and wanting to hurl myself off the top of the steps near the couch. What did I miss? How could a world have passed in front of my eyes and how could I have missed something so damn important?

"Hey, if it makes you feel better I never knew either. He really didn't figure it out until he left. There wasn't anyone to talk to, Mom, don't slap yourself about this."

"I tried so hard, you know, I did. I could feel him slipping through my fingers every day. It was terrible and I was, well, I was frozen."

Katie's hands move across my shoulders, pushing and rubbing, that comfortable push of hands, an instinctual feminine move that wants to knead a muscle and unknot a problem. She sees me smile and I tell her how I'm realizing touch is such an important part of everything we seem to do and she tells me to think about what I am saying.

"You have always touched people, all the time," she tells me, closing her eyes, perhaps to remember how old and far back this memory reaches. "It used to drive me nuts, and I would always back away from you, Mom."

"You didn't back, you jumped."

"But then one day I came home from track and you saw me limping, do you remember?"

"Sure, last spring when your heel was sore."

"You made me sit down and your hands worked on my leg and foot and it was weird because it felt like you knew exactly where the pain was, and I realized at that very second that your touch was a very big part of who you are and that maybe you had some kind of special gift for it."

"Really?"

"Haven't you thought about this, Mom? My God, you touch people all of the time!"

We sway like that talking about my gay son, my hands, the direction a life takes often without a map or a break at a roadside stand. We sit on the porch for an hour and I rest my daughter's head in my lap and rock her on the old couch that I have trained to move like a soft recliner. The legs creak as if they are screaming for help and we laugh, but mostly I just want to feel her there and remember the moment when our lives passed from one point to the next. I want to let her long hair slip through my fingers forever like she used to touch the light silk on the top of her blanket when she was a little girl; I want to feel her heart there, under my fingertips, and imagine where she is headed and what she is going to do and how free she must feel knowing that she has my own heart in her hand and any other damn thing she wants and needs. I want to point her face into the late-afternoon sky, just like this, and show her how to put her hands on the horizon and claim a spot for herself—even if I'm not quite ready to stake a claim for myself and I'm terrified to do so.

"One step at a time," I whisper into her open eyes. "One step, do you hear?"

"I hear, Mommie," she tells me.

I have never heard anything sweeter. Never.

My attorney, Bridget, is a bulldog who has the face of a beautiful woman and hair that stands up so straight, it looks absolutely terrified. Doors open before she touches them. Opponents leap behind walls. This woman does not walk, she swaggers. She is terribly funky and intimidating, which I think is a very good look for an attorney, especially my attorney.

Her receptionist is a man and her two assistants are young women, recent graduates is my guess, who look as if they could eat the hind legs off of any male who looks at them for more than five seconds and breathes in the wrong direction. These are the women I want in my court. These are the women I would want to help me if I ever have the good luck to be in a bar fight or in the middle of a jungle without water or a knife. Actually, they could probably arrange a bar fight for me or build a jungle within five or six seconds. When I sit across from Bridget I decide, just at that moment, never to leave her office. I'm moving in.

"So, you're ready?"

"Yes," I manage to say with only a slight quiver in my voice.

"I thought it would take you longer."

"Really?"

"I'm impressed."

"You should be a counselor."

"I sort of am."

Bridget and I have met several times. She's given me the gory legal details. Prepared me for battle, but she doesn't expect a whimper from Bob. She does, however, expect that I'll be happy when the whole mess is over.

Ms. Confident shuffles papers, lines a pile up for me to sign and then grabs my hand before I can begin this interesting task.

"Are you sure?"

I close my eyes once before I answer, and what I see is my Mexican house. I call it "Marcia's Palace." I hear a warm wave break across Bridget's desk and feel that occasional breeze coming in just across the far edge of her spiked hair.

"Damn sure," I say.

While I sign the sheets, she gets out a bottle of Scotch. It smells like a hard day's work when I raise it to my nose and then pass my tongue across its surface. Bitter. Scary. Certain. Lovely.

"It feels like a first kiss," I tell her, which makes her spit out her drink and swear.

"Jesus! I hate to waste a drop of this. It's a hundred bucks a bottle, but that was worth it. Honey, you are *ready*."

Bridget is not just my attorney. She's my friend now. I am certain every woman who signs papers just like this feels that way, but she will always be my heroine. She'll get me the Palace. She'll help me keep my father's bonds, she'll shame Bob into realizing he makes more than enough to support himself while he helps Katie and Shaun through school. She'll get me half the money for the house. She is the queen.

Everything is a honeymoon, until she asks me the next question.

"Now what?"

Without thinking, I push the glass toward her, and she fills it to the top. Damn it. Why did she have to do that? Now what indeed.

"First I move."

"Then?"

"Another week in Mexico."

"Then?"

"A new job."

She doesn't say a word.

I have no idea where any of that came from, but I write down the name of the Scotch before I leave and promise Bridget I will bring some to court in exactly 120 days, when I expect to be divorced, moved and very tanned from my recent trip to the sea.

When I leave the building, I sit in the car for a very long time. I have no idea what to do next. None at all. I think of calling Elizabeth, who came to help me the last time this happened, but this time I wait. I remember how to drive, how to breathe, how to move my hand from where it is resting on my thigh to my face, but I don't know where to go. I have just signed a piece of paper that will change my life in a way that seemed impossible just months ago.

I start laughing, and say, "Hi, I'm Meg. No, I'm not married. I'm single."

My laugh, a feeling of utter release tinged with just a small hint of panic, comforts me a bit. When I open my eyes, nothing has changed but nothing will ever be the same. The key fits into the long ignition hole. The car moves away from the curb and I am steering it. The car and I move forward. We are going some-place.

The Scotch has moved into my veins and is pummeling the living hell out of my bloodstream. I think I could pick up the car and swing it over my head. Without realizing it, I am looking for FOR RENT signs. I drive to a section of the city where I suspect the wild women might live. The section of the city where there is diversity in neighborhoods and where you can see the shoreline of Lake Michigan from the top floor. The section of the city where women can hold hands with women and men with men and no one thinks twice. I pull over eight times and write down phone numbers.

Driving back to my tidy suburb, I almost get lost. Everything seems unfamiliar to me, which is a terribly odd sensation. I de-cide to buy a bottle of the Scotch Bridget shared with me just so I can touch the label if I get frightened. But I don't get fright-ened.

Parking the car is easy, but when I let myself in through the side door, the door I have used for years, I feel as if I am sneaking into a house and a place that is as foreign as speaking Latin or eating upside down. I am uncomfortable. A bit lost. Alone in a world that was once all I knew.

"I don't belong here," I tell myself, and then without realizing it I start packing. The boxes on the back porch fly into my hands and I make the first move. I take my old pottery vase off the counter by the phone in the kitchen, wrap it in a long piece of paper towel and set it in the center of the box. I have started something. There is no place to take my boxes just yet but I have some direction.

"I know something," I say, as I look around for something else to set next to the lonely vase. "I. Know. Something."

As I walk through the house with the box tucked under my arm, I don't bother to turn on the stereo or the television. The quiet house walks with me, patting my knees as I move upstairs just for a quick look to see what might like to lie next to the old vase, rubbing my shoulders when I tense up because of the silence, moving my hands through my hair when I want to be certain that someone or something is close.

But I am alone. Gloriously alone and smiling as I open the door to what was once our bedroom. Ribbons of light from the bent shades pattern across the bed and land at the edge of the dresser. My eye lands on two framed photographs. Shaun in fifth grade, his hair a mess of curls, that goofy green shirt he wore almost every day and his father's half smile. The other photo is Katie that same year, in third grade. A little girl's face aglow with happiness, smiling as if she has it all figured out, teeth not yet straightened, one hand under her chin. My heart races. Such fabulous prizes from this part of my journey. How lucky I am. How goddamn lucky. I kiss the photos, holding them to my lips, their solid frames nudging me forward. Yes, it is definitely time to move forward.

That is all I take from the room. I've already taken everything else I need. The box is very light when I go back downstairs, wonderfully, wonderfully light.

20

Elizabeth comes to my front door and I want to run back inside and get her some candy. She is wearing an orange jogging bra under a white sleeveless T-shirt, a red bandanna, purple shorts and a red, white and blue pair of Birkenstocks, which I know for certain she picked up at a yard sale run by some paramilitary people.

"Are you trick-or-treating or did you come to get me?"

"Wiseass. You could look like this if you put a little energy into it. Get in the car."

Elizabeth could probably do stand-up comedy, run a hospital and juggle at the same time. My breath disappears every time I see her, and I have never had such a good friend, never ever, in my entire life. She has wanted to celebrate the signing and then the delivery of the divorce papers, but I have been too damn busy. Calling places to set up rental appointments, worrying about my mother, trying to reconnect with my son, helping Katie pack for Mexico, poring over bank books and digesting my supremely interesting phone call from Bob moments after the divorce papers were delivered to his office.

"Meg, what the hell!"

"Bob, you'll live."

"This is something. Jesus H. Christ. You could have warned me."

"How could I warn you? I have no idea where you live."

Silence. A very long chunk of silence.

"You know where I *work*."

I get angry. Just a little angry. I need my energy for more important things, like getting on with my life. My voice is very loud when I respond.

"Fuck you, Bob. One of us had to do this. It was long overdue. You are miserable, or you wouldn't be screwing some other woman on our bed in the middle of the day. So get over it."

There. That popped a wedge of restraint right out of me.

He's thinking. Imagining what it would be like if everything stayed the same and he made believe he loved me and had a life that did not really exist. Then the next thought is what his life could be like if he just kept a few pieces of the old life—pieces like a relationship with his children and maybe, just maybe, a somewhat cordial relationship with their mother.

He says: "I'm sorry."

Wow, Bob, wow.

"This makes sense, Meg. It's just, could we maybe talk a little bit about some of this?"

"Now?"

"No, I can't do it now. Dinner? Can I meet you for dinner?"

"If you buy."

He laughs, but I'm dead serious. I pick a place where they have an exquisite martini bar and salads designed by men and women who wear wings. He wants to do it that day while his feelings are fresh and I agree.

Dinner starts out rough. He's edgy, scared, I think. Mr. Bob has been limping along, sleeping with the geranium, and maybe someone or several someones. He hasn't had a lengthy discussion with me in years and something thin and yet very solid is being pulled out from under his size 11 feet.

I touch his hand after the second martini. He doesn't pull away. I tell him I loved him, and I did love him. I really did.

"Bob, we should both be happy. I've never stopped long enough to even wonder what that might be like. I'm a frigging mess. Well, I was a frigging mess."

He tries to interrupt me, but I have to tell him some things right now before I get too boozy, before I move from that sincere place of alcohol-induced honesty to the "tell everything" phase that will have me saying things I will deeply regret in the morning. I so want him to know these things and remember them. I have to say them.

"Bob, I loved it when you made coffee on Sunday mornings and left me a cup in the bathroom. I loved the way you taught the kids how to drive without yelling at them and how you took Shaun to college because I couldn't stop crying. So much of what we had was okay, you have to know that, Bob. So much of it was great, really great."

He cries, which is something I did not expect. He takes my other hand and tells me how he feels like an ass because he could never tell me I was beautiful and a wonderful mother. He apologizes for not buying me flowers the day I got my second master's degree. He tells me how it was just easier for him to back away and how it never even seemed like I missed him.

"You are very beautiful, Margaret," he tells me. "Smart and wise and kind, so damn kind. There isn't anyone else like you. I want you to be happy too, I do. I'm sorry. I'm so sorry."

Oh, Bob. Oh, Bobby.

We have a very long and wild dinner. We relive all the years we spent together, remembering the fights and the baby diapers stuck in the toilet and the way his mother tried to shame us into having another child and how he waited outside in the car while I finished my orals, so I wouldn't feel so alone. I had forgotten that. There are so many things we had both forgotten.

"Bob," I tell him after the wine and before the dessert and at the moment we realize we will have to take cabs, one back to the geranium's home and one to our little house in the suburbs. "Bob, we have to remember the good stuff. It might take a while because I haven't gone all the way through my horrid angry phase yet, but promise me that we'll remember the good stuff?"

"But I feel like it's all my fault."

How I wish, Bob, how I wish.

"It was me too," I tell him. "Never knowing for sure. Waiting for someone else to do something when I was the one supposed to be doing it. It was a we deal, Bob. Both of us."

In what I can only describe as the miracle of mixing distilled grains with a last glimpse of love, we agree to almost everything. Selling the house, splitting the accounts, me keeping the Palace—which results in a fairly huge amount of tears on my part—the kids' schooling. We decide to take turns going through the "stuff" we have accumulated.

"This seems too easy," I say as we try to douse the evening with strong coffee so we can at least walk to our taxis.

"There's nothing easy about it," he responds. "A part of me will always love you, sweetheart. We share those kids, a past, so many years. I owe you the dignity of this. Going out quietly. Getting on with it all. It's part of my penance, you see, but it's not painful at all. Not at all."

"Not painful?"

"The dignity part. Everything else is making me ache. Of course, it would have to be you who did this. It was always you."

Is it possible, I think as I balance myself on chairs on the way to the bathroom, that someone else could have been appearing in the bathroom mirrors all these years? Maybe my life has been one of those Blessed Mary events like the kind of miracle where women making punch see the face of the Virgin Mary when they pour the mix into the water. I never felt strong or powerful or in control of anything in my life. How could Bob think that I had a clue of what was happening?

In the end we share a taxi. He rides all the way home with me, walks me to the door while the taxi waits and holds me for a moment. "How familiar," I think. The way my arms remember their way across his shoulders, the way my head turns to the left when he tips his head, the feel of his breath at the very edge of my hair, the same cologne he has used for fifteen years, the way his heart sounds like a wild horn under my ear. We stay like that for a long time, the taxi driver reading patiently while we embrace. I want to remember. I want to remember everything about this moment and what is essentially the last second of my married life. Through the living room window, I watch him leave and my heart sails just a bit. It sails with him as he goes home to his lover, his new life, with my heart in his pocket at least until he gets to her door. At least.

Dr. C is amazed the following week when I tell her what happened. I almost think she is disappointed that I am getting better.

"I knew you would be fast, because everything was so close to tumbling over when you came in the first time," she tells me, fingering her coffee cup as if it were on fire. "It's good, it's all good."

But I want to know if it's over. She laughs when I ask her.

"Oh, I hope not, darling. Can't you see another mountain off in the distance?"

"It's cloudy."

Then I admit that I'm scared.

She knows this. Dr. C knows everything. We work on a small plan. She tells me I may be flying now, but a couple of good days aren't a sign of nirvana.

"Look what's happened to you in just a few months, Meg. When you stop, when you get to the next point, you have to be ready to crash a little bit. String it all out, say it now."

I do. Infidelity. Gay son. The Palace. Aunt Marcia's lover. Divorce. Looking for a place to live. A new career. My mother's breasts.

"Shit," I say, suddenly a bit panicked.

"It's a load. A lot of stuff. None of it bad. Can you see that?"

I have to close my eyes to do it. The breeze kicks up, but I would kind of like a strong wind.

As I leave, I make an appointment for the following week. Dr. C smiles because this was my idea. She knows I'm hunting for a place to live. She knows my mother's tests are due in. She knows I must call my son. She knows.

Elizabeth knows all of this also. She tells me she's in it for the fun. Apartment-hunting. Looking for a flat. She's the one who told me to move to Andersonville, the funky Chicago neighborhood where openness is a must. "Such diversity. You'll never have to go to a movie again. You'll just look out your window."

I agree that if I am going to change, I may as well get out of PTA heaven. It was never quite the right fit anyway. My cupcakes were never perfect. I just wanted to go home and read. Who cared if the kids had to miss one recess because not enough parents volunteered for playground duty? But I went anyway. I was always there. Smiling when someone showed me a catalog filled with baskets or plastic bowls. I never did fit, but there I was, and now I was cruising the funky streets in Andersonville.

We had five places to look at and Elizabeth was determined that I would choose one of them. I was determined to go one entire day without crying.

"Remember how we all had old bricks and boards for bookcases in college?" she says as I weave in and out of traffic, thinking that I may have to sell my car if I lived in the city. "I had a friend who almost drove herself mad after she was married and up to her ass in kids because she wanted to live alone with her books and bricks."

This is how Elizabeth talks, rambling on and on about people and places that she seems to think have a connection to what is happening now.

"Screw the bricks," I say. "It's hot. I'm going for windows."

We look at three apartments that make me want to weep. All are dirty, small and expensive. I have not done this in a long while. A really tiny part of me wants to go back to my home with grass in the front and a sidewalk that ends up in another little neighborhood where people grill pork chops and bounce balls against the side of a garage. Then that damn breeze kicks up again. It's not a city breeze either. It's gotten here directly from Mexico. I have not mentioned the occasional breeze from the jungle to anyone and I decide to wait before I say anything. I'll know when it's the right time. Even a blossoming woman such as myself can only take so many people looking at her sideways in one day. The breeze, however, is perfect—a woman could almost dance naked through a breeze like this.

"I think it's going to be the next place," I say finally. We have been drinking water and fanning ourselves with the rental section of the local newspaper. Two men are kissing on the corner when we pull down the street for the next viewing. There's a famous women's bookstore, Women & Children First, down the block, bars, coffee shops, a place to work out. If I don't like this place, Elizabeth might take it. It's sort of what heaven should look like if such a place exists beyond earth, she tells me.

I know right away, even before we go inside. It's the lower apartment, and there's a fenced-in yard that is very private. That's what the ad says anyway. We pull into the skinny driveway and there is a woman leaning against the side of the house in a beige linen suit, reading glasses on the edge of her nose, fortyish, tall, a string of silver pearls bobbing between her breasts. She owns the place. She apologizes for being in a hurry, smiles brightly at Elizabeth, who leans right into her when she talks. "Here we go," I think, "what was I doing bringing her out in public like this?"

And the house is red. Not a wild red, but a maple-leaf-turning-from-yellow kind of red, with a light purple trim and green doors. There are metal sculptures that could be whatever you want them to be lined up in two roving rows next to the house. Beds of wildflowers. Nice bushes. Looking at this house makes my heart happy. I'm smiling.

Everything is new old. She's redone the entire building, financed it herself, hired her pals to do the work while she runs a huge gourmet bakery. I'd be the first person to live there since she finished construction. The walls inside are a blank canvas. There's a fireplace. That's all I see before I say, "I'll take it."

"All righty, then," she responds, smiling. "Any chance you can tell me who you are first?"

I start laughing and cannot stop. I laugh until I can't breathe, and the landlordess, identified only as Sally, starts laughing too. She looks smart. Sally must know I am heading into a new life. She asks me what I do, will I live alone, asks for a reference or two, then asks me if I know three people who happen to share an office two doors down from me at the University. They are misplaced women's studies professors who are waiting for their new offices to be finished one building over.

"Small world," she says, still smiling. "I think you need this place, Meg."

We finish looking through the two bedrooms, the dining room—which I immediately know will become my office—and the small kitchen—perfect for someone like me whose meal of choice is wine and crackers. I want to sell Sally my soul, write out a check, lick the dust off her sandals, but she tells me she has to make a few calls first.

"I have a partner, and I really have to see if you are who you say you are."

There's that smart scent I picked up.

Elizabeth watches Sally as if she is about to light herself on fire. I can't imagine Elizabeth giving up her funky house and moving into the upstairs flat, but I'm pretty sure she is at least thinking about it. There is something terribly sexy about the city. Something wild and alive, especially if you are used to wide lawns, garages and all the useless space. It's a world I have only traveled through for a very long time, but I feel the weight of all its promises as I stand in what I hope will be my kitchen and write out phone numbers.

I try very hard not to be distressed about the possibility that Sally the Wonderful might not want a soon-to-be-divorced woman with a teenage daughter living in her light orange bedroom. I try not to be distressed about what I still must do and how I have to sort through all those years of shit and touch all the memories associated with the shit. I try not to be distressed about my first night alone in this new house and all the steps I need to take to make that happen. It would suddenly be very easy to lie down in the driveway.

"You know, I only rent to people who I want as neighbors and friends," Sally tells me. "It has to work all the way around. I live upstairs. It's a big deal to me."

Here it comes. I must be too frumpy. She can tell I used to bake cupcakes.

"I think it would be grand to have the energy of a teenager around, even for a little while. You're gorgeous," she tells me, resting her hand on my arm. "If you promise to invite your friend here over for sleepovers, I bet we can make this work."

My gawd. She's flirting with both of us. What will Tomas say? What should I say?

"Elizabeth may have to spend the night with you," I tell her, which tells her everything. "It might be crowded down here."

When we get to the car, Elizabeth roars. I could probably drive on her energy. I may never need to buy gas again.

"Do you realize how lucky you are to find this place?" she demands.

No.

"Do you know that you are the thirty-sixth person who has looked at it?"

Where have I been?

"Do you know who she is?"

No. Tell me, Elizabeth. She is having this conversation alone. I just turn occasionally and nod. She hasn't even bothered to put on her seat belt.

"She's on the City Council, for God's sake. She's one of the most powerful women in this city. She knows everyone. She's been an activist for years. It's Sally. Sally Flannery Burton. She's written a book. She has lunch with people like Hillary Clinton. She wants you to live in her apartment! Right next door to her!"

"I think she'd rather live next to you," I finally say.

"Oh, come on."

"Really. You drooled all over her."

Elizabeth pulls herself out of it and I pepper her with questions about how long it will take to check references and move and sell my house. I'm more interested right this second in how to get from point A in the suburbs to point B in the city than in living below the Feminist of the Year, thank you very much. Elizabeth assures me it's a done deal unless Sally the Wonderful discovers my felony murder arrest record or decides I won't fit into her backyard barbecue cycle.

We banter like this without even moving the car. Elizabeth suddenly hops out and decides that we need to walk the streets and get the feel of the neighborhood, even though we have both been here before for everything from book signings to wild wine-tasting parties. It's different, we decide, to walk and think of actually living here. She's on fire. I decide to appease her; after all, I did drag her through several apartments from Hell.

"Would you move?" I ask her as we look into windows and order coffee at a small café with a patio in back.

"I've actually been thinking about it. Really. The boys come home about once every month, and they don't stay very long. When I'm down here in the city, I feel as if my feet are on fire. Maybe we should buy our own house? Share the space, you know, up and down. Maybe we should ask Jane too. What do you think?"

"You're asking me—the Queen of indecision?"

"Not lately. Look at yourself."

"I know this feels perfect for me. I like the hum of the city. I won't be able to hide here. I can meet new people. It feels pretty damn alive down here. You're right. Let's think about it."

I put my hand on her knee and squeeze it hard. "I have to do this alone first for a while, but what you are saying makes sense. It might happen. Give me this first."

Elizabeth has her legs crossed at the ankles and her feet are resting on the spare chair. I've always wanted to be like her. Since the moment I met her. I've never known anyone as alive and sure.

"Are you prepared for how much your house will sell for?"

"Haven't thought of it."

"You'll shit in your pants. It's going to be close to $350,000. Maybe more."

My mouth flops open. I had no idea.

"What are you saying?"

"I'm saying you have more options than you think you have. Maybe you'll want to buy something. Or take a year off. There are still things you have to decide. Let me roll it over in my head too. As you know, sweetheart, lots of things can happen in a year."

No shit, Elizabeth. I've even started to swear.

"I'm afraid to stop right now. I don't want a rest really. I want to run. Do you know what I mean?"

"Sure."

"But I'm also exhausted."

"I wonder why."

We spend the rest of the day like this, walking in and out of stores, buying books, just standing and looking around. Elizabeth sees four people in different places whom she knows, and just like that I have the phone numbers of four people who may end up being my new neighbors.

Wow, Elizabeth. Wow.

By the time I get back home, Sally the Wonderful has left a phone message that will set the tone for the launch into the twenty-ninth phase of my new life. The apartment is mine. The yard is mine, one parking spot in the driveway that will have to be juggled to fit into two other schedules is mine and a space at the back of the garage for anything I may want to store outside and a washer and dryer space in the basement, which also includes storage space. Mine.

I share this news with no one, but immediately begin ticking off days in my head so that I can organize what to do to keep pace with my move-in schedule. While I am doing this, a dark van pulls up in front of the house. A man dressed in a blue blazer gets out, pounds a sign into the front yard and leaves very quickly.

"What the hell?"

It is almost dark when I walk outside to look at the sign. Katie is working, I imagine Bob is picking geraniums, and my son is most likely scrambling to finish the summer term and prepare for finals. I am alone on the front lawn, bending down to read the words on the sign. FOR SALE. The sign looks good. It's in a lovely spot and Bob had agreed to find a realtor. I just had no idea it would all happen so quickly.

My house is for sale.

I'm moving.

I'm getting divorced.

Within weeks I will be living in the city.

I own a cottage by the sea.

I hate my job.

I don't mean to cry. I really don't. I'm happy. I am finally pushing the world, just a bit, and the world is not pushing me, but when I put my fingers on the side of the sign to make sure that it is straight, something shifts a little bit. There is an ache alongside of the bone that runs from below my neck and down to my belly button that brings me to tears.

It is the root of me, I think, the root of me getting ready for a fast transplant. A move. A new life. And yet the roots, even here, in the center of the lawn I have always hated to cut, even here the roots run deep and linger as I try to pull them out.

Three weeks ago I would not have lain down on the front lawn and cried as cars passed and the neighbors looked out of their windows. A month ago I would never have cried at all. I would have gone inside of the house and busied myself with another load of wash, an e-mail to my colleagues in Brazil or France, who are always in bed when I am at work, or a phone call to my mother.

A year ago I would have gone right for the wine or the vodka. I might have cooked dinner and then read for two hours wondering what time Katie would get home or if Shaun would show up for dinner. Maybe about two A.M., sleepless again, I would have walked through the house and tried to remember what it was like to wake up before dawn and make love.

A week ago, just a week ago, I would never have lain on the lawn with one hand touching the FOR SALE sign, remembering how I caught Katie kissing a boy one night under the porch light when I heard something funny and decided to check. I would not have rolled over on my side and looked through the last light of a July afternoon into windows that I would never wash again and a roof that someone else could now shingle and into the upstairs bedroom, where I would never spend another night.

Never.

I would never have slipped to my knees to kiss the grass and hold a large sign a day ago, a mere day ago, and the thought of what I must look like, bare legs flung one way, shoes another, head on my hand and the sweet knowledge of how glorious it felt to lie with my face pushed against the old dandelion heads and my heart racing ahead of me—finally ahead of me—made me weep even more.

I lay there for a very long time. No one stopped me. Not a soul. And what I felt slipping away was a past that I would remember and eventually embrace and a world that I would now very carefully hand off to the next person who asked for the keys to the front door and was bold enough to walk into my old living room.

Then a horn beeped and I heard a car door slam, but I still did not move.

"What the hell."

It was not a question, and I recognized the feet before I heard the voice.

Jane.

"Did your Clapper break?"

"Fuck you."

She laughs and then I laugh.

"How stupid do I look?"

"I could make money off of this."

She knows. She knows without me saying a word, and her hand reaches down and I think she is going to pull me up, but instead she touches me gently and drops to the grass and curls around me like a grass snake winding its way around a tomato plant.

"It's time," is all she says, and her face in my hair is the scent of fabulous friendship and I think how lucky I am to be a woman, how goddamn lucky.

21

1990

Vandy came back on a Friday morning and the first person she saw was Meg Richardson dropping off her kids at Meadowbrook School, where she had come herself to catch a glimpse of her boys.

"Meg!" she shouted, and then motioned for her to come over to her car. "Have you seen the boys?"

Vandy Hanson looked like hell. She'd been "missing" for three weeks, and all anyone knew was that she had left her four boys with her mother while her husband was on an assignment in Australia and she just disappeared. No one knew if it was true or not, and there she was, whispering to Meg on a sunny morning in February.

Meg was startled to see her and she had no idea why the sight of this woman made her jump.

"They're fine," she told Vandy. Then she quickly added, "Do you want to talk?"

Vandy had circles under her eyes the color of Shaun's old dark blue snowsuit. Her hair was pulled under a baseball hat, and Meg could swear that the clothes she was wearing were the same clothes she had on the last time Meg saw her on the playground just before she took off.

"Can you?"

"I can be late. An hour?"

"Get in, okay?"

They drive off without Vandy bothering to look for oncoming cars and almost broadside a red Toyota.

"Jesus!" Vandy shouts. "I'm sorry. I'm a fucking mess."

"Want me to drive?"

Vandy looks at her as if Meg has slapped her across the face.

"Trust me. We'll get some coffee."

They drive to McDonald's and sit in the back beyond the slides and games. Meg can only wonder what this woman wants, where she has been, where she is going. Meg closes her eyes for a moment and feels her days close around her. Breakfast. Kids to school. Work. Phone calls at lunch to drop off homework. Girl Scouts. Soccer. Endless movement. Endless. She imagines slipping away for a day, a week, three weeks, and she wants to fall across the table and rest her head on Vandy's long arms.

"Sit." Vandy commands. "I have absolutely no one to talk to."

Meg has talked to Vandy dozens of times. Their sons share a teacher. They live two blocks apart. They wave after school. Last year they both bought the same gold jacket. Meg knows absolutely nothing about her. Nothing important, anyway. Nothing that could cross the line between waving and knowing.

"What are people saying?"

Meg takes such a large sip of coffee, her entire throat burns and she has to suppress a tight scream. She says, "No one knows anything. All we heard, from your mother, is that you left a note and took off."

"My mother."

"She hasn't said anything. Vandy, what is it?"

Vandy looks at her, eyes wide, hat pulled close to the top of her eyebrows, and when she pushes back her hair, Meg can see that her hands are shaking.

"I think I'm losing my mind. Brad is never here, the kids, the house..."

"Vandy," she manages to say softly. "What can I do?"

"Can you just listen for a little while?"

"As long as you want. I can listen."

The story is not that complicated. There are no secret lovers. No bag full of drugs. Nothing sinister. Just this terrible well of unhappiness that makes Vandy wonder if and how she can make it through the month, the year, the next twelve years until the boys are gone.

"That's how you see it? Just waiting for it to be over?"

"I feel like I've never belonged here. When I close my eyes, I see the desert and miles of highway, a stretch of water, this piece of sky that is endless, and I just want to go there."

Meg thinks of the ocean. An island where it rains once every ten years and never snows and where you wake up tan, eat fruit all day and no one calls your name or asks you anything for weeks and weeks and weeks.

"Where are you staying?"

"Edge of the city. A hotel, Dreamer's Way, that should be condemned, right off Highway 32. I call the kids every night. They think I'm helping someone move."

"What *are* you doing, Vandy?"

"I'm hiding."

She says it without hesitation, her hands jumping as if she has been drinking coffee for a solid twenty-four hours.

"From what?"

"This," she says, moving her hand, palm up, across the table, sweeping it from one side of the little table to the other. "Everything. If I didn't have the boys, I'd be gone."

"Gone where?"

Vandy starts to cry. Meg wants to catch the tears and let them fill up her hands like a slow fountain, but she sits there, not moving, not knowing what to say.

She cries, and Meg touches her hand and wonders what to say next. She wants to cry too. She wants to put her head on top of Vandy's hand and ask her to put her in the car so she can run away too.

"Vandy..."

Meg wants to say, "Take them with you and run." She wants to, for those few minutes, put Vandy in the backseat under a blanket, go get the boys out of school and drive them all to the airport. She wants to pack up their house and put it inside of a long trailer and send it to them wherever they go, wherever they end up.

"Is it your husband?"

"He's just a part. Throw him on top of the pile and it falls over."

Meg pulls at the plastic lid of her coffee. She feels as if someone has punched her in the stomach. She knows she should reach across the table and hold Vandy's hand.

"Before this, Vandy, who were you?"

Vandy smiles.

"God, she's beautiful," Meg thinks. "I never noticed her smile."

"No one asks me about myself. I'm Ben and Brian's mother. Brad's wife."

"So?"

"I was a singer."

Meg cannot keep her mouth from dropping open. "Really?"

Vandy keeps smiling. "I traveled all over the country singing at hotels, fronted several rock stars. Slept with Van Morrison, and well…"

Meg cannot speak. But she has to ask.

"You're not making this up?"

"Look it up. Vanessa Satterfield. I've done a dozen records."

"I don't know what to say. Do you miss it? Is that part of it?"

"Not at all. I just hate this kind of life. Everything is predictable. Nothing changes. I was done singing, singing that way anyhow. I'll get a studio when I move, take students, but I won't come close to being and doing what I did before."

Meg feels the sides of her black slacks, the ones she wears every Tuesday and most Fridays, and she wants to tell Vandy to run and keep running, but the words stick someplace low, someplace far down inside of her.

"Hey, you look pained, Meg. Are you okay?"

"Yes," she lies. "I wish I could tell you what to do."

Meg takes another sip, the coffee's not hot now and she holds it in her mouth, wanting the bitterness of it to hold her right there and not let her say anything she doesn't want to say.

"How about you, Meg? Are you happy?"

The coffee bumps past her throat and lands in her stomach as if it is full of lead. The color goes out of her face, and Vandy tries to get up but Meg grabs her hand to keep her in her seat.

"Meg?"

"Sorry, I…What happened to all of us, Vandy? What happened?"

Vandy smiles again and Meg can see her moving across a stage, hair flying, rows of men screaming, sweat dripping from the edges of her face and down the front of her very low-cut shirt.

"That's what I'm trying to figure out. I wanted this life, I really did, but it wasn't supposed to be this damn *serious.* All these patterns of sameness are driving me nuts. I'm going crazy living like this, and I don't want my boys to think that this is what it's supposed to be like."

"So what can you do?"

"I was hoping you'd tell me."

"Vandy..."

Vandy puts up her hands to catch Meg's hands before they begin to wave in the wind.

"Stop," Meg tells her.

"I'm a mess, I know that, I'm unhappy, I know that, but I also know I can't kick-start anyone else's stuff. I didn't mean to do that. I'm sorry."

Meg can't speak. She's had terrific intellectual discussions at work for years, shared stories about her own kids, walked into buildings where every single person but her had a PhD, and she has no idea what to say to the woman sitting across from her except something she has always heard. Something that has been whispered in her ear so many times it's written on her brain cells. Something she never asked to hear herself.

"Maybe it will get easier," she says.

The smile comes again. Larger and with a bit of help from a laugh. Gentle, not like the songs Meg imagines Vandy used to sing.

"You sound like my mother."

"Really? Well, I guess I don't know what else to say."

Vandy cries all over again. Meg feels like an ass.

"No one knows what to say; it's okay," Vandy weeps into her napkin.

The silence after that is embarrassing.

"It's that I know there's more and I'm very angry at myself for letting it get this far, you know?"

Meg might know if she stopped herself for three minutes and checked into the Dreamer's Way Hotel and lay down without a television or a book in her hand or a phone to answer or a meeting to attend. She might.

She tries hard to be the teacher that she is for just a moment. "Direction," she tells herself. "Give her direction."

"Two choices, it seems," she manages to say.

"Oh, really?"

"Go or stay."

"I've already decided, you know."

Meg can't be angry, because she feels like a loser. A shit. Useless to womankind, to any female, to this one beautiful tattered soul who needs her right this second. Goddamn it. She could be looking into a mirror. She could be a singer. She could be anything.

"You have?"

"Not really, but I can't stay. I'm just trying to decide if I should take the boys and leave a note or take the boys and not leave a note or take just two boys, the little ones—my babies—and leave a very long note."

Now Meg smiles, which is exactly what Vandy wanted her to do.

"Maybe I'd go," Meg says suddenly.

Vandy laughs. "You?"

"Maybe."

"Never. I bet you still bake."

Meg gulps. She imagines there is still frosting on her left pants leg.

"I just can't make believe anymore. I have to go back to California. Find my place. Show the boys there is more. Let them wake up on a beach and have no clue about what happens tomorrow."

"Is this wrong?" Meg asks, flying her hand through the air to mean her life, all of her life, every single moment of it.

"Oh, not at all. I just don't fit in. I'm one of those rough-ride girls. I like to be hungry and not know what's happening next. My gawd, Meg, if someone of color drives past my house, people still jump into the ditch. How do we do this? How?"

Meg thinks that she has not had a conversation like this since college, the early years when she talked on rooftops and smoked dope in the closet and everything seemed possible, everything.

"Vandy, go. I'll do what I can to pave the way after you leave."

Vandy looks at her as if Meg has just sat down in front of her with a cucumber on her head and she has never seen her before in her life.

"Meg...I don't care what people think. That's part of the problem here. I don't give a shit. Tell them I'm a hooker, a lesbian, an ax murderer. What matters is that I am showing my boys a side of life that I can't find here or..."

"Or what?"

"Don't want to find because it's probably here anyway."

When Vandy drops her off back at her car, all Meg can think of is cupcakes. She wonders if she put them back in the refrigerator or left them on the counter, and then for a second she thinks about driving to work the back way through a neighborhood that has made her uncomfortable and where a man was shot in the head while he waited in a parked car a week ago.

The second passes in a snap and she forgets to look in the mirror to see which way Vandy turns, never realizing until the following morning that Vandy parked her car in the handicapped zone, went into school, got her boys and headed west before Meg had turned into the parking lot behind the University.

But that night when she drifted to the couch, when Bob was late again, when she realized that she had let something important and wonderful slip away, she walked to the west window, the long window that always looked as if it had been the carpenter's afterthought, and pressed her fingers against the cold pane of glass.

"Good luck, Vandy," she said. "Good luck."

And something new started. A thought that placed itself inside of Meg and waited. How it waited.

22

The first four people who looked at the house found me sobbing in the bathroom just off the kitchen. I had tried to leave before the realtor came by, but the phone rang, I saw it was my mother and I took the call. There I was, trapped in the "blue bathroom conveniently located off the kitchen" when the Donaldsons, John and Jacob (possibly brothers, probably not), and Gretchen and Tom peeked in to see me crying on the toilet with my head in my hands—lid down, thank God.

I waved politely, pointed to the phone, and they moved on, kind, house-searching souls that they appeared to be.

"Mom," I whispered as I overheard a very lovely discussion about the cabinets that could be refinished "before the holidays," "did you find out?"

"Just come over," she told me.

Before I can answer, I hear the real estate agent say, "She *loves* this house. *Hates* to leave. She's been like this for weeks."

"Mom, tell me."

"It's fine, honey. Just come over for a while. I want to talk with you anyway. I'll tell you when you get here."

This has happened to me before. It will probably happen again.

When Shaun was five he tried to fly off the top of the swing set one afternoon. I watched him do this. I went to the door to check on him just before I was going to jog to the basement and throw in some wash. It was a Saturday. I could describe every single piece of the entire day—clouds wafting in long rows, Mrs. Sorensen's sheets playing tag with the juniper trees, Shaun screaming with Dustin as they raced across the bars and under the slide and into the sandbox. Then a single instant when the world pierced my heart.

Shaun bragging and me leaning to press my nose against the screen door.

"I can. I can."

"Can what?" I whispered, watching, breathing just a bit faster.

He climbs to the top of the slide and pulls himself across the bar before I can move my hand from the metal hinge on the door to slide it open. I push through the screen, not waiting for it to pop free, and shards of steel cut into my hands, leaving bloody trails like tiny etchings in my white skin. But this I see later.

What I see first is Shaun slipping.

Slipping.

He can but he can't.

When he rolls over the thin metal ledge above the slide, every-thing stops. My heart. My ears. My legs. The world. The whole world.

"Shaun...," I scream.

I know I scream, because I can hear it, and I cannot get there. I cannot catch him or save him. I cannot.

He rolls like a rubber string trying to move back into itself. Arms moving against his side, chin tucked so it touches his chest, hair dipping into the wind, wild and free. When he hits the earth, I feel as if it is me. My heart drops, a shaft of pain digs into my chest, I think it is me who has hit the ground.

There is a swift cry. Air leaving lungs, and me right there, knees in the sand, my hand on his heart, listening, and then screaming for Dustin to run to the phone. "Run," I scream. "Call 911. Go, Dustin!"

Shaun's eyes flicker open. He smiles.

"Mom, did you see me fly?"

"Don't move, baby. Do not even blink."

I hold his legs down, my fingers touching the blunt edge of his spine, and I wish for angels to land at my feet and touch him. I want a miracle, and I want it now. Shaun wants to move his hands. I tell him in a voice he has never heard before and will never hear again that he can only breathe. Nothing else.

His eyes are my eyes. Gray locks of steel that vanish into a bright blue when the light is perfect. He says nothing, but he is listening. He is not moving.

I do what mothers all over the world are doing at the same moment. I offer anything. I beg. I swear that I will sacrifice a lamb and never raise my voice again. I promise that when spring comes I will teach him how to run in the hills and that I will volunteer at the shelter for the rest of my life. I will never swear or drink. I will be faithful to my husband and work two jobs to put my kids through college. I will go back to church.

"Make him be okay," I plead with every god and goddess who ever lived, who lives now, who is being created as I kneel there next to my baby boy.

They take him away so fast, they forget to let me get inside the ambulance. The doors bang shut as they turn the corner, and I am running, running to catch it. Delores picks me up on the run and tells me she will pick up Katie from school. She lives two houses down and flings open the door as I am at a full gait. She does not slow down and we get to the hospital before the ambulance. This is something she tells me twice a week, even now. It was the highlight of her life.

Shaun is not hurt. Just bruised and battered and that is the memory I hold in my hand as I jump into my car and head toward my mother's condo. She is well. She is. She has to be, because I finally have figured out who she is and who I am becoming.

When I storm through her door, she is doing yoga on a mat the size of my pants. I see her body moving, silently, in a way I never imagined.

"Quiet," she says, putting her finger to her lips as if I am a child. Her child. So I sit and I watch and very quickly I realize that my mother has become way too centered and whole and together to have a lump that is a tiny, malicious ball of cancer. She has let go of something harsh and hard that held her in place for so long that a tiny lump formed in her breast. It was her place of sameness and security. She could reach her hand there, just below her heart, and know exactly who she was and what she needed to do next.

I let out a huge puff of air and she gives me one of those, "Damn it, I told you to be quiet" looks. But I do not listen to her silent scolding. I move from the chair to the floor and I put my hands on her head and then move them down so that I am cupping her face.

"I was scared, Margaret. I wasn't sure. I willed it not to be cancer, but I didn't know."

"What did they say?"

"They said do more yoga."

I laugh, but know that is probably exactly what they said. For years my researcher friends and I have felt that stress and living a life without honor and truthfulness, living a life designed by someone else, could cause cancer. We talked about it all the time as we digressed from our intellectual conversations and fanned our thoughts into places where we dissected the inner lives of people we knew who were ill. We seldom talked about ourselves.

"No cancer."

"Pre-cancerous cells. I have to be careful. Go in more often. Tons of mammograms. But…"

She trails off, and I want to know what she is thinking. I desperately want to know.

"But what?"

"Now that the lump is gone, well, I know, I just know it will never come back and that I won't have any other lumps."

"How? Tell me, Mom."

She moves against me and I think that this is the first time in my life I have been strong enough to support her, to hold her weight, to be able to understand and accept anything that she has to tell me. Anything, absolutely anything.

"When your father died, I started to let go. I couldn't do it before, we've talked about this, but every month, every week, I let something else slip away. Does this make sense?"

"Oh yes."

"Maybe it takes some of us longer. Maybe if your father were still alive I'd be dead by now from holding everything inside of me."

"What did you hold inside, Mom, what was it?"

"You know, the pieces of a life that fall away. Your brother… your aunt, my dreams of college… the way you drifted into the same place and made me wish I could have been stronger, could have changed the direction of my own life."

She stops, and I let her have her time. She is gathering up the power to tell me something important. I can feel it rise from below her knees and through her stomach. I can feel it, and when she talks she moves against my head as if it is something magnificent that has been dying, literally dying, to get out.

"I fell in love with someone else."

I am certain my mother can feel my heart accelerate. "Are you serious?"

She laughs, and the very essence of her laugh moves right inside of me, so that I feel as if her hands are dancing against my heart. Who? I want to know who it was. When? What happened? Jesus. Just when you think you know everything.

"It about killed me," she explains, nestling against my own breasts as if I am the mother and she is the child. "You were in high school. Remember those months when I came to work in the office because Mrs. Shompston was ill?"

"Keep going, Mom, get to the good part."

"It was John Halinger."

"Are you kidding me? The football coach? My chemistry teacher? Halinger?"

"Do you want to hear what happened?"

"Go, Mother. Talk."

Breathless. I am breathless inside of a novel that is being written at the edge of my own skin.

She tells me a story so lovely, I close my eyes halfway through the telling of it. He simply came to the office to get his messages, looked at my mother and their hearts jumped, my mother remembers having to grab the desk to steady herself, and Mr. H closed his eyes too, thinking he was dreaming, and when he opened them my mother was still there. They talked. They went out for coffee. He was married, she was married—and they fell in love. Love where you are throwing up and losing weight and where you can't sleep and your whole body is filled with such physical wanting that you forget how to breathe.

"It's the year I lost twenty pounds, started walking at night and cut my hair. Everything changed."

"Did you sleep with him?"

"Everything's about sex to you kids, isn't it?"

She is not laughing when she says this, but then I know that she did sleep with him, and I wonder if she will tell me about it.

"We both knew that we could never be together, that we had family obligations and that we had met the right person at the wrong time. My God, Margaret, it was the first time a man let me hold him and cried and told me every single thing I had ever dreamed a lover would tell me. We did sleep together, damn you, we did, and I have lived on the emotion from those few nights all these years. It has kept me alive. It has."

I wonder if she has tried to find him, and when I ask, she looks astounded.

"I never thought of it," she says, sitting up. "Why? Why have I never thought about that? Could you help me? Maybe, maybe he's still around. He retired. I remember that he retired, but . . . Oh, Margaret, why did I never think of trying to find him again?"

Why, Mother? "Because," I want to say, "we have both been trapped like so many women into believing that Magic doesn't exist. We have stretched our hearts so many times to cover things that we did not want to choose or acknowledge. We have watched our hearts shrink in size so that our chests cave in and we grow lumps in our breasts. We have given away the very power that fuels our souls and keeps our dreams in ovens the size of the Colorado River."

"Mom, if I have learned anything these months, it's that it's never too late. It's never to damn late. You can still look, Mom. You can find him. You can do *anything*."

She turns into me when I talk to her and grabs the sides of my arms as if she is hanging on to the only piece of wood in the middle of an ocean, and I see for the first time that she needs me and she trusts me and I have said something that can help her. My mother needs me. Not to drive her to the hospital or hold her hand, but to give her something truthful.

"Mom," I say, shaking her like a doll. "You have buried people you love, the man you married and your sister, you have raised kids and survived a cancer scare. You have made love to a wonderful man who touched your heart. A man who saw you, truly saw you. You can do yoga and live alone. Add it up. Mom. Count. Should I keep going?"

She looks away, past me and through the window that looks out beyond the driveway, where everything is green and trees the size of small mountains guard her little home.

"Mom?"

"It's wrong for me to be frightened now, isn't it?"

"Never wrong, Mom, it's not wrong."

"I never imagined I could even look for him. Why?"

I grab her close when she asks this. I want to pull my mother inside of me so she can see what I have just learned, what I know now as the truth and what I have chosen as a part of who I am.

"Mom, it's just the past. It's all those years of everyone telling you things and you imagining that they were true because it's all you heard above the roar of your own heart. You know he's out there. You know if you close your eyes you can see him golfing past this very house or picking up coffee at Slanger's down by the freeway or waving to you as he flies off alone to the Bahamas for a few weeks. He's there, Mom. He's always been there: it just took you a while to realize it was okay to go looking for him again."

We talk for a very long time about the things we did because we belonged to a church that told us when to sit and stand or a family that expected us for Christmas even if we really just wanted to stay home and read by the tree. We talk about sacred vows that can only be sacred if you *really* understand what you are saying, and about how obligations can get in the way of reality. We talk about nakedness and about letting go and about how lumps of fear can grow and turn into patterns of life that control every single thing that we do and say but not how we really feel when we stop to take a look.

"Here I thought I was going to be some brave hero for you and help you on this new life," she tells me when we finally gather our twisted arms and legs and stand.

"So?" I ask her.

"So I start calling and then I see," she says, moving her hips in a circle and stretching her hands over her head. A woman unlike my mother. This woman is new. She is.

Then she becomes my mother. She spins me toward the back window, where the garden is in full bloom, in the spot just months ago where I kicked my feet through the dirt when we moved her in and said I doubted if the sun would reach this spot.

"Remember?" she asks now.

"I remember."

"Your life now, it can be only what you want. Think of where you were three months ago. Think. Oh, sweetheart, isn't this all so great?"

We stay in our circle for a very long time, holding hands and dancing into a place that we both acknowledge will not always be easy, but it will be our place. A place we design and no one else. We agree on that. *It will be our place.*

The house sells in an instant. I am not kidding.

The very first couple who came to see it, not the guys, but the short man and the tall woman, write out a check before they leave the living room.

"What?" I say to Golden Dan, the real estate man, who is really Daniel G. Balestreri, a gorgeous Italian man with wide dark eyes who could make me buy back my own home for more than my own asking price.

"They want it. Have cash. Want to know if they can move in…"

He hesitates, and I think he might say "tomorrow," but he doesn't. Two weeks. They are willing to pay an extra $5,000.

"What the hell, Dan—are they your mobster cousins?" Bob asks him as we meet at Dan the Man's office to discuss the offer.

"No, it's the schools."

"You're kidding?" I say, not realizing all the mothers my age have helped turn this school district into one hot property. Parent volunteers. Great teachers. All the building referendums pass because the voters are terrified of what the mothers might do if there are not enough votes to build the new wing of classrooms or to put in a science lab or to purchase new computers.

"Didn't you know?" Danny asks in total seriousness.

Bob and I look at each other as if we have never heard the word *school.* Nope. We did not know. The house, which cost us $92,000, nets us nearly $400,000. That's what Bob and I will split. I want to run to the bathroom but I cannot move. I may have to wet my pants in front of Dan and Bobby.

"Bob, can you help me get out of there?"

He smiles and nods, but I quickly ask Dan to leave. I want to negotiate one more thing. I will not sign unless Bob agrees to put enough money in an account to pay for Katie's undergraduate schooling and to pay off Shaun's student loans. I really want to start over. I don't want to have to ask Bob for another thing. Ever again. Nothing but maybe a dinner every year or maybe not. We'll see.

He agrees. We settle on a price and write up a contract that he says he will have his banker take care of. Before we let Dan back into his office, I ask Bob for a good-bye hug.

"I can't."

"No?"

"It's too hard, Meg. It's harder than I thought it would be. I loved you. I need some time. I'll hug you again, I will, but I can't do it now. I just can't."

Okay. It's all okay. Selling the house is quite a sign, I tell him. It's the end and the beginning and it was—for all those years—it was us. You and I. Bob and Meg and Katie and Shaun. A family. We were not always happy or honest. But we *were*. And we, I tell him softly, holding on to the edge of his sleeve so neither of us will fall, we will always have all those memories and days.

"Take what you want from back there," I say, moving my hands in small circles on his upper arms because I have to touch him. "Sometimes I think what we remember will not be so good, but that was part of it too. I'm going to eventually get to the place where I choose to remember things, like how I never had to shovel the driveway, how much Katie loved to sit on your lap when she was a baby and . . ."

I can't go on. My throat closes up, and he moves his hands to cover mine, and without saying anything he tells me he will try too.

We devise a workable plan. He gets the first week to go in and take what he wants. "Not much," he says. He promises to call if he isn't sure about something he wants to take. I get the second week, and I will need every minute of the first to prepare the apartment, to what? Oh my God. My heart starts to move as if it has left me behind.

"Do you have any idea how much we have to do?" I wail.

This makes him laugh, and he touches me lightly on my arm again. A feather, his fingers not certain.

"Meg, all these years, one thing after another, you never thought you could do it. The babies, your degrees, the house, your father and aunt, Shaun pushing us away. You always questioned yourself, and look where you are right now, look what you have done."

Who is this man? Where has he been? More important, where have I been?

"What are you saying?"

"I'm saying you can do this, damn it, Meg. You can do anything. What do you want to do?"

This time I smile, and I put my head against his long arm even though I know it might make him uncomfortable. I do it because it is what I want, what I need.

"I guess I'm doing it."

He does not move, and I freeze the moment because I know I am not done with my stuff, with his unfaithfulness, with how each of us lingered too long in a place that had grown stale and sad. I want to remember the way he didn't move when I put my head on his arm and how when I shifted my weight just a bit he held me, without moving his hands. I want to remember how he didn't argue about the terms and how he agreed to go first and how he maybe knew me better at the end than at the beginning, when we were so fresh and wild.

When I lift up my head, he turns to look out the window, avoiding a kiss I might have landed on his cheek. I have not been this close to him since the night we had dinner, and before that it must have been months and months, maybe a year since I'd even kissed him or touched him or stood close enough to see if he was wearing cologne. I see how the lines around his eyes have deepened and how the skin under his chin has softened and how his hairline is starting to creep toward the back of his head. I imagine the geranium woman moving her hands alongside of his face and I have to stop myself from telling him that I am glad he has someone, that I think he cannot be alone, that when Geranium leaves, he will quickly find another, because the silence and aloneness would eat him up. He will find that out himself. He will, someday, Bob will know what I now know standing here for the last time in the tired hands of what was once us.

I know too that when we open the door and Dapper Dan comes back in to see our signatures and to count up his commission, that something huge will have shifted. A curtain will drop and everyone will have turned to face a new direction. The seasons will have rotated and the walls in the hall will have mysteriously changed colors. There will be a band in the lobby and the sunset will be pink twenty-six days in a row. Nothing will ever be the same, and that is a wonderful reason to hear new music and let the sky skip across my heart in an entirely new direction.

Before I open the door, while Bob shuffles papers and checks the figures, I say one more thing.

"Bob, I'm not guessing. I'm doing it."

"Oh," he says, not sure for a second what I am talking about.

"I'm doing it," I say one more time and the words become a tattoo, my mantra, the words that will flash in front of my eyes when my knees weaken and I might not be sure.

They become me.

23

I catch the phone a second before the recording clicks in. It is under a pile of towels, below the front steps and behind three sets of bookcases. The house has exploded, and the only things left standing are the walls. There are boxes everywhere. It's my week to recover what I desire to take to my next home, and there is Tomas on the phone. I hear his voice and everything stops.

"Beautiful lady, the doggies miss you."

"Tomas, how are you? Is everything okay?"

He is generous and polite before he gets to the point. His father has slipped into a coma. The doctors promise nothing but weeks and days of waiting for his lungs to fill and his heart to stop. My own heart stops with this news. I reach to steady myself against the bare wall.

"He drifted in and out for days. He talked mostly of your aunt. He whispered and talked for hours and hours. I think that he was going over every precious moment of his life so that he could hold it all one more time before he moved through his 'transition.'"

"His transition?" I ask, wondering how this nice man with the polite voice and the insight of angels has come to be in my life at such a rare and interesting time. Aunt Marcia would tell me it was because I finally "let myself open up." She would be right; she always was.

He laughs and tells me that his father had a dream years ago where a group of men and women dressed in red robes appeared to him and told him that life never really stops and is endless but that we just move from position to position, from one universe and dimension to the next, kind of like a soft transition to a new place.

"Really?"

I say this, and I cannot even believe I am having this conversation with a man from Mexico who helped me dance with the dogs and discover a perfect place to catch a breeze from the jungle, where I came very close to dancing naked. Elizabeth and Bianna would be jealous as hell. I sit down on a box of books and I wonder. I wonder while he takes me through his father's ride from one life to the next, and for a while I leave my own life and levitate. While Tomas and his soft, sweet voice parade over, through and around me, I float above a house I soon won't own and a life that seems to be holding on to me and taking my flailing limbs for a ride, and I remember something vague, a dèjá vu feeling, and while Tomas tells me that the secret of life is really death, my story comes back to me.

Girl Scouts. Camping along the Wisconsin River in a year that I could never remember. Becky and Karen and Barb and Mary Jo and Char and Patty and Gail and all the girls I loved and who laughed at me and told me things that no one else could tell me. All the girls who made me feel as if I belonged to something. We are canoeing and camping and having an adventure that will carry us with this one story through all the years of what we know will be long and interesting and often entwined lives.

Our leader is a woman who never says never and who with great grace and style takes high school girls with hormone levels that cannot be measured by conventional methods out in public and sometimes into wilderness areas where anything can and does happen. This trip is a challenge of strength and wits and survival. It snows and rains. The tents fall in, huge metal poles that were designed by someone who never ever put up a tent bend and twist into a pile, and then we have to canoe through the largest rapids any of us has ever seen.

"Shit," Patty says, standing on the edge of the river shivering like the rest of us. "Look at that bastard."

Patty's father taught her to swear and she in turn taught us. It made us feel strong and tough. We all swore standing there, looking at the water roll over itself and then tumble back into waves of frantic abandon.

"Shit."

"Holy shit."

"Goddamn it."

"Son of a bitch."

We didn't have to ride the rapids, but we *had* to ride the rapids. Who would go first? Not me. Never me. Karen and Barb. They launched the canoe and paddled to the center of the river. We stood in a small group and cheered. They raised their paddles, screamed and shot through the rapids like straight arrows.

Gail tapped me on the arm and said, "Let's go." The water was rough from the beginning and I doubted myself. I sat in the bow because Gail had more experience and because I was a wiener. I wanted to belong but I never took the first step, never took the first paddle and always did what I was told.

I remember water hitting me right away. Sparks of freezing wetness that stung when they flew into my face. It was seconds, maybe five, it was two slow fingers snapping and we hit the second row of boiling waves just inches short of where we should have, and the canoe went airborne.

This was defiantly a transition. I remember the sensation of flying and I let the paddle slip from my hands and I had the presence of mind to suck in a huge wad of air before Gail and I were under the water and being bumped and dragged by rocks that could only be described as small houses and everything floated away from me. There was a light, honest to God, and this small sensation that started in my chest and shoved against me until my lungs, my hands, my heart, my body disappeared and I was letting go so easily, so quickly without a fight, without reaching my hand for the sky. Then other hands reached for me, and just as if someone had slapped me with a long, hard plank, I was out of the water, coughing and back—another transition.

This is what I remember as Tomas tells me his father's story and the excitement of the journey that has now begun. While he talks about the hospital where he is staying and how the winds have kicked up and how the people in the village are still talking about the three American women who knew Marcia, I move my fingers up and down on the sides of the phone just as I would if I had been holding Tomas's hand. My eyes are closed and I ask him where he is standing while we talk.

"In my father's bedroom."

"What can you see?"

"When I lean over I can look out into the ocean and from the window the garden in the back that is slowly preparing for a rest."

"Tomas..."

"What, what is it?"

"My whole life is changing. Everything is new but it all feels comfortable, mostly comfortable."

"Change, if I remember, it looks very good on you, beautiful lady."

He's flirting and I love it but I am trying to tell him something beyond the attraction that has been building since we met. I want to tell him that I cannot come now. I cannot. I want to, it would be the kindest thing to do for him, for my aunt, for his father, but not for me. When the words come out I have to concentrate.

"Tomas, I cannot come now."

He is silent. I think he must have dropped his head and he is now looking at his feet. He is disappointed.

"I'm sorry," I say quietly.

"Listen, you," he begins. "I wanted you to come for me. My father said and did what he needed to do. I will be fine. I understand. I do understand."

"Tomas, I will come when I can stay for a while. I have to finish this part of my own transition."

I keep him on the phone for a long time. I tell him how I had said yes my entire life and how it became a word without thought or emotion to me. In a strange way knowing that I can say no, that I can do what I need to do, what I have to do has become a huge gift to myself.

"I am smiling," he tells me, and I am thinking that if I were there now, in his father's bedroom, I might lie down and ask Tomas to let me hold him. I do not need to be held just then but he does. "You sound good."

"I am good, Tomas. I am."

When we finally hang up I have a very hard time moving. Not going to Mexico just now, not rushing off to rescue Tomas and to touch my fingers to his father's face one more time is huge. Dr. C has helped me understand why I used to think it was easier to say yes. She has walked me through the social channels and past huge islands of disappointment and an isthmus of guilt. She has walked me backward for a while, showing me the movie of my life in reverse so that I can see exactly what happened and not what I simply think happened. She has also been pointing me toward a place of no apologies, a wide-open plain that barks out the days of my life so that I can take what I want and leave what I don't.

"It's your life, Meggie," she has said over and over. "Not your mother's or your husband's or your children's or your employer's or the church's or the woman begging on the street. Yours, all yours."

She is right and I know it now more than ever, but that does not keep me from crying throughout the rest of my afternoon before my mother and two of her friends and my wonderful neighbors come to help me finish boxing up this finished portion of my life.

Bob has taken some furniture, nothing from the kitchen, lots of tools, and I find missing holes in some of the walls where he has taken one photograph, a picture Shaun drew in kindergarten, a family photograph. I reach out and touch all the empty spaces, moving my fingers in a perfect square where one memory had been and then another.

There is a soft echo in the house that seems to grow louder and louder as rooms empty and boxes fill and the pile I have started by the back door grows deep and long.

"Shit," I say out loud. "Where did all this shit come from?"

I have a hard time moving my detailed operation from the living room and kitchen and into the bedrooms. Those spaces remain intimate segments of my life in this house, I explain to the refrigerator while I take a break with a beer on the kitchen counter. I want to have the house organized in piles before the gang shows up to help me with the final destruction of 2357 South Calvin Street. I also want part of the day alone to pick through the pieces without the heavy breath of a daughter or mother or friend on my neck saying, "Oh, don't you want *that*?"

I am finding that I want very little, hardly anything at all. I'm beginning to wonder who picked out the couch and the green chairs and that ugly metal bookcase. What was I thinking? I want to really start over is what I think as I look around at all my "stuff" that has the breath and life and fingerprints of someone else, someone who is gone, someone who has changed clothes and had plastic surgery.

Before I finish the first beer and while I am sitting on top of the counter, I call St. Vincent de Paul, not the real guy but the people who own the store, and ask them how they feel about lots of furniture and dishes and garden hoses. They feel just great, and we make a deal that they will come over tomorrow morning at nine A.M. and take my green chairs, and boxes of paring knives and empty flower vases, so that families and single women and men starting over from one end of Chicagoland to the other can get cranking on their new lives too.

I do pretty well until I get upstairs and realize that Bob has taken so little from the bedroom. His clothes are gone, the tiny wooden jewelry case Katie gave him last Christmas, shoes, the books that he always kept on top of the short dresser by the window—and nothing else. I know I don't want the bedspread, which should probably just be burned, or the bed or the dressers that I think we may have purchased from St. Vinnie's the first time around. I make a note on my directions sheet to just take the clothes, and then I back out of the door, making certain I do not touch anything. I turn to go into Katie's room next but then I turn back and close the bedroom door. I don't want to look. I can't. Maybe I'm not as close to my new defined self as I think I am, but even a woman who has been through several transitions in one week—well, even she has limits. I give myself permission for this and the permission feels perfect. I will never open that door again. Such power.

I discover that Katie has already packed. When? Yesterday when I was at work? Last night with her father? She's been gone all day organizing materials at school for her trip and she's been staying with me at Elizabeth's while her father moves and the painters ravage my new apartment. She has left me a note on top of her dresser. I am weak in the knees and have to sit down when I read it.

Mom, I thought you might want to be alone and I kind of wanted to be alone to pack my room also. Let's keep the futon. I remember when you got it for my birthday and it still makes me happy. If we can afford it, maybe I could get a new chair and dresser for your new house. The boxes on the left go—the ones on the right stay and my things for Mexico are at Jaime's house. I'm flying, Mom, and I know you are too. I want you to remember that this is best for me and it's best for you. I had to bag up my own memories—and just so you know, I've decided to leave the bad ones in the closet. Do not open the door. I'll know if you do. I love you, Mommie. Katie

I make it to the bed before I really begin to miss her. Katie's empty pillow smells like Happy. That is the only perfume she will wear, and I bury my head in the pillow and rock myself as if I am holding her. My baby. My girl. My woman.

Oh, Katie. Oh.

I cry not for what we are losing but for what we have gained. Would I have known my daughter like this if I had stayed? Would she have reached out to hold my hand and then all of me on the porch? Would I ever have given her the chance to do something for me? To pack her own clothes, make her own way, write me a mature note that I will never destroy?

Any mother's world, I know, is riddled with doubt and anticipation and questioning and failure. I will always feel as if I have failed Shaun, even if and when we reconcile. It is a slight cross to bear, one that can be set down when the time is right. And Katie, who is as wise and wonderful and stubborn and beautiful as anyone I have ever known, has turned into a Magical gift that overshadows every shouting match and missed curfew and wrecked bumper and flying shoe.

I want to know, as the snot drips off my nose, if this is how it is. Do mothers just get to know who their daughters are the day before they leave? Do we hold them and feed them and listen and walk them to the bus and then simply turn them loose? Do we?

It was my Aunt Marcia who turned me loose after the feeding frenzy, driving me hours away from home to college, because she said my mother couldn't bear to do it. What do I remember about that? Thinking, I suppose, that my mother didn't care, that she had to stay home and cook for my father, that they would turn my bedroom into a den the second I left. Did I miss it? Did I miss my own mother lying on the bed and crying as she watched the taillights flicker and then vanish as we turned the corner? Did I think that she simply carried on and never missed the way I always banged the door shut and never closed the kitchen cupboards and forgot to change my sheets? Did I think she didn't miss coming in at night when she thought I was sleeping, not to touch me, but to push back my hair, she always touched my hair.

Oh, Mom.

Oh, Mommie.

That is who finds me with my head under Katie's pillow, stretched out like a wailing widow.

"Relapse?" she says, which makes me laugh and is exactly what I need.

The yoga queen is standing in the doorway wearing a pair of bike shorts, a NOW T-shirt with flowers on it and running shoes. I like this woman.

She reads Katie's note, bends down to kiss me and to run her fingers through my hair, just as I remember, and I catch her hand, hold it to my lips, kiss her fingers, and I say, "I love you, Mom."

Before she answers, she looks at me. Not just at me but into me. Hard, past my gray eyes lightened by all the crying and into a place way beyond that. She's thinking, remembering something, and she tells me she loves me too.

"I know, Mom. I know you love me and always did. I know now."

I know, Mom.

Elizabeth and her friend Terry go with me to check out the apartment when the painters call to say they are finished. Terry is an interior decorator who helped us pick out the colors and who has this great idea for what I am supposed to buy—"simple, modern"—to fill up the rooms that will surround my new life. A decorator is a luxury I decide to embrace, a gift to myself, something I would never have considered a year ago.

We open the doors slowly and that smell of new paint fills my head before we step inside. The polished wooden floors glisten and we take off our shoes and enter as if we are walking into some wonderful holy place.

"Well, it is holy!" Elizabeth says loudly. "I don't even want to imagine what might be happening in this space during the coming year. The possibilities have me shaking, just shaking."

"Elizabeth, drama becomes you."

The rooms are absolutely glorious. I did not want to have one wall of white anywhere. The living room is red. The bedroom is purple, green halls, kitchen as blue as the ocean off my Mexican home, just as I wanted it, and even though I have always hated yellow, that is what I wanted in my bathroom, and Katie picked black for hers and that's what she got.

Terry is clearly smitten with the place. I have decided to do something more lavish than I ever have in my life. I am giving her money to buy me new furniture and set up most of the apartment. This was my mother's idea. She reminded me that I have a job, that I need to iron out that part of my life, get my daughter off to Mexico, go to Mexico, settle my papers ... well, clearly I have no time to shop for a bed or rugs for the floor or carrots for the refrigerator.

"Work," Elizabeth says, as the three of us sit in the middle of my floor making a list of what Terry will be allowed to buy. "Have you gotten to that part yet?"

I swallow hard. Damn Elizabeth. She knows that will be next. She knows I have burned both ends of that professional wire right to the middle. She knows that if I can travel this far I can finish the trip.

"A little, Elizabeth," I lie, because I have been thinking about it as much as possible in between packing and crying and drinking beer at kitchen counters.

Terry wants to talk about fabrics, which is about as much fun for me as poking a stick in my eye and taking a driving test. She's a sweetheart, who I instantly claimed as a friend when Elizabeth introduced us. She wears big earrings and has refused to give up her brightly colored tights and big shirts from the '90s. She also has a tattoo snaking up her neck and into her hair, which is something I have never, ever seen on an interior decorator—or any other human being, for that matter. This woman should decorate everyone's home.

"I want it to look funky and not, well, I don't know how to say this ... ," I say.

Elizabeth does, of course.

"She's starting over. It's a bold move. Let's go with the wild colors we already have plastered all over the walls. Nothing extravagant, because I don't think you'd spend a ton of money on 'stuff,' would you?"

I'm smiling. Nope, I wouldn't. Terry writes it all down and then races off to measure things that I would never in a million years think to measure.

"The job?" Elizabeth reminds me.

"I have a few ideas. Can you let me rest on it and then we'll talk when I get in here? I think I've reached my limit this month on big life changes."

Elizabeth laughs.

"You are just starting. Once you see how glorious change is, you won't be able to stop yourself."

"You think?"

"I *know.*"

Terry bounces back into the room just after Elizabeth tells me that on Friday night, before one single thing can be moved into the apartment, we must have a spiritual cleansing of the space. She instructs me to invite women who know my heart, who honor me, who love me.

"Give me a list and I'll call them. It will be the first party here, one of the best, and it will signal the beginning of your life in a space that is yours, all yours and free of any clutter that might have occupied it before."

What if I said no?

Elizabeth dismisses that with a wave of her hand that makes Terry laugh. She knows no one says no to Elizabeth. There's absolutely no reason to say no.

I leave the apartment last, lock the beautiful wooden door with a key. It is my key, and when I slip it into my pocket it feels as if there is a warm, inviting hand on my thigh.

24

1997

The parade of students and professors and office staff coming and going out of Carol Kimbal's office had been endless for weeks. Kimbal, as she loved to be called by her students, was heading west. Destination Unknown. Leaving. Packing up her twenty-three years' worth of books and photographs and handing out her collection of coffee mugs like Christmas gifts from the goddess of the literary world—which is exactly what Dr. Carol Kimbal was and would always be to hundreds of lovesick, drooling admirers.

Faculty members were beyond astounded when Kimbal, who had penned such literary works of genius while employed at the University as *Women Raging—A Historic Look at the Feminine Genius* and *Dumping Testosterone,* which was a funky coffee table book penned and photographed with the notion that women should never ever actually live with men, was leaving.

Her books, five and counting, brought Kimbal more than national respect and notoriety and interest, they threw her into feminist circles with the likes of Gloria Steinem and Jane Fonda and made scads of money for the University Press and a bit for Kimbal herself.

The words *Kimbal is leaving* spread throughout the campus as if a plague had erupted in the main cafeteria. The *Chicago Tribune* ran a full-page story about her in its Sunday magazine. Students actually wept in front of her door, and her department chairman offered her an outrageous sum if she would stay, just stay, on campus. No teaching, just a place for her to write, to remain a part of the University, to be, *be* The Dr. Kimbal of the University of Chicago.

Kimbal would not budge. "It's time to move to new arenas," she told the *Tribune* reporter. "Chicago is in my heart, always will be, but I don't think a woman has to pick something—or someone, for that matter—and stick with it the rest of her life. My God, the world is full of promise and places and people and experiences that are dying to be explored."

Kimbal, it seems, was living her life exactly how she preached it in her classes, which were a witty combination of inspired writing techniques, studying the classics and empowering women and men, if they could stand the sexism, to go to places personally and professionally with their writing and lives that they had never imagined.

Private with her personal life, Kimbal had not disclosed her next destination. Rumors throughout Chicagoland had her breaking up with a female lover, sleeping with the male chancellor, moving to Paris, living in a teepee in Colorado and changing her name and moving to Boise, Idaho.

None of the rumors were true, as Assistant Professor Meg Callie Richardson discovered when she walked past Kimbal's office, found Kimbal alone, slipped inside and closed the door.

"Margaret," Kimbal said, smiling, shuffling through a stack of papers and pausing to greet someone she had always considered a friend.

Meg sits in the wide chair next to the window. She wants to say good-bye, wants to know something, wants also one of the coffee cups she hears are being passed out as "I know Kimbal" souvenirs.

"I came by for a cup and a final good-bye."

"That's nice, but you don't have to say good-bye. I'm not dying. We're professional colleagues and I've always admired your work, how you interact with students and this boorish faculty. I like you, Meg."

Meg is astounded. Her sociology papers have been shared with all the faculty members and she's won a few minor awards herself, but she's never imagined someone like Kimbal taking notice.

"Listen..." Kimbal gets up to lock the door and moves a chair over to sit next to Meg. "Can you talk a bit?"

"I think I can squeeze you in, Carol," she says, laughing.

They talk at first about the University, and Meg can quickly see that Kimbal just wants to have a normal conversation. No admirers. No "Please don't go"s. Just a lovely, long conversation.

Meg gives it to her. She leans in toward the window and stretches her legs up, pushes her shoes off, takes a cup of coffee from the pot on the desk and they talk. They talk about salaries and Chicago politics and how feminism has taken it in the chops and how the younger women, their students, have given them great hope with their wild ideas and their carrying the torch and believing they can make a difference. They waltz through an update on Meg's kids, and she shares the story about the loss of her son, who Kimbal promises will eventually find his way back home.

"Are you tired, Carol?"

Carol smiles and puts a hand on Meg's foot.

"Exhausted. I am totally exhausted."

"Where are you going?"

"Meg, I have some things to say to you, and I'm going to tell you where I'm going. I know you won't say a word."

Meg holds her breath. She's read the books and listened to the lectures and had dinner in the conference rooms with other published professors and the great Kimbal. She had no idea, not a clue, that Dr. Carol Kimbal knew she was more than alive and simply breathing to stay that way.

"I'm a good girl," Meg tells her. "No one would believe I was sitting in here anyway, talking so openly to the campus goddess."

"That's what I want to talk with you about, but I also want to tell you what I'm going to do."

Meg leans forward now, pushing against the back of the chair with her arms because she wants to get closer. Kimbal dresses as if it is still 1963. She wears cotton skirts and long silver earrings and scarves that are as bold as the words she writes. She has huge blue eyes and skin that has kept its place for fifty-three years, and Meg thinks that she is beautiful. Beautiful because the energy she has given to her work and what comes from her is fine and wise and full of something that Meg can only see as pure.

They talk for almost two hours. There are knocks on the door and the phone rings, but they go unanswered. The story is as remarkable as Kimbal herself, and Meg whispers to herself that she wants to remember every word, every moment.

"A long time ago, I had a baby," Carol tells her. "It's true what you hear about me now," she explains, laughing for the first and last time in the conversation. "I live with a woman, she is my lover and partner, but before that, long before that, when I was a girl really, I had a baby that I gave away."

Carol stops for a moment. She reaches behind her to pull out a bottle of Scotch from her almost empty desk drawer. Without asking, she pours a glass for herself and one for Meg. The whiskey moves from lips to throat, burning out any hesitation. Meg cannot ask her enough questions and Dr. K needs to talk.

"I don't really care what people say about me," she explains, "but this one thing, this lost son, it's been a deep and horrible ache throughout my entire life."

Horrible, Meg discovers, because Dr. Carol Kimbal was raped when she was seventeen by an uncle. Every story, every word of what women like Dr. Kimbal have fought against spilled out in a story that made Meg ask for more Scotch before the story was finished. "Jesus," Meg thinks. "Jesus."

Her parents sent her away. She had the baby and was made to give him up and then come back and act as if she had been on a vacation.

"It has been the one horrid lie of my life. My partner helped me find him. I found my son."

The professor closes her eyes and Meg reaches out to touch her hand. Meg wonders how many times her friend has talked about her loss like this. She knows about lost sons and as she holds Carol she cries too for the loss of her own boy, a man now, who ran away and whom she will one day find again also. She has to. She has to find her son.

"You are going to live near your son, aren't you?" Meg asks.

Kimbal nods.

"There's more."

"Of course there is," Meg adds, which makes them both laugh.

"You won't believe it."

"After this? Are you kidding? You could tell me you are going to be a stripper and I wouldn't think it was unusual."

Kimbal is moving to Northern California to open a restaurant in wine country with her partner and her son.

"Wow."

Wow indeed, Kimball tells her. She'll write, she has to write, but she'll also wait on tables, clean the bathrooms, do some marketing, and she'll drink wine every afternoon.

So different, Meg thinks, so different from the world of academia and lectures and writing up a syllabus that you will never follow anyway.

"You are surprised."

"Yep, I lied."

This part is for you, Kimbal tells her. Listen now, Meg, listen. And Dr. Carol tells her another story.

"You know that I admire your work, but you are terribly unhappy. Everything about you, the way you walk and dress and how many hours you put in here when you don't really need to be here—it's very telling."

Meg wants another drink but she knows she'll never be able to drive home if she has one. What the hell, she thinks, what the hell, but she cannot speak.

"I would have come to find you, Meg, if you hadn't come in to see me. You have to know that you don't have to do this."

"This?"

"Yes, this. This work, this kind of life. You can do anything, be anyone. I get so pissed off at the world because it tells us to get a job and then keep it for fifty years. There is no fucking rule, Meg, that says we can't open up restaurants or find our heart or leave the men or women we live with. None of it has to be."

"None of it," Meg repeats, as if she is in a trance.

They both have another drink anyway. Carol is on a roll. Meg

wants to be on a roll, she does. She wants to absorb every word
and then be able to reach inside herself and touch them when
she needs to remember, when she needs to be honest, finally be
honest.

"Tell me right now, if you could pick something else to do,
what would it be?"

Meg does not hesitate. The words come right out of her in a
place where she has been storing words and uncashed gift cer-
tificates and dreams of which she has never been able to speak.

"A massage therapist."

Dr. Carol Kimbal sloshes back another drink and laughs.

"Oh, Meg, I knew it. I knew something was there that you
were thinking about that you have wanted to try to do. I knew it,
and that's perfect for you, perfect."

Carol takes Meg's hands, which are strong and hard and made
for touching, and she pushes them together. "It's hard, Meg, at
first it's a little hard even if you are brave and wild like me."

Meg cannot even finish a sentence. It's the booze, but it's also
the wanting, a small seed of wanting that has now been given its
first dose of sunlight and will never be happy until it gets more,
all it wants, all it needs.

"You have to decide that. You do. Think about it, let it come to
a place in your heart that keeps you up at night and makes it impossible for you to concentrate and makes you want to dance."

Meg tells her she sees now why women fall to their knees in
front of her office and why her classes have huge waiting lists
and why people buy her books and why the entire University is
in a state of mourning.

"I just put it out there," Kimbal says, dismissing the idea of
her greatness, of others thinking she is some sort of prophetic
goddess. "Anyone can go to the same place. You can go to the
same place, Margaret."

They talk until they both pass back to the clear side of drunkenness. Meg asks her about the restaurant and promises to visit when she is on a break from her massage patients, and just before she manages to wobble to the door and toward the cafeteria coffee, she promises that she will call Kimbal the minute she starts to dance spontaneously.

"I'll call," she promises. "I will."

When she leaves, Dr. Carol Kimbal leaves the door open and watches her friend weave her way past the front office and out the door.

"Hurry up, baby," she whispers, throwing a kiss after Margaret. "Hurry up."

25

The furniture comes when I am at the garden center. I know when it is supposed to arrive, but there is a huge sale at a wonderful boutique I have discovered, along with coffee shops, and terrific restaurants, and a park where I will once again play tennis, and bars where I have only seen women and other bars where there are men dressed as women and women dressed as men and couples of every shape and size. I have a hard time shopping for my apartment because I cannot stop window-shopping all the faces in my new neighborhood.

After several weeks of work, and some very interesting bills, Terry tells me it is now safe for me to come open the door into my new world, because the apartment, her portion anyway, is finished. My boxes of clothes and books and the few mementos that I have saved from the past will be delivered from Elizabeth's garage tomorrow. I am anxious. Ready. Excited. Disbelieving.

Katie has been gone three days and it feels as if she has been gone forever. When I push my hand against my chest, I can feel an ache that travels right through me and comes out the other side. It has been just over a month since the house sold, since the attorney wrangled us a fabulous deal and I signed a series of papers that will change everything from my marital status to my last name. My sweet daughter left in a blur of excitement and I was delighted to find her father waiting at the ticket counter when I went with her and three other students to check in at the airport.

"Bob," I say.

"Hey."

"Daddy, thanks for coming."

Katie is clearly happy to see him, and I back off for a moment while they talk and I see him hand her some money, a phone card, and then kiss her on the lips in front of her friends. When she reaches up to wipe a tear from his eye, I think for just a second about all the years we shared, a thousand hugs, and this new kind of good-bye. I want to put my hand on the side of his face and feel a tear, but I don't. I can't. The moment passes quickly and leaves me almost giddy with embarrassment.

When we leave our daughter at the gate, I turn to hug him and he tells me he is going away for a month with a friend.

"I'll have my phone if you or Katie need anything. Shaun knows too."

I don't ask him where he is going or who he is going with. It's his life; the place where ours now touches just got on the airplane.

"Have a terrific time," I tell him as I squeeze his arm. "Terrific."

Then he is gone and Katie is gone and I am alone. Alone.

Alone and totally comfortable. One foot in front of the other, turning my head to look at a man with attractive hair on the telephone, nodding to a woman struggling with a small baby, smiling at a stewardess. Alone. My daughter going off in one direction, my soon to be ex-husband disappearing into another woman's arms. Alone. Happy.

"I'm alone," I end up singing to myself all the way back to

Elizabeth's house. "I'm alone...a-l-o-n-e." The song is familiar. I love how it feels at the back of my throat as I bring the words to life.

People in passing cars must hear me. They surely hear me at the stop signs once I get off the freeway. I don't care. They need to know that I'm alone. Everyone needs to know it and then see me singing so they know I am happy.

The happiness just doesn't seem to end. My attorney calls the following day to say the divorce will be final before the end of October, and Tomas calls right after that to tell me that his father is still half delirious and sitting up in the middle of the night, speaking in whole sentences.

"'The wind in August will dance like fire when the night steals into our day,' he says or 'I held you close and soft remembering that every moment was a balanced, generous gift of time.'" Tomas says he is writing down his father's phrases to use at his funeral, which he will not call a funeral but a celebration of life.

"But he may go on like this for days and weeks and months, in which case I may need several assistants, because what he is saying is absolutely beautiful, it's poetry," he tells me.

"Maybe it's all the unspoken words he kept in his soul," I say.

"What?"

"The unspoken words he kept in his soul."

"My God," he shouts.

"What?" I ask him, just like he asked me.

"That's the title of the book."

"What is the title of the book?"

"The Unspoken Words He Kept in His Soul."

"You're kidding."

"Say them to yourself. They are as beautiful as the words my father is saying when he sits up without help and speaks as clearly as we are speaking right this moment."

There you have it. My first book title in just seconds. Tomas makes me laugh and says that when I am ready for my break after I am settled, he will pick me up at the airport and shuttle me to my house by the ocean and to see my daughter.

"The way my father is going, he will still be alive."

Maybe, I tell him, maybe.

And maybe I can change the world and make everything hurry. I cannot sit still. I have not been able to sit still. I want to run from point A to point B and then start all over again at a faster pace. Dr. C tells me this makes sense.

"It's like a thirsty horse that smells water in the desert," she told me during our last session. "You've had a taste of who you are becoming and you want to drink until you fall over."

Then she warns me. I hate this part. The warnings drive me crazy.

"We are all becoming every day, but people get hung up when they think that what we want today is going to be what we want tomorrow and the day after."

"What do you mean?" I ask her, thinking that now that I had taken three giant steps forward I am close to where I am supposed to be.

She tells me a story to help me out. It is a story about carpeting, she says.

"Carpeting?"

"Listen, Margaret. Listening to yourself is what this story is all about."

Once upon a time Dr. C's sister wanted carpeting. She knew that if she got carpeting, new carpeting for her house, that everything would be better. The sister had given up her job, a profession she adored, to stay home and raise her babies, and she loved that job too, but she was also miserable on many days, especially when the babies were taking naps and she could sit for five minutes and look out the window and remember how alive she felt when she was following her other passion.

"A few streets over, there was another woman who suffered from the same malaise," Dr. C tells me. "This woman also had two babies and had once been an artist who painted for hours in a studio in the city. Her babies exhausted her and she could no longer paint."

I start asking questions, interrupting as if I am a pre-schooler and can't wait for the end of the story.

"Were they good mothers?"

"Were their husbands kind?"

"Why didn't the men stay home?"

"Did she ever paint again?"

Dr. C finally leans over and puts her hand over my mouth.

"You are not listening, Meg. Do you want me to send you to your room?"

I finally shut up. The two unhappy women, who often drink beer together for lunch, walk to the park with the babies and then light candles and tell wild stories about what they did in college and how many lovers they had and who had the biggest penis. They tell these stories while the babies grow and begin to become friends too and then the two friends get this idea that if they could only get cranking on their house projects and get new carpeting, they will be happy. They know it as sure as they know that they could never trade the sweet morning touch from their daughters' tiny hands or their sons' feet warm against their bellies or the way they continue to check on the babies in the middle of the night every single time they get up to go to the bathroom or cannot sleep.

"They get the carpeting," Dr. C tells me, leaving her hands close to my mouth just in case. "My sister gets the blue carpeting because she thinks it will warm up the house and keep her company. The artist goes for a soft beige, the color of her favorite canvases just before she puts her brush to the paint for the first time."

They use the same carpet installers and they toast and celebrate as first one house and then the other is completed, and the carpeting is definitely magnificent. It stretches from room to room and it's as if they have started everything over again. New. Fresh and clear. The carpeting is everything they hoped it would be.

"But?"

Dr. C laughs. "Do you know that two months ago you would never have interrupted me. Now you sure are."

I know I should feel as if I have been given a great compliment from a powerful and very astute woman but I need to know what happened. I almost fall off the chair from the needing.

"Well, it's not enough. One day, months later, they are sitting at the artist's table while the babies all nap in one great pile in the bedroom, and their hands stretch across the table until their fingers touch, and they both say at the same time, 'It wasn't the carpeting.'"

It wasn't the carpeting.

I know what it is, and I finish the story, much to Dr. C's delight.

"It was the carpeting, but then the walls needed to be done, and your sister thought about what a fabulous vacation she could have taken for the price of the carpeting, and then there was another need and another want," I almost shout out.

"Exactly. So?"

I want to know what happened to the artist and the sister, but I know she has another point to make. Damn this therapy. I just want to hear the story.

"Tell me," I ask, back to being the student.

"The carpeting was okay, everything was okay. We change every day. Be open to change, Meg. Be open to what comes and goes and how the rhythm of your heart may change and move in many directions. Wherever it goes, it's okay. You are okay. Someday you might wake up and no longer want coffee with cream in it. What the hell. Don't let where you are hinder where you are going to be tomorrow."

What the hell indeed.

She tells me eventually, weeks later, because I am driving her nuts, that the artist threw away her brushes and turned to throwing pots because she felt she wanted something larger, something she could feel and touch in a way she never felt from the painting. Dr. C's sister divorced, went back to school, got a degree in social work and is now working in the inner city with the people most of the rest of the world would rather ignore— the men and women who are HIV positive, the drug-addicted mothers, the men who lost control of their minds and lives and who refuse to take their medication. She lives in a tiny apartment by herself, and it does not have carpeting. Both women are happy. Well, that specific week they were happy.

There is not one piece of carpeting in my new apartment. That is what I am thinking after I hang up the phone and throw Tomas a kiss across all the miles that separate us.

My last night at Elizabeth's, she plans a meal and we cook together in the kitchen. I am happy, imagining the nights she will spend with me when she is in the city, and I tell her I have already begun to design a trap to lure her into buying or renting a home in my neighborhood.

"I have the money," I say. "We could buy a place like the one I will be living in and start a little suburban commune."

"I've already thought about that," she admits.

"Really?"

"Yep. Still thinking. I don't need all this space, and you've given me the itch to make a few changes myself. How's that for switching roles?"

We wander back to her living room and I end up on the futon, where I thrashed uncontrollably and threw myself around just a few months ago.

"Did you think I was nuts?" I ask Elizabeth as she moves her legs to either side of mine so that our limbs are a tangled mass of ankles and knees and toes.

"Sure you were. Nothing made sense. You couldn't even remember how to turn on the car."

"But was I crazy really?"

"I've always thought that people who fight their feelings, who don't give in to the sorrow or anger or love or lust, can never really experience any of those emotions."

"Makes sense," I say, sipping my tea. "A couple of examples?"

Elizabeth tells me that she had a dear friend who had a phobia about taking her clothes off. The woman had been touched inappropriately when she was a little girl by two different men and had never gotten over what that felt like. She had never properly grieved or mourned or gotten angry as hell about what had happened to her. This woman could not believe that anyone wanted to touch her because she was loved. Trust? It was a word that did not exist for her.

"She talked about her clothes constantly, would never shower in front of anyone on trips, had lovers disappear because she hated undressing in front of them. She did make love, but it was always with great fear, under a sheet, with the lights off. She was totally ruled by those two incidents her entire life."

"Why didn't she get help?"

"I think any decent psychologist or counselor will tell you that you have to surrender to your fears and let them wash over you before you can get rid of them. My friend couldn't do that. Letting go of what happened was so terrifying, she chose to live with her sorrow and anger rather than give it up."

"So you telling me I really was about to lose my mind was just me surrendering to my sorrow and anger at myself for what I gave up, what I didn't do, all the things that made me at least peer over the cliff for a while?"

Elizabeth is smiling and pushing her toes into my thigh. "Exactly."

"What could have happened?"

"Well, look around. That's the easy question. How many unhappy women do you know?"

"Way too many, but I also know pretty many happy ones."

"Like Jane now—almost—and Bianna?"

"Yes."

"See, you have to surrender. Deal with what they had to deal with, wallow in it for a while, then get up and walk away. Gradually all the pieces that are still clinging to you fall away, vanish, disappear."

She's right. My mind whisks through the women I know who are happy, and every single one of them has come through the eye of a storm, mostly whole, changed, moving forward. Skinned alive, some of them, and barely breathing, but they made it. They came out alive.

"If they don't surrender to their own form of madness, nothing changes, does it?"

"Exactly. That's why you see couples arguing in their cars and men and women having affairs and goofy-ass doctors handing out Prozac like it's candy to women who can't quite take their clothes off when they make love."

"And what if I hadn't surrendered so quickly?"

"Well, let's see, this morning you'd be doing Bob's wash and then calling me to go to lunch and then you'd be sitting home alone with your feet propped up by your old desk the same way you propped them up for the past ten years almost every Saturday night while you were waiting for one of the kids or Bob to come back home."

"I was waiting."

"Yes, you were."

We talk for hours, which is what women do. Talk even though they have talked for days and weeks and years before. I hold Elizabeth's hand and thank her and let her know every twenty seconds that I would fling myself off a bridge for her. She knows this already, but women do this too. They tell each other. Always and over and over, because these things are so nice to hear and so wonderful to say. She wants to know what I am going to do tomorrow, the first day alone in my new home with my new life backed up against me and ready to climb over my back and right off the top of me.

"I can't tell you."

She laughs. That golden, deep sound that makes me close my eyes and think that those Catholics or Lutherans or Mormons have no idea what Heaven is like until they all have heard Elizabeth laugh.

"You can't tell me?" She sits up. Fakes looking astounded. Holds her hands to her chest.

"No, but I'll show you when you come over for my first real dinner in my new home on Sunday."

"That's better."

"But I have one more thing to tell you that I haven't shared with anyone."

She sits up fast. The hands go down. She's terribly quiet. I haven't spoken this out loud yet. I cannot wait to hear what it will sound like.

"I'm going to quit my position at the University. I am still working out the details, quietly, because they'll have someone in my chair before I leave the room if I'm not careful, and I have to figure out a few more things first, but it won't be long. I am going to leave."

"What? What the hell are you going to do?"

This is so much fun, I want to string it out for a while, but Elizabeth grabs my hands and holds them so tightly that I cannot breathe.

"Tell me before I pop you," she threatens.

"Ready?"

The hands clamp me harder.

"I'm going to go back to school to become a massage therapist. I'll open my own studio down where I live, offer funky services, walk to work, eventually maybe have a studio where I live."

"It's perfect, my God, it's perfect."

Then she turns over my hands and runs her fingers up and down my veins and across my palms and reminds me how I have always been a toucher.

"I know."

I say "I know" so many times that Elizabeth puts her hand over my mouth and I kiss her fingers, all the while thinking that within a few months I will be able to rub the soreness and sadness out of her fingers, anyone's fingers, the limbs of the entire exhausted world.

The truck from the garden store is waiting for me in the driveway.

"Damn it," I shout to myself, angry because I do not understand the tempo of driving life in the city. I'm shouting. I never shout—well, almost never.

I park behind the big red truck because the street is packed with cars, as I imagine it will be the entire time I live here. The two men are thumping on the hood of the truck.

"Hey," the big one yells. "Where do you want this stuff?"

I stop yelling. Right then. I stop.

"How long have you been here?" I ask as I look up into the big guy's face.

He steps back. Most people, I already know, are so elated when anyone in the city actually shows up to do what they say they are going to do, they pretty much bend over, but I paid for this shit. That's what I'm thinking. These guys are working for me.

"Five minutes," he answers.

"That's worth a six-pack in the backyard when we are done. Let's go. Follow me."

The rocks cost me almost as much as my living room furniture. The two men from the garden store are pissed. No one orders quite this many rocks, but I tell them right away that besides the beer there is a tip if they can shut up and just haul the rocks.

"Just haul them," I plead. "See how beautiful they are."

I say this as I am rubbing one against my face, and then I hold it out to them as if I have just turned one loaf of bread into twelve.

"Okay, lady," they finally say, looking just a bit frightened.

I know they want to know what in the hell I am going to do with them, but it's my secret, my rocks, my life. I'm guessing they have helped haul stones for backyard ponds and sidewalks, but the flat, river-bottom kind of rocks that we are moving from the truck to the backyard are absolutely beautiful. They will not touch water from a lake, river or sea or be stepped on. They will not.

I work for about fifteen minutes with them and then it dawns on me that I am paying them and they can probably haul rocks alone. I have not even bothered to look inside of my apartment.

The key to my house is as warm as my skin. It has been tucked in my shorts pocket, and when I take it out, I press it against my face and it brings back a memory of my first apartment. College. Sophomore year. A studio so small that I had to sleep in the closet when I lost the coin toss and my friend Lynn got the far side of the only other room we shared besides the bathroom. It was one of the most remarkable and wonderful years of my life. A first taste of freedom that slipped away from me way too fast.

My tennis shoes come off easily and I leave them by the front door, and then in a moment that I can only describe as pre-Christmas-like excitement, I close my eyes and step inside.

Wow, Meg. Wow.

The apartment is beautiful. I am dead. I think I am dead, and turn immediately to look in the small mirror that Terry has hung by the door. I bend over and see that I am alive and here, standing in front of a mirror in a room that is filled with bright throw rugs, and lamps, and a couch that is whispering, "Meg, Meg, come lie on me." The living room and kitchen are works of art.

While I walk through the kitchen, which is the color of a summer morning sky—blue, yellow towels, red thingamabobs on the counter—I wonder why I never thought to make my space so lovely. Why did I never think to hang something like that there, place a table at that angle, put a photo so low on the wall like that?

Somehow this decorator woman figured out who I was in our few brief meetings, and when I move into the bedroom, my bedroom, where untold tales and adventures (how I hope!) will unfold, I cannot move. A brass bed and nightstands, bedside lights lined with bright beads, a gold and burgundy and green bedspread that rocks against the dark walls, candles everywhere. I imagine my "things," the photographs and few mementos that I chose to take from my last life, in the places where they will eventually lie the second I look at the dresser top and walk into the bathroom.

"It's perfect," I tell myself. "Totally perfect."

Katie's bedroom hasn't been touched and that makes me laugh. That is also perfect. She will need to design her own space and I'll help her pick out her dresser and chair when she gets back.

On a small table, placed in a spot that seems almost strange but then suddenly perfect because it is where I can set a coffee cup, my gloves, a book, before I go outside, Terry has placed a note.

> *Meg,*
>
> *I know that you will fill this space with your favorite thirteen coffee cups—you like the one from the spa in Rhinelander the best—the silly school photographs of the kids—your three diplomas—your "stuff," as you like to call it. Before you hang or place anything, I want you to think about how you will live in this space. Feel it for a while. This is your house and it will become your home the very first night you sleep here. In the refrigerator you will find a $50 bottle of champagne—but you must drink it alone. Tonight, when you have unloaded your few boxes, sit where you will always end up sitting and drink the entire bottle. I admire you for changing your life, for finding who you are. My commission for this job covers only my expenses. Elizabeth told me that you are going to massage school. I want a massage a month for as long as you can stand me.*
>
> > *You rock, baby. Now live—just live.*
> > *Terry*

I feel as if I have won the lottery. Since the watching I have met the most extraordinary women. Women who are bold and beautiful and brilliant. Women who have seen the dark edges around my eyes and who have reached out to put a hand right there, below my eye, in that deep spot of wanting. Women who would cross borders at midnight for me, walk on coals, give me the last sip of the best wine, hold me when I cry, be there at the end of every goddamn phone line—wonderful, glorious women.

Terry. Oh, Terry.

I have her note in my hands when I go back outside and then rush back in to get the beer and some tip money. The boys are almost done and they have put all the stones, two huge piles, right where I asked them to, against the deck that comes off my living room. This makes me very happy and will save me hours of work. I set down the money and put the beer on top of it.

"When you are done," I tell them, "I have to haul boxes."

Which is exactly what I do next while I wait, not so patiently, for them to leave. The car is packed, but it doesn't take me long. There is half a pickup load left in Elizabeth's garage, but that's tomorrow's chore. This day—I have the stones.

They are almost too perfect, flat and soft. When I touch them, hundreds of them, maybe thousands, I imagine what my finished product will look like, and it helps me to keep going. What I also have to imagine is the length of my body, curled just a bit at the knees. First I lie at the edge of the deck and then place a stone just beyond my head and another at the end of my foot.

Within an hour I realize I may have underestimated the time needed to complete this terribly important job, but I am dauntless. I see that there are two lights at the edge of the porch roof. I will work all night if I have to. And it's hotter than Hell. I strip off my shirt, go inside for a beer, then another one, and work placing the stones one on top of the other for two, three and then four hours.

By four P.M. I am further than I thought I would be. The stones are beautiful, solid, a ring of life that is becoming my fortress. Every stone tells me something. I wonder where it came from, who touched it first, how many years it bounced along the bottom of a river. Some of the stones are so beautiful, flecked with gold and green and blue, that I kiss them, and each rock holds a part of my story, my life—up until this moment.

I think about my parents, my brothers, my Auntie Marcia. While I put the rocks in place, winding them in a long oval, I try and remember as much of my life as I can. My first period, a kiss, the night I made love with a long-legged boy from Florida on a beach, the dancing dogs, the sounds of my babies waking up while I stood and watched.

I remember the pain of childbirth and my wedding and my father's funeral. I am sailing and running and crying and laughing with every rock that I place, and then I am finished.

Meg, oh, Meg. Wow.

The circle is waist high. It curves perfectly. I love it.

It is just getting dark on this summer Saturday evening. The sky, blinded by the lights from the city, is still the champion, and while I walk to the car to retrieve two large plastic bags, I feel like everything I see is twinkling, whispering hello, saying, "Welcome back, Margaret." I am trying to imagine feeling happier and I can't.

I set the bags down outside of the rocks and go inside to wash my face and to grab the bottle of champagne. I linger too. My apartment is dazzling, absolutely dazzling, and I am in love.

Back outside, the rocks look as if they are glowing. This makes me laugh out loud. First I walk around the edge and run my hand over all the stones, a thankful caress. The bags untie easily and flower petals spill out before I get a chance to line the inside of my fortress. Rose petals fall everywhere when I tip first one bag and then the other into the center of the rocks. Flakes of yellow and red and white. It's snowing for just a few minutes, and the scent is overpowering, wild, beautiful.

Getting inside of the rocks is easy. I take the bottle with me and slide down so that I can lie with my legs stretched out. The flowers are soft and silky against my legs, hands and arms.

I pop the bottle right away. There is no fancy glass, just the joyous sound of an expensive bottle of champagne breaking itself free, an exotic and sensual explosion that streams down my legs and drops into the flowers.

The wine is fabulous. I think I may never use a glass again. I think there are many things that I may never use or do again. I drink for a while and settle my ears into the new city sounds that will eventually become familiar to me. Beyond the lights and buildings and light poles, I can make out a few stars, fighting furiously to be seen beyond the soaring city.

"I see you," I tell the stars, and then I say the same thing out loud to myself. "I see you, Meg. I see you."

When I set down the bottle and curl around myself, a tiny breeze moves in between the holes I have left in several places in my rock house. My mind floats back to my Mexican jungle when an occasional breeze woke me up, showed me the way home, helped me stand with my feet at the edge of the ocean, the edge of the world, the edge of my life and see who I could be, wanted to be, had to be.

I tell myself that this breeze from the jungle has followed me and that I can have it and feel it and taste it anytime I want, wherever I am. I let the air curl around me and then I wrap my arms around me, myself, just a bit tighter, and I feel the glorious fineness of myself, and then I laugh, alone—happily, gloriously alone—into the breeze that has found its way into my heart.

26

"Something is happening at seven tonight," Bianna says as if she has been talking and I just jumped into the middle of a long conversation she thought she was having with me.

"Huh?"

"My house, in the back studio, seven P.M."

"Is this an invitation?"

"No, it's an order."

"What?"

"It's what you asked for the last time we talked. You are beyond ready. Be there."

She hangs up and I look down into the glass that covers my desk to make certain that I am really alive and standing in my office. I bend down so that I can see the bridge of my nose, my hair tumbling into my eyes and the confused look that has settled into the heart of my pupils.

"I have no idea what is going on," I say to myself. "What in God's name is going on?"

Bianna's studio sits behind her garage on the middle half of two rolling acres just south of the city. It is one large room that is its own country, and from my new home in the city the drive takes seventy-nine minutes. She does all her work in the room, on scattered pillows, with the soft wave of ancient music, under the glow of flaming candles and through a veil of incense so thick, it often feels as if the room is on fire.

I arrive at exactly seven P.M., floating in on some kind of soft air that has me wondering what in the hell is going to happen to me next. Before I get out of my car I run through every major thing—screw the minor stuff—that has happened to me since the morning I watched Bob and the geranium woman. Could it be possible that their sex act unleashed something magical that has cascaded into my life and filled up all the empty holes that I had been unwilling to plug myself? When I walk into Bianna's chambers, I am laughing, propelled by the thought that my husband's affair has changed my life in ways that I now must be thankful for.

The room is full of more than incense smoke. There are at least eight or nine women milling about in the glow of dozens of candles.

"Darling," Bianna calls to me, and I see her walking through the thick air with her arms open, her long caftan trailing behind her like an obedient servant, her smile wide and just a little scary.

I don't say anything, but fan my hand around the room as if to ask, "What the hell?" She keeps smiling and places her hand on the side of my perplexed-looking face.

"We are doing something I call a Reverse Bridal Shower," she tries hard to say.

"What the hell?"

"Well, it's a way for you to kick off the final stages of your divorce proceedings with help from some very smart experts and a few people who simply love and care about you very, very much."

Do I laugh now or cry? I tumble to the edge of both emotions and stand still.

"Bianna..."

"It's a lovely ceremony. You'll see."

"Do I have a choice?" I whisper.

"Of course not," she laughs.

I feel as if I am floating above my body. Bianna introduces me to Samantha, Lisa, Carrie, Pat and Lee and Audre. Dark hair. Lovely eyes. Hair as short as a Jack Russell. Long legs. Acne scars. Plain. Beautiful. Tall. I am in the midst of a glorious group of women who are throwing me a Reverse Bridal Shower. A Reverse Bridal Shower. I have never seen any of them before. I smile. I have absolutely no clue. Then Elizabeth appears from the back room and she is holding hands with my mother. When I look as stunned as I am, my mother simply puts her arm around me, kisses me on the cheek and says, "Isn't this fun?"

Bianna offers tea and coffee for all those in recovery. I choose the wine. If this is a shower, my shower, I will have at least one part of it my way, wondering the entire time what in the world a Reverse Bridal Shower could be or do or become.

On the table with the drinks I see packages. My shower gifts. They are wrapped up in newspaper. The energy from the women sparkles through the studio. I swear to God before I take my first sip of wine that everything and everyone is glowing. When I look down to make certain that I am not on fire myself, I see a soft light moving off the edge of my fingertips. Something is already happening at this Reverse Bridal Shower.

Something is happening.

Bianna has us bring our drinks and sit cross-legged in a circle. We drop obediently onto pillows as soft as summer clouds. She has on a series of funky CDs, so that in the background it seems as if there is an orchestra playing in the bathroom. Echoes are bouncing everywhere.

"Are we ready?" she asks.

Everyone is ready. I am still smiling. I may need a much bigger wineglass. The shower has very simple rules. There will apparently be no male stripper, which is good news for me. There is no cake, and we will not go barhopping. I am certain no one in this group has wrapped up Tupperware or sexual devices as part of the shower gift-giving. I am starting to feel much better.

Bianna keeps talking. The shower rules are brilliant and beautiful.

"These women are all clients and friends of mine," she explains. "Each one of them has been through a life transformation, a divorce, falling in love, loss, grief, rediscovered love. Each one of them has a short story and a gift for you. They are going to help you by sharing a part of their story, give you something tangible that you can take with you, and your simple job is to give them something, unburden your fears, so that you can move into the next stop on your own life ride with power and strength."

The woman next to me, Carrie, gently touches my hand and smiles at me. I put my head down, shake myself into a place of acceptance, openness, extreme gratitude. Let the Reverse Bridal Shower begin.

Lee goes first. She has long dark hair and winds it in and out of her fingers as she talks. She only looks at me occasionally. I think this must be terribly hard for her, but she talks softly and there is firmness in her voice that is reassuring and strong.

"My husband wanted to leave me and I fought it for a long time. Months turned into years and then one day I got out a calendar and counted the exact number of days I had spent trying to save something not worth saving, and I was astounded," she tells me. "It had taken me two years to realize my marriage was over. I could not waste another minute, another second. I put the calendar down, signed all the papers and called someone to change all the locks on the house."

Lee, who is sitting on the other side of the circle, says, "Catch," and throws me her package. I unwrap a calendar. There are no photos on it, no glorious sunrises, just days and days and months of blank spaces. I want to cry, but I just say, "Thank you, Lee."

Carrie, with the ancient acne scars, tells me how she was pregnant when she married her husband and how she would wake up every morning and imagine that she was alone and raising her baby the way she wanted to raise her baby and not the way her husband, who tried to guard and guide every moment of her life, wanted her to raise their son.

"The only quiet moments I had were those fifteen or twenty minutes each morning when I woke before he did and could stare out the window and imagine a life that I thought was impossible to have," she says, while balancing on her hands and leaning very far into the circle. "I felt so damn alone and found myself wishing away every day until my son was grown and I could leave."

Carrie does not seem weak or weary. I find the dips in her face terribly attractive. I wonder if she could lift up the entire room with the simple strong tones of her voice.

"I found myself always looking out of the window. One day, when my son was eleven, I asked him what he wanted for Christmas. He turned to me very slowly, smiled, and I imagined he was going to ask me for something like a computer or the keys to a pickup truck. He told me all he wanted was for me to be happy."

Wow, Carrie. Wow.

"That's when I went through the window. I literally went through the window of my bedroom, jumped onto the downstairs porch and called an attorney the second I walked back into the house."

Carrie's gift to me is a photograph of the window she climbed out of. I smile at her, imagining what that Christmas must have been like. I imagine the morning she rolled over in bed and could move her arms without touching a man she did not care to be with. I imagine she slept with the window open every night, even when it was twenty below zero.

"Thank you, Carrie. Thank you for the window."

Samantha is quiet. I do not think of her as a woman who could be wild and brassy. Her legs take up almost two of the floor spaces. Her long fingers are laced together when she speaks, and it looks as if she is praying.

"I was in love with another man," she confesses. "My husband was not bad or evil, he was just, well, he was just my husband. We never made love, he worked too much, and I fell in love with a man from college who moved back to town and called me. I could not bring myself to move the love affair past meetings for coffee, phone conversations, a gentle kiss on the cheek. My husband always looked desperate, and we were simply sharing space, a kitchen and a place to park our cars."

Samantha has us all spellbound. She did not want to cheat on her husband but she was desperately in love with someone else. She had an official piece of paper that announced to the world that she was married, but she did not feel married. Her friend was also desperately in love and desperate to make her see that her husband was equally as miserable.

One afternoon, she found a note in her car, the key to a hotel room and a bottle of wine. She went to the hotel room, sat alone on the bed drinking the wine, and then her man showed up.

"I could not have done it without the wine," she says, blushing. "I stayed in the hotel room with him for two solid days.

When I came home to tell my husband, he was happy for me, re-lieved, thrilled. It's unusual, but we are still very good friends. Once a year my new husband and I go spend an entire weekend in the same hotel room, but I don't need the wine anymore."

She tells me that as she remains friends with her ex-husband, she wants me to never give up on love. She tells me the world is full of kind, wonderful, generous men and that some of them will find their way into my arms.

Samantha's gift is a tiny bottle of wine. "Whatever it takes," she says, smiling wildly and pulling at the top of her sweater as if she is trying to let out a long wave of hot, exotic air. "I wish to hell I would have done it sooner, so much sooner."

"Samantha, bottoms up, baby. Thank you."

I take breaths now, deep and wide, filling my lungs with the same air that these women are sharing with me, waiting desper-ately to fan myself with the same wind that has given these women whatever they needed to step forward. They are lovely, so damn lovely.

Pat, short and round and with eyes as wide as the top of my glass, tells me she is embarrassed to even say why she could not dive into a divorce. But she does, dropping her head into her hands and then rising with a simple smile to say: "I thought my mother would be mad, because the wedding cost so much."

We all laugh, but we also know exactly what she means. The embarrassment of failure, the elaborate charade of ceremony, the unnecessary extravagance, the piles of useless gifts and, of course, the most ridiculous bridal showers one could possibly imagine.

"It wasn't one thing, it was more like three thousand things that led me into a total pile of unhappiness," she explains. "I limped along waiting for someone to come pluck me from my life and drop me into another one, but no one ever showed up. It wasn't my husband's fault. It was my fault for not realizing the failure of my marriage and my life up to that point was all of my own doing."

She takes a breath, and we all wait. What could it be?

"I got really sick one morning, just violently ill, and I went to call my husband to take me to the doctor, and when my hand was on the phone, I realized that he was the last person I wanted to be with when I was ill, the last person I would call if I was an inch from being delirious—the one person in the world who was supposed to love me, who probably did not love me at all," she says, closing her eyes so that she could recall exactly how she felt. "I decided to drive myself to the doctor. I was drenched in sweat, had a horrific pain in my abdomen, and I realized the second I put my hand below my waist that I probably had a burst appendix."

Which is exactly what Pat had. From her hospital room as she was prepped for surgery, she called her best friend and not her husband. When she woke from surgery, with rocks in her mouth and her entire body floating in narcotic ecstasy, she looked up to see her friend, standing guard over her wedding ring wrapped in a wad of Kleenex on the table, and a bright light shining above the door—which was really the bathroom light—but she decided that the light was her path to singlehood.

"The first call I made from the hospital room was to a divorce attorney," she says, smiling. "Here," she says, pushing her gift toward me, "I threw away the appendix, so this will have to do."

Her gift is a Barbie doll–sized hospital kit that makes me laugh, which I am discovering from these terrific women is a fine and wonderful thing to do.

"It's lovely," I tell her.

Elizabeth gets up then and comes over to hand me a piece of paper. It is a note from Katie.

"She knew we were doing this and she wrote this for you."
I take one look at it and ask Elizabeth to read it for me.

*"... Mom, my gift for you is myself, everything that I am
becoming, the woman I am going to be. When you thought
you were failing me—you were not. Without your help and
encouragement, I would never have the courage to go to
Mexico for six months or to work so hard for the grades that
got me here. The divorce does not change anything about how
I feel toward you or Dad. Sometimes people just fall out of
love, and that is an important lesson as well. I just want you
to be happy, Mom, just really happy, and to know that I am
really excited about your new life and our new home. You are
a wonderful mother, and I will always be your daughter. As I
am a gift to you, you have always been a gift to me.*

                                                    Love always,
                                                    Katie"

Oh, Katie.
"Thank you," I tell her, throwing a kiss into the air that I hope
will land right on her lips all those miles away in Mexico.

Lisa has a tale of great sadness. She is our domestic-violence
statistic, and for her to simply voice her past is a leap of generos-
ity that makes me reach out and take her hand halfway through
her Reverse Bridal presentation. It is impossible to guess her age.
Lines long and hard move to the very edge of her eye, where I always raise my eyeliner, out to the side of her face and down to a
valley of red streaks that fan across her face. I think of a valley of
tears. I think that she has been crying for such a long time that
her face turned into a river. I think that compared to her story
mine is a free lunch at a cheap restaurant.

"You think it cannot be happening. You think that it isn't happening when it does happen and that when it stops it is never going to happen again."

Lisa speaks quietly, her voice rising in the middle of every sentence and then dipping to the edge of the last word as if she is trying to hold on to something she knows is slipping away. Everyone is looking at her, no one is moving, even the incense seems to be paying attention, and even though I suspect they have heard her story before, they have to listen. They have to hear it again.

"So much of what happened to me is classic domestic violence stuff," she explains. "He was a professional who had a violent temper that was accelerated when he drank, and he drank pretty much all of the time."

Lisa was embarrassed and lived in a place so surreal that she became adept at using makeup, forgiving; saying the limp in her right leg was from an old running injury, passing on family gatherings because of his workload, disappearing from any portion of her former world. Her life within three years became nothing more than a fearful attempt at survival and denial.

When I look again at Lisa, when I really look, I see that there is a tiny, soft spot in the center of her eye. I see that she has surrounded that soft view of the world with a hard line that must now and forever be the place she turns to for protection.

"I went to a terrific college and have half a master's degree. I have been to Europe and the Caribbean and I am well read and have a mind that can wrap itself around views of the world that are complicated and sophisticated and wild," she tells me. "But I could not leave this man. I was just as sick as he was. Just as sick."

There is something, there is always something, Lisa tells us, moving her eyes from face to face and then back to mine. For Lisa it was not one single act of violence. It was not a kick to the womb that killed her baby or a bullet aimed at her heart. It was a single streak of light that worked its way into her dining room window one night.

"I was just sitting there, and this odd light moved across the window, like the shadow of a ghost, and it fell across my arm— right over the top of my hand where there was a scar...."

She hesitates, a memory rising like a ring of pain from her face, trapped for seconds, a minute, then two in a place that is dangerous to revisit. An old scar, long, horrific, terrifying.

"It was from him, from something that he threw at me, and I put my hand into the air to save my face, and my hand from finger to wrist sliced open, blood everywhere, him yelling that I was a stupid fucking bitch and I could not go back to the hospital, so I bandaged it myself."

Lisa raises her hand and moves it from face to face. There is a jagged red scar that moves east and west and then back again. It is the kind of scar left by rough steel or broken glass. It will never go away.

"When the light hit my scar, it stopped moving and stayed right there, and I thought if I could save my face, if I could save that, then why could I not save my own life?"

Why not, Lisa? Why not?

"I got up from the chair and walked out of the house without one single thing, and I never went back."

I am breathless. Worlds of sorrow and loss and dreams melted into piles of grief have settled in my heart, but Lisa touches me softly and places her package into my fingers, and that weight disappears.

"So you can always have that beam of light, Meg. Always."

My new flashlight is red and will fit into the small pocket of my Levi's. It has one of those fabulous batteries that never runs out. I turn it on and flash it into everyone's eyes, and then I simply hug Lisa, because I am unable to speak.

My mother's gift comes before her words. It is a travel book filled with blank pages and a small beautifully framed photograph of my father. I look at her in wonder and she speaks softly but firmly about life and changes, and I look at her in astonishment.

"I loved your father, I really loved your father, and yet there were things that I hated about him too," she explains. "It took me a long time to forgive him and myself for everything that went wrong and was hurtful in our lives, but at the bottom of it all was the fact that we did love each other. Times now are not like they were back then, and the gift you have is what the power of this day brings you."

My mother talks too about the goodness of kind men's hearts. She tells me I will love again and that I should remain open to every chance, every touch of a man's hand. The light of passions, she says, is always brilliant. "Embrace your past, Margaret, just as you must embrace your future."

The travel book, she explains, is for me to know that if love does not come to me, then I must go to it.

"Mom, that's beautiful. Thank you."

Audre, who has jet-black hair and green eyes, tells me that the luck of her life has been the ability to finally know a good thing when she sees it. When I unwrap her gift, it is a compact pair of binoculars so that I might be able to find my own good things and then keep them.

"I have been married for twenty-one years to a man who was relentless in his pursuit of me," she explains. "I had a series of tough relationships before I met Jim and was determined to stay single and be alone. But he would not give up, and one day he wrote me this terribly beautiful love note—and when I put it down, I looked up and into his eyes...and I decided I had not been looking at him at all."

Audre tells me not to be afraid to love again and to look into the eyes of any man who might have a kind heart with an open heart myself.

"I'll be looking," I promise her. "Thank you."

Elizabeth, my wonderful Elizabeth, is next. She is sitting in front of me, smiling widely. In her hands she has nothing. Empty palms. Long lines of life.

"Do you know?" she asks me.

"I'm not sure. . . . What is it?"

"Honey, everything you have always needed has been right inside of you. You are strong and beautiful and wise. The world is yours. Continue to get to know yourself. Be brave. Don't back up. You have it all, baby. You do."

"Elizabeth, I love you. Thank you."

"When you are not sure, simply look into the mirror. You will see exactly what you need to see."

Then Elizabeth finishes and I put the flashlight away and look up to see them all watching me, and I know that it is my turn to give them all something at this Reverse Bridal Shower.

I think that I can give them a promise.

"You have given me courage and hope and stories of your life that are precious and intimate," I tell them, feeling about for the right thing to say, the right way to say it. "I cannot say that I am not afraid to sign the final papers and move into the next phase of my life alone, but I promise that I will do it with a full heart and with the knowledge that I am doing what is best and right for me—*me*."

They clap, but I am not finished.

"And soon—when I have filled my own space and I can feel my own life, my life, lifting me and holding me—we will have a party, all of us, we will have a party, and it will not have a damn thing to do with brides."

The laughter carries us to our feet, and then the Reverse Bridal Shower shifts its tone toward celebration, and as women always do, we take care of each other and the food appears and we continue talking. Women. How wonderful they are. Sisters. Friends. Daughters. Women are so absolutely wonderful.

"Elizabeth..."

"Yes, baby?"

"Thanks."

She surrounds me with her arms, arms so familiar to me now that I fold into her as if we have done this every day of our entire lives.

"It's what we do, Margaret. It's what women who love each other do."

"It is," I echo.

"We can do anything."

Elizabeth. Oh, Elizabeth.

I get home close to three A.M. and I can see dawn peeking its head around the corner. The world is asleep and I may never be able to sleep again. I do not bother to see if anyone is watching me from the window next door. I do not care.

When I slip off my top and then my shorts and sandals, I think I hear music—something ancient and pure, the whisper of wind that catches my hair and helps me circle slowly on the deck overlooking my rock fortress.

Then I dance for a long time. Alone. Naked. And when dawn breaks across my roof, I can see the edges of tomorrow.

Epilogue

*i will
dance naked
when i first
learn
to walk...
and there
will be
a rainbow of light
colors
to blind
the binding minds
the closed hearts
of the men and women
who said
"never"
i will not
simply walk
but
fly
with wings of gold
woman*

warrior
feeling with a heart
the fineness of the journey
and dancing naked
at the edge of dawn
is the gate
that moves my soul
into the endless
realm
of possibility

—Chesnay Susan Thomas
Chicago
From: Passing the Light—Women in Transition—1968

Meg finished dancing naked before the neighbors looked out their windows, and claimed her house that night as her new home, which was a major part of her new life.

Just before Christmas, she resigned her position at the University and spent a month in Mexico. She visited her daughter in Mexico City and then went to see the dancing dogs, Tomas and her cottage by the sea.

She spent almost all of her time at the cottage and visiting with Pancho Gonzales Quintana, who, whispered into her hair, kept uttering unbelievably beautiful phrases of love, all the while in and out of a coma that kept him in one world one minute and another the next. One afternoon Meg decided to tell him what he needed so desperately to hear.

"Pancho, go to her, she is waiting for you. Marcia is waiting."

The funeral was a grand affair that took place at his estate. Tomas set the casket in the living room so that his father was facing the sea. The dogs danced and there was music in the gardens, food, people laughed and talked about what a wonderful man

Pancho Gonzales Quintana had been—generous, kind and fair. Several hundred people came by to pay their respects and they all brought flowers.

"My father was the one who put the dried flowers in the rocks by your cottage," Tomas told her. "We would always find baskets of flowers by the road. People knew he loved dried flowers."

One night, two weeks after the funeral, Tomas and Meg walked on the beach. They talked about Marcia and Pancho, and how the events of the past year had forever changed them. Meg instinctively reached down and took Tomas's hand while they sat on the beach, and then she turned and asked him a very important question.

"Tomas, do you think you could make love to me?"

They talked for a long time first. Meg said she wanted to feel the hands of a man on her who cared about her. She told him that it would not bind them, that he must see it as a gift to her and a gift from her.

"I trust you, Tomas," she told him. "I know you would not hurt me. I need this. It is the last thing that will really set me free."

Tomas was a sweet and gentle lover and they discovered that two people could spoon together and fit into the Stone Palace at the same time.

When Meg came back to Chicago, she began her classes at the massage school that was within walking distance of her home. The very first second of the first day of class, she knew she had found a place to rest her heart. She loved every single thing about her new profession.

During her yearlong program she took a job at the coffee shop on the other end of her block, where she met and dated several men. She made love in her bedroom with several of them, and when Tomas came to Chicago, he joined her there too and was pleased to discover that Meg's backyard rock house was also big enough for both of them.

Halfway through her massage training, Meg struck up a wonderful friendship with a woman in her class and they developed a business plan, arranged funding and located a suitable building for their massage practice. Meg made certain that her new partner realized she would be gone several months a year to Mexico.

Katie had the time of her life in Mexico, and Meg was not surprised to learn that Tomas helped her gain entrance to the university in Mexico City. He also helped her find a suitable place to live and part-time employment.

In January, during a long weekend off from school, Meg took the train to Denver and showed up at her son's home. Shaun's boyfriend answered the door; she embraced him and they were drinking wine together when Shaun got home from work.

They talked for hours, reconciled, and Shaun and his partner, Kevin, traveled to Chicago the following month to see Meg's house and to take a major step back into her life.

Shaun and Katie's father stayed with the geranium lover for less than a year and then immediately moved in with another woman. He helped Katie with her school costs, helped pay off Shaun's bills but gradually drifted out of Meg's life and world. He called her from work every other month or so to see if she was okay, and Meg was always glad to hear his voice.

Meg's mother continued her search for her lost lover, and by late winter was planning a trip to South Carolina, where the former football coach had moved. He was now a widower. Single. Free and absolutely healthy.

Jane fell back into her life as a writer with great enthusiasm and success. She put her house up for sale and began looking for an apartment closer to the heart of the city. She started dating, reconnected with several college friends from the past and began volunteering at the rape crisis center and homeless shelter. Meg threw her a huge Reverse Bridal Shower, which was featured on the front page of Jane's own newspaper.

Aunt Marcia's foundation flourished, and Meg attended her first board meeting, where she was introduced to a world and a cause that she would take on as her own. She immediately recruited her friends Elizabeth, Bianna, her new business partner, the members of the original Reverse Bridal Shower and her landlord to the cause, and within six months they were all working on fund-raisers and planning a trip to Mexico to work at the clinics and visit Meg's cottage.

By mid-summer, Elizabeth was spending so much time driving into the city to see Meg and meet with all her newfound friends that she was looking for a town house to purchase for herself. Meg would often come home from school and find her sitting on the deck, drinking wine, with her feet propped up on the rock structure.

Sometimes the two women would get into the rock palace together and talk for hours.

"Someday you'll have to put an electric ramp in here that will lower us in and out when we get arthritis," Elizabeth told her. "One of these days my damn knees are going to blow out."

Bianna's business continued to flourish, and Meg became a regular part of her Reverse Bridal Shower therapy sessions. By the end of the year, eight more women had found the courage to change their lives following a shower.

Dr. C broke all of her professional rules and struck up a wonderful friendship with Meg, and finally admitted that she and Elizabeth had been friends and a bit more for many years. When

Meg was making the plans for her business, Dr. C proposed that she move her practice in with the two massage therapists. That led them to find a bigger building which they decided to purchase and restore. The women added a Reiki practitioner and are now in the process of turning the business into one of the most successful treatment centers in Chicago, where women can get everything from a massage and facial to a psychological overhaul. They also started a Reverse Bridal Shower group that has downtown divorce attorneys more than excited.

One summer afternoon, while Elizabeth, Katie, Meg, the funky landlord and her partner and the three guys from across the street were celebrating Meg's two-year anniversary of moving into her home, Linda, the guide from Mexico who had helped Elizabeth and Meg find the dancing dogs, showed up miraculously in the backyard.

"What the hell!" Elizabeth and Meg shouted at the same moment.

"How did you find us?" Meg asked Linda.

"I've been back in the United States for a few months, trying to decide what to do next, and I turned my head one day and I swear to God I could feel an occasional breeze from the jungle, and I followed it right to your backyard, Meg."

Tomas, Meg thought.

That night, while various assortments of men and women and women and women and men and men took turns going in and out of the rock palace, Meg sat on the steps and called Carol Kimbal. She told Carol everything and then asked if she could come for a visit and drink that wine they had talked about so long ago.

"I thought you'd never get around to it," Kimbal said. "I've kept the light on Margaret Callie."

"It took me a while," Meg admitted. "But I did it. I'm dancing."

Then the wind blew across Chicago, an invisible sweet tornado that brushed against the smiling faces of all the men and women in Meg's backyard oasis, and within seconds a million flower petals were dancing everywhere as if they had just witnessed the infamous dancing dogs near a lovely cottage in Mexico.

About the Author

Kris Radish is an author, journalist, public relations executive and nationally syndicated political and humor columnist. Her first novel, *The Elegant Gathering of White Snows,* was a Book Sense 76 selection and appeared on national bestseller lists. Radish is also the author of a true-crime book, *Run, Bambi, Run,* and a psychology book, *Birth Order Plus.* Her writing has appeared in magazines and newspapers throughout the country.

A lifelong supporter of women's issues and feminist causes, she travels throughout the country to speak about her novels and to empower women to seize their own personal power and to dance naked as often as possible. She lives in Wisconsin with her partner and two teenage children, who think it's normal to have a mother who rides a motorcycle, has written about everything from wars to windows, follows the very loud dreams in her heart, embraces change and still tells them to put a hat on in the dead of winter.

Visit the author's website at www.krisradish.com.

If you enjoyed Kris Radish's heartwarming DANCING NAKED AT THE EDGE OF DAWN, you won't want to miss her bestselling debut novel, THE ELEGANT GATHERING OF WHITE SNOWS. Look for it at your favorite bookseller's.

And read on for a tantalizing peek into

THE

ELEGANT

GATHERING

OF

WHITE

SNOWS

Kris Radish

THE ELEGANT GATHERING

OF WHITE SNOWS

Available now

Just a glass. Balanced for a moment as brief as a breath. Like a confused dancer undecided about a direction here on the edge of the ancient yellow Formica counter. A speck of light filters through the crystal etchings on this last, best glass, one of three remaining after years and years of life following the goddamned wedding.

Susan watches the glass, her hand stretched out in a flat welcome, her stomach moving in waves as the glass falls and Susan, always anticipating the next movement of everything, moves with it.

"Shit!" She screams as the glass punches through the soft skin in the folds of her fingers. "Shit! Shit! Shit!" The blood gushes, covering the spot where she used to wear a ring and then down onto wrists that are as thin as the stem of the broken glass. Before a drop of blood hits the floor, before Susan can raise her hand, before a thought can form, the women come running.

There is a concert of unrehearsed movement on the kitchen floor. Alice runs for the dishcloth; Chris is on the floor cradling Susan in her arms; Sandy is looking to make certain the good bottle of wine has not spilled. Joanne and Janice are crouched like frogs close by, their hands dangling between their legs; Gail guards the small door between the kitchen and the living room, and Mary is poised to grab more towels and maybe, if the cuts are deep enough, those big bandages she knows Susan keeps on the shelf behind the kitchen sink.

"Is it deep?" Chris asks, extending her fingers around the tiny bloody wrist where a red-colored stream begins moving over her own fingers.

Everyone waits. There is a silence that reaches toward Susan, who answers by pushing herself into Chris's chest, bending her head so she can lie against her friend. Then there is the unspoken gesture of Alice slipping the stained dishcloth into Chris's free hand, and Chris placing it around the bloody wrist once and then twice like she is wrapping a holiday gift.

"Hey," Susan stutters, a whimper visibly rising from her stomach through her chest and toward any opening it can find. "I'm fucking pregnant, fucking, fucking pregnant."

There it is, suddenly as plain as the long splinters of glass. Forget the blood, forget the crystal glass, forget every damn thing. Everyone moves closer, except Sandy, who reaches for the bottle of wine, grabs the plastic cups off the side of the table and then sets them down in a circle around the bottle of wine.

"Oh honey," Alice says, reaching without thinking to run her fingers, already bent with arthritis, into the edges of Susan's incredibly short hair. "It's okay, sweetie, we're here now, we're here."

Susan weeps into Chris as if she is a giant Kleenex, and although Chris has never rocked her own babies, she rocks Susan. Back and forth, back and forth, while the other women slide closer, reaching first for a glass of wine until the eight women are touching, breathing, drinking, sitting in a mass that has quickly surrounded Susan and Chris.

"How pregnant?" asks Gail.

"Just barely," whispers Susan. "I found out yesterday."

"I take it this isn't the best news you ever had?" Chris already knows the answer. "Oh, you poor, poor girl."

Everyone knows right away. They know without Susan saying a thing, without looking into anyone else's eyes, without a single movement in the room. Susan knows they know. These women have seen the lining of her soul, the secrets of her heart, the insides of her mistakes and faults. When they walked into her house thirty minutes ago under the pretense of one of their charmed female gatherings and saw the circles under her darting eyes, saw her hair matted to one side, saw the newspapers stacked on the living room table, saw only one car in the driveway, they knew.

"It's not John's baby. Oh Christ, it's not John's baby."

While it is impossible for the women to sit any closer to each other, they quickly try, tucking under legs, clasping their plastic cups, scooting sideways, brushing shoulders and pushing their rear ends just another inch closer to Susan and Chris.

"Does John know?" Mary asks quietly, knowing already that the one thing John is ever in and out of is a hell of a lot of trouble, and definitely not a wife he most likely hasn't had sex with in twenty years.

"I don't even know where John is," Susan answers. "A clinic in Milwaukee knows, but that's it. John hasn't been here for a long time. He's gone, he's always gone, he's always been gone."

Now there are a thousand things to say and the women are restless, tapping the plastic cups with nervous fingers, holding back questions, wanting to skip over the obvious and find a solution, solve a problem, help their friend, a woman they love. But they wait, because they know this has to happen slowly, and they want it to be perfect and right and cautious, just a little bit cautious, because Susan has never been like this, and it's important, so important.

"Let's pull the glass out of that hand before we go any further," Alice says. "Here, just open your fingers, and let me clean this up."

Alice, with her bent fingers, is the one who knows about babies born and unborn, alive and dead, and when she touches Susan, picking the little shards of glass out one at a time and dropping them into Janice's outstretched hand, she tries hard to think only of that. "There now. We'll just put a few Band-Aids on those fingers, and I think you'll be fine."

The Band-Aids are passed over, more wine is poured, and Sandy and Mary quickly pick up the remains of the glass and drop the pieces onto the shelf where Susan keeps her recipe boxes and cookbooks.

Susan shifts, turning to face the women who surround her, but Chris won't let go of her and pushes in her legs to hold the tiny woman against the full frame of her body. The women talk then, the same easy conversation they might have had in the living room, without a broken glass, where Susan would have eventually told them in greater detail about the boyfriend who has been standing in the wings for years, more—always more— about John, the missing husband, about the risks of a baby when you are past forty and tired and angry and sad and don't want any more babies anyway.

Another bottle of wine comes off the top of the counter, and this sad circle of friends becomes lost in remembering and talking and simply being there together on Susan's kitchen floor. An hour passes, and the voices rise and fall and rise and fall like a wave moving from one wall to the next and then back again.

The women talk about abortion, and they talk about what bastards half of the men they have married and loved and slept with are and always will be. There is a chorus of sorrow that floats from one woman to the next, and these women who have spent time together for years and shared their loves and who have talked about lust and hate and crime and passion don't see that the early evening has passed, and that there is a half moon rising outside of the high kitchen window.

They talk with great sincerity and kindness about helping Susan and driving her to the clinic and helping her to get that damn attorney to file the divorce papers and getting off the fence with the jackass she's been screwing for twelve years. The women talk about these things mostly without anger, but that rises from them too, in an unseen layer of life's tragedies and sorrows that always seems to hover close.

As the women talk, they don't see themselves as separate entities even though they are each as different from one another as the proverbial fish is to the bicycle. They are grandmothers and career women, housewives, a secretary. They are divorced, married, grieving, wildly happy, conservative, liberal and a combination of every sad tale in the universe. But those differences are overshadowed by the fact that they are all women and friends, and because they have shared their secrets and because now they are lying on the floor in Susan's kitchen and they have made the world stand still.

When their words begin to slide into each other after the fourth bottle of wine, Sandy decides they must eat. No one rises from the floor though, and the time or the place doesn't seem to matter. It becomes clear first to one and then to the next that they matter, just them, and nothing else matters for these hours, not another person or thing or problem.

"Well," Sandy finally says, "I'm just thinking, 'Thank God that Susan threw that glass on the floor.' I haven't done anything like this since the last time I got stoned in college."

"Oh, Sandy," laughs Chris, leaning back to shift her weight, "the last time you got stoned was probably this afternoon. Isn't this the day that kid drives through from Madison?"

No one looks shocked or stunned, especially because it is

Sandy who has always had a hard time remembering it is no longer 1968, and they are once again and always talking about the unspeakable, about what really happens in a life, about what really matters most. There is shifting, the flush of a toilet, bowls of red Jell-O and a tuna salad, and chips and salsa, and whatever else Sandy can reach by crawling to the refrigerator and then shoving the plastic containers across the ten feet of space from the open fridge door to the pile of women on the floor.

Something else is happening during the sharing of food. There is the flow of erotic energy that has the scent of people in love in those first months when there are hours of talk and always a communication with bodies and eyes. Women especially know about this phenomenon. Women who cling to each other and who flock to female friends and say everything and anything with such ease it is often embarrassing to watch. It is like the magic moment of discovery when something finally makes sense, when someone finally says the right thing, when the pieces of life finally flow in the correct line. It is bright and sexual and the release of a thousand demons when a simple idea begins to grow until nothing can stop it, and then something that just an hour ago was unbelievable and unthinkable makes perfect sense.

Chris gets the idea first, and it comes to her just as quick as every other wonderful thought that has helped her escape death a hundred times and tackle life in every conceivable fashion. The idea is hers because she has missed this the most, this love affair women can have with each other. These hours where women talk and hold each other and pass on whatever bits of courage they need to get on with it; the times when they can become emotionally naked and turn themselves inside out and continue to love what they see anyway; and a moment just now, when you can tell someone you are pregnant and don't want the baby and hate your life and your husband and the man who made this baby with you and "could you please, right now, tell me what in the hell I am going to do about this mess of my life?"

The others, often sidetracked by the very things that they now discuss, have missed it too. It has come to them sporadically in their lives, and not often enough because there is never enough time. Luckily, during these last months these women together have become an electric charge. There is a current of life running among them, and somehow a spark of magic has risen up and the women have become powerful and invincible and now they can do anything they want.

"What time is it?" Chris begins, and the question startles everyone because they don't care what time it is and they think with great joy that they may never care again.

"Geez," Janice says, rolling over on top of a pile of potato chips, "it's probably late, but screw it, let's just stay up all night and have a slumber party."

Mary rolls toward her with outstretched arms. "Let's make it a party that lasts ten years, and we'll just live on the floor and eat and drink and talk and never let anyone else in the house."

"Oh God," remembers Joanne, moaning as if she has just had an incredibly personal physical experience. "Once when I was living in Chicago, I did that for three days but it wasn't with a room full of middle-aged women."

Everybody smiles and Chris knows that her simple question, like the broken glass, has changed everything. She smiles. "Quick, tell me something you have always wanted to do but never did, everybody think of something, just tell us all whatever pops into your mind."

Everyone begins dreaming. The women slide around on the floor, roll their eyes, and their thoughts come to a mutual conclusion. In unison they dream of leaving. Simply walking out the door and moving on from something or someone. The magic of friendship has spoken to each one of them so they are dreaming the same dream.

Chris says what will happen next is just for them and absolutely no one else. "No one," she emphasizes with a half scream, because she has done this in her life a thousand times and she knows that to do it, even once, is necessary for survival, for change, for forgetting and moving on. To do it together would be a miraculous occurrence.

"We could do it, you know," she tells them, becoming the teacher they are waiting for. "None of us have babies, hell, half of us don't even have a uterus anymore. Imagine it, just imagine it and don't think about anyone else but yourself. That's the secret here."

The women are thinking and Chris urges them on. She reminds them of the months and months they have tried to talk away everything from menopause to rape. She tells them that sometimes a simple movement, a simple act, can be more therapeutic than a million meetings around a living room coffee table listening to old records from the '60s and drinking wine that isn't quite as good as you'd like it to be.

"Are you trying to convince yourself too?" Sandy asks her, leaning across a set of legs to bring herself closer to Chris. "Where are your demons, dear friend? You've been everywhere and done everything. We have to be in this together."

Chris is the only one who has never cried during all these months of meetings and shared secrets, and when Sandy sees that her question has made Chris weep, she is momentarily startled. When she reaches beyond Susan to wipe Chris's cheek, she doesn't say anything else but waits. Everyone waits.

"I've never had real friends," Chris tells them as softly as they have ever heard her speak. "My life has been so different from yours, but I would have given my left tit or any one of my adventures to have had an hour like this just once ten, twenty or thirty years ago. I could never be careless with any of you, with all of the things you have told me and being with you like this or wherever we choose to go, would just mean so much to me."

No one is stunned by this confession or by the tears or by Susan's unborn baby. Among themselves they have seen and heard and felt so much and now they are tired, so damned tired. It is the tiredness that somehow gives them strength.

"Of course," Chris adds, not as an afterthought but as part of her confession. "I've never been much of a friend myself, it was always too frightening for me. So I didn't quite know how to do it until I met all of you."

There is nothing else to say then as the women bend to touch Chris as a silent way of thanking her. Susan moves out of her arms and without realizing it at first, all eight of the women—wearing glasses and stretch pants, old tennis shoes, loafers, mostly jeans and socks that are too thin at the heel and toe, find they are sitting in a perfect circle.

Everyone is anxious, ready, pensive about what will come next. They feel it coming but for minutes they can't move, and then Alice—of all people—starts them out. Alice who has a hole in her heart the size of Miami is the one to bring them up and out of their woman circle one at a time, reaching first for one hand and then the next, then pulling with such a fierceness it's a wonder her back doesn't go out. Even in this extraordinary moment she is still Alice—kind, gentle and firm all the way.

"We'll go," she says. "I think we'll all go. Enough with all of this suffering and sacrifice and waiting for something to change. Just enough is what I say."

Alice pauses to shift her thoughts back toward the direction they usually travel. It's a worn path of practical things like coats and warm soup and keeping your head covered in the wind, but even Alice feels a change in that wind. She shudders with pure excitement as she adds what she hopes will be the last perfect thing she ever utters. "It won't be cold even if we stay out at night because I've been watching the weather, and it's not supposed to get below fifty at night. Let's try and do the best we can for clothing with whatever Susan has around here."

No one has exactly said what is going to happen next or what they are about to do, and that is the wild beauty of all the sudden movements, of the giggling, of the not-at-all-frightened looks the women exchange.

There is a quick raid of socks and only one shoe exchange because Susan is so small that no one but Susan can wear any of her shoes, although Sandy puts on a pair of John's hiking boots. She can't bring herself to leave them on for more than a few seconds because the thought of anything that is his makes her want to vomit. "We should throw these right out the window," she says, flinging the boots down the basement steps. They bounce into the side of the dryer and leave a two-inch dent.

Alice makes everyone take a coat or a sweater. When they are ready, they huddle by the door waiting for the right moment to push it open and walk out into the night.

"What an unlikely marvelous mix of womanhood," Susan shouts as she kicks open her own front door with her size-four feet, forgetting about the baby and John and her throbbing hand. She screams, "Let's walk!"

In the darkest part of the night, just after midnight, the women crush the dewy grass without hesitation, heading north down a highway that is as black as hell, but as inviting as anything they have ever seen.

Associated Press, April 26, 2002
—For immediate release.
Wilkins County, Wisconsin

WOMEN WALKERS SHAKE UP LOCALS

Police report that a group of eight women are walking through this remote county on a "pilgrimage" and refuse to talk to authorities or to relatives who have tried to stop them.

"It's the craziest thing I have ever seen," said Sheriff Barnes Holden. "They are out there just walking and they won't talk to anyone."

Holden said he received numerous calls from people who have passed the women in the middle of the night and wonder if there is something wrong.

"Apparently they are on some kind of pilgrimage, and they won't talk to anyone but each other until they are finished," said Holden. "I tried to stop them but there's no law against walking down the side of the road if you want to."

He said he met early this morning with a husband of one of the women, who said he thinks a study group the women have been attending may have gotten out of hand.

"The husband told me these women have been meeting for several years every Thursday night. He thinks they just got carried away and started walking and praying," said Holden.

Jeanette Sponder, 68, who lives near Granton, where the women have been meeting, said county residents who have heard about the women walkers have been leaving food and water for them along the highway.

"Obviously this is something important to them," said Sponder, who said she knows all of the women. "If they are smart, they'll keep walking and get the heck out of this county."

Paul Ridby, of Granton, said his wife, Janice, is one of the walkers and he has no idea what is going on.

"I thought these meetings were just some excuse for the women to get together and eat and gossip," he said. "I suppose they will just stop when they get tired, but I hope it's soon because I'm kind of lost here."

The women are now heading south on Wittenberg Road and refuse to talk with anyone.